Born and bred in Yorkshire, A. L. White is the author of *Ravenswyke*, *The Homeward Tide* and *The Vanishing Land* – as well as *Kibbutz*, *The Long Day's Dying* and *The Long Summer*.

By the same author

Ravenswyke
The Homeward Tide
The Vanishing Land
Kibbutz
The Long Day's Dying
The Long Summer

A. L. WHITE

The Years of Change

PANTHER
Granada Publishing

Panther Books
Granada Publishing Ltd
8 Grafton Street, London W1X 3LA

Published by Panther Books 1984

First published in Great Britain by
Granada Publishing 1983

Copyright © A. L. White 1983

ISBN 0-583-13409-2

Printed and bound in Great Britain by
Collins, Glasgow

Set in Times

Part One

CHAPTER ONE

Matthew Aysgill looked at his wife Mildred as he came in the door of their mean house in Hunslet. She was sitting at the table with a large sheet of paper spread before her, a pot of tannin by her hand and a pen she'd made from a quill. Despite the paucity of the light, she had no candle beside her to help her to see, but then Matthew knew how carefully she hoarded their meagre supply of mutton fat.

'Nay, lass, tha'll damage thy eyes like that,' he growled.

Mildred looked up when she'd finished the stroke of the quill. 'Oh, Matthew,' she said anxiously, 'I never thought to see you back this early. You'll think me a sloven, with no food on the stove for you . . .' She glanced across at the iron stove they now used instead of an open fire; it was much more economical to run, and kept the house warmer with the few coals their two sons were able to bring home from the mine whenever they were in work, which wasn't very often.

Once Matthew too had been a coalminer, but he'd abandoned the mines in favour of travelling round the district with itinerant Wesleyan preachers. Sometimes, if the preacher didn't arrive in time, Matthew himself would mount the hastily erected platform to deliver the message of Methodism. Mostly he preached in the open air: on the commons, in the beast-market, sometimes even outside the Wool and Corn Exchanges. He always drew a large crowd, for he was gaining a local reputation and following, much to the annoyance of the clergy whose indifferent teaching and care for their flocks had driven many from the established Church. Many of Matthew's meetings ended in violence, however, since some of the locals regarded him and all the Methodist followers of the Wesley brothers as heretics and anti-Christs.

'They were out in force today from the parish church,' he told Mildred now. 'Even the parson was standing by listening to them shout, doing nothing when they started brandishing sticks and throwing stones they'd brought with them.'

Mildred got up from the table and quickly crossed the room to his side. 'They didn't hurt you again?' she asked, examining his face for wounds. It was so battered and carried so many scars she could hardly tell if any were new.

'Nay, lass,' he said, 'I'm all right. The beadle made me move on, and the constable was with him. They said there was a danger I'd cause a riot – I reckon as the parson himself must have put them up to it, through his connections with the gentry. Any rioting came from the members of his Church, and not the folks as were quietly listening to what I had to say.'

'Sit down,' she said solicitously. 'It'll not take me a minute to rake the stove and warm you a bowl of soup.'

He sat at the table and began to examine her work. She saw what he was doing, blushed, and tried to take it from the table. 'Nay, lass, let's see what tha' spends thy time on when I'm away.'

'It's nowt,' she said. 'Just something I'm doing to amuse the lads.'

'Aye, well, what is it to be?'

'It's a plan of the Aysgill family, don't you see? Starting with your father, John, back in Barthwick, then all the brothers and sisters, with their wives and husbands. Next I'll put in the names of all the children. I thought I'd get our

Richard, who has a nice hand with a brush, to decorate the sides of the paper and make it look like one of those scrolls.'

'The Aysgill family, eh? All set down on paper.' He pointed to an empty box at the top left-hand side. 'What are you going to put in there?'

Mildred put her hand on his shoulder. 'That's for poor dead Simon,' she said. She knew Matthew had never forgiven himself for the death of his older brother who had left his house one morning four years ago and drowned himself in a dew pond. Matthew had always felt that he should have been more sensitive to his brother's feelings, should have visited him more often and encouraged his brother to talk about his despair, to release the dreadful sorrow that had impelled him to take his own life.

'Now that you're the head of the family,' she said gently, 'I thought it fitting that we should keep a record of all the Aysgills.'

He stared at the paper. 'It's a sad family,' he said, shaking his head. 'Gertrude away in service in Whitby . . .'

'Nay, not in *service*, Matthew,' Mildred interrupted. 'She's the *housekeeper* to Mrs Edgecombe now, no less. We can be proud of her.'

'Peter grown so grand, even if they wouldn't elect him to Alderman because of his background . . .'

'It was his hatred of Lord Barthwick that did for Peter, not his background.'

'And sister Dodie going the same way – we haven't seen her to talk with, as one of God's families should, in a six-month.'

'Perhaps, if I keep a record of us all, it might suffice to bring us all closer together,' Mildred suggested.

He looked up at her. 'You're such a simpleton,' he said, though not unkindly. 'When I first married thee, tha' wert a firebrand, always urging me on. Well, now I'm doing God's work the way I suppose I always wanted, you've settled into contentment with your home – such as I've been able to provide for you, and that's not much – and your lads who've turned out a credit to you. Why do you seek to blow flames into a family that's become cold as the ashes of yon stove? We've gone our separate ways, Mildred. Tha'd better face up to that fact and save thyself the worry and the work of trying to bring us together again.'

For a second he saw the old vehemence cross her face, a flash of the spirit that first had attracted her to him. 'I'll never do that, Matthew,' she said. 'Never! You're an *Aysgill* of *Barthwick*. That makes me an Aysgill too, and our two lads heirs to the family name and the line. I never intend, so long as I draw breath into my body, to let them forget that!'

CHAPTER TWO

Dodie Ottershaw moved cautiously in the large wooden bed, trying not to waken Titus Waverley, who was breathing heavily in what seemed to be a deep sleep. She could sense that daylight would soon be here, and she must make haste to return home in time to waken the two lads to send them to their last day in school, and to prepare breakfast for her husband, Mark, when he came home after his night's work in the foundry. She'd lain awake in the big bed Titus had brought with him from his father's grand mansion near Wakefield, thinking of the many things to be done this day if she was to advantage herself and her family. For this was Dodie's sole pastime: wondering how best she could raise them from the lowly position into which they'd been thrown when she and her brothers had been forced, by the new land enclosures, to leave their father's home and the village of Barthwick. Her brother Peter had succeeded and now was wealthy beyond all their aspirations – Dodie was determined that, come what may, she would follow in his path as soon as she could. Sharing the schoolteacher's bed had been her way of securing an education for her two sons; she was prepared to do anything to see they acquired a good education and a start in life.

She slipped slowly from the bed, shivering, clad only as she was in a thin cotton shift, and padded silently across to where she had left her clothes on a chair in the corner of the room. She clambered into the long cotton hose and the heavy cambric bloomers that would keep out the worst of the chill of the cold May pre-dawn, then her woollen dress with its high neck and long skirt. She had seated herself in the chair and was pulling on her boots when her thoughts were interrupted.

'I suppose this will be the last time,' Titus said quietly.

She gasped with the sudden shock of hearing him; she had been so occupied with her plans for the day that she had forgotten he was there. She looked across at him as he struggled to sit up in bed. Really, he *was* a handsome man, with his long thin face and tender eyes the colour of lavender flowers. He had such a gentle manner, she thought. In all the years she had been coming to him, he had never treated her roughly. Though both knew she was giving him such pleasure as he could find in her body as a means of paying for her sons' education, he had never treated her as a common doxy, been coarse or crude with her. He had never caused her to expose her naked body to him, but had taken care to leave the room while she prepared herself for bed. He had always been respectful – yes, that was the word – despite the difference in their rank and station. And always so humbly grateful.

'The boys must leave school, I fear,' Dodie said sadly. 'Lacking financial means, they must seek employment now to further their prospects.'

'Stanley is nobbut ten years of age,' he said gruffly, 'and Claude nine. Both are doing extremely well in Latin and some Greek, and Stanley has mastered Mathematic. Both can write with a fair hand, and I'd a notion to prepare them for advancement . . .' His voice dried, and he looked directly into her eyes. 'I shall miss you, ma'am,' he said. 'You've brought much joy to my heart.'

She crossed to the bed and gently patted his cheek. 'And you to mine, maister,' she said. 'But I am a married woman,

12

and my husband has never wronged me nor lifted his hand to me in anger. I would like our relationship to end, now, before we are discovered. It's becoming increasingly difficult for me to escape from the house without alerting the boys, who have reached an age of understanding. It was never my intention that I should sleep beside you, but I have to confess . . .'

'I pleased you so much?'

Dodie laughed. 'Nay, maister, you have such a comfortable mattress I couldn't forgo to enjoy it a while longer! Our straw and shoddy ill compare with yon goosedown. Nor our calico with yon linen, I'll be bound.'

Titus held out his hand. 'We part friends, ma'am?' he asked.

'More than that,' she said sincerely. 'You have my undying gratitude for what you've done for my two lads.'

'And for you?' he persisted.

She coloured. 'Nay, maister,' she said softly. 'Tha'll not trespass on my modesty, surely. Tha'll leave me that to take away wi' me?'

Titus placed one hand tenderly on her shoulder. ''Tis often said that an excess of modesty betokens a lack of generosity, but in you I have always found it to be a virtue. And no man will ever take your virtue from you, ma'am, no matter how he may oblige himself of your talents and abilities. I adore you, ma'am, as much at our parting as I did at our first meeting. I bid you and your two lads well in whatever life may offer you.'

Dodie hurried through the streets after she had let herself out of the back door of Titus Waverley's house attached to the school. They'd struck a bargain all those years ago; he had educated her sons and she had obliged him with her body in default of money to pay his customary fee. Though it had seemed a purely business transaction at the time, she realized now how much she'd learnt from him and his

13

gentle manner. Her thoughts lingered with him as she made her way through the crowds of people already hastening to and from the factories that were springing up everywhere in Hunslet, the spinning sheds and the water-powered weaving mills. Carts lumbered along the lanes through the mud and mire, carrying a vast variety of wares to feed the hungry new industrial urge; one was laden with wooden poles from which the bark had been stripped, and Dodie was reminded again of the village of Barthwick where she'd been born and had lived her young days in blind contentment, not knowing the tragedy that would befall them as a family. If the Aysgills had been able to afford poles such as those on the back of the cart, they could have fenced off the land apportioned to them by the Act of Enclosure. If her father, John Aysgill, had been a prudent man rather than a goodnatured open-handed spendthrift, they could have done as Sam Weighton had done and bought other people's portions, even built their own house and left the tied cottage to Lord Barthwick. She'd heard that Sam Weighton had virtually become the new squire of Barthwick, that his holidays increased every year with the size of his flocks and that he now owned as much of the village land as did Lord Barthwick himself. She'd even heard that his lordship had sold much of his woodland to Sam Weighton, since he husbanded his newly acquired land so badly and derived so little income from it. It might have been the Aysgill family that owned the woodlands now, if only their father had been less inclined to give money to every needy man he met.

Dodie sighed bitterly as she walked along the road towards the small house that was all they could afford on her husband's wages at the foundry. She'd pressed him many times to try to educate himself, to seek a better paid job. He was a willing worker and the foundry master knew it. If only Mark had studied pattern-making or any of the

14

many tasks that paid better money. So many new things were being invented, so many new ways of doing old things, that a man prepared to study them could advantage himself greatly. She thought of Ezra Wilkins who'd come from Betlaby, worked day and night to improve himself and was now employed at a large wage by the *Leeds Intelligencer*, the newspaper that had been started six years ago – and he a man who, as a lad, could neither read nor write! All Dodie's frustrations, all her rage came to the surface as she thought of her own husband who was still doing the same job he'd done the first day he went to work in the foundry, and doubtless would die doing it.

'Oh Mark,' she said to herself, 'why couldn't you be like our Peter who rides in his own carriage? I too could be riding in a carriage at this very moment!'

A passing horse stepped into a pool of excrement and mire, splashing as it clattered along, doing nothing to lighten her spirits nor abate her ill-humour.

The two lads were up and dressed when she arrived home, though her daughter Jennifer who was seven years old, lay still abed. Dodie looked at her fair hair spread across the horse-hair stuffed cushion on which her head rested. Though her anger had not abated, nor her feelings of frustration, her mood softened as she gazed at Jennifer. With God's grace she'd grow to a beauty, and would not lack for advantage. Life could be very different for a well set up maiden who had the ability to make profit from her own natural endowments. Dodie was resolved to teach Jennifer all she knew of the womanly arts, the wiles that had won an education for her two sons.

'Tha'll never lack for coin, my lass,' she murmured as she tucked the calico sheet round her daughter's chin.

She scolded the lads when she returned to the downstairs room in which they lived. 'You should have been left ten minutes ago,' she said. 'Now you'll have to run to school and you'll arrive like a pair of ragamuffins. You must learn that a gentleman behaves with dignity at all times, and doesn't scuttle through the streets like an urchin. Get away now, and mind you pay attention to Mr Waverley on the last day, for he'll have good advice for you, that I'll be bound.'

She watched them leave. Aye, it was a pity they couldn't stay in the school, but she had other plans for their futures. They'd learnt enough from books; now was the time for them to learn more practical matters.

Dodie knew Mark would go to the coal tip on his way home, to scratch among the flints and slates to glean what pieces of coal he could find; she woke Jennifer and instructed her to have her dad's brewis ready for when he came in.

'I have to go out,' she said, 'but you can straighten the covers on the bed so that your father can take a few hours' sleep. I'll be back afore midday, and I'll want to see you've taken a broom across the floors and are reading your book.'

'Nay, Mama,' Jennifer pouted. 'That Mr Defoe is a boring man, wi' too many long words for my comprehending!'

Dodie fetched her hand sharply against the side of Jennifer's head. 'Don't you ever say that again,' she chided. 'There's many a young lass down the mines, or in the mills, as'd give her right arm to be able to sit on the doorstep conning a book. Tha's going on eight years old and it's time you had something in that head of yours to talk about when gentlemen begin to notice and address you. Else what will you say if your Uncle Peter takes you under his wing, him having only two boys and no girl in his household?'

'Shall I ride in his carriage, Mama?' Jennifer asked, her eyes gleaming. She loved to hear her mother talking of what might come to pass, and best of all she liked the stories in

16

which she rode in Uncle Peter's carriage to attend some grand occasion, peopled by ladies in elegant gowns and gentlemen in fine coats.

Mark Ottershaw, sitting by the fireside resting after his labours at the foundry, would snort and say to Dodie, 'Nay, missis, tha' moan't turn the lass's head that way,' but Jennifer would plead with her mother to tell more of the wonderful stories on which her dreams were built.

'Aye, Jennifer. I promise as you shall ride in a carriage of your own, one of these days,' Dodie said indulgently, 'if only you'll stick at the reading, as I beseech you.'

Jonas Clegg admitted Dodie Ottershaw to the private office on the ground floor of his new-built mill. Situated behind the clerk's office and the counting house, it commanded a view across the whole ground floor, overlooking the worsted weaving looms on which he had ventured so much precious capital.

'You come highly recommended by Maister Waverley,' he said as he offered her a seat by his desk. 'Though I'd have thought it was more fitting for the lad's father to come on his behalf.'

'My husband is an honest working man,' Dodie said demurely, her eyes cast down, 'and must take his rest between labours if he is to give his master good service.'

'Maister Waverley has told you what I want?' Clegg asked.

'Yes, he has explained that you wish someone to give your apprentices an education.' Dodie had been surprised when Titus Waverley told her of Clegg's visit to the school. Most factory owners bought apprentices from the orphanages, housed them in miserable conditions in the factories, keeping them virtual prisoners. They fed them meagrely, and took as much work from them as they could before turning them out on to the streets at fourteen or fifteen

17

years of age. But Jonas Clegg appeared to have a conscience: he wanted *his* bought apprentices to be *educated*. When Dodie heard this from Titus Waverley, she had quickly seen a way in which her son Stanley could be advantaged. 'My son is rising eleven and has a grown way with him,' she told Clegg now. 'He has mastered his Latin, Greek and Mathematic, and—'

'Aye, missis, I've had word o' that from Maister Waverley,' Clegg interrupted.

'Stanley will do as you wish in the matter of educating your apprentices,' she went on desperately, for his mien now seemed somewhat unfriendly.

'I shall want them taught in a practical way,' he said, 'wi' nowt fancy.'

'That is the way Maister Waverley has instructed my son,' Dodie said.

'He'll need to work alongside the 'prentices,' Clegg persisted. 'The education can only start when there's no more work to be done. He'll have to live with them, share their lot in all matters . . .'

'My son will be agreeable to that,' she said.

'Aye, well, it'd be better to hear that from the lad's father. Many a woman spoils her lads wi' soft ways – tha's not made thy lad to be a softie, has tha"?'

Now Dodie realized he was being deliberately belligerent. Was that to test her? She had been told by Titus Waverley that Jonas Clegg was a kindly man, with good Christian intentions. Many were saying that he was too lenient in his treatment of the people who worked for him, in the space he had provided in his new factory which certainly appeared lighter and more airy than any she had previously seen.

'No lad o' mine could become a softie,' she retorted, raising her eyes to look into his face. 'In this modern world we must be strong to gain advantage from what we do. I

18

think my son can advantage you, and you him.'

'Nay, missis, tha' goes too far,' said Clegg. 'How can your slip of a lad advantage me as has all this?' He waved his arm round to indicate his wealth and privilege, his new factory building, the deployment of his capital. 'I think tha's too bold for me,' he said.

'Bold I may be, master, but I mean no mischief and no disrespect.' Dodie swallowed hard. Was she pushing him too far? There were hundreds of boys who could do what Clegg wanted. Was she throwing Stanley's chances away in the manner of her address? 'My Stanley can indeed advantage you,' she said firmly. 'He's been brought up in humble surroundings and has gone from them to acquire an education for himself, the better to fit him for life.'

'I assume you had something of a hand in that, missis,' Clegg growled, 'to judge by the warmth of Maister Waverley's recommendation.'

'I did no more than any other mother would do,' Dodie said, wondering if Waverley had been speaking too warmly of her. But she knew in her heart that he would never have disclosed the full nature of their relationship.

'Aye, that's as may be,' Clegg said. 'I shall need to see the lad afore I take the matter any further.'

'I thought we might discuss the nature of the lad's recompense,' she said softly.

'Recompense, missis? He'll get wages, like everyone who works for me. No more, no less. I'll start him on wi' a tanner a week, and we'll see how he does.'

Sixpence a week! Dodie thought immediately how much that would help the family income, especially since Stanley would be fed with the apprentices. It was tempting, oh so tempting . . . But she pushed the thought resolutely from her.

'I'd hoped,' she said, taking all her courage to help her, 'that we might come to an arrangement.'

'An *arrangement?*' Clegg repeated, his brows beetling down in a frown. 'Think carefully, missis, afore tha' throws away thy good name wi' talk about arrangements.'

'I'd hoped I might strike a bargain with you,' Dodie said, persisting in her course despite the fierceness of his manner. 'Instead of wages, I want you to teach my son about practical matters. Maister Waverley told me you've a strong knowledge of all matters of making machinery, and inventions. He said that you've put ideas into this factory that are ahead of the times. I want you to teach my son in the same way my son will teach your apprentices. Only they'll learn to read and write and do mathematic, while you teach my son the making of machines and all their workings – you'll have to forgive me, but I know nowt of any machine nor how it can be made to work.'

Jonas Clegg was grinning hugely, and he slapped his hand on the desk. 'I've wronged thee, missis,' he said, 'and I'm happy to acknowledge it. I thought with *arrangement* tha' meant . . . Aye, well, never mind what I thought. I'll take your lad. Titus Waverley gave him a good name at his schooling, and I can see that with a brave mistress like thee for his mama, he'll have strength and character where it matters the most, at his own hearth. Aye, I'll take him in; I'll pay him his tanner, and he can be by my elbow. I've not made a lad of my own. Your lad can stand by my side and I'll teach him what I know. I'll make an engineer of him, mark my words.'

'An *engineer!*' The very title sounded magnificent to Dodie's ears. 'You'll make my son an engineer?'

'Aye, missis, that I shall. He shall start in the morn as soon as the papers have been drawn. I'll need him bound to me, until he comes of age at seventeen. Twixt the two of us, we shall see him right. I'll knock some engineering into him and tha' can make him into a man!'

* * *

Jonas Clegg's establishment was part mill, part machine-making factory. Most of the ground floor was taken up with looms on which workers drawn from the surrounding district wove the worsted threads into fine cloth. On the floor above, the spinners worked on machines devised by Paul and Wyatt and patented in 1738. Clegg himself had adapted the machines, using a smaller roller system to draw out the fibres. The machines, as yet, didn't work as well as he would have liked, and the skeins of yarn often varied too much in thickness for the fine cloth he specialized in weaving. It took five or six spinners to keep one of his flying-shuttle looms occupied, and even then he had to send some of the wool out to people's cottages for spinning, to keep his looms going.

Clegg had travelled to Birmingham and to Northampton to see the experimental mills that had been built to exploit the Paul and Wyatt invention, but he had not been impressed by what he saw, and had resolved to work on the matter himself. His own mill was, in essence, a proving ground for his own inventions. His great dream had always been to harness the great power of the engines used for bringing water from coalmines to the mechanical business of spinning and weaving. Many people laughed at him and thought him mad. How could two such dissimilar endeavours, each with its own difficulties, be harnessed to a mechanical monster, they asked. So far he had not found the answer.

Jonas Clegg had married early, but his wife had developed consumption and now spent most of her life in bed ailing. He'd plunged into his mechanical work as a compensation for the domestic life that was denied to him by his wife's illness, for he was not a man to frequent the Assembly Rooms or the ale-houses, and he had scant interest in gaming, cock-fighting or wenching, the usual pursuits of a moneyed gentleman.

He took a fancy to Stanley Ottershaw immediately. The lad was well-mannered and deferential, though Titus Waverley had warned Clegg that he had a strong spirit and a temper when aroused.

'Tha'll call me Master,' Clegg told the boy, 'and I s'all call thee Stanley. Tha'll be at my beck and call morning, noon and night, understand?'

'Yes, Master, I understand,' Stanley said, liking the man's direct blunt manner. He knew he'd always understand exactly what Jonas Clegg meant, and that way they'd get on.

The Clegg works were a revelation to Stanley. He'd seen the inside of mills before – but never the inside of a machine shop, where iron was forged and worked, where there were all manner of strange tools, the odour of grease and oil, the grating screech of the pole lathes and the pounding of the battering hammers. Jonas Clegg was prepared to take on any form of metal manufacture and had stocks of iron, brass, bronze.

During their tour of the works, Stanley noticed one of the 'prentices crouched inside a vast cylinder, rubbing the inside with a shaped stone dipped in sand and water.

'Yon's one of your lads,' Clegg said. 'You'll be teaching him Mathematic, reading and writing after work has stopped.'

'What's he doing?' Stanley asked, fascinated by the work that proceeded all around him.

'He's smoothing the inside of a barrel for the steam engine, so's to make a tight fit. If the steam blows out past the collar, the engine loses its power. The thrust of the rod is proportionate to the pressure of the steam . . . I can see by thy face tha' knows nowt of what I'm saying, but that's what you're here to learn. You'll need to pay close attention, mind. I'm a man as doesn't care to say owt twice. If I catch thee daydreaming, tha'll feel the hard edge of my hand round thy ears, I can tell thee.'

That first day Stanley resolved that his new Master would never catch him daydreaming. Not that he was afraid of a clip round the ears – Titus Waverley possessed a hand as hard as the next man and had used it unsparingly if he caught any of his scholars dozing. But Stanley had been infected with a sudden enthusiasm by the works he saw about him and though he couldn't yet know it, the smell of machine oil and grease would always be an elixir to him, as vital as the blood that flowed along his veins. To be an *engineer*, to be able to take these heavy pieces of metal and bend them to his will, forge and hammer them into useful shapes and objects, surpassed his wildest aspirations. Though he had worked hard in school, conscious of his good fortune in having the opportunity of bettering himself, Stanley had conceived no desire for a bookish life, working over ledgers in some cramped office. It was all a will-o'-the-wisp existence. Metals, machines, engines, wheels and rods turning under strong force and doing work to replace man's puny energy, that was a magnificence he could immediately comprehend.

'I'll not be caught daydreaming, Master,' he vowed. 'If I could only ask your patience. I learn but slowly, but I learn well.'

'Aye, Maister Waverley gave thee a good name for that,' Clegg nodded. 'He said tha's slow to grasp owt, but when tha' has it, tha'art like a bulldog as never lets go. Now, we'll start at the beginning. Yon's iron, and yon's brass. Yon's bronze, yon's white metal for bearings . . . Aye, and look over there at that lad dozing by his machine. Yon's a lazy 'prentice – you'd better learn to recognize him as quickly as tha' tells iron from brass. I hope tha's not afeared of sticking thy foot up a lazy 'prentice's backside?'

'No, Master, I'm not,' said Stanley, stifling his doubts.

'Right, then. See what tha' can do to waken that one a

bit. He's supposed to be attending to that piece of stuff in the loom, making sure that no faults are missed. How he can do that wi' his eyes closed is beyond my understanding.'

Stanley's heart sank as he walked across the weaving floor. The 'prentice was nearly half as big again as he was, with a thick arm and fists like hams. Stanley reckoned he must be at least twelve years old. He was dressed in ragged trousers and a torn jerkin that came only halfway down his trunk and arms; the rag round his throat defied description, with globs of fat and grease on it, the obvious remains of half a dozen meals. He was lying on a pile of bobbins from which the weaver would thread the flying shuttle; despite the clatter of the machine beside him, he was fast asleep, with his chin on his chest. Stanley walked carefully behind him, studying his sleeping form.

The weaver raised his eyes from the weft and warp of his weave, and winked at Stanley, then nodded approval of what he hoped Stanley was about to do. A lazy 'prentice could waste a weaver's time if he wasn't alert to give notice of when the shuttle would be emptied, if he allowed broken threads to spoil the quality of the cloth, if he failed to make correct joins so that the threads parted and the finished worsted pulled a hole when it was being stretched.

Stanley drew closer; the 'prentice was totally oblivous of him.

Now the other 'prentices had seen what was happening and had stopped work to gape. Stanley looked up and saw Jonas Clegg eyeing him, a smile on his face. Suddenly Stanley realized he'd come to his first testing time all unawares. The event had been staged deliberately. His future success with all the 'prentices would hang on how he dealt with this one, twice the size of all the others and no doubt twice as strong.

Luckily, a memory of Titus Waverley sprang to his mind, and the way he had dealt with Stanley one day when

24

Stanley had complained that his soup was too cold, not knowing that the Master stood behind him.

'Stanley quickly reached both hands forward, grasped the 'prentice's ears, and twisted hard. The 'prentice woke with a roar and lurched forward to escape the pain. Stanley twisted tighter, then suddenly released his grip and pushed – the 'prentice went sprawling on the floor, howling with pain. The bobbins on which he'd been lying were unbalanced by his violent lurch and fell clattering and rolling around his head.

Stanley seized one of the bobbins and rapped the back of the lad's head with it. 'Tha's supposed to be watching these,' he shouted, 'not ligging abed! Now pick 'em all up and stand by thy machine, and if I catch thee dozing again, I'll knock the sense out of thee.'

'Aye, Master,' the 'prentice said fearfully, thoroughly cowed by Stanley's fierceness.

'I'm not thy master,' Stanley retorted sternly. 'Mr Clegg is thy Master – *and* thy benefactor, and every moment tha' sleeps when tha's supposed to be working, tha' steals a coin from his pocket. Tha' can be transported to America for that, remember.'

The 'prentice scrabbled about the floor, picking up the bobbins, stacking them beside the machine.

'Right,' Jonas Clegg shouted above the hubbub of laughter 'that's the end of the show. This ain't a fairground, so tha' can all get back to work.' He came over to Stanley and clapped a hand on his shoulder. 'I hope tha' didn't damage yon bobbin when tha' hit him wi' it,' he said, grinning. 'Bobbins cost money, tha' knows. Next time tha'd better use thy fist.'

CHAPTER THREE

Gertrude Fossett primped her hair anxiously beneath the modest mobcap she wore, and beckoned for her son Walter to sit on the chair beside her in the outer room of the Whitby hiring hall. Many times during her life she had felt a nervousness, but none so severe as this one. She felt nervous all those years ago when she'd come to Whitby alone in the stagecoach, and had been hired as a servant by Mrs Edgecombe. She'd felt nervous when Mrs Edgecombe had entrusted the position of housekeeper to her, nervous when she and Luke Fossett had been married in the local church, with Captain Edgecombe himself as her sponsor. Now that her first-born, Walter, had reached ten years of age it seemed as if all her nervousness was for him, not for herself. But the letter she carried in her reticule comforted her; she held the bag to her stomach, guarding it as if it contained her life's savings.

Men came and went in the long low room and there was a constant bustle of activity as crews were signed on and paid off. The ones here for signing were clean and tidy, their beards and moustaches neatly trimmed. Some of them were bleary-eyed from a surfeit of on-shore drinking – a few days at sea would soon clear out their systems. Others, back from long voyages across the world, looked tired, often unkempt, all smelling strongly of the sea, tar, wax and resin – aye, Gertrude thought, and of personal indifference to cleanliness. She noticed the scrimshaw in some men's hands, pieces of whale-bone on which they'd whiled away what idle hours were given to them by carving ships and seascapes; there'd be many a customer to buy the scrim for good prices to adorn a mantelshelf or a cupboard. Captain Edgecombe himself had a fine collection of pieces that had been carved by men under his command when he went to sea. The most beautiful he possessed were carved in real ivory he'd obtained along the coasts of Africa and even India, where he'd taken aboard loadings of spices.

'Nay, Walter,' she said testily, 'stop thy fidgeting else I'll think tha's caught a flea. Tha'll be seen soon enough. Tha' mun learn the virtue of patience if tha's to succeed.'

Unlike his brothers Reuben and Daniel, Walter had never acquired the art of sitting down and attending to his lessons. Captain Edgecombe had arranged for all her boys to be accepted into the Endowed Grammar School on North Hill, overlooking Whitby harbour. The building had formerly been a house, built of stone with a large walled garden about it. Captain Edgecombe and local business-men had acquired the house and had installed no less than two schoolmasters in it for the benefit of local children. Most of the scholars were the sons of masters and crews of the Whitby fleets; it had been a rare privilege for her boys to attend alongside the sons of such men, people of substance, if not of quality. Mostly the boys were taught arithmetic, Latin and English writing, but, as befitted a community that derived its living from the sea, they were also instructed in the elements of geography and of navigation. Many of the boys were also taught, if they displayed an aptitude, one of the sea-going skills such as carpentry, sail-making, rope-handling.

Mr Fennel, the head schoolmaster, had spoken to Gertrude the previous month. 'Madam,' he'd said, 'I'd be talking with your husband if he were not away at sea and not expected back for a six-month. Though your son

27

Walter is industrious and pays good attention to his teaching, I fear there is a restlessness in him that often diverts his attention from his books. It seems to me that your son would be better employed learning some useful trade in which his hands can be occupied while his mind pursues whatever flight of fancy takes it. Some boys are clearly made to learn from books – your son Reuben, even at nine years of age, shows signs of absorbing knowledge like dry ground absorbs the rain. Walter, it is my regretful belief, will never learn from books.'

Gertrude had wept with sorrow. 'What then is to become of him, Mr Fennel?' she'd asked tearfully. 'I'd built my hopes on the lad acquiring an education to fit him for life.'

'And so he shall, Mistress Fossett,' the schoolmaster had said reassuringly, 'but he'll do it by experience, and not from books.'

Though Gertrude was devoted to her duties as housekeeper, even Mrs Edgecombe had seen that some inner worry was troubling her.

'Mistress Fossett,' she'd said one morning, 'I do declare that the mantel in the morning room was fair covered wi' soot this morning. Have you become short-sighted? The Captain would have died of apoplexy had he seen it.' When Gertrude burst into tears, even at so mild a rebuke, Mrs Edgecombe made her sit down. 'Come now, Mistress Fossett,' she'd said, 'I have seen for many a day that thy mind is distracted – shall you not take me into your confidence?'

Gertrude had blurted out her disappointment over the matter of Walter's schooling. 'It seems such a poor way to repay the Captain's generosity,' she said as her sobs subsided, 'when he has so charitably arranged for them to attend the Grammar School to receive an education above their station.'

'A pox on that!' Mrs Edgecombe had said, with a

coarseness calculated to shock Gertrude from her misery. 'There's many a man i' Parliament today who could hardly tell you which way a book should be held. The good Captain himself could take a vessel out in all weathers before he could write a hand you could read.'

'But what's to become of my Walter?' Gertrude asked, tears threatening to return to her eyes.

'I don't know,' Mrs Edgecombe said. 'It's the Will of God. And I shall do what I have always done when confronted by the Will of God.'

'Go to the church and pray?' offered Gertrude timidly.

'Nay, Mrs Fossett. I shall speak to the Captain.'

It was Captain Edgecombe who had found the answer. 'The lad shall leave the school,' he'd said. 'There's no reward in him occupying a chair that could benefit another. He shall be articled and 'prenticed to a good devout captain and be taught the trade of the sea. If he applies himself to his tasks he shall follow in his father's footsteps and become a ship's mate. Aye, and who can know – one day he might also follow in my path, and become a captain wi' his own vessel.'

'Tha' must be Mrs Fossett, ma'am, and this must by thy son, Walter.' The large bearded man, who'd come unseen to her side, had a voice that, without being a shout, would certainly have been heard and understood at the top of a yard-arm.

Gertrude rose nervously to her feet. 'And you, sir . . . ?'

'Captain Bishop, ma'am, at your service.' Bishop spoke to her, but his eyes were already on the boy. He approved of the way Walter had jumped swiftly to his feet and held himself tall and erect. He could see the boy bubbled with suppressed energy; his eyes were bright and intelligent but not cheeky. 'Give me thy hand, lad,' he said, offering his own paw in which Walter's smaller fist was engulfed. 'Tha's a firm hand lad, and I like that,' he said, noting the way the lad regarded him fearlessly without looking away as he applied a gentle squeeze. 'Captain Edgecombe has spoke of thee but aboard my vessel a man or a lad must needs speak for himself. Tha' can come wi' the highest recommendations but there's nowt I can do if tha' falls from the yard-arm, save to scrape up what's left of you on the deck and scour away your blood wi' soapstone.'

'I shall endeavour to be careful on the yard-arm, Captain,' Walter said.

'Aye, well tha'd better.' Bishop turned to Mrs Fossett. 'I'll give him one voyage, ma'am, on account of Captain Edgecombe's recommendation. On that voyage we'll find out if he has the makings of a man and a sailor in him. If he succeeds, and I warn you I'm a most demanding taskmaster, he'll get papers of indenture wi' me. If he fails, he'll be paid his mite and I shall wish him good luck in his future, which won't be spent wasting my time on my vessel. Is that clearly understood, ma'am?'

'It is, Captain. And I'm very grateful to you.'

'There's no call yet for gratitude. He'll be worked like a dog and he'll live like one for we have no comforts on board. There'll be nights he'll cry hisself to sleep wi' pains and aches. He'll be wet and cold – aye, frozen to his marrow, if he's got any. And he'll work alongside grown men, wi' no quarter given nor taken. Any man who walks aboard should be in Bedlam if he know what's good for him. But 'tis a man's life, miserable though it may be at times. I hope your lad will fit in with it, and make something of hisself. One thing is certain: if he don't, then the sea shall have him.'

'His father said the same,' Gertrude said with a half-smile. 'After his first voyage he swore he'd never go to sea again. He went on swearing, right up to the moment of signing on again.'

'And now he's got his mate's papers. Aye, I've heard tell of your husband, ma'am. It's because of him as much as Captain Edgecombe that I'm taking your lad aboard. One more matter. I've heard as Walter here cannot abide to have his head in a book. Well, I'm not of the same mind as some of these modern schoolmasters. There are some things to be learned only from books. Some things, I'll grant, have got to be learned in the doing. Your lad will get a bit of both. He'll work hard, but he'll also study books – I've a full book-box in my cabin, and your lad will not touch food until he's done his daily reading. You understand that, Walter?'

'Yes, sir,' the boy said bravely.

'Right. Tha' can come inside and sign on. We sail on the evening tide and thy mam will want to shed a few tears o'er thee before tha' departs.'

CHAPTER FOUR

Jabez Broadley confronted the miners gathered round the steps of his office. Tarn Fowles stood by his side, a long-shafted cudgel held loosely beside his leg. The mood of the miners was ugly, but Broadley knew he had the best of them. He looked at their hungry faces, their pinched cheeks, looked across their heads at the crowds of vagabonds at the gate, waiting to be given employment to earn a day's crust. No, none of the miners would rebel.

'The upper level's closed,' he said. 'The seam's running thin and full of flint. It's time we opened the lower level.'

'We tried to work the lower level, Master,' Wilfred Oates protested, 'and lost thirty men, women and babbies when it flooded.'

'Aye, well, now we've refitted the collar on the gin, we'll get the water down again. Job Bentley's been drawing wages night and day to get the lower levels dry. Tarn's been down there and come back wi' his boots unsoiled. It's either the lower level – and I'm kindly giving you all the first chance of signing – else I open the gates to yon crowd as'll be glad of work, I'll be bound.'

The miners didn't need to turn round to know the truth of what he said; they could hear the shuffling of feet and the hungry murmurs coming from behind them, the pleas of the women and the children.

'That pump will never keep the lower level dry,' Frank Aysgill said quietly to his brother Richard. 'Mark my

32

words, once he gets us down there, he'll open the gates on yon lot and they'll be working the upper level The pump will never cope wi' both levels. We'll be stifling down there.'

Richard spat on the ground. 'I've no coin in my pocket, Frank,' he said. 'Us cannot go home wi' nowt to show for the day. Now that our father spends his time preaching, our mam looks to us to provide. Us have to go down to the lower level, come what may.'

'We could hazard our luck elsewhere,' Frank suggested.

'Nay, th'art dreaming,' Richard said disgustedly. 'That many folks are coming into't town from't countryside – there's many coming over from Ireland and other foreign parts – for every job of work there's four or five waiting. We *mun* go down to't lower level, we mun.'

'Aye,' Frank admitted. 'I reckon that's the truth.'

The miners were all watching him. After his father had departed from the mine to follow a preacher's life, the men had looked upon Frank as their natural leader and spokesman. At seventeen years of age he'd filled his frame to manhood and hard work had firmed his shoulders and his back. Though there wasn't a spare ounce of flesh on him, he was tall and strong and could heft a hammer or swing a pick with the best of them. Even Tarn Fowles, the master's bully, was rumoured to be afeared of Frank.

'Right,' Frank said, 'we're earning nothing standing here. If't Master says it's the lower level, then down we go, and quick about it if we're to take home a crust.' He looked at Jabez Broadley with intense eyes that burned with his father's passion. 'In this life, Master Broadley, us can have nobbut one satisfaction. When we pass on, we're all going to answer to the same God. He'll judge me and mine, aye, and he'll judge thee and thine. I'd gi'e a week's wages to be standing by His side when He looks thee, Master, in thy eyes and judges thee wanting.'

With that, Frank turned abruptly on his heel and headed

for the top of the ladders that led down, past the upper level, to the dank foulness of the lower levels of the coalmine. The other men followed him, each one descending into a private hell. Then the women and the children, some of them no more than six years old but grimed and calloused already, with a cunning on their faces that belied their tender years. As the stream of humanity flowed down the ladders, the air rising past them became hotter and fouler with all manner of underground gases released from the workings of the coalface. Many were already coughing by the time they reached the lower level where they'd spend the day in semi-darkness, their progress lit only by the few rush lights clamped to the walls or the mutton fat candles burning in bowls set on hewn ledges.

They had barely started to hew out the coal – to be loaded into baskets dragged back through the tunnels by women squatting on their knees like dogs, then carried by children up the long ladders, since the whim-gin had not yet been extended to this lower level – when the two men they'd seen in Jabez Broadley's office climbed down the ladder, each with a pack on his back. The strangers crawled along the first passage and came to the start of the pillar-and-stall workings, where men were hacking at the solid rock wall that lay between them and the richer seam beyond. One of them took a long pointed-nosed hammer from his bag and began to tap the rockface, moving along from point to point, grunting with satisfaction about every fifth tap, and marking the place with a few deft hammer blows. Where the marks were placed the other man worked with a hammer and a chisel with a rounded face, hollow in the centre like a piece of pipe. As he hit the chisel, he carved a rounded hole into the hard rock. He took another such chisel from his pack and gave it to Frank Aysgill.

'Do as you see me do,' he said. 'Hammer and turn, hammer and turn.'

Frank, mystified, did as he was bid. Any fool knew how all that solid rock face had to be picked out before they could earn any money, but what was the point of tapping away with this dainty little chisel? It needed the power of a big swing, and the full force of a prise-bar to shift rock as strong as this. However, he supposed the man knew what he was doing; he seemed to have the authority of a specialist about him, like the men who'd come down to construct the rest of the whim-gin to extend it down to the lower level.

'What's tha' doing, then?' Frank asked.

The man smiled at him. 'Tha'll see in good time,' he said.

It took about an hour to chisel five holes in the rock face, each about fifteen inches deep and a couple of inches in diameter, corresponding to the length and width of the chisels. Frank had seen that they seemed to have a special edge to them, and had not blunted despite the work they'd been made to do under the repeated blows of the hammers.

While they were cutting these holes in the rock, the work of the mine continued where it could. Three of the stalls had already been opened, and there was a constant flow backwards and forwards of women carrying, dragging, pushing, heaving the baskets of coal, each in her individual method. All the women had taken off their outer garments and their torsos were covered only by shifts to preserve their modesty. Several of them were in advanced stages of pregnancy, and they moved along usually backwards, dragging the baskets after them; no woman wanted to risk banging the head of her unborn child on the stone jutting from the uneven floor. None could pause or rest since the line must be kept moving constantly, and none shouted louder than the young ones if an older woman should delay their progress. The women were paid by the number of baskets they hauled, and any impediment meant a loss of coin.

When the holes were cut, the two newcomers conferred. One looked at all the people going into the tunnels of the mine-working, the men labouring at the opened faces which here, fortunately, were five feet high so that the men could almost stand upright to work.

'We ought to clear them, do you think?' he said.

'Aye, we ought,' agreed the other man. 'But what'll Broadley say? Us'll get no more work from him if we clear out his mine afore we proceed.'

'Us'll get no more work if we kill his miners.'

'Nay, Nathaniel, there's plenty more waiting outside the gate.'

'So we take the chance?'

'We could send them back to the bottom of the ladder.'

'Aye, I reckon that's what we'll do.' The one called Nathaniel beckoned to Frank. 'Tell them all to go back to the bottom of the ladder, and put their hands over their ears.'

'What are you going to do?' Frank asked, his suspicions already aroused. Suddenly a thought occurred to him. 'Where do you come from?'

'Halifax,' Nathaniel said with a smile on his face.

Frank threw down his hammer in rage. 'I ought to have knowed it,' he said 'Halifax! You're explosives men!'

Every coalminer knew and feared the men from Halifax ever since the first explosives had been used to open a mine in 1743. When a mine was opened by hand, the miners were able to see what was happening to the rock above them, to hear it creak and rattle as it tried to subside. A skilled miner knew where to put a pillar of stones to support the roof, on which the strain was felt gradually. When explosives were used, no man could judge where the strains would come. Several mines had caved in after explosives had been used, delivering their powerful thrusts through the cracks and crevices in the rock without regard for the line of the coal seam. It had been bad enough when the explosives men were called in at night when the pit was not being worked, and the day men, the following morning, had descended into unknown dangers. Some of the greedy owners, however, had started blowing the rockface while the mine was still being worked, and many people had died of a mysterious head-blast that brought blood streaming out of their nostrils and their ears.

'Tha'll not blow the mine while we're down here,' Frank said. 'We're getting out before you do your mischief!'

Nathaniel looked at his partner. They'd discussed the matter at length with Broadley.

'I can't thoil to have idle workers climbing into and out of the mine while you blow a few cracks in the rock face,' Broadley had insisted. 'If tha' can't control the blast I s'all have to pay my coin to somebody who can. My man tells me there's nobbut a few tons of rock between the workers and the coal seam – I'd have thought tha' could have shifted that without wasting time to bring the folks out and put them back in again.'

'The master has told us to blow it,' Nathaniel said, 'and blow it we must. You can take everybody back to the foot of the shaft. They'll be out of harm's way there. It'll take us that long to get everything prepared.'

Quickly Frank began summoning the miners, starting them on the crawl back to the shaft. There was much confusion in the tunnels since they were already filled by women and children crawling each way with their baskets, and there was hardly room to turn around.

The men scooped out some black powder from the bags they'd brought, rolled it in greased paper and thrust it into the holes that Frank himself had helped them chop. 'If only I'd known,' he said as he watched them working, 'I'd never have helped you do the Devil's work!' When the holes had been half filled, they sealed the remainder with stones, tamping them home with the wooden shaft of a hammer. Despite himself Frank watched with some interest. 'It doesn't explode, then, when you hit it?' he asked, mystified.

'It won't explode until we put a spark to it and light it,' Nathaniel told him.

'And then what happens?'

'The force will go inwards and crack the rock.'

'And if it doesn't?' Frank had heard too many stories about the effect of these explosives in the confined space of the mines where they were being used increasingly to open the faces.

Nathaniel smiled. 'Why then,' he said, 'us'll have nowt to worry about. Us'll all have gone to meet our Maker! Now, tha'd better get back to safety at the foot of the shaft. Bend down, and clamp thy hands over thy ears. Aye, and a prayer might help since, to judge by what tha' said to Jabez Broadley, th'art a believing man!'

Some perverse force took hold of Frank, some previously unfelt proprietorial sense. 'I work here,' he said. 'It's my living. I shall stay by thy side while tha' blows my mine.'

Nathanial glanced at his partner, amused. 'Ah, *thy* mine, is it? Tha' sang a different tune afore when tha' accused us of doing't Devil's work.'

'I shall stay,' Frank said in a voice that brooked no dissent. 'Tha'd better get ahead and blow it and we shall see what happens.'

He watched with great interest as the men prepared a trail of the black powder grains – not an easy task since there was so much water about, and the level seemed constantly to be rising. Finally, they were able to lay a continuous trail of about twenty feet, ending in the paper tube that went through the tamped stones into the centre of the explosive itself.

Nathaniel pointed to one side, out of the direct line of the impending blast. 'That's where us'll go,' he said, 'but since

38

it's thy mine, tha' can suit thyself.'

Frank walked to where Nathaniel had pointed, hunkered down and raised his hands, ready to clasp them over his ears as they had instructed. He watched Nathaniel strike a spark with his tinder and flint; it took four tries before the spark finally caught, and the black powder began to splutter and smoke. The two men walked leisurely across the open space of the stalls, came beside Frank, and they too squatted. Frank watched fascinated as the tiny flame moved slowly along the powder trail, flaring sometimes, seeming sometimes to have expired in smoke, but moving constantly along. Only when it had disappeared into the tamped hole did Nathaniel signal for them to cover their ears and turn their faces away from the explosion.

Frank was trembling with fear as he waited, his early courage quite dissipated. 'What am I doing here?' he asked himself, knowing he could have been with the others at the foot of the mine shaft, a good hundred paces away.

The explosion was more hellish than he could have guessed. It seemed as if a fat hand hit him heavily between his shoulder-blades, driving him forwards towards the rockface. Then he felt a second hand slam into the back of his neck, jerking his chin forward. He had felt both blows before he heard the almighty thrump of the explosion itself. It was as if a hole had been blown through the centre of his skull; his ear-drums rang with the shock of it and the blinding, excruciating pain was worse than anything he'd ever felt in his life. Next came the flying stones and slivers of rock that tore into his back. He heard a piercing scream nearby, but the air was so turbulent he couldn't move. He crouched down, wondering only when the agony of this hell would be over, when once again he'd feel able to breathe. His lungs had been emptied by the blast, and he tried to gasp as he pitched forward under the violent force behind him, the whee of the stone fragments in the air, the clatter as they rattled from wall to wall and thudded into the ground around his feet.

When finally he lit a candle, Frank saw Nathaniel's partner spreadeagled on the ground beside him, the back of his head a bloodied mess. A fragment of rock shaped like a chisel protruded from his neck. Nathaniel himself was lying face down with a large rock beside his head and blood seeping out of his ears. Frank felt a wetness run down his lips, raised his hand to wipe it away and found blood pouring from his own nose.

The shape of the stalls had changed completely and the rubble of the rock had covered the faces of two of them entirely. Much of the force seemed to have gone upwards and the roof had belled. As Frank looked up he saw water trickling down from inside the bell; the roof was beginning to creak and to alter shape with the pressure that had been forced up into it. He turned to Nathaniel, flipped him over, but quickly saw he was dead. Nathaniel's partner was obviously as dead as a pole-axed bull. Frank climbed to his feet and, stooping, tried to find the tunnel that led back to the foot of the mine-shaft. The movement of the rock had so changed the structure of all about him that he had no idea where the tunnel might now be. Panic flashed through him and he began to pull at the rocks, casting them wildly aside without finding any trace of an opening.

After a few minutes he began to lose the first flood of fear, and took himself back from the rockface to squat and consider his situation. The candle burned bright enough but he had no way of knowing how long it would last. He would have to conserve his own energies if he was to succeed in getting out. The rest of the miners would already be making their way along the tunnel to reach him; he could sit there and wait in the hope they'd get through before the air ran out, or the water rose high enough to drown him.

'Dear Father,' he said, 'pray for me . . .'

Another fall of rock from the roof of the bell the explosion had created sent Frank scrambling back to the rockface. He saw that the water was now a foot or more deep and must engulf him within minutes if he didn't get out. This time, however, he managed to bring his panic more quickly under control. Trying to think clearly and logically, he reasoned that the tunnel entrance had been directly facing the rock wall in which the explosion had been created. He walked back as far as he could and turned his back to the rock wall.

'There,' he said out loud, 'there, straight ahead.' He scrambled over the fallen rock back to where he believed the tunnel entrance to be, and began to tear at the rocks, throwing them violently aside. But as fast as he removed one, another three or more fell down from the pile. Already the water was two feet high, and now that the numbing shock of the blast itself had gone he began to feel the pain in his back where the rock had smashed into him. When he rubbed his hand over his jerkin, it came away covered in the blood that was flowing from his wounds.

'At least,' Frank told himself, 'the candle still burns and I can see.' To have been trapped in total darkness would, he knew, have driven him out of his mind.

All his emotions, all his feelings, were directed into bitter hatred of Jabez Broadley who tried to use these new methods to secure an advantage for himself, no matter what the cost in lives of other people. Nathaniel and his partner had accepted the risks of a dangerous trade, but presumably they had been paid enough to make it worthwhile. Of course it would advantage the miners if the rocks, on which they spent so much time without earning money, could so quickly be driven out of the way. But miners accepted rock, shale, clay and flints as part of the normal hazard of their trade. No man would ever be able to dig a ton of pure coal without having to dispose of a quantity of wasted material.

How could a man so debase human life as to permit such terrible risks, for the sake of earning more coin, taking more advantage for himself?

For the first time, Frank understood something of what his father, Matthew Aysgill, had vainly tried to teach here in the mine, on the moors, in the markets. That all men should have a respect for the lives of others suddenly seemed to Frank, trapped hundreds of feet below the earth's surface, to have a true meaning. If only he had learned that sooner, he thought as he tore at the stones, he could have offered comfort and assistance to his own father, could have helped him more than he had.

He resolved that if ever he escaped from this hellish tomb, he would look again at what his father had always said. He knew he could never accept anyone's teachings without considering them. But at least he could try to understand.

A stone came away, and only one jagged lump of rock fell. He hauled out the fallen lump, lacerating his hands on its sharp edges as he heaved it from him, but ignoring the pain as a gasp of relief burst from his lungs: there before him stretched the tunnel mouth, dark and empty. As he watched, a faint glow of light appeared at its far end as someone began to crawl along with a rush-light, then another with a candle, then another. He pulled more rocks away, careful not to cause a further rock-fall that could entrap him again.

'Frank!' It was the voice of his brother Richard calling.

'Aye, Richard, 'tis me,' he said, though his voice was so hoarse he knew none would hear him. He dragged himself forward beyond the rock-fall and waited there, crouched on all fours like a dog. His back hurt abominably and there was an acrid taste of bile and blood in his mouth. His ears pained him and his senses had begun to reel.

'Art alive then?' Richard said as he drew close. Both knew it was a daft thing to say but the brothers had an affection for each other that rarely found expression in words.

'Aye, I reckon I am, but nobbut just . . .'

'I've never heard nowt like it,' Richard said. 'It come out of 't tunnel like nowt I've ever heard before, and brought stones wi' it, and rocks, and a stink of gas. Four people's been killed by it. Nobody we know, all late-comers. I thought tha' were gone, and I was thinking what to tell our mam.'

'The Halifax men were both killed,' Frank said. 'They mun have used too much powder.'

'I thought you mun *all* be dead. Stones came flying big as a man's head. That young lad as were cheeking me yesterday caught one in his chest. It broke his bones. His mam were right beside him. He were nobbut seven, the poor lad.'

The ones who were uninjured went back to work immediately. There was rock to be shifted and coal to be won for coins – none could afford to stop when there was work to be done. Now that the tunnel was open and the pump had begun to function, the water level slowly subsided.

The dead were carried to the lower level on strong men's backs, then tied to the baskets of the gin to be hauled to the surface.

'Art going up?' Richard asked his brother.

'I don't reckon so,' Frank said. 'I can still swing a pick.'

'Thy back's a mess. We ought to get summat rubbed on it.'

'Mam'll rub it wi' grease when we get home.'

'I'm going up,' Richard said. 'I've had as much as I can take down here.'

43

Frank held his arm. 'Nay, lad,' he said, 'it's me as were caught, not thee . . .'

'It doesn't make any difference to me,' Richard said adamantly. 'I can't take it no more. Tha' can stay if tha's a mind, but I've got to get up and out of it, else I shall suffocate.'

Frank eyed his younger brother. Richard, though only sixteen, already displayed strains of restlessness and malcontent. When their father had taken to the life of an itinerant Wesleyan preacher, Richard had expressed contempt for his noble teachings.

'It's very well for him to take his ease roaming the country spouting beliefs as interests and benefits nobody,' Richard had complained once, 'while we're down yon mine earning enough for only a handful of oats and sometimes a marrow bone to suck.'

'Nay, th'art exaggerating again,' Frank had replied. 'Our mam feeds us right well on what we gi'e her, and still there's summat left over for our father. In human charity we mun look after our own father, Richard. That's the way of the Aysgills and we mun be proud of it.'

'I'm not interested in the Aysgill way,' Richard had retorted vehemently. 'Our mam is always thrusting the family name at us, but I'm not concerned to be an Aysgill. I seek to better myself and that means I need to jingle a few coins in my pocket.'

Frank had hoped that Richard was beginning to settle down and accept their lot; certainly he'd seemed less complaining and quieter lately. He'd taken himself out of the house for hours on end and when Frank asked him where he'd been going instead of taking his rest for the next day's toil, Richard had flared like tinder.

'It's nowt to do wi' thee,' he'd said.

Frank had assumed Richard had found a lass for himself. These days, he thought, morality was low and lasses and lads met openly on the streets, could even visit the ale-yards together if they had a mind and a coin, aye, and lie with each other in the fields.

'Tha's not giving some lass babies, art tha', Richard?' he'd asked. Since their father was often away from home, he felt responsible for the younger lad.

'Babies? What are you talking about?' Richard had said.

Unconvinced, Frank had continued to worry about him. Now he rested one hand on his brother's shoulder and asked: 'What ails thee, Richard?'

'I mun get out of't mine, Frank,' Richard said. Frank had never seen such a look of desperation on his brother's face. 'Not just now, after't explosion, but for ever!'

Frank turned to look at the miners who'd already gone back to work. 'Aye, lad,' he said, 'I can see the way tha' feels about it. Tha'd better get back up't ladder, and us'll talk about it when I come home tonight.'

'Tha'll not hate me, Frank?' Richard asked anxiously.

'Hate thee? Th'art my *brother*. No matter what tha' does, I'll never *hate* thee.'

CHAPTER FIVE

When he left the mine, instead of going home to Hunslet, Richard Aysgill walked swiftly in the opposite direction. Leeds had grown vaster even in the short time they'd been living there, and new houses were springing up like fungus everywhere, many built for the people who were becoming prosperous as traders, some by enlightened owners of the new factories who knew they'd keep their work-force together and better disciplined if the tenancy of a house was bonded to the employment. People would be less likely to ask for more wages, or to absent themselves, if the loss of a house was one of the possible penalties.

Richard skirted the houses and the thickly populated area, and headed across the wooded moorland. On the way he stopped beside one of the many streams and washed his hands and face to remove some of the coal dust. He'd never felt clean on his skin since he'd gone down the mine as a lad of eight. After all these years the blackness of the coal had embedded itself in his pores, deep inside him. 'Aye, and more than that,' he said to himself. 'The damned stuff has embedded itself into my nature, into my very being.' He knew it would be harder to cleanse his spirit than his body, to make a clean free man of himself.

And a free man he was determined to be, no matter what it cost him, no matter what manner of thing he was obliged to do.

He strode vigorously across the heath in the sunlight. The

air was crisp, and he could taste it already on his coal-rimed tongue. He hawked and spat, gulped in more of the fresh air, and spat again. Ahead of him, approaching slowly, he saw several packhorses, in the charge of a man who carried a stout stave, doubtless against the cutpurses, vagabonds and robbers who were all around these days. Another man walked behind the three laden packhorses and he carried a pistol in his belt. As they spotted Richard they stopped the horses and the taller man who'd been at the back went behind, shielded by their bulk. Richard knew the pistol would already have been primed and cocked and was now most likely aimed at his body.

'Nay, you can put up your pistol,' he said. 'You have nowt to fear from me. I'm a simple working man as wishes you no harm on your way.'

He could see the packhorses were burdened with lengths of cloth that would have been woven in one of the small outlying villages from wool the merchant himself had provided. When the merchant left on his rounds, he'd take unspun wool with him to the spinners, then the spun thread to the weavers, ending his day by bringing the finished cloth back to the Wool Exchange where it would be sold the next day, probably for export. Richard eyed the merchant's fine though serviceable clothing: the green velvet travelling coat, the white cotton hose now spattered with mud, the soft leather boots, the three-cornered hat which he wore straight across his brow. His man was dressed in rougher wear but there was a healthy bucolic shine to his reddened cheeks that spoke of the outdoor life, with plain but ample food.

Richard watched them enviously as the two set off to continue their journey. He himself had not eaten that day and it was apparent the two of them had dined well at some wayside tavern. His stimulated senses could even detect a strong odour of beer on the air as they passed by, and a

47

more pungent waft of strong hollands with which the merchant had no doubt settled his stomach after the meal. Richard imagined the taste of the food on his tongue – and suddenly felt a fresh surge of determination to finish with the life of a miner, the unending toil of dust and dirt for scant reward, the thin meagre brewis on which they fed each evening since much of their money went to Matthew, their father, to permit him to travel far and wide on his preaching mission. What did it matter to *him*, Richard thought, if some fisherman in remote Robin Hood's Bay, where his father had gone with John Wesley himself, should hear the word of God? Richard didn't even know where Robin Hood's Bay was. All he knew, and it rankled sorely with him, was that Mildred, their mam, had dipped into their scant supply of coins to provide Matthew with travelling money. Half those coins had been earned by Richard – surely he had some right in their disposition? He hated to see them squandered on some distant enterprise, no matter how godly and moral the mission might be. Richard's feeling of rebellion had been growing in him for some time, heightened by the sense of great injustice that his coin should be so used.

'I'll not go back down the mine!' he said. 'I'll *never* go back down the mine!'

Only when a crow rose cawing from a tree nearby did he realize that he had shouted his thoughts aloud, as an act of defiance to the heavens above.

The tavern he was heading for was a mean place, set on the edge of a copse of trees that occupied the crest of a hill – a man could easily slip out of the back door and be away with no one the wiser. The tavern was thatched and beside it, to the right as Richard approached, were a sheepfold, a cows' byre and pig pens. It was apparent that the tavern-keeper gave as much time to husbandry as to serving his customers; in this remote spot, travellers would be few and far between, and ill-inclined to linger when they smelled the rude farmyard odours of the establishment, saw its smoke-blackened interior, sensed its atmosphere of conspiracy and evil-doing.

When Richard stepped across the threshold, the men seated round the smoking fire immediately ceased their conversation and stared at him. Accustoming his eyes to the gloom and the smoke, Richard looked around. On each of three sides of the room, which measured at most five paces by eight, were closed doors. The one to the right of the fireplace, which was deep and carried benches on each side of the open grate, was a stable door. The top part was open, but the view beyond was hidden by a muslin curtain through which, Richard guessed, the proprietor would be able to see without being seen. The room must formerly have been a barn; the upper part revealed the cruck-truss and the wattle filling to the ends of the walls. The timbers were now smoke-blackened and gleamed with the oily soot of mutton-fat candles.

Three tables in the corners held pots of ale and platters of chunks of meat; the men had doubtless eaten a meal and were now relaxing by the fire. Richard's mouth began to salivate when he saw the leavings – what remained on the platters would have fed him for a week, and the ale would have quenched his thirst for a day. The men were huddled together by the modest fire, as if they had been playing some game in its embers, but more likely conspiring in some enterprise.

Suddenly one of the men leapt to his feet. 'Aye, 'tis the lad!' he shouted boisterously. 'We never thought you'd come!' He charged across the room, seized Richard's arm, and dragged him over to the fireside bench. 'Now, Tod,' he said, 'this is the lad I was telling you of. Strong'i'the'arm, we should be calling him, for he certainly bested me, and there's many a grown man tried that to his cost and sorrow.'

Tod, the man he had addressed, eyed Richard coolly, without favour. 'Looks a bit young to me,' he said, dismissing Richard at a glance.

'Young or not,' Richard's champion said, 'he's the lad for us! He has reading and writing, a strong back and a wicked powerful arm. What better combination could we seek for our enterprise?' He looked across at the table. 'Has tha' eaten, Richard?' he asked. 'Tha' mun gobble some of yon fare down afore we start to talk, since tha' can't speak wi' a grumbling belly.' He lifted his head to shout. 'Emily! Fetch us a pot of ale – and sharp about it, else the lad'll die of thirst!'

The curtain parted instantly to reveal a woman of indeterminate years wearing a heavy cotton mobcap over unwashed hair.

'Aye, and who'll pay me?' she bellowed, loud as he.

''Tis all on the one account,' he cried. 'Tha' knows when us'll pay thee, old crone, and wi' what!'

She cackled coarsely, retired inside the room, opened the door, and came out with a pot of ale in her hand. She slammed it down on the table and some of the beer slopped on to the bare boards. 'I'd like to see the day when tha' comes wi' coin in thy hands,' she said, 'and not tomorrow's promises.'

Richard was already seated with a well fleshed lamb knuckle in his hands, tearing wolfishly at the meat. The woman regarded him and her eyes softened. She reached out her hand and stroked the side of his cheek.

'I had a lad like thee, once,' she said, 'till the pox got him. Tha'd do a lot better to get home to thy mam than laiking about here. I can see by thy face tha' comes of a good home, and despite the coal-dust, th'art the cleanest lad as has been in here for many a year.'

'Shut thy mouth, Emily,' the man said suddenly, all traces of former joviality gone. 'It's thy choice to run a thieves' kitchen and profit from it – tha's got no call to interfere wi' my side of the enterprise. The lad will make up his own mind wi'out advice from thee.'

Emily flounced from the room and the man beckoned the others to come to the table.

'I'll gi'e thee a few names, lad,' he said, 'as a token of our good intent. We're all woven of a piece, tha' mun understand that – one man's warp is another's weft. In, th'art in – if tha' betrays us, th'art dead.'

Richard nodded his head, unable to speak for the full mouth of food.

'Right. I'm Joe Grice, as tha' knows already, and I'm to be followed without question in everything, understand?'

Richard nodded, still more interested in food than anything else.

'This is Tod Lackley, and he's been wi' me the longest,' Joe went on, indicating the man Richard had not previously met.

Richard had gone from his home one night, in despair over the amount of money he felt his father was taking from the household accounts with no return. He'd had just a penny or two in his pocket, but it was enough to buy sufficient beer to drown his sorrows.

He was sitting at the ale-house table with his first jug before him, overhearing the conversation of a party travelling on the stagecoach now being re-horsed in the yard. He liked to come to the staging post; he saw adventure in all the travellers and dreamed of a time when he'd be able to escape from the mine and go adventuring himself to London.

One man was arguing loudly about the new Customs Law they were trying to pass in Parliament, protesting that it would give Excise men the right to enter any premises without so much as a by-your-leave. The man was expansive, including all the table in his monologue.

'*For a man's house is his castle* – isn't that what Sir Edward Coke said, young man?' he declared, seeming to address Richard directly.

'Without doubt, sir,' Richard said, smiling secretly at the man's pomposity. Then he added, '*Et domus sua cuique est tutissimum refugium.*'

The man stared at him, his mouth opening and closing, like a fresh-landed carp. 'I took thee for a coalminer,' he said, 'by thy garb and colour, yet th'art versed in Latin . . .'

'Yes, sir, I may make that small claim in all modesty, for my mam has taken a leather to me a score of times on that account.' Richard did not reveal that he had been a miserable failure at his studies and his mam had finally despaired of teaching him anything other than to read and write and do simple calculations. He did remember the words of Sir Edward Coke, however, for his father was wont to quote them as part of his humanist teachings. All men, his father frequently declared – too frequently for Richard – had a right to peace and quiet in their own homes, and a right to determine what they themselves would make of their own lives. This was a new teaching, of which few approved; more than anything else, this was what was responsible for the difficulties Matthew Aysgill encountered when he preached in the 'Changes or at the gates of the new manufactories springing up everywhere. Few members of the established Church and even few land and business owners could countenance such revolutionary teaching – it would only cause discontent among the common run of folks, they argued.

By the time the stagecoach left that night, Richard had drunk – at the travelling gentleman's expense – as much beer as his belly could hold. Rising unsteadily to his feet, he lurched into a corner of the yard to empty his swollen bladder and was sighing with relief when he heard a voice bellow beside him. He hadn't realized that a man was crouched in the dark recess of the corner, pulling the ample nethers of a servant girl on to himself in pleasure. Richard's stream of urine was coursing down the girl's naked buttocks on to the man's hands and his parts.

The man threw the girl aside and, despite his exposure, launched himself at Richard in fury. Richard's years in the mine stood him in good stead; his frame was hard as iron and the man's blows did him no harm. Drunkenly deciding he must defend himself, he struck out wildly and felled the man with a couple of blows to his chest and face. Then he felt a sudden remorse.

'I beg your pardon,' he said as he helped the man to his feet. 'I hadn't seen you were taking your pleasure in the corner.'

The man recovered quickly and began to laugh at himself. 'Who'd have thought,' he said, bursting with laughter, 'that Joe Grice would get himself pissed upon! And by a young Latin-spouting lad at that! Gi'e me a moment to repair myself, and us'll go back inside to celebrate such an event!'

They talked half through the night, long after the others were all lying down in corners, seeking rest. Richard found himself expressing things he'd not been able to say at home, pouring out his feelings of the vast injustice of his present life. Joe Grice, for the most part, merely listened, urging the lad on and on.

'Aye,' he said finally, 'I can well understand what tha' means. Th'art being hard done by, as are most men who don't take matters into their own hands. Tha' should be like me – free as a crow to fly anywhere I choose. I take my food and my pleasure where I find it, and no man can say me nay.' He chuckled. 'Except thee, who's the first man to piss on me, in all manners of speaking, since I chose the free life. At least, tha's the only man to do it and live to tell the tale.'

Suddenly Richard realized what manner of a man Joe Grice was. The mists of drink that had befuddled his brain had long since disappeared, and now he could see the hardness beneath Joe Grice's amiable surface.

Joe Grice perceived the change in the younger lad's manner. 'Now tha' knows me for what I am,' Joe said. 'Free as a wind, I travel where the will and the lust take me. I eat where I may, take my ease in whatever grove or chamber suits me at the end of the day.'

'And for coin . . . ?' Richard asked hesitantly.

'Coin? Nay, lad, I take where I might. I engage in bold enterprise with my lads about me. We take from a coach here, from a laden traveller there. We rob only those who can spare what mite we lift from them.'

'Tha' steals? Th'art a thief?'

Joe's face darkened. 'I take from those who can best spare it. If tha' wants to dub it thieving, then tha's not the man for me. I thought I saw a spark of adventuring in thee, and hoped I could join thy efforts to mine. In truth, we lack but one in our band of men. We lack only a man who can read and write, who has education and can speak well wi' those who'd call themselves his masters. I see th'art such a one. Once we get the coal-dust off thee, tha' could advantage us by sitting in the coaching inns and the staging houses, gathering intelligence of departures, of men a-jingling wi' coin. That we cannot do, for we're all of a rough cast and no man would speak before us. Thee, wi' thy Latin, could coax a casual intelligence from the over-fed pox-raddled persons it is our pleasure to take from. But if tha' dubs it thievery—'

'Nay,' Richard said hotly, 'I had no wish to offer thee an insult, Joe Grice. I've been brought up in a Christian household and must shed many of its teachings afore I can come to an understanding of what tha' says.'

'When tha' understands, and if tha's of a mind to adventure with us, tha' mun come to the inn by Shapwell Top. We mostly set our adventures from there. If we come across a piece of goods wi' money in the selling, the innkeeper takes it from us at a fair price. I've disposed of many a watch and jewelled stick-pin that way. But, lad, I warn thee. If the constable should appear before tha' does, I shall know tha's lain an information against us to advantage thyself, and then thy life wouldn't be worth the living.'

It had taken Richard a month of soul-searching; everything his father and mother had ever said to him was in conflict with Joe Grice's teachings. Each day he'd resolved to put all knowledge of Joe Grice and his way of life from his mind, but each day some new incident had come to affect his reasoning. Why should some men wear a diamond in their stocks that would feed a family for the rest of their lives? Why should well-clad ladies carry a fortune in jewels on their fingers? Why should Jabez Broadley dine each day on roasts of pork, beef and lamb, the odour of which drove the hungry workers half crazy as it wafted over the mine-top? Aye, and when he'd gorged himself and his favourites had been given chunks of the meat, why should he throw to his dogs bones with meat clinging to them that would make brewis for a large family for a week? Young Billy Vertue, who knew no better at seven years of age, had once attempted to snatch a bone from one of the dogs and had had his hand and arm lacerated by the brute's savage teeth. And then had seen his mam, his dad and all his five brothers discharged from employ on the spot, with not a coin to take home.

Surely, Richard had thought, that was not in accordance with Matthew's teachings – that all men were born equal in the sight of the Lord? Joe Grice's philosophy was no more than an extension of that; if the Lord took no hand in making men equal, then it was up to men to help themselves.

The explosives men, the wanton injury to the workers, the near-entombment of his brother, the foul stink of released gases and dusts merely provided Richard with an excuse for a resolve he had already reached. He would join Joe Grice in his adventuring, wheresoever it might lead.

Richard looked around the faces of his new-chosen companions. 'I'm glad to meet you, Tod Lackley,' he said, when Joe Grice introduced them.

'Tod's a good lad wi' his fists,' Joe said, 'but he's not much for talking. This one, on the other hand, would talk his way into the sweetest bedroom in the land, given but half a chance. His name is Dick Berry, and his father's father, some say, were a gentleman of quality, high-born and honoured. Not much of that shows in our Dick's face, however!'

Dick looked like a simple yeoman farmer. Broad-shouldered, with thick arms and huge hands, he had a sweet soft smile to his face, and glistening hair the colour of walnut dye. Richard shook hands solemnly with him, pledging himself to their joint enterprise.

Stephen Lumme and John Hirst were as even as a pair of whelps from one litter; both were well-founded but thin, both had sharp fox eyes and close-clipped hair. Neither one appeared able to smile. Richard reckoned them to be around twenty years of age, whereas Joe, Tod and Dick were, he estimated, going on thirty.

'Stephen and John make a point of assaulting lawyers,' Joe said, 'for it was with a lawyer's connivance that their families lost their holdings, to make way for house-building by the Earl of Morley. The lads joined together in enterprise; I met them in the most coincidental way, when they chose

56

to waylay the York coach at the same time and in the same place as ourselves. By the time we'd sorted out who was trying to take who, the coach was well on its way past Tadcaster and we made no coin that day, though we entered the brewery and made ourselves comfortable on their sweet-water ale at their expense. We've coached, ridden, floated, walked – aye, and run together ever since.'

'And doubtless will hang together,' Emily snorted as she came to clear the platters from the table. 'It's been a long time since tha's tasted meat straight off a knuckle bone, lad,' she said fondly, placing her arm round Richard's shoulders.

'Tha' mun take her in the back and gi'e her a tumble,' Joe said, 'else she'll never let you in peace.'

Emily saw Richard's face redden, glanced at Joe, and winked. 'I reckon as the young master doesn't know what you're talking about, Joe,' she said. 'While tha's instructing him in the ways of the road, happen I'd better show him a bit about life.'

'You're not trying to tell me that our Richard Aysgill is a virgin, Emily, are you?'

'I'll wager a coin on it,' she said.

'Tha'll lose for sure,' Joe said. 'Won't she, Richard? Tell me, dear lad, tha' ain't still a virgin?'

Richard stood up at the table, realizing they were making fun of him. Now was the time to establish himself. As the youngest member of the band of men, he had no intention of being bullied. 'Why, Joe,' he said, 'haven't you seen me pissing on girls' arses afore now? Don't you remember? Or must I recount the tale?'

'Tha's no need of that,' Joe said hurriedly. 'I believe thee to be a man in all tha's done.'

'We shall see about that,' Emily said, as she removed the platters and went back into her smoke-filled kitchen.

CHAPTER SIX

Sleightholme's Mill, where Arthur Aysgill worked as a fourteen-year-old apprentice, was the first mill in the district to have one of James Hargreaves's newly invented, and as yet untried, spinning jennies.

Hargreaves had been a weaver who lived and worked at Stanhill, near Blackburn in Lancashire, in the already thriving cotton trade for which the moist atmosphere of that county was much suited. The hand-operated machine he'd invented consisted of a wheel which powered a number of spindles, and a clasp which drew a spun yarn from each spindle at the same time. When the clasp had drawn the yarns forward it moved back and the yarn was wound on to a cop. Since all the yarns were drawn together, they all achieved an even quality and were suitable for weaving. Hargreaves had tried to interest the Lancashire spinners in his invention, but many feared that this monster would take their employment from them and he received a poor reception wherever he went. Thomas Sleightholme had been in Manchester when he'd heard of the 'Spinning Jenny', as it was called, and he asked Hargreaves for a demonstration. Despite the fact that it broke down twice, Sleightholme was fascinated by the new machine and insisted that Hargreaves put one in his mill in Leeds. After all, he reasoned, if it would spin cotton fibres, it should spin woollen ones just as effectively.

Sleightholme bought the machine outright; he wanted

nothing to do with paying James Hargreaves royalties and he knew the man was desperate to see his machine installed somewhere. So far Hargreaves had not been able to complete the machine satisfactorily to apply for a patent; Sleightholme realized he could advantage himself if he obtained one before the patent was granted.

So the machine was duly installed on the second floor of Sleightholme's Mill, a vast building of stone and brick. It had eight spindles and required but one operator to turn the wheel, to watch that the spun yarn didn't snag or break as the frame moved along the metal tracks in which it was housed. At the completion of each cycle the yarn was spun on to the cops, all regular in size and twist.

The mob of apprentices gathered round while Tomlinson, the foreman, stood beside the jenny, twisting the wheel. Thomas Sleightholme himself had come to watch the first trials of the machine; even he exclaimed with delight when he saw the spun yarn on the cops. James Hargreaves, who had travelled from Stanhill to supervise the installation, stood there beaming, covered in the grease with which he'd lightly smeared the tracks to assist the trolley's movement; then, wiping his hands on a swab of wool waste, he accepted the handshakes – first of Thomas Sleightholme, as was befitting, then the gentlemen of the Partnership, most of whom were Sleightholme's relatives, then finally Tomlinson, the jenny's first operator.

'There can be but little doubt, Mr Hargreaves,' proclaimed Sleightholme, 'that what we have achieved this day will go down the long annals of history. I predict, man, you'll be famous in your own lifetime – aye, and wealthy!'

Neither could foresee the years of struggle, of agony and enmity, that would ensue before James Hargreaves finally established his own mill in Nottingham, where he fled to escape the wrath of his fellow Lancastrians.

The partners held a celebratory luncheon at the mill

when the machine was working and Hargreaves had departed for Stanhill. After the luncheon, Thomas Sleightholme sent for his foreman.

'The jenny goes well, Tomlinson?' he asked, puffing at the pipe filled with American tobacco which he had recently affected, as befitting a man of his stature.

'Aye, Master Sleightholme, it goes well; the yarn is spinning from it at a fair rate,' Tomlinson reported. 'We've had a few moments of care, but nothing our new engineer can't cope with. Jonas Clegg has paid us a visit, and thinks he can copy the machine quite easily. In a six-month, we can have five or six of them working on yon second floor, and we can keep all the flying shuttles busy wi'out need to buy in from the countryside.'

'Five or six, Tomlinson? You must lift your expectations higher, man. If Clegg seeks a contract from me, he'll guarantee to have twenty of them operating by next Quarter Sessions.'

'Then I'd better inform him so,' Tomlinson said. 'I think he's still on the second floor, copying his measurements.'

'Aye, and while you're about it, you can suggest he increases the number of spindles,' said Sleightholme. 'Even a non-engineer like myself can see the jenny would carry twice, three times, even four times as many spindles. We must extract the full amount of work from our machines as we do from our workers. 'Tis God's way, Tomlinson, God's way, since idleness in machine breeds rust as readily as idleness in workers breeds sloth. While you're about it, man, you'd better dispose of six of our spinners – I'll not have them standing by idle while a machine does their work for them.'

'*Six* of them, Master?'

'Aye, Tomlinson, six. We cannot throw money away on Idle Jacks when we have other means of doing the work. That would *not* be God's way, Tomlinson, not at all.'

* * *

Amelia Aysgill stirred on her pallet, wondering who could be disturbing her in the middle of the afternoon in their mill cottage. Recently, the pain she had felt in her stomach had grown and grown, almost as if another child were feeding on her insides. It had been several weeks since she had been able to drag herself into the mill to work, though Arthur had warned her that Tomlinson's patience would soon be exhausted. Mill cottages were supplied only to those who actually worked in the mill. So far, Tomlinson had been unusually lenient when Arthur had told him of his mother's sickness.

In the four years since his father, Simon Aysgill, had killed himself in a fit of depression, fourteen-year-old Arthur had had to provide for the two of them, his mother and himself, as best he could. Gone were his boyhood games with Ezra, the bought apprentice. Gone was his foraging for food from tavern tables. Now he had to maintain the cottage, feed and clothe himself and his mother with the meagre wages he earned, as well as do the cooking, the cleaning, all the things a woman would normally do for herself. It seemed as if Amelia had lost heart and the will to live these days.

'Can that be you, Arthur?' she asked querulously as she heard his footsteps on the flagstones of the kitchen.

'Aye, Mam, it's me.' Arthur appeared in the doorway, his shoulders slumped.

'What are you doing home at this time o' day? Has summat happened in't mill?'

'Aye, Mam, summat's happened,' he said wearily.

'Is it that new jenny you were telling me about?'

'Aye, I suppose it has to do wi' the new jenny . . .'

She struggled to sit upright on her pallet bed, sensing his great despondency. 'Nay, what is it, lad?' she asked. 'Why such a long face?'

'I've been laid off, Mam. I've been dismissed from't mill.'

'You've *what*? I thought Tomlinson liked you. Have you been mischieving?'

61

'No, Mam, I haven't been mischieving. Six of us is laid off. Just when I were making a success of the spinning he's laid me off.'

The awfulness of it suddenly struck her and Amelia began to cry. 'What's to happen to us, Arthur? What about the cottage? What about the roof o'er our heads?' she sobbed.

'We've got to get out, Mam,' said Arthur bleakly 'Since we're no longer working in't mill, we've no right to a tied cottage. We've got to get out. Mind you, he's been decent enough. Seeing as I paid him the rent only yesterday, he says we can have until the end of the week to find somewhere else.'

It seemed as if misfortune dogged Arthur's footsteps as he wandered the district, looking for somewhere to live when he and his mother were obliged to leave the mill cottage at the end of the week. Fortunately, he'd been prudent with the small hoard of coins earned by the spinning he'd so quickly mastered, and he could afford to spend a few days roaming from place to place in search of lodgings.

There was a great movement of people around the district as some left to seek their living in London and others came in from the country, dispossessed by the Acts of Enclosure or thrown out of employment by the new agricultural methods that meant that one man with a horse and a deep plough could do the work of four or five. Many had to leave their cottages because they could no longer find employment to pay their rent, and some were reduced to sleeping rough on the moors and in the woods. Crime abounded around Leeds, and Arthur knew neither he nor his mother would survive long if they had to become vagrants and live rough in the open air.

Finally, his fortune changed. He knocked on a door to ask the woman within who had the renting of the humble house next door, which appeared to be empty.

'Aye, what a pity you weren't here an hour ago,' she said. 'A young man fresh in from Birstall wi' his wife and babby has just taken the renting of it. They seem a clean respectable couple. It'll be good to have new neighbours instead of the slattern as were here before, wi' her drunken husband as used to abuse her day and neet.'

Arthur's face fell at the news that he was too late. ''Tis my mam', he explained. 'There's nobbut the two of us, and she's ailing. We're being thrown from our tied house by't mill, since the machine had done me out of a job.'

The woman took pity on him, and invited him into her simple but clean two-roomed home. Introducing herself as Nancy Boothman, she placed a bowl of brewis before him; he hadn't eaten all day in his need to find somewhere to live, and gulped down the oatmeal.

'Happen I can put you in the way of something,' she said. 'Mind you, it's not much. How do you fare for coin?'

'I've enough to keep us simply for a week or two while I find another position,' Arthur told her, 'and enough to pay an honest rent.'

'There's a small place behind here,' Nancy began. 'I happen to know as the man did a moonlight flit last neet, on account of he couldn't pay his rent when the agent comes round today. I reckon as he owes the agent all of five shillings. If you and your mam were inside, and you had the five shillings in your hand, the agent wouldn't hardly throw you out, now would he? Mind you, it's nowt special – nobbut one room and a share of the privy. And doubtless it's filthy dirty. Thy mam will need to scrub it out, to judge by them as left it.'

Arthur's heart sank when Nancy Boothman showed him the simple one-roomed house, built of brick, with a slate roof and a shed stuck on the back. The room measured four paces by four and had an earth floor on which the filth and degradation of years had settled. There was no glass in the solitary window, only a rag stretched across the frame. As

63

he went out at the back; a horde of rats scuttled from a pile of bones of some dead animal, likely a dog. In one corner of the outside yard was a stone sink under a slate-covered canopy; the privy at the bottom of the yard stank of multiple use without adequate cleaning. The room itself contained a single bed; the stains of squashed ticks could clearly be seen on the straw mattress, half covered by a length of cloth, frayed at the edges, whose original colour could no longer be discerned. The fireplace was lined with brick and, surprisingly, carried one of the new cast-iron grates in which no fire had burned for many a month. The grate was flecked with old dry spittle, as was the coal-blackened kettle that hung over it; Arthur had known many men whose simple habit was to spit into the grate, and the previous tenant of the house must have maintained the habit even though he lacked money for coals with which to light a fire.

Despair engulfed Arthur as he stood in the centre of the room and looked about him. Would he and his mam never rise out of the stinking mire of Hunslet? Would they never be able to live somewhere clean and decent, to hold up their heads in self-esteem and respect? He was still standing there when the agent knocked on the door.

A fat red-faced man wearing a top hat, thick cotton breeches and solid boots that came to just below his knee, the agent smelled well-fed and well-content. His brown jacket came to his knees, half covering a leather purse that was strapped around his waist by a heavy belt. He took a book from the purse and perused it. As his eyes lit on the figures, he became immediately aggressive.

'Now, young man,' he said, 'my master's patience is exhausted. I'm here under instructions to tell thee either to pay what tha' owes, else get out of the cottage.' He looked straight at Arthur without seeming to realize he'd never seen him before. 'If you followed some honest employment,' he added severely, 'instead o' laiking at home in the middle of the working day, you wouldn't be so indebted to my master, would you? Fine healthy lad like you ought to be in't mill, else down't mine, where there's good money to be earned.'

'I have the owings here,' Arthur said, showing the man the coins that lay in his hand.

'Aye, well, tha's come about them by God knows what devious means, I'll be bound,' the agent said. 'But a coin's a coin. Give it here.'

Arthur's hand closed over the coins. 'What name is written on yon paper?' he asked, pointing at the book the man held.

'Why, thy name – Bickerstaff,' the agent said.

'I want the name changed,' Arthur told him. 'To Aysgill.'

'The name changed? Whatever for?'

'To make it all legal. If I'm to pay my coin . . .'

'Dost mean to tell me tha's not *Bickerstaff*?' the man interrupted, suspicion dawning.

'Aysgill – that's the name I want on the book,' Arthur insisted.

'And what about Bickerstaff?'

'I know nowt of him.'

The agent pushed past him. 'Tha' hasn't murdered him to get his renting?' He looked around the room, saw no signs of violence, though his nose wrinkled, as Arthur's had done, at the foul odour of the premises. 'What's happened to Bickerstaff?' he asked severely.

'He's gone, and I'm here – wi' five shillings in my hand.'

The agent looked at Arthur with cunning eyes. 'There's a list of folks waiting for one of our fine cottages,' he said. 'I couldn't see my way clear to putting you at the head of the list. I've been offered shillings by some folks, just to advance their names on the list.'

'I'm offering thee nowt,' Arthur said, 'but I'll tell thee this. It'll take a constable and a bailiff to get me out of here.'

'Why, you young whelp, I could take thee out of here myself!'

Arthur was at the end of his patience. Everything boiled inside him at that moment, all his frustrations, all his misery, all his anxiety for his mother. He reached forward, seized the tail of the agent's coat, swung round, and spun him out through the door before the agent could know what was happening.

'Why, you young whelp—!' the agent spluttered, repeating himself, unable to form a new idea in his astonishment at being so treated. 'I'll have the constable here to throw you out,' he said.

'Now sithee,' Arthur said, his voice dangerously quiet. 'I don't know thee, and I don't know thy master, but I vow to thee I'll find him and I'll report to him thy words. "Folks have paid me shillings to be advanced to the top of the list," is what tha' said. When thy master hears that, he'll have a stick between your legs fast as may be. Now, there's the five shillings. Write Aysgill in that book, take the five shillings, and be off wi' you.'

The agent knew he'd been bested. If Silas Moroney heard he'd been taking coin to advance folks for rentings, Moroney would have his head. 'Th'art lucky as I'm in a benevolent mood today, young lad,' he said gruffly. 'Tha' can have the cottage long as tha' pays the rent on time. But I warn thee, if th'art a week late wi' the money, tha' comes out wi' no more of this blether about going to my master. In honour, trust and faith, do I have your hand on that?'

'Aye, you have,' Arthur said, shaking the man's hand to confirm the deal.

When Amelia Aysgill saw the house her son had rented, she was too far gone in apathy to comment upon it, but retired instantly into the bed. Arthur had cleaned the grate and lit a few coals. The kettle was boiling cheerfully and Nancy

Boothman had given him a few scraps of meat to make a stew in it. Nancy was obviously pleased to have new neighbours over whom she could fuss. She told Arthur how her husband had been a careful man who'd saved his money. When he'd died a few months previously, she'd found enough money sewn into his mattress to keep her for a year or two. Now she'd put the money in the Merchant Bank and was living off the interest. Occasionally she took boarders into her home: travellers passing a few days in the city who didn't care to go to an inn, or didn't have the money to afford it. It was clear to Arthur that she took people into her home to relieve her own boredom rather than for the coins she earned. He was happy to know that when he was away at work - assuming he could find other employment - his mother would have somebody to talk to. Nancy was a cheerful friendly soul, with no malice in her speech, and laughter often on her face. Already Amelia had reacted to her, her eyes following their movements round the room as Arthur and Nancy set things to rights. They'd brought a few things from the mill cottage, including a sampler on which Amelia a long time ago had worked the Lord's Prayer in coloured silks.

'Why, that's beautiful workmanship!' Nancy exclaimed when she saw it. 'I'd be awfully obliged, Missis Aysgill, if you could instruct me in the art of such fine work, for I've but a coarse hand with a bodkin and none for fine needlework such as this.'

Arthur left the two of them already discussing needlework and realized he hadn't seen his mother so animated for many a long month. 'Good comes from evil,' he thought as he set off along the mean slum street. 'If we hadn't been forced to leave the mill cottage, we wouldn't have met with Nancy Boothman . . .'

CHAPTER SEVEN

The circle Arthur trudged in search of work grew wider and wider, with always the same answer. With all manufactories growing more efficient in what they did, in the way they grouped their machines to be operated by fewer people, most of them were laying folks off, not taking them on. Add to that the vast flood of folks coming in from the country districts, even from foreign lands like Ireland, and Arthur began to realize that his was a hopeless quest. Many were setting out on the long road south.

'They say there's work and lodging to be had in Sheffield, Nottingham or even London,' Arthur was told by one man marching south with his wife and his family of twelve children. 'A young lad like you would do best to throw in your lot wi' us.'

Arthur shook his head. 'My mam's ailing,' he said. 'The journey would do for her, I'll be bound.'

The man gave him a sad goodbye. He had several lasses nearly of marrying age and a fine-looking lad like Arthur could have relieved him of the burden of at least one of them.

Arthur walked along the main road out of Hunslet; he'd heard there was work to be had in the bell mines along that way, with not too many willing to volunteer for the arduous and dangerous task. He remembered his cousins had worked a bell mine and they had survived, though he knew his uncle wanted no more of it and he'd heard that his

68

cousin Richard had left home a few months ago to seek his fortune adventuring. Many folks were heading in the same direction, since it was one of the main roads out of Leeds to the south, along the coach route. The new big waggons trundled along, churning the surface of the road with their great wheels, the hooves of the teams of horses stirring the mud. The side of the road had been laid in part with timbers and crushed stones, but it was not wide and any fat burgher carrying his big belly before him would force lesser thinner people off the paving into the mud. Here were many rows of houses mingling with small and large factories, yards in which blacksmiths forged iron with ringing clangs on massive anvils. Arthur had loved to stand and watch them at work in their yards, blowing the coal fires into white heat with leathered bellows, taking out the heated metal and banging it with big hammers that sent showers of sparks everywhere, fashioning waggon wheels, hinges for doors, gates for fine houses, shoes for horses, bracket lamps to hold candles and lanthorns, all the gallimaufry of metal attached to waggons and coaches – and, Arthur thought bitterly, to machines that replaced men and made them idle against their wishes. There were yards where timber was worked, with men standing in pits while sawdust from the big splitter saws rained down on them, men splitting logs with chisels and wedges, even turning fine wood between spindles using a treadle for one part of the motion and a springy pole for the other. Normally Arthur found a tremendous fascination in wandering along this road on which, every day, some new enterprise formed itself. He smelled the lye in the leather yard, where skins of beasts still carrying their natural hair were dipped in the lye vats to remove the hair prior to the leather being tanned with oak-chips. At each place, Arthur went to the yard and asked: 'Any work?'

Everywhere they shook their heads. 'Not today,' they'd

say, if they were kindly and well-disposed. If they were otherwise, they'd brandish a stick at him and shout: 'Get away you thieving ragamuffin!'

With that number of desperate people walking the roads, Arthur could well appreciate that a yard-owner would need to keep a careful eye on his property, especially if it could easily be carried away by hand.

Arthur quickened his stride when he saw the crowd that had assembled at the staging yard a few hundred yards ahead. Despite his morose feelings, he still had an interest in all that was happening, and he remembered that sometimes an impromptu display took place in the staging yard, with itinerant tumblers and jugglers, travelling feast people from all over the world, who went round the country entertaining at wakes, feasts and fairs. Sometimes, if the feast had been badly attended or if the spectators had been lean of coin, they'd put on a show beside the road, hoping to coax the cost of a meal or a night's lodging from the passers-by. When Arthur arrived at the staging yard, he saw only a low platform and no sign of performers. Men were thronging around the platform, and a burly man was arranging those on the side into some sort of order. Arthur stared at the man seated on the platform, sensing something strange about him. When he'd managed to push his way through the throng, he realized what had attracted his attention. The man was blind.

The men at the side of the platform were being presented, one by one. The blind man listened to each man give his name and speak a few words; he would consider for a moment or two, then say firmly 'yes' or 'no'.

'What's going on?' Arthur asked a man standing next to him, who'd received a 'yes' shortly before.

'Us is signing on for work,' the man said.

'And the men who got a "no"?'

'Blind Jack'll not have 'em. It's uncanny. He can tell a

70

man's character from his voice – they say as he's never wrong. Tha'd better join the line and let him have a listen to thee.'

'Is that John Copley I can hear in front of me?' Blind Jack suddenly said, his sightless eyes seeming to stare directly at them.

'It is, Jack.' Copley turned slightly and whispered to Arthur. 'What did I tell thee? He's nobbut heard my name and voice once.'

'And who's that with you, John Copley? Have him address a few words to me.'

Arthur realized his chance had come, and spoke up boldly. 'My name, sir, is Arthur Aysgill, and I'm born of a good family that prides itself on honesty and hard work. I'll serve my master well in whatever job he entrusts to me.'

'Arthur Aysgill, eh?' Blind Jack said. 'Is it thy uncle, Peter Aysgill, as I've heard on?'

'The name is the same,' Arthur said sadly, 'but, that apart, there's nowt in common.'

'Matthew Aysgill, as preaches for the Wesleyans?'

'Aye, sir, he's my uncle.'

'Tha' rejects the one but speaks for the other.' Arthur's voice held a note of pride now, observed Blind Jack. 'Aye, lad, you've a lot to learn – but us'll teach it to you. Sign him on, Mr Binford, if he's a mind to earn a honest coin.'

'That is my fondest wish,' Arthur said simply but vehemently.

Blind Jack leaned forward. 'Tha' mun learn, lad, as tha' grows older. There's roguery in thee, aye, and honesty too. Thy nature will be a battleground on which both will strive for supremacy. I'll have thee by my side on the works. If Sir Roguery triumphs in thee o'er Dame Honesty, I s'all send thee packing, without a crust to thy name. Dost tha' understand?'

Arthur was flabbergasted.

71

Copley, beside him, was grinning hugely. 'Didn't I tell thee as Blind Jack would read thee better than a fortune-telling gypsy?'

'I mun run home straightaway and tell my mam I have a job,' Arthur said happily.

Copley shook his head in mirth. 'What are you going to say to her, lad, when she asks what you're going to do – how much you're going to be paid, where you're going to work?'

'I care nowt for that,' Arthur declared. 'If yon blind bugger can trust me to work for him in honesty, then I'm bound to trust him to pay me for my endeavours. I care not where or for how much. All I care is that I'm in work again. I've got something to do with my life.'

'In my lifetime,' Blind Jack said, addressing the men who'd gathered to his banner for work, 'I've been many things. Ye'll all readily see that the Good Lord saw fit to deprive me of my sight when He gave me the smallpox. Be that as it may, I've learned myself to play the fiddle, to be at home wi' Nature in all her glories, to develop within me a sense of intuition and understanding that most men with full use of their eyes neglect. I've walked the fields and the moors, can tell you to a rood where I am by the sounds and smells, by the press of the ground under my feet. I married a lass, Dorothy, as fair as any in the land and have lived in connubial bliss with her ever since. Some of you may have heard of how I raced from London against Colonel Liddel, him in a coach and me on my feet, and beat him into second place.'

Arthur was thrilled to the narrow by this gaunt, tall man who was addressing them all. He'd never conceived that such a romantic figure could exist. As for a blind man walking all the way to London and back . . .

'Aye, and some of you will have heard stories as I've

engaged myself in smuggling tea from time to time from the coasts of Yorkshire – well, be that as it may. I'm not a man to deny a good story! I raised a private army of a hundred and forty men, and marched at their head in the service of King George the Second, may the Lord have mercy upon his soul, offering myself and my platoon to General Wade at Newcastle. Aye, we fought the damned accursed Jacobites at Culloden and at Falkirk. Aye, well, be all that as it may. I can hear the shuffling of restless feet and I was never a one to bore another wi' tales of times past. Now we're going forward into times future, my lads, and we're going forward together. Times are changing; new ideas, new methods are upon us. Some of you may know of the tree that's been travelling, if you take my meaning, from York to Hull for the past two years, lying by the side of the quagmire roads in winter. The reason the tree is taking so long on its journey is because of the condition of the roads, which every day are being forced to carry more and more waggons, more and more heavily laden carts of all descriptions.

'What we're going to do, my lads, is to work out together a new system for making roads stronger and safer. We're going to offer ourselves to any Trust as will have us, to ease the passage of transports from one place to another. We're going to make them all bless the name they'll remember: John Metcalfe – as some calls, in their ignorance, Blind Jack o' Knaresborough!'

'We're going to build the roads?' Arthur said excitedly to John Copley, who had already adopted him as a friend in the enterprise.

'Aye, lad, I reckon we are. One thing I can promise you: any man who follows Blind Jack will never want for adventure.'

'I'm going to be a road-builder, Mam,' Arthur announced

when he returned home that night. 'I'm going to travel round the countryside building roads. Tha'll stay here, and Mrs Boothman will see to you, mark my words. You're already in better health now you've gone back to your samplers. Soon us'll have you back on your feet again. I shall leave you the small store of money I still have and you can use it to reimburse Nancy Boothman if she's out of pocket.'

'I shall miss you, lad,' Amelia said tearfully. 'You've been a great comfort to me since your dad died.'

'Aye, Mam, and I shall miss you. But work I must, and since there's nowt for me to do hereabouts, I mun adventure wi' Blind Jack if I'm to earn a coin. There's all the work a man could desire on the roads, wi' new ones being built for the Trusts every day, and new turnpikes replacing the old systems of payage and pontage.'

'My, what a lot of words tha's already learned,' Amelia said admiringly. 'Behave thyself when tha's away from home and don't get into bad company. It was bad company as did for your father, never forget.'

Arthur knew well enough that his father had killed himself because of a defect of character, a weakness he could never overcome since he had inherited it from the Aysgill line. The Aysgills were either very strong or very weak. There was no in-between. Arthur was determined that he would be strong in all he did.

Blind Jack had worked out what he considered to be the best way to repair the old roads, and had received his first contract from one of the Trusts: a stretch of road along the direct route between Leeds and York, which carried much traffic.

Arthur set off for work with the other men, walking in a pair with John Copley. It took them three days to reach the site, a stretch two miles long on low-lying ground, where the mud was churned sometimes two feet deep. In parts the road was a hundred paces wide, where carts had diverted to avoid the worst of the mud and pot-holes. Blind Jack had ordered waggons to come carrying stones, tools for the men, and food.

After their three-day walk, the men were glad to set up an encampment on the dry land some small distance from the road, among trees and shrubs. John Copley helped Arthur make a lean-to shelter against the weather, for though it was June the evening winds could blow chill and sometimes a fine rain fell. Arthur quickly learned how to take the bunches of ling and twist them together to make a waterproof shelter for himself, open on one side but protecting him from the cold night air.

They did no work that first day, since Blind Jack was re-surveying the site. It was uncanny to watch him walk slowly along with his long hazel stick in his hand, placing his feet carefully, avoiding the worst of the terrain, glancing from side to side though all knew he couldn't see. He would pause, make a motion with his hand, and they'd know he could 'feel' the patch on which he stood.

'We shall have to level it here,' he'd say, 'and get the drainage working more quickly.' Or he'd suddenly point ahead and say, 'Those shrubs will have to be moved back, since they stand in the path of the ditch we'll dig.'

None of the men with him, all of whom had become his disciples, could understand with what senses he could 'feel' and 'see' the undulations of the ground about them, but it quickly became apparent he knew the lie of the land as perfectly as if he could see it.

The following day, they unloaded the stones from the waggons, and some were set with hammers to crack them into smaller sizes. Others were sent away with the waggons to fetch loads of ling and heather. Others, Arthur and John Copley included, were shown the side of the stretch of road they were to repair.

'You'll dig a ditch along here,' Blind Jack explained. 'The bottom of it will have a small slope which I will show you as you go along. The ditch will have smooth sides, three hand-spans wide, and you'll pack the earth firmly along the sides and the bottom. I shall want you to navigate a straight line until I show you where the bends will come. Is there any among you who doesn't understand?'

They all understood, and set to digging the ditch as Blind Jack explained it. Arthur set himself in its path, shovelling out the first spadeful of earth, which John Copley then moved to the side. Here the ground was soft and heavy with moisture; it clung to the curved blade of the shovel. Arthur was surprised by the weight of that first load; quickly he realized that the work would be hard and taxing, but resolved to stick to it as best he might.

As they worked, they saw how many people passed along what had been this deserted stretch. Coaches came, and waggons, many men with pack-mules carrying goods from one village to another, or taking cloth into the nearest town. On one occasion, as Arthur paused to wipe his sweat-drenched brow, he saw a post-chaise pulled along by four harnessed dogs. All the men laughed as it came by, but Blind Jack shouted imprecations after it for the owner had harnessed his dogs merely to avoid the payment of tolls at the turnpike. The law specified the tax should be paid on the horse or 'beast of burden', which no dog could claim to be. Arthur often saw the waggons harnessed in a strange way, with the four horses proceeding in single file on long traces. Copley explained that many Trusts would not permit horses to work side by side, since they would destroy a greater width of the road surface. Such surface as the road had known had vanished beneath the thick slimy mud. The local parishioners had been responsible for the maintenance of this stretch of road under an elected man; each six months the elected man was changed, and with him the responsibility for the road's repair. It had not proved an efficient system, Copley explained, and now Acts of Parliament were being passed to put the responsibility for the roads into the hands of Trusts who, by charging tolls, could recover the costs of road work from the travellers themselves.

After the first hours of work, Arthur ceased to care for the motley crowd who passed by; he was too concerned with the enormous pains in his back, arms and legs, with the mists that swam before his eyes. Work in the mill had been hard enough, especially when he had tended the fulling machine on his own. It had been heavy when he became a spinner and had to fly to keep a supply of thread for the weaving machines. But this work – this constant stooping, pushing the blade of the shovel into the ground, tilting it, extracting it from the sticking soil, heaving its load on to the side of the trench – was unlike anything he'd ever known.

Unbeknown to Arthur, Copley had been watching him work, and Blind Jack himself, though he kept his blind 'eye' over most of the working, was never far away. When, finally, Copley saw the lad had had enough, he beckoned silently for Arthur to jump from the trench and replace him, while Copley himself went into the soggy bottom. Though no word had been spoken, Blind Jack understood the change that had taken place and came to stand beside them.

'You mun learn to work more slowly, young Arthur,' he said. 'I've been heeding you. You go at your labours like a bull at a gate on the other side of which the cows are waiting; tha' mun learn that a slow, steady pace can be as effective as short sharp bursts of endeavour from which a man needs must rest. That's how I bested Colonel Liddel for he was ever wont to gallop his horses, while I moved forward at a steady rate, making progress when the Colonel was resting his wearied animal. Copley here will show you, Tha' mun watch him, listen to him, and learn from him in all things. Aye, and I'll gi'e him a handful of mutton fat to rub in thy back afore tha' settles to thy rest this even.'

Arthur was amazed to see, the next morning, how much moisture had gathered in the trench they'd dug, and how smoothly it ran away along the puddled side and bottoms. Most of the moisture seemed to be draining from the bed of the road, and Blind Jack had diverted the traffic so that the horses and waggons passed along the side. When a sufficient stretch of the road had been drained, the men came forward with the ling and heather which they laid along the road's surface in swatches, binding them together with a stick poked through them into the mud, to prevent them moving sideways. Meanwhile, the other men had been breaking the stones into small pieces less than the size of a fist. Slowly, the men spread these pieces neatly on the bed of ling and heather, treading them in, banging them down with heavy sections of tree-trunks that smashed the stones together.

The road bed was at least six inches deep when Blind Jack instructed them to bring the waggons along it; the ten-inch-wide waggon wheels pushed the stones further down into the ling, creating a flatter surface. The waggons were driven forwards and backwards over the surface; each time a depression was made, more stones were packed into it, to fill it to the road surface level. Despite his fatigue, Arthur was mightily impressed by the speed and despatch with which Blind Jack organized the men's labours; walking along the road surface before the waggon he would stop, poke down his stick, then cry, 'More stones here!' It was as if his feet could read the imprint of the road bed as a man's fingers will read the texture of a cloth, the markings on a coin.

They stopped work when the sun went down and already had achieved a stretch of finished road, or so Arthur thought, about twenty paces long. Three men had been laid off work to cook the food in large pots, which they suspended from tripods over wood fires. This was no thin brewis like that to which Arthur had become accustomed; the stew was heavy with meat and grains, thick and bubbling hot, made tasty by handfuls of salt and wild-growing herbs. Each man had his own tin plate, which he was permitted to heap as many times as he felt inclined. Arthur took three plates of the stew, amazed by his own appetite, and a can of water from the nearby stream, taken from above the place where the men had washed.

As Arthur lay back beneath the June night sky, he heard a waggon approaching, then a sudden burst of laughter – some of it, to his amazement, from female voices.

'Nay, what's happening, John?' he asked, mystified.

Somebody started to play a lute, and a man was singing tender songs. It seemed as if, in a clearing in the heather above where he lay, the folks had started to dance. A fiddle joined in, then another; then John Copley, sitting not five feet from Arthur with his hands clasped round his knees, also began to sing.

Love, love, nothing but love still more, for though love's bow shoots buck and doe, the shaft confounds, not that it wounds, but tickles still the sore . . . Aye, 'tis Shakespeare,' he said. 'I know it well.'

'Sing some more, John,' Arthur urged. 'Yon's a sweet voice . . .'

'*These lovers cry, oh, oh, I die* – nay, I'm not certain of the words. *And that which seems . . . the wound to heal . . . doth turn oh, oh, to ha-ha-ha, so dying love lives still* . . . I think it goes summat like that. My mam used to sing it to me when I were a nobbut a bairn, and I know not where she got it, for she could nor read nor write. I'll teach it to you by rote, if tha's a mind to learn it . . . Yon's the doxys from some tavern nearby, I reckon, come to offer themselves for pleasure and to earn a coin. Tha'd do well to avoid them, if tha' knows what's good for thee, else tha' might catch summat as'll take a long time to leave you in peace. Dost hear me, young lad?' He turned to look at Arthur lying on his back beneath the stars.

Arthur had fallen into the deep sleep of exhaustion.

CHAPTER EIGHT

During that summer of 1761, the outdoor life, the good food and the healthy toil put pounds on to Arthur Aysgill's city-bred frame, tanned his cheeks a ruddy bucolic colour, straightened his back and hardened his muscles. Spending his time exclusively with men, except when a waggonload of doxys came from the nearest large village, had made him independent in argument, prepared to state his beliefs and fight for them if necessary. John Copley became his inseparable companion, his guide and his mentor in all matters to do with practical living, for John had led an adventurous life and had even served with the military in France.

Blind Jack also took an interest in Arthur and frequently the three of them sat together after the evening meal, discussing the affairs of the day. From Blind Jack Arthur learned of the doings in the greater outside world, of London and of Parliament, as Blind Jack patiently explained to him how decisions taken in London could affect the lives of all of them. 'If it were not for these Trust Acts and Turnpike Laws – why, we'd all be out of jobs,' Blind Jack explained.

One day Arthur saw John Copley gazing thoughtfully at him as they prepared to work. 'What's amiss, John?' Arthur asked.

'I've just been looking at thee,' Copley said. 'Tha' must have growed three inches since we started here, to judge from the fit of thy clothes. Us'll have to find another outfit for thee to wear, since tha's already bursting out of the seams of thy jacket and trousers.'

It was Blind Jack who provided the new suit of clothes for Arthur. Soft black leather boots with a brown top tied with a leather thong. Brown breeches he tucked into the boots. A white cotton shirt, with a blue neckerchief. A red cord waistcoat that reached down to his thighs. As a final gesture, he gave Arthur a black velour hat; the hat was a touch too big and hung to his ears.

'Tha'll soon grow into that,' Copley said smiling, 'the way tha's starting to speak thy mind on all occasions!'

Arthur had never had such an outfit in his life and felt a real swell as he strolled up and down. 'I don't hardly like to get my clothes sullied,' he said apologetically, 'since Blind Jack was kind enough to gi'e 'em to me.'

'Aye, well, I reckon he didn't give 'em to thee so's tha' can stand about all day admiring thyself,' Copley said. 'Tha'd better start the day down't drainage ditch, puddling them sides. Then us'll see what tha' looks like when the day's work is done . . .'

Blind Jack had heard the exchange, and laughed. 'Nay, gi'e the lad his first day,' he said. 'The two of you take Seamus wi' you, and fill in the few pot-holes near the toll-house, as I showed you yesterday.'

The section of road on which they were working was the responsibility of a Trust that had formed from local inspiration and stimulus. Though it had formerly been a pack road, carrying only packmen and their mules from one village to the next and running parallel with the drove road along which the cattle were moved in season, the increased amount of traffic caused by the new enterprises, by the increased demand for coal, for wood, metal and ores, had resulted in the road becoming almost unusable by the local people. They did not see why they should pay the excessive charges to repair the road when it was used principally by people passing through the district, from whom they derived no profit. The local landowner, who found it increasingly difficult to move from one part of his property to another for the constant stream of heavy traffic, had been the instigator; following the first Act of Parliament of 1663, he had petitioned for an Act for their own district, and one had been granted in 1759. Immediately three toll-gates had been established along the stretch of road, charging one penny for each horse, ten pence for a score of cattle, and five pence for a score of sheep or pigs. These were modest charges compared with the prices for waggons, carriages, goods and passenger vehicles of all descriptions, for each of which the charge was twenty pence. The only exemptions were to travellers on foot, to local people, and to waggons whose wheels had a width of at least nine inches, since the Trust reckoned that such wheels would not cut the road, but help to roll it flat. Perhaps the Turst erred on the punitive side in their toll charges; their land lay on low ground, much subject to seepage in the rainy season, with correspondingly high costs of repair. Blind Jack had promised them that he would cure that seepage by taking the water from the road bed by drainage – they were happy to permit him to try knowing that they would recover his costs through the increased sums they'd collect at the toll-gates, should the experiment prove a success.

Ironically it was the waggoners, whose vehicles had done the most damage over the last few years, who caused the most trouble. A waggoner contracted to take materials from one place to another at a fixed price. The new imposition of toll cut his profits considerably, but the people whose goods were being carted would brook no rise in the fee they paid.

Arthur was working in sight of one of the toll-houses that

had been erected at the side of the road, with a solid gate that crossed the road to prevent passage of any man or vehicle until a fee had been negotiated and paid. This part of the road was on rising ground and drier than the section in the valley behind him; with Copley and an Irishman they all called Seamus, he was filling in the few pot-holes with stones they'd brought in a wheelbarrow from the main working. Copley was breaking the stones by the side of the road, using the long-shafted heavy-headed hammer designed for the purpose.

As Seamus arrived back from the main workings with more stones, Arthur regarded the Irishman. A great brute of a fellow, he was dressed in a blue calico jacket over a bleached cotton shirt and wore leggings of canvas instead of the knee-length boots Copley and Arthur wore. He had no hat on his head, which was almost bereft of hair except at the sides above his ears. He paused in his labours and wiped his forehead with his sleeve. Arthur took the rag from round his own throat and wiped his face with it; the day had turned hot, the weather sultry and sticky.

'It'll storm later, mark my words,' Seamus said.

Arthur imagined for a moment that he could even hear the storm clouds, the mutter that coming winds throw into the air. Copley stopped wielding his hammer and stood listening.

'Are we to get a storm?' Arthur asked.

'Aye, but not the sort you mean,' Copley said. 'Look yonder.'

Arthur turned around. In the distance he could see the plume of smoke rising vertically into the sky with no wind to disperse it; between the smoke and the toll-house, a crowd was advancing, some riding the tops of waggons, some walking beside, several clutching flaming torches on the ends of poles.

'Rioters,' Copley said tersely.

Arthur had heard of the waggoners who stirred crowds against the Turnpike toll-houses and Copley had told him that he'd read, in a copy of the *Leeds Intelligencer*, an account of their mischief along the Wakefield road. The waggoners were claiming that the tolls were doing them out of a livelihood; that waggons should be allowed to pass freely; that the roads belonged, free of tolls, to all men and not just to a few Trustees who'd set themselves up in Parliament to cheat and rob the rest of the people. It hadn't been long before inflammatory speeches had turned into flaming toll-houses, as men followed hasty impetuous words with burning brands. Once or twice Arthur had felt a billet pound into him, flung from some passing waggon, but he'd thought nothing of it at the time, not realizing it implied a personal animosity.

'We mun get out of here,' Seamus said urgently, 'for they regard the men who work on the roads in the same light as those who demand the tolls.'

'We can't leave the master's goods behind!' Arthur cried. 'They'll steal his barrow and shovel!' He grabbed the hammer, rake and shovel and put them in the barrow. John Copley and Seamus had already started on their way back to the workings where the bulk of men were assembled; Blind Jack would know how to deal with a few rioters especially since he always carried a brace of pistols. Arthur started to walk away from the mob, wheeling the barrow before him, not wishing to start to run as Seamus was now running. His pride wouldn't permit him to scurry away with his tail between his legs like some coward.

The mob swarmed round the toll-house, dragging the toll-keeper and his family from within, yelling and shouting at him. Arthur, vastly afeared, glanced behind and saw the flames begin to lick from the windows of the booth, where one of the waggoners had flung shale oil which quickly ignited amidst the flaming brands.

'Nay, Arthur,' Copley shouted back, 'leave't barrow and come on!' Now he, too, had broken into a trot, seeking to catch up with Seamus.

But Arthur could not leave the barrow and the tools; he'd vowed to serve Blind Jack faithfully, and that meant protecting his goods as well as giving him a good day's work. He increased his pace as much as he could but the barrow was unwieldy to push and not well balanced on its small single wheel at the front; he tried to trot but his legs caught the legs of the barrow and he would have fallen had he not regained his balance quickly, desperate to advance.

Now there was no time to look behind him. He heard the shouts – 'There's one of them! There's one of the roadmaking rascals!' He heard the mob start to bay behind him, like a pack of wolves, and then heard the pound of their feet on the road he'd just been repairing. Sweat streamed down his face as he tried again to run; blinking it out of his eyes, he saw Copley had stopped and was running towards him. He felt a surge of gratitude that Copley had not abandoned him in his need.

'Drop the cursed barrow, Arthur! Drop it and run!'

But Arthur knew a stubbornness he couldn't control. He could hear the shriek of the mob drawing nearer to him, the yells as they bayed after him like hungry dogs after a stag.

Copley came level with him, wrested the barrow from his hands and flung it to the side. 'Silly bugger!' he said. 'Art trying to get us both killed?' He grabbed Arthur's arm and pulled him forward. 'Come on, you daft ha'porth, us can allus come back for't barrow later.'

Arthur set off running, but it was too late. The impetus of the mob carried it forward and around them. Arthur felt a stick go between his legs and himself somersaulting over it. Copley was down and the mob had settled on him like bluebottles, hitting, punching, biting, yelling with glee. Arthur struggled to rise but they leaped upon him. He bent his head down and put his hands behind his neck as he crouched over, knowing he couldn't escape the violence of the blows that were being rained upon his shoulders, his back, his buttocks, his legs. They were using blackthorn sticks, lumps of stone, anything, and already Arthur felt his senses going from him in the whirling maelstrom of the savage attack. Voices yelling in his ears, spittle flecking the exposed side of his face, the hot smell of pounding boots, the stamped dust of the road rising into his lungs to choke him, his senses were slipping from him.

Suddenly the note changed. Now he heard familiar voices, the bellow of Blind Jack, the boom of his pistols. The roadmen had counter-attacked in force, brought from the workings by Seamus's warning shouts. They'd seen Arthur and Copley set upon and had launched themselves into a flood-tide charge with hammers, shovels, rakes, all the roadmaking tools they had been using.

When Arthur dared to raise his head he saw the broken and bleeding bodies that littered the battlefield. Most of the mob were in flight being wildly pursued by Blind Jack's men, but some there were, lying on the ground, who'd never flee again, never burn another toll-house, never shout curses nor raise a blackthorn stick against another man. Blind Jack's pistols had taken away half the head of one man who'd been belabouring Arthur with a chain, had spread a stain of blood across another assailant's chest, whose blooded spittle drooled from his open mouth beneath sightless eyes.

John Copley was dead. A blow at the back of his neck had broken his spine and his head lolled at an impossible angle.

Arthur couldn't walk; when he placed his weight on his leg it gave way beneath him and he sprawled on the ground, near enough to Copley, his friend and benefactor, only to touch his dead face.

'He came back to save me,' Arthur sobbed, all his own pains forgotten in the stunning sorrow of Copley's death. He beat his other hand on the ground. 'He came back to help me . . .' he yelled in the hysteria of despair.

Blind Jack knelt beside him, touched the side of his face with his long fingers. 'Aye, he was your friend in all things,' he said. 'Tha'll never know a better.'

They buried the dead without ceremony in graves beside the road – one for the rioters, one for the roadmenders. They beat the wounded rioters out of the district, driving them mercilessly back to where they had come from. Blind Jack confiscated the waggons that remained, commandeering them for his own service. Arthur was the only roadmender seriously injured. Blind Jack felt with his sensitive fingers and pronounced his leg broken. The lacerations about his face and body would heal; he'd need a bone-setter for the leg. Blind Jack thought for a while, and as he thought, he stroked his own leg in the same place Arthur's had been broken. He crossed to where the lad had been placed on a pallet; Arthur was sweating profusely and moaning in agony, though his tears had now dried.

'Tha' needs a bone-setter, lad,' Blind Jack said, 'and quickly at that. At thy age, bones set together quick; if we leave that leg the way it is, it'll set like a corkscrew and tha'll never walk straight again.'

'What can I do?' Arthur asked quietly.

'I'll tell thee what tha' can do. Tha' can trust in the Lord and me. I've no expert knowledge, but I reckon I can set that leg back straight. But tha'll need to trust me.'

Arthur attempted a smile but it came through the pain as a grimace. 'It seems I have no alternative, Blind Jack,' he said. 'But tha'll do it quickly and sharp?'

'That I will, lad,' the blind man promised

Two men held Arthur's shoulders back, imprisoning his head, and they gave him a rag to hold in his mouth.

Another man held his waist down. A fourth man held his left foot, exactly at the angle indicated by Blind Jack, and a fifth man held the foot of the broken right leg.

'Tha'll pull when I say,' Blind Jack instructed the latter, 'and then tha'll twist as I say, then let go. At the full of thy twist, tha'll be at the same angle as Simon there – understand? But first tha' mun pull the bones apart if we're to achieve owt.'

Fortunately, Arthur had no idea of what was to come; he thought of it as the pulling he used to do to annoy Ezra to crack the knuckles of his fingers. He'd always been able to crack each one in turn and the noise had always made Ezra go green . . .

'Pull!' Blind Jack said. He was resting his hands on Arthur's leg, spanning the break; he felt the bones come apart, and all could hear the grating sound as they were twisted on each other.

Arthur felt one monstrous stab of pain that seemed to run clear from his toes to the top of his skull. The pain engulfed him, washed fire over him, drew him down and under before he could even emit the scream that had formed in his throat.

'Pull again,' Blind Jack said urgently. 'Harder!'

Arthur, unconscious, knew nothing of what they were doing.

Blind Jack grunted with satisfaction. His sensitive fingers had felt the ends of the bone go into each other like a scarf-joint. 'Hold that leg still,' he said, 'and you, Will, wrap it up wi' some of this wet clay on this shirt o' mine. We could be doing wi' Plaster o' Paris but we have none by, and the wet clay will take some of the heat out of it. I reckon as the lad'll be all reet now.'

They crowded round him and slapped his back. 'Th'art a wonder, Blind Jack,' one of them said but Blind Jack waved his hand to disclaim all credit.

'Yon's the wonders,' he said, 'as makes me humble. A lad who owes me nowt risked his life to save my bits of property, and another gave his life to save the first – there's the wonder, lads. We may not see their like again.'

Blind Jack o' Knaresborough, a caring man, sent Arthur Aysgill back to Leeds on a waggon in the charge of Binford, his foreman; Binford also went to tell John Copley's wife the sad news and to give her all her husband's earnings, plus a small sum Blind Jack paid out of his own pocket in lieu of a pension. He estimated it would take Arthur's leg a full month to heal properly and gave him a sum equivalent to wages for twice that period. Thus, when Arthur arrived home, he had more money in his pocket than ever he had seen at one time before.

Though Amelia grieved over her son's injury, she was overwhelmingly pleased to have him back, even though it meant surrendering the pallet to him until his bones had knit. It became, in fact, something of a blessing, since once Amelia left the pallet she showed no inclination to lie down again, except at night for sleeping, when she made up a bed on the floor.

When Nancy Boothman came in to see Arthur the next day – she'd been away overnight, she explained, visiting relatives near Wakefield – she was amazed at the change in him, his vigorous colour and the muscle on his frame.

'Why, lad,' she exclaimed, 'tha's growed a year since't last time we saw thee and got so much colour in thy cheeks I'd hardly have recognized thee!' She'd have offered Amelia the spare bed in her house, she went on, but she'd brought her niece back from Wakefield to stay a few months with her, to keep her company in her loneliness. Also, the room she rented out occasionally was now occupied more or less permanently by a man who worked as a winder in one of the collieries, and she felt it hardly fitting to share her roof with a single man without someone else to guard her reputation. 'You know the way people will talk, Amelia,' she said.

Arthur lay on the pallet, listening to the two women chatter together. For months now he'd been so used to the company of men who talked but little that it amused him to hear the pair of them cackling like geese, seeming to say nothing in as many words as possible. He was happy that his mother had found somebody to talk to; she seemed to have blossomed while he'd been away and to be recovering some of her former liveliness. Happen she'd be able to go back to work soon, he thought, and take her mind off herself. There was no hurry. The store of money he had set by from the roadmending would keep them for a long time to come, even if he weren't able to walk or work for a month or two.

The ride on the waggon had jarred his leg a bit; wrapped still in Blind Jack's shirt, with the clay now baked hard by his body heat, the joint couldn't move. The skin beneath the clay dressing itched like the very devil, but there was nothing he could do about that, other than to poke a thin stick between the clay and his leg, to give it a bit of a scratch. Blind Jack had said he must keep the clay on for as long as he could bear it, that he must spend time each day flexing his foot, bending it back and forth, twisting it at the ankle. He must also wrinkle his toes as much as he could to keep all the ligaments in good working order.

'If tha' smells owt funny, if thy ankle and foot seize up and cannot be moved, or if they turn blue, tha' mun go to't Free Infirmary immediately, understand?' Blind Jack had said.

Arthur had promised to do that, but so far there seemed no problems; his foot and toes moved freely, there was no smell other than the normal smell of body sweat, and certainly no discoloration.

He'd been lying in bed three weeks when he woke up one

morning to find the clay had cracked during the night. When he touched the leg cast, bits of it came away in his hand. Amelia was still asleep in the corner of the room and judging by the light it was only shortly after dawn. He could hear the clatter of feet in the street outside as workers hurried off to the mills and factories, and the snort and wheeze of horses dragging waggons. He swivelled on the bed and gently picked as much of the clay as he could from the cotton shirt in which Blind Jack had wrapped it. Then he prised the solid bits of the cast loose. At first he was horrified to see his leg looked considerably thinner than the other with which he quickly compared it. The skin had a dreadful tinge of greeny white, and was as wrinkled as tripe. There seemed to be dirt accumulated at the bottom of each ripple and the surface of the skin came away beneath his fingers when he rubbed it gently, as if it had decayed.

Slowly he swung the leg round, feeling no pain; he bent his knee much further than the limited flexing he'd been able to achieve with the cast on, and again he felt no pain. The last time he bent his knee he let his foot go over the edge of the pallet until it touched the ground. He moved his backside so that he was standing upright on his good left leg and then gently, oh so gently, allowed a little of his weight to fall on the right leg. Still no pain. More and more pressure downwards, and still no pain.

'It's a miracle!' he exclaimed. He was so excited he called to Amelia. 'Mam, Mam! Look at this!'

Amelia came alert instantly and had sprung to a sitting position before her eyes were fully open. 'What is it, lad?' she asked anxiously. 'Gi'e us a minute to get my eyes open.'

'Look at it, Mam!' he said, jubilant. 'There's no pain! None at all!'

When she saw him standing, she leapt from the palliasse on which she'd made her bed since Arthur returned. 'Take it steady, Arthur,' she cried, fearful he might injure himself

92

further. She put her arm round his shoulders. 'Don't try to walk on it,' she urged. 'Get back into your bed – at least for another day or so.'

'Nay, Mam,' he said proudly. 'Now I'm on my feet again, I mun try to walk, I *mun*!'

Seeing he wouldn't be dissuaded, she held her arm as best she could round his waist while he essayed his first steps. His movement was slow, deliberate and careful, but he managed four steps successfully.

'Now let me do it on my own,' he said.

She stepped before him, her arms outstretched, ready to catch him should he fall but, after the first difficult manoeuvre of the turn, he was able to stand upright and step out with only the slightest wobble when all his weight fell on that right leg.

'I do believe it's mended,' he said. 'I do believe it's right as rain again.'

She came beside him and stroked the side of his face. 'It's God's miracle,' she said, 'it's God trying to repay us for what happened to your Dad.'

He shook his head. 'Nay, Mam, it's Blind Jack's miracle. We owe it all to him and I s'all never forget him as long as I live – aye, and walk!'

'Get back to bed,' she said, 'and I'll make thee a breakfast.'

He relaxed back on the pallet, his mind buzzing now with future possibilities. He realized that the road-mending work would be too taxing on his leg for some time to come, though he would dearly have liked to hasten back to the road workings to show Blind Jack his success, to take his place with the men. Somehow, instinctively, he knew that that phase of his life was over, that he'd need to go on to other, hopefully better, things.

'I s'all have to think about getting back to work again, Mam,' he said as he wolfed down the meat stew Amelia had

93

made the previous evening. 'We can't sit idly by and watch all our coin disappear down our bellies.'

'There's no hurry, Arthur,' she said. 'I've been thinking, these weeks since you've been back, that I might try a job myself. I hear that, since the spinning jenny doesn't work too well in't mill, they're setting on hands again, and I'm well versed in spinning. Or I was, once upon a time. It'd do me no harm to get back to earning again. Help to take my mind off myself.'

Had they both but known it, the decision was taken and already out of their hands. Later that same morning Amelia was giving Arthur a wash on the bed, trying to get rid of the dead skin that coated his leg where the clay had lain, when they heard a loud knock on the door.

'Who can that be?' Amelia asked, instantly worried. 'It's not rent day, and Nancy Boothman would never give the door such a clout.'

There was another knock.

'S'all I open it?' Amelia asked, afeared.

'Well, Mam, tha' won't know who it is if tha' doesn't,' Arthur said, smiling at her timidity. She had no need to open it for the man outside had pushed it open and both heard the well-remembered voice.

'Arthur Aysgill, art tha' there? Don't try to get out of bed, lad. I'll let myself in, wi' your permission.'

'It's Master Tomlinson,' Amelia whispered. 'What can be wrong wi' him?'

'Come in Mr Tomlinson,' Arthur called out. 'Mam, fetch yon box for him to sit on.'

Tomlinson's bulk filled the room. He was wearing the outfit Arthur remembered as his best working clothes. Whenever important people had come to Sleightholme's Mill, or there'd been a meeting of the Partners, he'd worn this same black coat, cut long and full, with light tan trousers, not breeches.

94

He was carrying the hat he wore on those occasions, with its stiffened narrow brim and its heavy silver buckle that some folk said wasn't really silver but white bearing metal. His long hair curled down the side of his head and almost concealed his ears. This was the first time Arthur had ever taken a long look at the man who had employed him, who'd bullied him and all the apprentices, who'd spouted Holy God at them on all occasions. What he saw now was a severe but handsome man who, he was astonished to discern, had kindly eyes.

'I were sorry to hear about your misfortune,' Tomlinson said, addressing himself to Amelia, 'and I hope as now you're feeling better. There's a place for a spinner at Sleightholme's, if you've a mind to come back to us, ma'am.'

Amelia didn't know what to say. Fancy being addressed as *ma'am* by no less a person than Master Tomlinson himself! 'Why, Master Tomlinson, I thank thee kindly,' she said at last. 'I'd be right happy to come back. We were nobbut talking about that very thing this morn.'

'I'll see thee when tha' comes, Missis Aysgill.' A smile flitted across his face. 'Tha' knows the way reet well, I reckon.'

'That I do, Master,' laughed Amelia.

Tomlinson, the courtesies observed, now turned his attention to Arthur. 'And you, you rascal – what's all this I've been hearing about you?'

'I broke my leg, but it's mended now,' Arthur told him.

'Is that all you have to say?' Tomlinson asked. '"I broke my leg but it's mended now . . .?" Tha' doesn't say anything about facing a mob single-handed, trying to protect thy master's goods, until another came and joined you, and paid dear for it.'

'That weren't my fault,' Arthur said, tears springing unbidden to his eyes at the memory of John Copley. 'He

95

were like a father to me. I never wanted him to run back to me. I've been lying on my bed reproaching myself. If I hadn't been pig-stubborn and had left the barrow when he said . . .'

'Tha' weren't pig-stubborn,' Tomlinson said softly. 'Tha' were loyal to thy master. It was God's will that Mr Copley should die that way.'

'How do you know his name?' Arthur asked, surprised. 'It hasn't been written about in the *Intelligencer*, has it?'

'I heard his name from an old friend of mine,' Tomlinson said. 'You may not know it, Arthur, but I was born in Knaresborough, too. I've known John Metcalfe, as some call Blind Jack, all my life.'

'He never said owt,' Arthur protested.

'That's his way, lad. He wouldn't let on to you that he knows me, lest you judge us both by the same yardstick. I seem to remember that you didn't take too kindly to me letting you go out of't mill. I had to do it, lad. I take my orders from the master, you know, just as you take your orders from me. I had to make a choice, a cruel choice, between men and women with a lot of bairns to keep alive, or thee, who's quick and nimble and has only thy mam to take care on. Tha' saw which way it went and tha' hated me for it, quite rightly; I knew, and tha' knew, tha'd always given the master value for his coin. Tha'd never been lazy, never stolen owt, never been slack in whatsoever job I gave thee . . . Well, now here we come to the heart of the matter. Blind Jack has told me about thy leg, and says it'll unfit thee for working on't roads. But it won't bother thee in't mill. I'm getting older, lad, and I need somebody to do a bit of my work for me, under my eyes, of course. The master has given me the right to pick any God-fearing man or boy I please. I've a mind to offer the position to thee. It pays as much as you've been earning on't roads, and a bit more. You've Blind Jack to thank for it – I'd never have thought

96

of thee if he hadn't penned me a letter, and in such glowing terms I felt obliged to wear my best working suit before presenting myself to this paragon of godly virtue he were describing.'

Arthur could see the smile in his eyes as he said this, and knew that Tomlinson was going out of his way to offer a new relationship. It wouldn't be the old fearing time when he'd dreaded to hear Tomlinson's footfall, when Tomlinson would cuff him for the least infraction, the least lack of attention. In a way, Arthur knew, his whole status was changing. He'd be on the other side, with all the responsibility that would mean. He'd be a man in his own right.

'I'd be honoured to take the position, Mr Tomlinson,' Arthur said, 'and promise to serve thee right well.'

Amelia was looking from one to the other. She had not understood what was happening, only that Arthur was being offered a job again, just as she had been. She had no idea of the special relationship that Arthur had understood and had grasped at so hungrily. 'God bless you, Master Tomlinson,' she said. 'You've greatly advantaged us this day.'

'I think I might have advantaged myself more,' Tomlinson said, as he gathered the skirts of his coat about him and prepared to leave.

CHAPTER NINE

Dodie Ottershaw wiped one hand across her face in the overheated atmosphere of the hospital ward where, with Titus Waverley's intervention, she had been given a situation as a nurse. Though she had lacked training when she first took the situation a year ago, in 1762, she had been quick to learn and was already trusted by the overworked doctors and surgeons of the Free Hospital to perform all manner of routine operations, such as the re-opening of festering wounds, the swabbing of throats, the application of calamine pads to smallpox victims in whom the virulent stage of the killing disease had passed.

She now had a number of assistant nurses under her and could leave the more basic tasks with bed-bottle and bed-pan to them, while she concentrated on dosing and physicking the sixty or so patients in her care. She had taken this supervisory job because it meant a rise in her wages; now she was earning an unbelievable twelve shillings a week – as much as a skilled glazier or cabinetmaker, and four shillings a week more than her husband Mark received for his heavy work in the iron foundry.

Over the years, a lust for money had become Dodie's passion. At first, when they were obliged to leave Barthwick, she had merely wanted a bit put by as a means of bettering themselves. She had induced Titus Waverley to educate her sons for that same reason, and hadn't considered it much of a sacrifice to become his temporary mistress in lieu of paying school fees. After the birth of her daughter Jennifer, her relationship with her husband had changed. Mark was a sensitive man, despite the brutality of his employment in the foundry, and had quickly seen that his sexual demands had become a great burden to Dodie: these days he approached her seldom and that side of his nature appeared to have withered. Dodie had no lust within her other than to acquire as much money as possible. She'd given her son Stanley the best possible start in life, she hoped, by having him trained as an engineer by Jonas Clegg. Now Stanley was engaged in helping Clegg improve the spinning jenny that Sleightholme had bought, and Dodie had heard that her son had suggested several modifications which Clegg adopted.

Her second son, Claude, had been a great disappointment to her. Though she had taken him from Titus Waverley's school in 1760 when he was nine and had apprenticed him to a lawyer, he didn't seem to be making any progress within the firm and spent all his time running round the town with messages, briefs, all manner of papers. None of this used the Latin or English that Titus Waverley had given him, but the lad seemed content to while his life away without ambition.

At least Jennifer continued to fulfil her early promise. One day, Dodie knew, she'd be a beauty and could claim any highborn man she would attract.

Mark Ottershaw could not understand what now drove his wife onwards. Though his wages were meagre, they could live frugally on what he got, plus the money they received from Stanley's apprenticeship to Jonas Clegg. Claude hardly earned enough at his job to keep him in boot leather, but he was permitted to feed with the other lads at the lawyer's table, and his work clothing was paid for, since the lawyer wanted his runners dressed alike, in simple black worsted breeches, with black top coats, silk waistcoats, stockings and shoes, and a tricorn hat, the edges decorated with some silver stuff. Anyone could recognize one of Lawyer Wormsley's lads, even across a crowded courtroom – which was, of course, the motive behind the lawyer's expenditure.

When Dodie had told Mark of her hospital appointment, he'd taken her face in his hands and looked deep into her perpetually troubled eyes.

'Nay, lass,' he'd said tenderly, 'why must tha' always run so? Can't tha' abide to stop at home wi' a bit o' knitting or needlework to keep thy hands busy?'

'I've better things to do wi' *my* time, Mark Ottershaw,' she said, pulling away from him roughly.

As usual when he tried to be tender with her, Dodie's response took on the edge of an attack upon him. She would never forgive him for his lack of ambition, for not thrusting himself forward to try to improve his position. He'd mastered his job and was content. He did his job so reliably and so efficiently that no one had any intention of promoting him to some other position.

'Besides,' she'd said, 'the money I earn is going straight into my box. We shall not be dipping into it to provide unnecessary luxuries.'

'I'd never think of dipping into yon treasure chest,' Mark said grumpily. 'It's thy money, and I want nowt of it. The money I bring home is more than enough, wi' careful husbandry, to provide what we need. It's not my fault if tha's too busy traipsing around advantaging thyself to save a bit on the buying and the cooking.'

Dodie blushed. He'd scored a point there, had touched her on a sore spot; she was often obliged to buy quickly and hurriedly since she was so busy elsewhere. She knew that other housewives bought their foodstuffs much more cheaply by going to different places, by waiting until they saw a bargain in the way of a piece of fly-specked meat. Only last week she'd paid a penny a stone for potatoes, when one of

Mark's workmates had told him his wife gathered seven stones for a penny at the market, with only a few that had gone rotten.

'If you only knew how much I have to pay for bread these days,' Dodie said, seeking to defend herself by attacking. 'But then, tha' knows but little of what goes on outside thy foundry or the ale-house where tha' drinks thyself to a stupor for a penny . . . while I have to find a penny farthing for every pound of bread tha' scoffs. Do you know that last week alone you ate eight poundweight, and if it hadn't been for the Assize of the Bread refusing the bakers their increase it'd have been a penny ha'penny! A quarter of thy wages goes on bread alone, did you but reckon it.'

Mark didn't want to argue with her, for she'd best him with her vitriolic tongue and her quick ways. He reached out his hand and banged the side of her head.

'Tha' gets above thyself, lass,' he said. 'I'll not have thee allus talking back to me, no matter how much tha' brings home in wages.'

Dodie had bitten her tongue; no matter how much she resented his complacent ways, he was still the man of the house to be obeyed in all things. More and more, these days, she sought consolation in her work at the hospital. There, at least, she could be a person in her own right; there she had the command of a number of nurses, all of whom were obedient to her, and the respect of a number of educated doctors and physicians, all of whom respected her efficiency.

She looked round the ward now, assessing the jobs that waited to be done, seeing the number of deficiencies of the girls who worked for her. 'Annie,' she said, 'take that bed-pan out, empty and wash it. It's been lying beneath that bed for at least a couple of hours, and fair stinks the place out.'

The bed-pans produced only one of the many unseemly

smells that plagued her nostrils; worse, by far, was the putrid odour of some of the bandaging, the personal smells of some of the patients. Really, she couldn't comprehend why the Free Hospital had to give bed space to old men and women who were so obviously incurable. They didn't accept such people in the other hospitals in Leeds. Why should they? A hospital should be where people went to be cured, not to die, she thought irritably. They could just as easily die at home, or up on the moors and in the woods.

'Nurse, my arm is paining me so,' the man in the nearest bed called out to her.

She went to him. 'Aye, Jacob, and so it will until it heals.'

'Couldn't you give me summat, Nurse? A little laudanum, perhaps, to take away the pain?'

'Th'art a great booby, Jacob,' she said. 'Look at young Tommy there – had his foot taken off, and never a word of complaint.'

Tommy in the next bed had worked in the mill and, one day, had caught his foot in the waterwheel. They'd taken him home, and it was only when the stench of the gangrenous bone had become too strong to support that they had thought to bring him to the Free Hospital. It was too late by then for anything to be done to save the lad's foot, and the surgeon had been obliged to amputate it. The shock to the young lad's system was great; he lay on his bed wasting away, barely half conscious from the loss of blood and the poison that had invaded his entire system. Dodie would have bled him but already he was so weak from loss of blood that she feared she might kill him if she tried to draw anything from his wasted body. She would have to speak to the doctor about him when he came the following day into the ward. Meanwhile, she'd get one of the nurses to spoon raw liver into his mouth. Liver makes blood, one of the doctors had told her, and she always believed what they said.

The man in the cot at the end of the room was still unconscious and suffering a high fever. They'd brought him in the previous day, already unconscious, running with sweat. The doctor had examined him the previous afternoon, but had not been able to say exactly what was wrong.

'Just keep an eye on him,' the doctor had said, 'and we'll wait to see what develops.'

Dodie looked down at the man, who appeared to be having trouble breathing. She opened his mouth with the wooden spoon she kept in her top pocket, and peered down his throat. His tongue was covered in a thick coating of yellow fur, as was the back of his throat where several large red spots had also appeared. It was like nothing she'd ever seen before and she resolved to ask the doctor to look at it when he came round the beds the next day.

The next man was recovering from smallpox: he was one of the lucky ones, for most of the victims of smallpox died in the building behind the hospital in which they were confined. Now her task consisted solely of trying to heal the scabs that covered the man's face and would mark him for life. Cool calamine pads would help reduce the itching and stop the man scraping at his face, increasing the damage already done to his skin.

'Just lie still there,' she said, 'and we'll see what we can do.'

'Aye,' the man said. 'I'm reet grateful to thee, ma'am, for what tha's doing for me. I've got a bit of a sore throat, is all.'

She took the wooden spoon again, used it to examine the man's throat. 'Why,' she said, 'that's summat similar to yon man in't next bed.' She could clearly see the start of the yellow fur on the man's tongue, the red patches at the back of his throat. 'I s'all tell the doctor about it when I see him in the morn.'

Dodie could not know, as she walked home through the

streets after work, that both the men were dying of the virulent infection whose symptoms she had seen but had lacked the knowledge or experience to diagnose. The plague came in many forms; some were instantly affected by it, especially if they'd been weakened by another disease. Some caught a small infection but, if their bodies were strong, they developed their own cures. Could she but know it, Dodie's work at the hospital had given her so many of these small infections that now she had developed an immunity to most of them; though she might be carrying the infection on or in her person, it had only the slightest effect upon her. On this occasion she felt a bothersome headache, nothing more, which the air of the streets she passed through on her way home helped quickly to dispel. Anyway, Dodie had no time to indulge herself thinking of headaches.

Ever since she had met Basil Townley and listened to his scheme, Dodie had had other things in mind, of far greater importance. The money in her 'treasure chest', as Mark derisively called it, had quickly accumulated over the year she had worked at the hospital, and now, in every sense of the word, weighed heavily with her. Like all people who acquire a little money, Dodie had a passionate desire to see the sum grow. And that meant, so Basil Townley had explained, putting her money to work.

'Idle money locked in a chest at home will avail you nowt,' he had said. 'In fact, if you think of it in real terms, it will quietly wither away. If you think, for example, of five pence. Yesterday, when the price of bread was a penny a pound, five pence would purchase five pounds of bread. Today, bread is a pennyfarthing, and five pence will only buy four pounds of it. Tomorrow, it could be a penny ha'penny, in which case you wouldn't even get four pounds of bread for your money.'

Dodie was not skilled in Mathematic, but she could understand *that* simple equation and its meaning. With the prices of everything increasing all the time, the value of idle money could be thought to be decreasing in like measure. The answer was simple. The money must be put to work, must be made to produce more money, to beget more money just as a man and wife begot children. But how could the money be put to work to best account?

Basil Townley had the answer. 'There are a number of folks wi' small sums of money,' he had said. 'I think we should put all these small sums together and buy shares of cargo in cargo vessels. I know a number of people, each of whom can raise twenty guineas or so—'

'I can manage a bit more than that,' Dodie had interrupted. She had never told anyone how much was in her box and many would have been amazed to discover that she had hoarded, over the years she had been married to Mark Ottershaw, the queenly sum of over sixty pounds. At first she had thought to use it to buy a better house, in a better neighbourhood, but with Mark content to spend his days in the foundry, she had reasoned that the money would be wasted. Mark was a journeyman in the foundry – he'd found his place, and nothing would move him. If he had become a foreman, or something . . .

She had thought that perhaps she'd send the boys to better schools, where they could learn more and perhaps associated with better-class boys, but then prudence had told her it would be too big a leap. Gradually, the idea of doing *anything* specific with the money had disappeared, until Basil Townley had come along with his talk of the value of the money decreasing.

'The money would be safe?' she had asked.

'Safe as houses,' Townley had assured her. 'Whenever did you hear of anyone losing money by financing cargoes?'

'And if the boat should founder, carrying our goods to the bottom—?'

'Why, these days all cargoes and vessels carry insurance,' he had told her.

'I'm afraid you'll have to explain that.'

'Insurance means that if a boat goes to the bottom with its cargo, the value of the vessel *and* the cargo can be recovered from the Insurance Society as takes on the risk. This is how it works. Very few vessels ever founder. The Insurance· Societies insure most vessels that go to sea, taking a small payment in advance from the vessel owner. That's known as a premium payment. The Societies make a lot of money, since they get all these premiums and seldom have to pay anything out.'

Dodie couldn't quite grasp such an arrangement, but she was prepared to believe what Basil Townley said. Anyway, in her cautious manner, she intended to verify that everything he said was true, that everything he proposed be done in a legal manner, before she ventured *any* of her precious capital.

Theirs was a most unlikely relationship. She had met him one evening as she was leaving Titus Waverley's house after obliging him; the next time she'd gone to the house, he'd been on the point of departure and Titus, with apologies, had been obliged to say he couldn't spend time with her. The young Mr Townley had offered gallantly to escort her home. On the way he'd asked, most politely, if she would share a glass of cordial with him at a staging post they were passing. His manner being most correct, she'd accepted his invitation. They'd seated themselves at one of the tables in the centre of the room and had conversed. He informed her that Titus Waverley had spoken of her in glowing terms and had explained how Mrs Ottershaw, seeking to improve her mind, had come to him for private tuition. Dodie had been relieved to learn that Titus had not disclosed the true nature of their relationship. Many men, she knew, would have boasted of their conquest, seeking to aggrandize themselves.

Just as they were about to leave the staging house, Basil Townley had touched her hand, though not in a forward or unseemly manner.

106

'Mrs Ottershaw,' he'd said, 'I have something to say to you which I will say in a direct manner, for I'm not a man to beat about the bush. I find you very attractive and desirable – will you share a room with me upstairs, if only for a fleeting hour?'

She'd laughed at the forthrightness of his manner, which was neither coarse nor demeaning. 'Nay, Mr Townley,' she'd said. 'I thank thee for thy offer, but I'm a respectable married woman who must return to hearth and husband.' The touch she'd given his hand had relieved any harshness in the rejection for, in truth, she found him most fair and, had she not been engaged with Titus Waverley at the time, might have considered indulging herself with him. It would be a welcome change to joust with a man between the sheets rather than servicing her husband's requirements from time to time as part of the matrimonial pledge and duty.

'Then say we may be friends?' Townley had asked passionately.

'Aye,' she had said, 'friends we may be, but first tha'll have to come to the house and meet my husband. I'll have no hole-in-the-corner relationship with you for I suspect we might greatly advantage each other, if only in conversation. My husband is a worthy man, Mr Townley, but not versed in the gentle arts of talking.'

His face had fallen. He'd wanted to befriend her alone and for himself, and the prospect of trying to stir life in some dull stick of a husband did not appeal to him. He was, however, pleasurably surprised when he met Mark Ottershaw: though the man was little versed in the affairs of the day, he had a ready wit and seemed anxious to expand a friendship with this unlikely man.

He worked in an office in the town, Townley told the Ottershaws. 'But 'tis a dull job and I'll be happy with it only until I have my own business.'

Now Townley had the entrée to the Ottershaw home, and even sometimes met Dodie on her way back from the hospital so that they could converse alone together. On these occasions, mostly they talked of how they would improve their situations by reaping the benefit of the sums of money they'd managed to accumulate. Townley's father was a parish parson near Dewsbury and had given his son the rudiments of an education, the better to fit him for life in the thriving city of Leeds. So far, though Townley knew a score of people, he'd formed no attachments, and seemed perfectly content to pass a couple of evenings each week at the home of Mark Ottershaw, whom he greatly liked, and his wife Dodie, whom he quietly adored for her strength and determination.

It had taken Dodie two months of intense contemplation to decide to do as Townley was suggesting and venture her capital on a cargo. 'I'd prefer, however, to do it on my own,' she had said once, 'and not in company with others. That way I should more easily be able to control what happens to my own money.'

'So you shall, my dear Dodie,' Townley had said, 'so you shall. I'll introduce you to Hawkins forthwith and you shall see what you make of him.'

Hawkins was a typical product of the second half of the eighteenth century, a man who rode the fringes of all the changes then taking place, an agent who relished an entrepreneurial role. Sometimes he introduced a wool merchant to a cloth master, sometimes a cloth master to a cargo agent. If a man wanted to solicit a builder to work for him, Hawkins would not only find the builder but the architect too, and would even supply the materials the building itself would eventually require. From each transaction, Hawkins took a small commission, never large enough for folks to accuse him of complicity with either side, but large enough for him to make a splendid living for himself, with a large house in the centre of Leeds, not far from the Free Hospital.

Townley and Dodie walked there one evening after her

work. Hawkins received them civilly in his office; he was a robust man with a large stomach, florid and jovial cheeks. His appearance was as much an asset to him as his honesty and his vast circle of acquaintances. He offered them a cordial, which both accepted, then stood before the fire whose generous helping of coals threw out a welcome heat, lifting the tails of his coat the better to warm his backside. Even though summer was upon them, the nights still struck chill.

'We ain't had a decent summer since I were a lad,' he observed. ''Tis very rarely I have no fire lit these days.'

He was used to assessing the people who came to him; Mrs Ottershaw seemed overly nervous and he wondered if the handsome young fella, Townley, had any part in that. He knew Townley for an honest man, though his head was sometimes full of dreams. Once he settled down . . .

'In what manner may I be of service to you, ma'am?' he enquired, after the common courtesies had been completed and he was seated again behind his desk. Dodie looked at Townley, who understood.

'I think Mrs Ottershaw would prefer to speak to you in private,' Townley said, 'so with your permission, I shall wait outside.'

'As you will,' Hawkins said, mystified. He looked at the lady before him, seeing that what he had taken for nervousness had fled with Townley's departure.

'I have saved sixty pounds,' Dodie said firmly. 'I have been persuaded to invest it, in the hope it might grow apace. I have also been persuaded that you are the man to help me in this matter.'

Hawkins was tempted to smile. Usually, he felt like saying to this fiercely determined woman, the people who sit in that chair talk to me of thousands, not tens. The last occupant had been the Chairman of the Board of Trustees of a school, who wished Hawkins to act for them in the building of a new extension involving a matter of some £15,000.

'I shall do my best to advise you, madam,' he said gravely.

'I shall want everything done in a legal manner,' Dodie warned him.

'Aye, madam, that shall be so. All my transactions are completed in a legal manner, for I'll have nowt to do with jack-o'-lanterns or will-o'-the-wisps. I have become accustomed to availing myself of the services of Messrs Elland and Peecham, and can highly recommend them, though of course you can choose to make your own appointment. I should warn you, however, that I should not use half the lawyers in this city, for a scurvier set of knaves I've seldom seen as many who embrace the legal profession.'

'I would be quite content to accept your recommendation of Messrs Elland and Peecham,' said Dodie.

'Good,' said Hawkins briskly. 'Now, in what manner do you care to venture this capital of yours? There are many possible ways – even if one only counts the legal and honest ones and I realize the others would interest neither you, madam, nor me.'

'I am advised to invest in cargo for vessels proceeding to foreign ports,' Dodie announced.

'Yes, I see. Well, madam, 'tis without doubt a good investment, though long in the term. By the time the goods have crossed the ocean . . .' Hawkins finished with an expressive shrug.

'I am in no hurry, but have been told the return on cargo is very high.'

'That it is, madam, since few these days are prepared to venture on the long term, preferring a short quick turn round of their capital sums.'

'I have been told that it is not unknown for the investment to double itself with each voyage.'

'That it can, madam, that it can. Cloth bought here in the

110

piece can fetch twice, three times, the amount in Europe, and even allowing for costs, the return to the original investor can be high.'

'And you can arrange this for me?' Dodie asked. 'In legal manner?'

'I can take charge of the entire transaction, madam,' Hawkins said gravely. Though they were speaking only of a woman's mite, he liked this fierce lady and wished her well. The sixty pounds could only be a part share of a larger whole, he realized, but he'd soon whistle up someone to add the balance to the cost of a small cargo. He'd not make anything for himself from the investment since he only charged one, or at most two per cent, and by the time he'd worked with a lawyer . . .

'If you are to do this for me,' Dodie was saying, 'you'll need to extract your own fee. Though I am willing to pay any man for his services, I have no desire to see my profits gobbled by middlemen.'

He laughed and slapped his knee. 'That's rich!' he roared. 'I was just thinking the same thing myself. Nay, I'll not rob the account – that's not the way of Hawkins, I assure you.'

'We should discuss the exact amount and come to a clear understanding,' Dodie persisted.

'And so we shall, Mrs Ottershaw,' he said, 'so we shall.' He took a slate from the drawer of his desk and a triangular piece of French chalk. 'Now, let's see . . . It'll all have to be reckoned mathematically. What would you say to one per cent of the capital sum invested, to which is added a further one per cent of the difference in the value between gross receipts and net earnings? Or alternatively, we could . . ' He chuckled at her bemused expression. 'I can see you've no mind for Mathematic, Mrs Ottershaw,' he said. 'Why don't we agree that you'll pay me one pound for all my services, and that is to include a contract drawn up by Elland and

Peecham. That way, you'll have the balance, fifty-nine pounds, to venture.'

'A pound?' Dodie gasped. 'For a few hours of work at most! My husband works for fifty hours or more each week in the foundry, and earns less than a pound!' She was visibly outraged by his suggestion.

Hawkins didn't inform her that his minimum fee was normally ten guineas. If the person in the chair had been anyone else, he would have terminated the conversation at that point and have shown them the door with scant courtesy. But there was something about this woman, some naïve but indomitable spirit that endeared her to him.

'Well, madam, might I make so bold as to ask what you yourself would suggest as a fair and honest recompense for my labours?'

She made a quick calculation. She had no wish to insult him by offering too low a sum, but thought a counter-suggestion might be acceptable. 'I realize that since your work is of a highly skilled nature, and cannot be performed by any Tom, Dick or Harry, I ought to offer you a good fee. I would suggest that ten shillings – enormous sum though it may be – should secure good and honest service.'

'Ten shillings—?'

'Generous, I admit,' Dodie said, 'but I feel sure your services are worth it.'

There was nothing Hawkins could say without bursting into violent and hysterical laughter. Silently, he offered her his hand to conclude the deal.

'Is it agreed?' asked Dodie. Then, as he nodded, she grasped his hand and shook it vigorously. 'Thank you, Mr Hawkins, thank you!'

'Th'art a remarkable woman, Mrs Ottershaw,' he said, finding his voice at last and trusting himself to use it. 'Perhaps I should persuade thee to forget adventuring capital and come to work in this office for me.'

112

CHAPTER TEN

The following weeks were filled with anxiety for Dodie, with her life savings at risk. Everything had gone well and Hawkins had honoured his word by introducing her to Mr Peecham himself, who had brought the contract to Hawkins's office for signature. The money was invested in fine worsted to be despatched to the Dutch market, where they'd achieved a good price and a fast turn-round of capital, or so everyone believed. Each week, Dodie went to see Hawkins and he reported progress. He grew to enjoy the arrival of this unusual woman who asked so many questions, seeking genuinely to inform herself of the ways of commerce and trade. After the third week, Hawkins was able to inform her that the worsted had arrived in the port of Yarmouth whence it would be despatched across the North Sea as soon as the vessel which was to carry it had arrived from Spain.

'Intelligence has it, Mrs Ottershaw, that our schooner will make land within the week,' he told her. 'It carries a cargo of sherries and sweet oportos, so must be boarded by the tide-waiter who will assess the value of the cargo before the vessel is allowed to make landfall. The Customs men are ever active and despatch their duties quickly; we will not wait long afore the vessel puts to sea again carrying our joint hopes and aspirations.'

Hawkins himself had provided the balance of the money to comprise a full cargo; Dodie was relieved that his own investment was so much greater than hers, for his honesty was thus ensured.

During this intolerable waiting, her work continued at the hospital. A new ward had been constructed for women, and Dodie had been given its charge. Now she commanded a staff of ten, with call on two surgeons and a doctor. The hospital did not deal with maternity cases; most of her patients came in either with infections or with the wasting disease that was so common among women, whose bodies sseemed ill-equipped to fight; many had large lumps in their breasts and bellies that grew and grew despite the efforts of Dodie and the doctors. The best treatment they had yet found, apart from the knife, was 'breathing' the veins to take off quantities of blood – Dodie remembered the village where she had been born, and the leeches that were taken from the river for the same purpose. In the hospital they were more modern and advanced; the vein would be gripped tight just above the elbow, punctured, and the blood which spurted out caught in an earthenware bowl. The surgeon explained that, if the arm were held below the incision, the blood would spill from a carelessly cut artery, which could prove fatal to the patient. Several times Dodie went into the operating room and – despite the odour, the blood smears everywhere, the foul-smelling liquids which drained from sick bodies – she examined opened arms the better to know which were arteries, which must not be punctured, and which were veins. She also learned how to use the specially sharpened knives with which incisions were made, and how to bind the wounds securely afterwards, even how to sew them with washed cat-gut and a fine sail needle.

From time to time she encountered the same throat disease that had killed the two men in her charge in the other ward. She now knew the condition was fatal, and would promptly arrange for such patients to be transferred to some other ward, or discharged, since she felt a death in her ward reflected badly on her efficiency – too many patients lost, she thought, and her position would no longer be secure.

The vessel that would carry her wares arrived in Yarmouth where Hawkins had an agent who sent immediate word on its sighting. Dodie waited in nervous anticipation until word was received that the cargo was aboard and the vessel had set sail. Finally the word came through: Dodie's cargo was safely on its way to Holland. But her anxiety continued unabated.

On the night after the sailing, a tremendous storm set in, with gale-force northerly winds and icy conditions. Early next morning, and each subsequent day, Dodie went to Hawkins's office, desperately hoping for news. Each day Hawkins would give her the agent's report, information gleaned from some passing ship that had subsequently made landfall. Many vessels had been blown off course by the terrible gale which had raged continuously for four days and nights. One vessel that had set out from Scotland to go to Hamburg had made its landfall in Brest, France, having run goosewinged before the fierce winds with no hope of turning on to an easterly course for fear of being capsized. There were reports of wreckage, of men overboard being thrown ropes which their numb fingers couldn't grasp and vanishing in the tempestuous seas. Beachy Head claimed a number of victims returning from the Baltic trade and baulks of timber were reported washed ashore over a ten mile shore line. A Customs cutter had been thrust on to the cliffs south of Whitby; the brandy it had confiscated the previous night was washed into a cove and, reportedly, salvaged by smugglers who left the Customs Officers to die on the rocks. One of them escaped and, though badly injured, lived to tell the tale and identify the smugglers' leader.

After three weeks without news Dodie, hollow-eyed, could only drag herself to her work at the hospital, and lacked interest in her patients. She was distracted during the day while her nurses took advantage of her inattention, then dragged herself home when the night-watcher came to relieve her. Basil Townley had been sent to London by his employer – she would dearly have loved to speak to someone about her plight and couldn't introduce the subject to her husband, who was quite unsympathetic about anything to do with her money.

After five weeks the vessel was found, unharmed, in the harbour at Ostend. The Master of the vessel explained that only by lightening the ship had he been able to save it, since the weight of the cargo had caused the vessel to swing dangerously abeam under the strength of the wind, and he had feared being driven on to rocks if he took down all sail. He'd made the best progress he could under storm sail alone, but even then the pendulum motion of the boat across the waves had threatened to capsize them. He'd thrown the cargo overboard, his first concern being to save his ship.

Hawkins was thin-lipped as he explained this to Dodie. 'We cannot blame the man,' he said. 'Any Captain would seek to save his command rather than his cargo.'

Dodie was relieved that at least they knew what had happened. 'Now Elland and Peecham will doubtless invoke the insurance,' she said, 'and we shall, at least, see the return of the value of our investment . . . ?'

Hawkins had spread the insurance document across his desk and was looking at it and shaking his head. 'Alas, Mrs Ottershaw,' he said, 'you have forgotten the provisions of the insurance. If it should happen that the Master of the vessel shall take it upon himself to jettison his cargo, and then subsequently bring his vessel safely to port, the portion and clauses of the Insurance Contract relating to the value of the cargo will be deemed ineffective,' he said, paraphrasing the cumbersome legal jargon of the document itself. 'They always put that clause in an Insurance Contract, Mrs Ottershaw, since many unscrupulous ships' captains have been known to jettison cargo into a waiting cutter, and then to claim they were doing so only to protect their vessel from foundering. The cutter, meanwhile, has made for the shores of the nearest country where the cargo is sold, and the spoils divided.'

'You mean . . .' Dodie whispered, though her tongue was unable to complete the sentence.

'I mean our venture has failed, Mrs Ottershaw. Our money is irretrievably lost.'

When Dodie arrived home that evening she little knew how she'd got there; she'd walked through the streets like someone in a trance, quite unaware of her passage. All she could think of was that all her savings on which she had counted so heavily to improve their situation in life were lost. Though she had always been a positive person, determined to make her own way in life, without permitting herself to become a straw blown by each and every wind, she could not accept this most crushing blow with her normal fortitude.

'If only I'd never met Basil Townley,' she said to herself. 'If only I'd not permitted myself to be led, to be influenced by Hawkins!' It mattered naught to her that Hawkins had lost far more than she; he was a man used to venturing and could take a gambler's view of it.

'If only I'd never met Basil Townley!' The thought kept ringing through her mind, making her oblivious to her passage along the streets on her way home. Several times she stepped off the pavement to the curses of waggoners and coach-drivers as their horses reared to avoid her.

Her heart had never been so heavy as when she entered

her humble house, to which she saw herself now condemned forever. She'd dreamed her dreams of a better place, perhaps even with a small garden and its own well and privy. She'd seen her money, doubled and redoubled, providing them with peace and dignity in which to live; she'd seen herself setting Stanley into his own business when he'd learned enough from Jonas Clegg; she'd seen Mark working alongside him, using his journeyman skills and strong muscles to aid his son's more educated figurings – even Claude, always in her dreams miraculously awoken from his youthful sloth, handling all the ledgers and paperwork. And herself in a carriage with Jennifer, going the rounds of the silk merchants to buy ever prettier clothing for her beautiful daughter, being admired by bucks and gentlemen.

The reality was impossible to face.

She went into the room, expecting to find Mark sitting in his chair by the stove with the brewis for their supper bubbling. Jennifer had instructions to get it all ready; Mark would have been home an hour, but always said he preferred to wait for her arrival before eating. But Mark was nowhere to be seen.

'He's upstairs, in bed,' Jennifer told her mother.

'In bed? At this time of even?'

'He said he was not feeling well.'

Dodie climbed the stairs to their one small bedroom; Mark was lying atop the covers and to her great annoyance hadn't even troubled to pull off his boots or remove his jerkin.

'What ails *thee*?' she said impatiently. 'Has tha' supped too much again?' She knew he often went into the ale-house these days on his way home, giving as his excuse the heat of the foundry, the fact that his throat was parched. Once or twice he'd arrived home long after she'd returned from the hospital, much the worse for wear.

He groaned, and didn't speak.

Dodie placed her hand on his brow; he was already running a high fever. She called down the stairs: 'Jennifer, fetch me up the bit of stick you'll find on the mantelshelf.'

She felt Mark's throat while she was waiting for Jennifer and her fingers could easily outline the lumps she had come to know so well. When Jennifer arrived, she opened Mark's mouth and had but little need to poke in the stick, since she could already smell the familiar odour. His tongue was coated in the yellow fur; already the red spots were showing on his tonsils and the roof of his mouth.

'Dear God, let it not be the plague!' she prayed silently. 'Hold the candle close, Jennifer,' she said. Her mind was racing through the possibilities. 'Stay here with your father,' she said. 'I'll return as soon as I can.' She raced downstairs again, picked up her outer coat and reticule from where she had placed them when she arrived home. All thoughts of her lost money were gone from her as she dashed into the street, looking wildly about in the hope of seeing a passing fly. It would be unlikely to find one in this part of the town, she knew, but she kept looking as she made her way rapidly towards the main Hunslet Road. Often a fly would trundle along here after delivering some gentleman at one of the manufactories or someone's grand house. She'd gone almost a mile before she saw an empty one passing by. She held up her hand and shouted at the top of her voice.

'*Stop!* For the love of God, stop!'

The driver reined in his horse and stared down at her from the bench. 'What's amiss wi' thee, ma'am, that tha' scares my horse so?'

Already she was climbing on to the step. 'Take me to the Free Hospital,' she cried, 'and quick about it!'

'The Free Hospital would be twopence, ma'am,' he said, looking at her dubiously.

'I can pay,' she said, 'I'll pay when we get there.'

He smiled knowingly. 'I take my payments in coin, ma'am,' he said. 'I've known o'er many bawds as thinks they can pay wi' a token of their affection and esteem – aye, and other matters I'll not mention!'

Seeing he was obdurate, she fumbled in her reticule and extracted two pennies. She gave him one, allowing him to see the other. 'You'll receive the other when we arrive,' she said, 'provided we proceed with despatch.'

'Ah, the grand manner, is it, my dear? Well, you'll find as Albert Humble will get you there as fast as any fly-driver on the road.'

He set the horse to a brisk trot despite the number of people on the road and the pavements, weaving among the heavy waggons and coaches that clogged this main artery into and out of the city. Whenever a clear space presented itself, he lashed the horse's flanks and encouraged it into a canter. Dodie bounced up and down on the seat, oblivious of her discomfort, praying only for more speed.

When they arrived at the hospital, she thrust the penny at the coachman with a brisk enjoinder – 'Wait there for me!' – and hurried inside. She knew Doctor Bartholomew would still be working, or would just have finished, for there had been many cases awaiting his attentions when she had left to return home that evening. She found him in the doctors' sitting room, a glass of port by his hand. His black frock coat was stained with blood, and his hands were streaked with all manner of vile substances, though she knew he'd wash himself and change his clothes before he departed for his home.

'Doctor Bartholomew, you recognize me?' she asked hurriedly as she braved this holy of holies, this inner sanctum.

He frowned when he saw his peace disturbed. 'I cannot say as I do, madam,' he said, 'and I'd be obliged—'

'Nay, Doctor, forgive me, forgive me disturbing your rest, but I mun speak with you, I mun!'

He had immediately assumed she was the relative of one of his cases, perhaps come to upbraid him for his failure. Several times he had been abused by wives or mothers, and once had been set upon by an entire family whose mother had perished under the knife. 'If you do not leave,' he said sternly, 'I'll be obliged to call the porters.'

She snatched her nurse's mob-cap from her reticule and placed it on her head. 'The new Women's Ward, Doctor,' she said. 'Surely you remember me?'

'Aye, I've a memory of your face,' he said, 'but that in no way excuses—'

'My husband,' she interrupted, 'has taken bad. Will you in mercy's name spare a few minutes to examine him, to recommend what is best to do?'

If that would get rid of her, he thought, and allow him his rest, his glass of port, time to compose himself before he returned home . . . 'Which ward is he in?' he asked.

'He's not in a ward,' Dodie cried impatiently. 'He lies in our *home*!'

'Then bring him to a ward, ma'am, and we will see him in the morn.' There, the matter was settled. He turned from her and raised his glass to his lips in a gesture of dismissal.

She dashed forward and struck the glass from his hand, the wine spilling down his frock coat.

'You go too far, madam, too far indeed!' He raised his head and was about to shout for a porter when something in the woman's eyes, some near-madness in her face, arrested him.

'Please, Doctor Bartholomew,' she begged, 'I mean you no harm! I was carried away . . .'

He reached out his hand to touch her, saw the condition of it, and pulled it back. 'Give me a moment to wash myself,' he said with compassion, 'and I'll come wi' you to his bedside.'

121

She almost swooned with relief. 'I've a fly waiting outside,' she said.

'So much the better, for my man will not come for a half hour. Have you paid the driver?'

'Yes, I have, but I told him to wait.'

'Then get outside quickly, and hold your foot on the coach, for there's many a rascal will take your coin then sell himself to the next buyer. I'll be out as soon as I've washed, for I'd not like to bring this muck to your husband's bedside.'

Something about Dodie's earnest manner had appealed to Doctor Bartholomew, just as once it had appealed to Hawkins, to Jonas Clegg, to Titus Waverley – even, in the dim days of the past, to the young lad Mark Ottershaw who had anchored his dreams to her side.

As they travelled along the roads, she described Mark Ottershaw's condition to him, described how she had seen similar infections in the ward. He listened gravely; he knew the condition well enough and had lost many a patient through it. When they arrived at her home, he bade the driver wait, refusing to give him a coin 'on account', and hurried inside the house.

Jennifer was curled up in the chair by the fire, almost asleep. 'You ought to be upstairs, watching your father,' Dodie chided her, but Jennifer pouted.

'There's such a stink up there,' she complained.

Dodie brought her hand smartly across the girl's cheeks, then hurried up after the doctor. He stood by the bed.

'Fetch the candle,' he commanded and she did as he bid. He'd brought a bag with him and from it he took a brass spatula with which he opened Mark's mouth. He grimaced when he saw the condition of Mark's throat. 'Aye, 'tis the plague,' he said.

He went down the stairs, took the spatula and held it over the flames of the fire until it was soot-blackened, before wiping it clean on a cloth from his bag, then carefully threw the scrap of cloth into the centre of the fire and watched it burn, thinking the while. He walked slowly back up the stairs. Dodie was sitting on the bottom of the pallet and tears streamed from her eyes; her hand clutched Mark's ankle beneath the cover.

''Tis the plague,' Doctor Bartholomew repeated in a matter-of-fact voice, accustomed to offering bad news to loved ones.

'He'll die?' she asked quietly.

'Nay, Mrs Ottershaw,' he said, 'you know the answer yourself. I'll not give you false hope. The hospital records show—'

'That five in a hundred survive,' she finished for him.

'If they're lucky.' He looked around the room, saw the wooden spatula on a chest of drawers by the bed, picked it up and examined it, then went downstairs and threw it into the fire. He reached into his pocket and extracted a coin. 'Run to the chandlers,' he commanded Jennifer, 'and bring me two sulphur candles.'

When he returned upstairs, Dodie had not moved. Mark Ottershaw was still unconscious. Doctor Bartholomew held Mark's wrist, then placed a hand on his forehead. He could read the whole story. The man was burning up as the plague took hold of him. Soon the black spots would appear on his skin; his breathing would become more laboured; he would literally burn to death. And there was nothing any doctor could do about it. Breathing an artery would prolong the patient's life, but only for a short time. Some people were fortunate; in the cauldron of their own heated blood they seemed to create the necessary substances to effect a cure. Doctors did not understand how this could happen – someday, Doctor Bartholomew passionately hoped, they would. Many men were studying the secret workings of the human body to try to uncover these mysteries.

'Should we try to bring down the heat, Doctor?' Dodie

asked suddenly, seeming to waken from a reverie. 'We have water in the house.'

'Nay, Mrs Ottershaw,' he said. Some fevers responded to cooling and could be brought under control. Others needed to burn themselves out, or so he had observed. Someday they'd know which was which. 'The only cases I have seen which have recovered,' he said, 'are those which have passed through a heat. Cooling seems, if anything, to increase the fever's passion.'

Both of them heard Jennifer return. 'Where has she been?' Dodie wondered aloud.

'I sent her for sulphur candles,' Doctor Bartholomew said gravely.

Dodie sobbed once, loudly. 'Then you think he's going . . . ?'

'Aye, Mrs Ottershaw. I'll not speak falsely to you. I think you should muster strength within yourself, and prepare to pray, for your husband is in no condition to ask the Lord's forgiveness.'

Mark Ottershaw died at four o'clock in the morning, by which time Stanley and Claude were in the room with Jennifer and Dodie, who was holding Mark's hand and bathing his forehead with a wet cloth from which steam was rising. Mark's eyes had been open for the past hour but had seen nothing, recognizing no one. When they had spoken to him he'd given no signs of hearing them – his breathing, laboured and shallow, had not altered until the last moment, the last tormented gasp which ended in a rattle from somewhere deep within him.

Stanley put his arm round Dodie's shoulder. 'Father is dead, Mam,' he said.

She shuddered, her eyes closed, her frame held stiff. Then she collapsed on to Stanley's shoulder and a multitude of tears suddenly poured from her. Stanley helped her from the room, down the stairs.

'Light the candle,' he whispered to Claude, who took one of the sulphur packets and a brand from the fire. Soon the heavy sulphurous odour wafted downstairs to them as the candle spread its cleansing vapour round the room in which their father had died, taking away the last of his infection, purifying the unknown source of evil.

'Us'll need to take the sulphur bath', Stanley said, ever practical. The sulphur baths were an innovation. Attached to hospitals, they provided a free cleansing facility for any infested by lice or ticks or suffering from infectious diseases of the skin such as scabies or psoriasis. They were also used by people whose close proximity to a dying person might have infected them.

Dodie sat in her chair with the others about her, knowing Stanley was only speaking of these practical matters to hide his feelings. Of all the family he had always been closest to his father. They had shared the same streak of practicality, of resignation, of contentment with their lot. But Stanley, of course, with the benefits of an education denied to Mark Ottershaw, had seized the opportunity to improve himself while Claude seemed to have inherited his father's complacency. Dodie knew Claude would never strive, as Stanley was doing.

'Your father was a good man,' she said, 'and I always loved him . . .' She broke down again, and now was inconsolable. The loss of the money which earlier had seemed the worst tragedy that could befall had faded into insignificance in the darkness of this new misery. 'He was a good man, and he never knew that I loved him so . . .'

CHAPTER ELEVEN

When his son Gavin reached the age of five in 1762, Peter Aysgill gave a large celebration in his honour, to which he invited all the commercial barons of Leeds, most of whom had prospered from beginnings as humble as those of Peter himself. Thus the Assembly Rooms that night were filled with rich merchants – although Peter would much rather have used his friendship with several members of the aristocracy to spread his net throughout the social élite.

When Peter had left Barthwick with the rest of the Aysgill family, after the death of their father John and the enclosure of their land, he had refused to resign himself to his lot, as had his brothers and sisters. Instead, by devious methods – some of which would not stand the scrutiny of honest men – he had amassed a large fortune and had married Tessa, the daughter of Sir Ian Clether of Wakefield. He had believed that his alliance with this titled family would open all doors to him, and for a while it had promised to do so. He had been greatly helped by his friendship with Lord Percival and, in 1759, had aspired to public office as one of the Aldermen of the City of Leeds. Being snubbed by the Philosophical Society, whose aristocratic members he needed to endorse his candidacy, had temporarily soured Peter against the high-born knights and barons of the wealthy county; he had thereafter concentrated all his energies on the acquisition of a fortune so great that none would dare gainsay him or his family. The years 1759 and 1760 had been the most lucrative for him. His wealth was invested in countless ventures; his commercial and political intelligence was bolstered by the many informers he secretly employed; his shrewdness and business acumen were talked of and admired in the coffee-houses, the Assembly Rooms and the Gaming Houses. Most important, however, he was becoming a man of power.

In all matters, Peter maintained a clear conscience. It was not his concern, he would tell himself, if others behaved foolishly and permitted astute people to profit by their mistakes – like Brian Broacke.

Broacke had so impaired his family fortune that he had been required to sell the goods in his store-house quickly in order to obtain cash money, since none would accept his note-of-hand. Peter Aysgill had discovered Broacke's exact cash requirement, and had offered exactly that sum for goods *and* a warehouse worth twenty times that amount. When Peter had realized his investment and had cleared yet another fortune, Broacke had come to him, again in need, again requiring financial assistance. Now he had nothing to sell, and Peter refused him. Broacke pleaded that Aysgill had made a fortune from Broacke's goods – surely he ought to recompense him by sharing a part of the profit? Peter had refused. That night, Broacke had put a pistol into his mouth and shot himself, leaving a letter behind cursing Aysgill and giving all details of the transaction.

Peter had known that, if he now displayed the slightest weakness, his fellow merchants would be on to him like a pack of moor dogs to tear his own fortune from him. He therefore sent, by a member of the staff of the *Leeds Intelligencer*, the derisory sum of ten guineas – 'to be used by the widow in any way she sees fit and in full recognition of her late husband's value to the community.'

The *Intelligencer* had printed the message in full.

Peter was a good judge of human reactions. At first Society was outraged. But when it became known, as Peter himself quietly ensured, how many debts Broacke had left behind him, how many humble workers on his estate and tradesmen had not been paid, sympathy swung away from Broacke. Peter Aysgill, people argued approvingly, had seen Broacke for the wastrel spendthrift that he was. Aysgill understood the two interlinked facts: Society in Leeds depended – say what the snobbish gentry might – on financial resources, and the acquisition of those resources depended on ruthlessness in business.

Peter was equally ruthless in his private life. Long ago he had cut himself off from the rest of the Aysgill family. His brothers and sisters never visited his house, and he had had no contact with them of any kind, especially since the night in 1759 when they had inadvertently caused him to lose the Philosophical Society nomination for Alderman.

For the time being, Peter Aysgill was content to expend all his energies on his first love, the acquisition of wealth. He would fill his social life, such as it was, with the other merchant princes, who made up in joviality what they lacked in social graces. One or two of the more rakish fops of the district were happy to join one of 'Aysgill's rough-and-tumbles', as they called them. They knew there'd always be adequate food and wines, plenty of lusty young wenches, and the chance to pump Aysgill for a business suggestion. Aysgill played fair with them: if anyone of good family came to one of Aysgill's parties, he always left with some small venture intelligence on which he could earn a score or two of guineas. And, coming from Aysgill himself, that would be as sound an investment as any man could wish. Lord Percival, who had acceded to the title on the death of his father, had been made a wealthy man by his continued loyalty to Peter, by being the vanguard of the few aristocratic friends Peter could boast and by sponsoring Gavin, Peter's son, on any possible occasion.

It was Lord Percival who had introduced Gavin to the extremely exclusive School for the Sons of Gentlemen that Keith Semple had opened on the outskirts of York.

'Don't send the lad to Eton,' Lord Percival had told Peter. 'He'll learn precious little there that would fit him for any other life than lounging about in Parliament. Folks send their second and third sons to Eton, the ones who will inherit neither title nor estate and be obliged to go into politics, the Army, or the Church. First sons go to Semple, where they learn nought at all except to mix with the rest of the lads from the district. That way, the web of privilege through personal contact is maintained, long after the lads succeed to the family estate.'

So Gavin, Peter decided, would go to Semple's while Robert, his second son, would go to Eton. There would be no more sons.

Gavin's fifth birthday party in the Assembly Rooms quickly divided into three sections. Nannies and their charges – with some mothers who had not yet learned the aristocratic way of entrusting the welfare of their children to professionals – went into one large room where there were all manner of gifts to be distributed, unwrapped, fought over, played with, broken. Mostly the gifts were the new toys that were being imported from France and taken round the country by packhorse pedlars. There were rag-dolls with lifelike wooden heads into which flax had been fitted for hair, wooden carts and horses, carriages on wheels that could be pulled along by a thong or a silk ribbon, all manner of cup-and-ball games to play, even one game with carved wooden rings which one had to try to throw around sticks fixed into a board. Of course, there were many skittles sets, some with ingeniously decorated men and ladies, all to be knocked down, hopefully, with the throw of a soft ball or the rolling of a hard one.

Older wives and mothers, grown tired of childish noises, retired to a room set out with chairs and tables where, inevitably, they gathered into small social groups, exclusive enclaves in which privilege was clearly defined.

Lady Rounham, as the undisputed social queen of the occasion, had gathered a small court about her that all longed to join but none dared approach without specific invitation, which would come in the form of a called name, a wave of the hand.

'Ah, Mildred,' Lady Rounham called as she saw one passing group, 'we haven't seen you in ages.'

Mildred had been avoiding Lady Rounham, for the older lady's prattle bored her, but now she abandoned the other strollers. Not mentioned, they were not invited. More than that, they realized, they'd been judged, found socially wanting, and had been excluded.

'Mildred,' Lady Rounham began, 'you are so *intimate* with the Aysgill family. Tell us all, since we're dying to hear, why Tessa Aysgill, Peter's wife, is not to be seen on these occasions any more. I've heard that she's grown gross fat through eating too many sweetmeats and drinking too much of that oporto that seems all the craze these days.'

An insatiable busybody, Lady Rounham always chose one person as her target at any soirée, and surrounded herself with the people she felt best able to fill her cup of vitriol with spiced, malicious anecdotes. Little did she realize how often she herself formed the subject of such a symposium of malice and gossip.

The men, meanwhile, had gathered upstairs in the drinking and gaming rooms, with the salon that linked them being the only place where widows and groups of 'ladies' could congregate. No one ever seemed to know where they came from or where they went to, these 'ladies'. By the tone of their voices, their dress and deportment, many had been accustomed to a rich style of life and, though they ultimately plied the same profession, were a world apart from the common doxys who frequented the taverns and ale-houses of Boar Lane and Briggate. No one ever invited them, for no one ever knew where to make contact with them, but if the affair promised rich pickings and if they were not rigidly excluded by command of the host – or, as more often happened, his wife – they would arrive in plenty of time to be given food, drink, conversation, and any other benefits they could glean.

It was in the upper foyer, just outside the salon, that Peter now stood. Neither a drinker nor a gambler, he was willing enough to hold a glass (which he seldom drained), to throw a pair of dice in jest, or turn a card. Gavin had run up the stairs of the Assembly Rooms ahead of his nanny, Mrs Pocock, who had taken charge of him ever since his birth. When she arrived at the top of the stairs, Peter was already fending off his son's clamorous attentions, trying to maintain his poise and dignity in the face of the child's excited noises.

'I'm sorry, Master, but he did so want to come and see you – I just couldn't stop him,' Mrs Pocock panted as she stood with her hand on the shoulder of her charge.

'Perhaps we should chain him to you,' Peter suggested, 'like the man chains his monkey or the pedlar his bear.'

Gavin squealed with delight. 'Oh, wouldn't that be fun!' he cried, his young voice already strengthened by the singing lessons he was having, along with dancing and music.

Mrs Pocock coughed to catch Peter's ear.

'Yes, Mrs Pocock,' he said, recognizing her manner and inclining his head towards her, after a quick glance around to make certain they could not be overheard.

'Milady Rounham, Master, has seen fit to choose your good wife as her subject this day . . .'

Peter frowned. He knew there was speculation about the fact that his wife was no more seen in public, but he'd no intention of informing even Lady Rounham of the reason he had thrown a ring of security around his marital relationships. 'And who are the idle-headed chatterers she has selected to wallow in her swine-pool tonight?' he muttered.

Mrs Pocock grinned with delight. Her master could bandy words with the best of them, but was always reduced to abuse when he was sorely affected. She knew she'd have sport from this conversation. One by one, she listed the ladies gathered around Lady Rounham, noting the expression of her master's face as she mentioned some who obviously had a deeper meaning for him.

A nod, a sharper look – those were the wives of men with whom he had business relationships. Her master would not let insult go unavenged: each man would pay for his wife's gossiping.

'Go back now,' he commanded, 'and position yourself where you can the best hear what is said. Note the speakers carefully; I shall need a full account from you at the party's end.'

Mrs Pocock dropped him a curtsey, though there was nothing servile in the sparkle of her eye, took Gavin's hand in hers and descended the stairs, carefully keeping to the balustrade to permit the gentry to occupy the centre as each sought to make his grand entrance to where Peter stood, in the upper foyer, to meet and greet them.

Peter adjusted his wig, smoothed down his rose-coloured velvet and satin coat over his white silk breeches and extended his hand.

'Lord Rounham,' he said, as he made a small bow in recognition. 'Just the man I want to see . . .'

Part Two

CHAPTER ONE

Tomlinson had been as good as his word, and had taken Arthur Aysgill under his wing. At first it had been because of a sense of obligation to Blind Jack o' Knaresborough, but as the young lad worked alongside him in the mill and grew in physical stature and authority, Tomlinson began to leave more and more of the responsibility of his daily supervision of the workers to Arthur's care. Arthur, of course, had risen from among the workers themselves; Tomlinson's only complaint was that he could be too lenient in dealing with their transgressions.

One cold day in January 1770, Tomlinson instructed Arthur to come to his office. Arthur still went in fear of Tomlinson who had continued to deal harshly with him; a summons to the office implied no small matter and, once again, Arthur was afraid for his job. Was Tomlinson going to put him back among the spinners, or up in the top floor with the fullers, manning the giant waterwheel to pound fuller's earth into the fibres of the woollen cloth? It was an arduous job, and not well paid, but at this very moment Arthur had need of all the coins he could muster.

'Shut't door, lad,' Tomlinson said as Arthur timidly went in.

Sleightholme had provided Tomlinson with an office that abutted his own. Though by no means as sumptuously furnished as Sleightholme's – which had a thick Axminster carpet on the floor, furniture specially made in seasoned woods, including a set of walnut arm-chairs with padded seats and ladder backs – Tomlinson's office was comfortable enough and even contained a padded library chair in which he sometimes took the opportunity to nap, though only when none of the partners was about. As Tomlinson now settled himself in the library chair and motioned for Arthur to take a seat on a stool by his side, Arthur noticed how aged his benefactor's face had become in the years they had worked together.

'You've a radical streak in you,' Tomlinson began, 'and I've no notion how to rid you of it. It'll be your downfall in life, believe me, for you'll find many as'll think nowt o' taking advantage of it. Tha' mun learn to be harder, Arthur, if tha's to serve our Master in the best ways. Tha' should have fined Molly a penny yesterday morning, for coming late like that and then slobbering o'er her machine for half the day.'

'She's just lost her lad wi' the consumption,' Arthur said hotly. 'I couldn't add a fine to what she's already suffering.'

'There you go again, lad,' Tomlinson said sorrowfully. 'It matters naught what happens outside these walls; we're not a charity, nor one of these new-fangled benevolent societies that'll be the ruination of man's God-given natural will to work. It's bad enough that our Master, by iniquitous taxation, has to contribute to the Poor Laws income to maintain every beggar who cares to lodge himself hereabouts. Damme, Arthur, the parish provides amply well for those who cannot or will not work, wi'out us having to let the workers make a mock of us by bringing their private woes down upon our heads. I want you to see that every man-jack in this mill gives our Master a fair day's work for the fair coin he pays them. And what's private is private. Sometimes, my lad, you go too far wi' your sympathy for these people. You must harden your heart if you aspire to continue on the upward track on which I've set your feet.'

136

'I'll try, Mr Tomlinson,' Arthur promised. 'I really will try.'

Inwardly he sighed. It was so difficult. He wished he knew how to reconcile the two opposing factors in his mind, as Tomlinson so successfully had done. Arthur saw all the human suffering about him; he always noticed when a woman dragged herself to the mill in an advanced state of pregnancy or suffering one of the many women's wasting diseases that were so prevalent. He wanted always to relieve such suffering by any means at his disposal. Thank God Tomlinson had never learned that, on some of the occasions when he'd been absent with the Master, Arthur had permitted several of the pregnant women to drag up a box and sit on it while they were working. Tomlinson would have skelped Arthur's arse a time or two if he had seen some of the things that went on with Arthur's connivance.

'I know you'll try, Arthur. I have every confidence in you. And, I might add, so has the Master. He's spoken your name to me several times in commendation.'

Arthur's heart leaped. Fancy Mr Sleightholme noticing him, let alone praising him to Tomlinson! My, that was a prize to take out with him tonight, when he went to see Sally.

'There's more, Arthur,' Tomlinson continued in his heavy voice. 'I'm to give you extra wages, the Master says, in keeping with your position as my assistant. As from today, you're to have a pound a week.'

Arthur's head reeled. At the age of only twenty-four, he was to earn a pound, a whole pound a week! More than the mill's engineers, more than the skilled craftsmen carpenters, more even than the highly paid croppers! He hardly heard Tomlinson's next words for the buzzing of pleasure in his ears.

'Mark you well, Arthur, the Master is putting a lot of

trust and faith in you. More than I would have agreed to, knowing some of your radical thoughts and ways. I know you've been letting the lasses sit down to work when I've been away wi' the Master on business. I know you've been letting them stop work to take a sup o' water from time to time. Aye, well, I'm getting on in years and perhaps the good Lord had a purpose in sending you to me, to show me a new way o' conducting business. Mind, I'm not agreeing wi' this radical nonsense of workers talking back to their masters, trying to tell them what they will and will not do! I'm not agreeing wi' all the new societies that are being set up secretly – largely, I reckon, as a result of the agitations of your ungodly Uncle Matthew and his Wesleyan lot. Happen there's summat i' the Aysgill blood as makes you act the way you do. But I'm willing to give you one more try. You've had the power these many years, and now you've got the brass. I want to see less of this humanitarian stuff that I think of as weakness, and more discipline and holding to the old ways, understand?'

'I understand, Mr Tomlinson,' said Arthur, 'and you have my word I'll try.'

'Aye, lad, I know tha'll try. But I can ne'er forget that tha's an Aysgill. Too bad tha' couldn't have been cast in the mould of thy Uncle Peter.'

Arthur rushed home after work, bursting to share the good news. His mother was home before him, since the spinners were laid off as soon as enough thread was on hand and ready to lace up the machines the following morn.

The last ten years had brought a change to Amelia and though she was often tired and wasted, her spirit was ever strong. These days she hardly ever talked of her dead husband, Simon. Her friendship with Nancy Boothman had flourished and often the two women would pass the evening together, sewing their samplers so long as the candles gave light. Nancy liked to escape from her own home of an evening and, despite the poverty of Arthur and Amelia's hovel, she'd come there and sit with them, bringing one of the wax candles that were everywhere replacing the mutton fat, and gave so much more light for sewing. Arthur never objected when he saw Nancy arrive, since she always brought news of some little task for him to do at her home.

'Nay, Arthur,' Nancy would say, 'the damp's got into the wattle in that far corner – could you go round and daub a bit more on for me, there's a good lad?'

Arthur would be delighted to accept, for it would mean a couple of hours spent alone – if the lodger wasn't at home – with Sally.

Arthur and Sally had known each other since Sally first arrived from Wakefield to live with her Aunt Nancy. She'd been a shy little girl, ten years younger than him, but Arthur had been kind to her and their relationship had immediately become that of devoted sister and doting brother. Arthur had enjoyed showing her around the district, and looked forward to every feast day when he could take her walking up over the moors, or teach her how to catch sticklebacks with a piece of netting wrapped round a wire ring held in a wooden pole. They'd once sneaked under the canvas of a travelling circus, since neither could afford the threepence to go in by the front entrance, and clutched each other in awe as they watched the man who rode a wheel along a slack wire hanging high over the crowd's heads, the swarthy-skinned acrobats who built pyramids, the Fattest Lady in the World, the Thinnest Man, the Sword-Swallower, the man who threw knives at his own wife.

Now Sally was fourteen and a little girl no longer.

And now Arthur had the unbelievable income of a pound a week.

Ever since his meeting with Tomlinson, his mind had been circling around the two facts which were inseparably intertwined in his mind.

'I've come to daub a bit on that wattle in the corner,' he told her now.

'Yes, there is much need of it, Arthur. A piece fell out on my head only this afternoon. Look . . .' Sally parted her thick chestnut-coloured mane of hair, inviting him to examine her scalp.

A foot taller than she was, he bent his head over to look directly down upon her, drawing her closer to him the better to examine the wound on her scalp. In truth he could discern a break in her skin . . .

'Tha'll need to look after this,' he said, 'else it'll become infected.'

'You should have been a doctor, Arthur,' she said, 'for you have wonderfully delicate hands.'

He allowed his hands to fall down behind her until they were resting on her shoulders, and then embracing the small of her back and her delicate waist. She tilted her head back to look up at him. Her tiny face was rounded by a gentle smile; her eyes, the colour of hazel leaves, were opened wide as she gazed up at him. Her complexion had not been coarsened by rude sun and winds, since she spent her days in Mrs Little's workroom on Boar Lane, sewing the millinery for which Mrs Little was becoming famous throughout the district.

'I have news for you – wonderful news,' he said softly, still holding her close.

'Then pray don't keep me waiting with my neck bent back this way!' Sally laughed.

'Come and sit on't settle,' he said. Some years before, when Nancy had complained she had nowhere comfortable to sit, he'd brought pieces of wood he'd found behind a furniture makers, and had constructed what they now called the settle. Nancy had woven a cover for it which Amelia and Sally together had embroidered with leftover coloured cottons and silk scraps from Mrs Little's workshop. They sat down, side by side, and Arthur took her hand.

How many countless times had he done that, he asked himself, in order to emphasize some point he was telling her? She'd always been interested in everything he had to say of the wider world. He'd told her of his boyish adventures with his friend Ezra, roaming the bustling streets of Hunslet and Leeds at night, mostly searching for food but often just for sheer daring, and of his time with Blind Jack o'Knaresborough, learning how to build roads. Always she'd sat here, silent, beside him, her wide eyes enlarged by his stories. And holding her hand had become as natural as holding his own.

Why, then, did holding her hand *this* evening cause such deep stirrings in him? Why could his eye not meet hers? Why did he feel a rush of blood to his face? Why was he breaking out in a muck sweat? And, what was worst of all, why did he feel a stiffening in his breeches . . .?

He crossed his legs, though it meant sitting in discomfort. 'Aye, well, I've good news,' he muttered.

'You said that before, Arthur,' Sally smiled.

'Aye, well, you'll never believe it. The Master, Mr Sleightholme, has been talking with Mr Tomlinson about me, he's been commending me.'

'He's *never*!' she cried incredulously. 'Mr Sleightholme commending *thee*?'

'Aye, and why shouldn't he?' Arthur said defensively. 'I gi'e him a fair day's work for a fair day's pay!'

'Aye, Arthur, and what about all the ladies you let sit on't boxes? Your mam's told me how they take advantage of your soft nature.'

'I just try to help them a bit. Anyroad, that's got nowt to

141

do wi' it. I'm trying to tell you summat, Sally.'

'I'm sorry I interrupted, sir!' she laughed. Arthur could be very pompous sometimes, she thought, especially when his dignity was ruffled. 'Come on, what is it so special you want to tell me? I'll not interrupt, I promise.'

'They're paying me a pound a week,' he blurted out, cursing himself for his ineptness. He'd meant to make it a guessing game with her, to enjoy watching her face as the sum mounted to these incredible heights.

'A pound a week? A *pound*? I don't believe it!' Sally gasped.

'It's the truth. Tomlinson showed me and it's written in't wages book. Starting as today, I'm to get a pound a week.'

Her eyes shining, she threw her arms around him and hugged him. 'I'm so happy for you, Arthur,' she said. 'Now you can be a swell like you've always wanted. It'll be tuppence to speak to you, afore we know!'

'You've no call to be cheeky,' Arthur said, withdrawing his hand from hers.

But Sally couldn't hide the mischievous glint in her eyes. She was so pleased for him, so proud of him, that her pleasure and pride had to escape somehow. 'Happen,' she said, 'now you'll have so much coin in your hand, you'll be taking a wife for yourself?'

'Aye, that could be,' Arthur said gravely. 'When a man is succeeding in life, he has to think about the future. I've been giving it a bit of thought myself.'

'And what conclusion have you come to, Arthur?'

He took her hand again. 'Tha' knows, lass,' he said softly.

'Aye, I reckon I do. But say it, Arthur. A lass likes to be told.'

'I reckon as we'll be getting married,' he said, his face solemn and unsmiling.

'Why ever would you want to marry *me*, Arthur?' she

142

said innocently. 'Why ever *me*?'

'Why ever not you?' he retorted. 'I don't know anybody else, do I. Anyroad, except when you're being cheeky, we get on nicely together and I reckon as you'll make a good wife when you've been taught a bit about looking after a man.'

He didn't see the new look in her eyes, didn't sense her sudden rebellion.

'I'm glad to know how the master thinks,' Sally said, springing from the settle. 'But, alas, at this moment I have no plans to get married to anybody – ever!' She stood before him, her slight figure held tense as a sprung bow. 'I thought tha'd come to smear a bit of daub on the wall. If tha's going to do it, tha'd better get on wi' it, since I wouldn't like Aunt Nancy to come home and think we'd wasted the evening laiking about!'

She turned and slammed out of the room to the backyard. He watched her go, astounded. By God, he thought, she's like a little vixen. He shook his head in puzzlement. 'Who can know the ways of a woman?' he asked himself as he got up and brought the sacks of earth and dung to mix for the daub. There was no sign of Sally, but the door to the communal privy, recently installed, was closed.

'I never meant owt wrong,' he called out as he started on the mixing.

There was no reply.

Sally kept Arthur waiting a whole year before she finally agreed to marry him. During that time, she played him on the end of a line as she would a fish in Middleton Ponds. Perhaps she foresaw difficult times ahead if she let him dominate her completely. Perhaps, in the new spirit of freedom that was abroad in the 1770s, she felt a need to preserve her human independence. She'd seen the way

Amelia acted, subservient to her own son; she'd watched Mildred tolerating anything Matthew Aysgill cared to do. She'd also taken particular note of Arthur's Aunt Dodie, as different from Mildred and Amelia as it was possible to be. 'How would Aunt Dodie have survived,' Sally asked herself, 'if she'd always given in to her husband Mark?' It seemed as if Mark's passing had made little effect on Dodie's life; she continued to work at the hospital and now had a job of great responsibility in the Almoner's Office.

Sally was determined that she wouldn't be submerged under beneath Arthur's will. Arthur was an Aysgill, wasn't he, and no matter what Mildred might say with her lists of names and dates, there was some weakness in the Aysgill strain, some inevitable softness and lack of purpose. Take Arthur as an example. Look at the way he behaved with the women of the mill, permitting them to take advantage of him! Although by his charm and pleasantness he was able to keep the volume of work higher than under Tomlinson's bleak regime, still the women slackened off whenever they could, or so Amelia had told her. Take also the matter of the money. Though Arthur was now earning this incredible sum of a pound a week, he still had but little to show for it. A coin here, a coin there, a bit of meat for this person, a few pounds of bread for another. Always, it seemed, there was somebody in need, somebody Arthur felt he should give a helping hand. And always, his pound a week vanished into the ocean of his kindness, with not a ripple of gratitude to show for it.

Amelia and Sally talked about it many times during that year.

Arthur would come home, look about him, and say, 'Soon, Mam, I'm going to move us out of here and into somewhere more fitting.'

Even Tomlinson would ask Arthur, 'When are you going to set your mam into a better house?'

But always there was some other demand on Arthur's money. 'Liza Rishton,' he'd say, 'she has to get off to London to see her husband who's been put into't Fleet.' It mattered naught to him that Liza Rishton, besides working in the mill, also spent most of her time in the Cock Tavern, half downstairs in the public rooms, half upstairs on her back, earning an extra coin by obliging the gentlemen travellers. All Liza's own money, Amelia explained to Sally, went on fripperies, yet when her husband was thrown into Fleet Prison she had no hesitation about borrowing a coin from Arthur with a sob story. The mill was full of Liza Rishtons and Arthur could not see it.

Sally saw that if she didn't put herself into a position where she could exercise at least some control over him, then his financial gains would naught avail them and he'd go through life as poor as he started. But gradually she grew more confident that she'd be able to manage him.

So, one evening in the autumn of 1771, when Arthur came round after his work and Nancy Boothman – as prearranged – went across the yard to sit with Amelia, Sally took Arthur's hand and led him to the settle.

'Do you find me attractive, Arthur?' she asked coquettishly.

Arthur looked at her cautiously. He was not going to risk yet another rejection. Every three months or so during the previous year he'd asked her to marry him, but she'd repeatedly refused him. Each time he'd resolved to forget about her, to start casting his eyes over the many other girls in the mill who'd be more than happy to give him a tumble. Once, when he was working on the road with Blind Jack o' Knaresborough, he'd tumbled one of the doxys who'd come from the village to earn a coin. Though he hadn't enjoyed waiting while all the other men took turns, the experience had been satisfying and certainly novel. Recently he hadn't been able to stop speculating what it would be like to tumble Sally. Despite her slight, slender figure, her breasts had grown full and white, swelling invitingly over her tight bodice. More than once, Arthur had needed to sit with his legs crossed, or go out to the privy. He looked at her now, sitting beside him on the settle. She was wearing a pretty day gown with a low neck, and two of the thongs that should have secured it were unfastened. Damn it, if he looked directly at her, bending slightly forward as she asked her question, he could see . . .

'Do you desire me, Arthur?' she asked.

'Aye, that I do,' he gulped.

She came closer to him, tucking herself into his arm which had been resting along the back of the settle. He could smell the soap on her hair, and the scent of lavender.

'I washed myself afore you came, Arthur,' she said, 'all o'er.'

'Did you, lass?' he croaked, unable to control his voice.

'Aye. Feel my skin, how clean it is . . .'

He touched her shoulder gently. 'Aye,' he said hoarsely, 'it feels reet clean.'

She turned towards him and without him realizing how, the hand that had touched the skin of her shoulder was now plunged deep into the neck of her bodice and touching her breast, holding it, stroking it. The pain of pleasure rose swiftly in him and she said his name softly as he covered her lips with his.

'Do you want me, Arthur?' she whispered as at last his lips left hers.

'You know I do,' he said as he turned her, so that she could lie along the settle, with him beside her at first, then atop her. Then, after her first pained cries, he plunged deep inside her.

When it was all over he stroked her tear-sodden cheeks. 'It's all right,' she said, 'Arthur, it's all right. Mam told me it always hurts the first time, but then never again.'

'Nay, lass, it weren't my intent to hurt thee,' he said, full of remorse but full, also, of a pleasurable ache and deep satisfaction. 'I reckon us'll be getting married, now,' he said quietly, praying to God she wouldn't reject him again, not after that . . .

Sally knew she had him now. By giving herself to him she had gained a power over him. If she had married him, he would have taken her as a natural right, and she would have been obliged to serve him as her *duty*. This way, he was bound to her. She had given him the privilege of her body, and could use that as a weapon against him.

'Aye, Arthur, I reckon we shall,' she said.

From the very beginning, Sally took charge of the family money, a thing unheard of among other wives who had to make do with whatever their husbands gave them. Sally was a good manager; she kept on her employment with Mrs Little which brought in four shillings a week. Amelia earned another four shillings, all of which went into the pot with Arthur's pound. By agreement, Arthur was permitted to keep three shillings a week; though it was reckoned to be his 'man's money', they both knew he spent little on himself, but mostly gave it away – 'loaned it', as he called it, without hope of return – to the many who came to him with stories of need. At least, Sally and Amelia consoled themselves, Arthur had never formed the habit that had led to his father's downfall, of patronizing the ale-houses and the gin or brandy shops.

Sally remembered the advice that Dodie Ottershaw had given her immediately before the wedding. 'Don't be in too much of a hurry to start with bairns,' she'd said. 'Wait until you've been married a year or two, and until your man has settled down, before you add to the number of mouths you'll have to feed.' Sally knew that Amelia had started Arthur before she and Arthur's father were married, as

frequently happened all around them. The women who
were firmly married in church, as Sally had insisted – with a
licence and banns being called, according to the Marriage
Act of 1753 – were still comparatively rare in Hunslet,
where the couple usually moved together only after the
woman was visibly pregnant.

Within six weeks of their marriage, Sally had saved a
sufficient sum of money to be able to take the renting of a
house nearer the town, on the edge of a piece of common.
The house was one of two in a block built by one of the
Jewish merchants as a speculation. Though it was expensive at nine pounds a year, it had two good rooms
downstairs and, unbelievably, three bedrooms upstairs. It
was five minutes' walk from Nancy Boothman's house, but
that walk made all the difference to the environment. The
new house, being set on the edge of the open common, was
light and airy, with a constant supply of clean water from a
deep well, and a privy which was used only by the eight
houses the merchant had built and was enclosed in a brick
building a small distance from their own house.

There was even a small patch of garden at the side of
their house. 'Look, Arthur,' Sally showed him delightedly,
'you'll be able to grow vegetables here.'

Arthur was bemused by the speed with which it all
happened. It seemed only yesterday to him that he had been
married and already here he was renting a property at nine
pounds a year, with a wife and mother to keep. 'It's a big
responsibility, Sally,' he complained as they looked round
the house. 'I'd have thought summat a bit smaller might
have been more suitable. After all, you're the one is allus
saying I gi'e too much away – and now I'm to g'ie nine
pounds just to keep a roof o'er my head! Aside of what it'll
cost to have a man to furnish it for us . . .'

Sally and Amelia caught each other's eye. Let him
grumble all he wanted. It was *their* house, a place for them

to be, and against the combined strengths of two women there was nothing Arthur could do about it, their look seemed to say. They threw themselves into the arrangement of the house with great energy, buying scraps of cloth to make spreads, edging fabric for curtains at the windows which were of glass, finding furniture in the workshops of carpenters or persuading them to make a piece cheaply.

Gradually Arthur formed the habit, after the end of his day's work, of calling at the ale-house along Hunslet Road, where he knew he'd find good companionship and relaxation. He had no lust to go home to a house turned topsy-turvy by the women's endeavours to bring everything to what they called 'an orderly disposition'.

CHAPTER TWO

Lord Porter was sitting across Aysgill's chest on the dormitory floor, Aysgill's stubby nose between his thumb and forefinger. As he spoke, he twisted Aysgill's nose vigorously from side to side.

'Say it, you turd,' he hissed. 'Say it! I am a piece of dung. I was born a piece of dung. I will die a piece of dung.' The fervent light of cruelty shone from Porter's eyes as he licked his lips.

The others in the circle all bent forward, a variety of smiles on their faces. 'Say it,' some of them repeated, 'say it, Aysgill, you turd!'

Aysgill looked up at the ring of faces. They'd already taken down his breeches and had smeared his genitals with melted tallow mixed with feathers from one of the pillows. Lord Porter, the school bully, had already buggered him twice and he could still feel the dreadful pain in his anal passage. Now he could hardly breathe for the weight on his chest and his arms. He looked up into the cruel face of his tormentor. 'I am a piece of dung,' he said, his voice quavering. 'I was born a piece of dung. I will die a piece of dung . . . There, I've said it. Now get off my chest, I beseech you, else I shall suffocate.'

'Dung can't suffocate, you turd,' Porter said, climbing reluctantly from his victim's chest.

Gavin Aysgill didn't know what gave him the courage to act as he did, but as Lord Porter was rising from him, leaving his middle exposed, Gavin brought back his foot as if intending to rise, then jerked it forward with all his force, straight into Lord Porter's testicles. Porter screamed as he staggered back, his face ashen, his lips blue with pain. He couldn't speak, could only gasp and clutch his balls in anguish. Another of his victims, William Holmfirth, realizing that for the first time they had the school bully at a disadvantage, brought his foot up between Porter's open legs from the back. Holmfirth was still wearing his boots with stout leather soles. Porter screamed again as the kick sent him sprawling on his face on the floor. Walter Tadcaster, yet another of Porter's past victims, stepped in, his eyes gleaming, and his kick took Porter under the chin. Now the room had gone crazy as old scores were settled and sporadic fights began.

Gavin Aysgill crawled out from beneath the kicking, punching, pummelling bodies. He went to his own bed, pulling his breeches up and securing them. He opened his locker, took out the purse containing his allowance, picked his cloak from the hook, opened the bottom of the window and dropped to the grass below. As he left he heard the dormitory door open and the bull voice of Keith Semple himself bellowing for them all to stop. As Gavin hurried away, he heard the swish of the cane with which Semple sought, often fruitlessly, to maintain discipline.

Semple's School for the Sons of Gentlemen had proved to be a nightmare to Gavin and now, at thirteen, he could take no more. The school was a dreadful place, he thought, as he set out across the moorland in the starlight of early night, plotting his route as he went. None would think to pursue him in this direction and eventually he would arrive at the hamlet of Boroughbridge from which the coin in his purse would buy him a passage to Leeds and home.

Semple, Gavin had soon realized, had no knowledge of education. He was running a private club for young gentlemen in which the class system of the county could be perpetuated. The boys learned only sufficient to be able to take their places in Society – the French language seemed the most important of their acquisitions, and the simple reckoning of acreage, the skills of the field, fencing, and dancing. For the rest, the pupils spent their time gaming, drinking and, whenever they could visit the nearby village, whoring and wenching if they were of that persuasion. Many, like the sixteen-year-old Lord Porter, found their satisfactions among the younger boys who quickly fell victim to their perversions, with a certain beating should they refuse or protest.

Lord Porter had shown no sign of leaving the school to live on his estates with his mother and grandmother, both dowagers with an enormous sense of discipline and correctitude. He treated Semple's as his private fiefdom, where even the school's owner and master, Keith Semple, deferred to his whims and wishes. He'd quickly formed a dislike for Aysgill, called him the son of a tradesman and, over the years, had made the younger boy's life hell.

Only Peter Aysgill's insistence had brought Gavin back each year to continue his 'education', but now Gavin could not support any more. 'If Father tries to send me back,' he told himself, 'I'll run away to London and seek my fame and fortune there.'

Of course, if Gavin himself had been more resolute, he could have stood up to Lord Porter who, though school bully, was not in prime physical condition due to his many self-indulgences. Gavin, given determination and fortitude, could doubtless have thrashed his tormentor, as could many of the other boys. Gavin, however, had been born with a deficiency of courage and resolution; he was a coward who knew himself for what he was.

'I'll tell Father,' he resolved as he tramped over the moorland, seeing shapes and evil forms behind every patch of scree and scrub, 'that I am not going back.'

Several times he wanted already to turn back; the way to Boroughbridge was long and the night grew constantly darker as clouds obscured stars and moon. He had left the hard going of the open moor in favour of the moorland track, which wound between the drystone walls that were being built everywhere. When he heard the clip-clop of horses' hooves approaching, he scurried behind the wall, and saw a packman leading his mules carrying bales of cloth, doubtless from some upland hamlet. Gavin was tempted to leap out and speak to the packman, if only for human contact on this awesome night, but the humiliation of Lord Porter's assault and the pain it had caused was constantly with him, and he held his tongue until the packman had disappeared from view, then hurried on his way.

Several times during the night he had similar experiences when packmen came along the track, and once a band of three he reckoned were villains who, had they seen him, would certainly have robbed him of his meagre possessions. Mercifully, he reached Boroughbridge just as dawn was appearing; without the darkness to conceal him he would have been prey on the open moor to every passing marauder and villain.

Boroughbridge had one coaching inn; he trudged, exhausted, into the yard and flopped on to a bench. The serving wench came quickly, bringing him a flagon of home-brewed beer and a cutting from a piece of pork, fresh from the oven, with fresh-baked bread. He gulped down the food and drink hungrily, then, resting his head on his arms, fell asleep at the table.

The next he felt was a rude hand shaking him.

'You for the coach, young sir?' the serving wench was asking.

He shook his head, wondering who she was and what she could be talking about, when suddenly the memory of the night flooded his brain. 'Aye,' he said hurriedly, 'I'm for the coach.'

'Then tha'd better make haste, sir,' she said. 'He's already blowed the horn twice.' Her eyes twinkled. 'I could hold him, young sir, for a token . . .'

'Aye, hold him,' Gavin said. He had a terrible need to relieve himself before he could countenance a ride in the jogging vehicle. When he stood up, the girl's eyes went to his groin. He looked down and saw with embarrassment that the tallow fat they'd smeared on him had penetrated the fine cloth; a dark stain was spreading across his groin, as if he'd already urinated. He picked up his cloak, flung it round himself to hide his embarrassment and went out into the back of the yard, hearing the serving wench's mocking chuckle.

He was obliged to change coaches three times on his journey to Leeds, and arrived home at noon the following day. Dirty, exhausted and completely dishevelled, he was met by a shriek from his former nurse who had stayed on as housekeeper. She immediately ordered a hot bath to be prepared for him, but he insisted on having the wooden tub carried into his dressing room, shutting the door firmly on Mrs Pocock before opening his cloak and removing his stained breeches and undergarments.

Mrs Pocock stood in the corridor and smiled. 'It's about time yon lad came of age,' she said to herself. Then she turned and made her way below stairs.

Peter Aysgill scowled when he saw his son at home. 'I suppose Master Semple has dismissed you from his Academy,' he said icily. 'What foolish mischief—'

'I've run away, Father,' Gavin said timidly. His father was so certain of himself, so confident in his manner. Gavin himself longed to have such strength but feared he'd always be a weakling, knuckling under to anyone who seemed stronger than himself.

Peter couldn't believe his ears. 'You've run away, you whelp? *Run away*, like some cringing cur? On what account?'

'I couldn't abide it there, Father,' Gavin said. 'And I was learning nothing.'

'*Learning*? I never sent you to *learn*! I'll teach you all you need to know when you take your place beside me in the business. I sent you there to come into intimate terms with the quality, to learn their manners and behaviour so you could be a gentleman. Have you learned nowt of that?'

'I can fence, Father; I can dance and I can speak the French tongue passably. I know the value of paintings and can tell a good horse by its head and haunches.'

'Then what more do you want?' Peter bellowed. 'There's many a gentleman sitting in Parliament today who knows less than that. Many a gentleman comes to my bank and cannot even sign his name to a Deed of Loan, nor read its provisions.' Then Peter stopped and looked deep into his son's face. 'Come here, lad,' he said gently.

Gavin flinched, expecting a blow, but Peter gathered him round his waist and drew him to his side.

'What are you afeared of, Gavin?' he asked, mustering all the tenderness he could. The boy's narrow shoulders were shaking with sobs as he buried his face in his father's worsted coat. 'Come now, lad, tha' mustn't sob like a lass,' Peter said, holding his son ever tighter.

'Don't send me back to that horrible place, Father,' Gavin pleaded. 'I'll do owt except return to that place.'

'Have they been bad to you, lad? You mun expect a bit of high-spirited horseplay among lads. It don't amount to nowt, you know; it isn't meant personally.'

'Don't send me back, Father,' Gavin said, regaining

control of himself. 'I've quite made up my mind. If you send me back I shall run away again, this time to make a life for myself in London or the Colonies.'

The new note in Gavin's voice cut through Peter's sensibilities. He'd never heard the lad speak with such a determined voice, such a strong manner. 'What'll you do for money, lad?' he asked brusquely.

'What did *you* do for money, Father?' Gavin asked with inescapable logic. 'You managed to make money and so shall I. The boys at school were saying you started life with a hole in your breeches, that you came out of the gutters. They called you a self-made man. I can be the same.'

Peter hugged his son more tightly, his eyes, filled with pain, seeing some distant horizon. 'Damn them,' he thought, 'will they *never* forget? Will they torture my son with my origins?' It seemed to matter nought to these people that they came to his bank looking for all manner of services, and he was ever ready to oblige, often at a cost to his own pocket. 'Can they not see how much they *need* me to keep their affairs in order?' Of course he had been ruthless with a number of people, so far gone towards bankruptcy that none could save them. He'd refused to pour more money into the hands of foolish gamblers, most of whom had already squandered fortunes before ever they came to him to help them out. But many men, ill-versed in the handling of capital, had come to him for advice and had been made wealthy beyond any previous possibility. How many sons of gentlemen had he steered along a sensible path of practicalities? Would they always despise him and his family for being *successful*? Was it a crime to be able to manage money matters with the same flair that landed gentry should, but all too often didn't, manage the grand estates of their forebears? Were the great landlords not as ruthless with their peasants as he was with defaulters? He would never forget, so long as he drew breath, how little concern Lord Barthwick had paid to the families who'd contributed to the Barthwick wealth over the generations – wealth which the new Lord Barthwick had largely squandered in inefficiency and by profligate indulgence in his own base perverted pleasures. His lordship was known to be a sodomite, an unprincipled hedonist, and yet he was accepted in salons to which Peter Aysgill would never gain admittance.

Among the many places Peter knew he would never be invited to visit was Temple Newsam, largely reconstructed by Sir Arthur Ingram, but now occupied by his descendant Henry, the seventh Lord Irwin and the present leader of Leeds Society. Sir Arthur Ingram had made his vast fortunes by moneylending and by dealing in Crown Monopolies and had bought Temple Newsam in 1622. It was a success story that Peter longed to emulate. Would his family, too, need to wait a hundred and fifty years before honours and prestige would attach themselves to Peter's descendants?

He knew that his son was dreaming falsely if he hoped to emulate his own success. Only Peter could know how ruthlessly he had needed to behave in the early days to secure the foundations of his wealth. His fortune, he secretly admitted to himself, had been built on a staddle of lies and deceit, on cheating, forgery and treachery. Gavin lacked the inner strength such a course of action necessitated. Of course, now that Peter was wealthy he could afford to carry out all transactions with scrupulous honesty, thereby hoping to build a reputation for probity that his humble beginnings had denied him. Yet still he remained tainted by his early reputation. How often had the indolent peers of Leeds society assumed that, since Aysgill was involved, the transaction must of necessity be dubious? But, on the other hand, how many had over-ridden those scruples when necessity pressed heavily upon them, when the need to resort to such a man as Aysgill had been forced upon them by demanding money-lenders, by the needs of an estate impoverished by foolish spending and reckless high-living?

Now Peter turned decisively to Gavin. 'I'll not send you back to yon school,' he said. 'Perhaps later you'll give me all the details of what passed there, for I can see you have been mightily disturbed. I'll engage private tutors for you, secure you an education that way that none can deny. I had hoped to give you the easy life of acceptance by membership of the exclusive club of Semple's but, if that's not to be, we needs must try other means.'

Gavin was overjoyed. His first thought was, however, that his father should never learn about Lord Porter; he knew he'd never be able to speak of the abject humiliation of that dreadful penetration. 'When I am become rich and important,' he secretly vowed, 'I shall work my own revenge on my tormentor.' For the moment, it was sufficient that he was free, to live at home, to study as best he might under whatever tutors his father provided. He hugged Peter gratefully. 'You are so good to me, Father,' he said. 'I shall do my very best to be worthy of you.'

CHAPTER THREE

Gertrude Fossett strolled down the main street of Whitby in a reflective mood. It had just occurred to her how many changes had taken place in the small fishing port since she had arrived all those years ago, changes which, coming slowly one by one, had gone largely unnoted and unremarked except as an eight-day wonder, soon to be forgotten in familiarity. She tried to remember when Mr Fairclough, the haberdasher, had opened his shop to which she was even now making her way through the crowded streets; she tried to recall when Mr Penberthy had begun to sell chinaware and glassware and when he had installed his new bow-window, the better to enable prospective customers to see his interior displays of Wedgwood, his Bow and Chelsea figures, his elaborate displays of fine Matthew Boulton cutlery. No longer did anyone in Whitby need to send south to furnish their homes; the local carpenters made excellent copies of all the best known designs of furniture, and the local tradesmen sold all the domestic accoutrements one could wish. Even Captain and Mrs Edgecombe had entirely refurbished their home in keeping with the modern times, thought Gertrude approvingly; the heavier furniture had largely been replaced by graceful light oak and figured walnut, and the windows of the house had been enlarged and fully glazed, many opening directly on to small balconies set in wrought iron into the wall of the house itself.

How the style of life had changed! Gertrude had seen the fine new theatre being built, where actors now came from London, where singers from Italy gave musical performances that were always thronged, where one could as easily hear a pianoforte recital as a chamber ensemble playing the works of Handel, Mozart, Tartini, Nardini or – her favourite – Vivaldi. Only the previous month Mrs Edgecombe had insisted Gertrude accompany her there to a performance of *The Beggar's Opera*. Gertrude hadn't enjoyed it very much, though she knew it was very popular throughout the land; she didn't like its low-life scenes. Always something of a romantic at heart, though intensely practical by nature, she preferred the magnificence of some of the modern high-society dramatic works, or the magic of the Italian operas. She couldn't understand the words, but fortunately the management always provided a book of the story of each of the foreign works, and the sheet music that was everywhere available these days always gave the words in both Italian, or German, or French, and English.

Whitby, she felt, was becoming quite a centre for the new fashion of what they were calling *ton* – what she preferred to call 'style' since she didn't enjoy foreign speech affectations. Even dear Mrs Edgecombe, with her plain looks, her large body, her reddened face, tried to adapt to the new manner, and was forever punctuating her speech with what she imagined were French and Italian words, though none could have recognized the origin from her pronunciation.

Gertrude herself was becoming quite well-known in the town, and a number of local dignitaries raised their hats to her as they passed in their cabs or briskly on foot from one 'change to another. She smiled as she remembered how, as a young girl, she would have considered such gestures quite improper and would have shunned them; now she raised her hand in a gesture of recognition – though it would not be seemly to speak – and passed on her way.

Mr Fairclough himself was waiting for her within his new shop, with its large tables, the three shop assistants and the apprentice standing by with his measuring tape. All knew that Mr Fairclough himself would attend to his most important customer so, beyond a deferential nod of the head, each kept his position while Fairclough sailed forward, a barque under full wind.

'Ah, Mistress Fossett!' he exclaimed, as if he were addressing royalty.

'Mr Fairclough.' The acknowledgement was brief, almost perfunctory. Gertrude was here today on her own behalf, not in the service of her employer.

'I have all in readiness, madam,' he said. He flicked his fingers without turning his head. 'Jack!' he called

Jack appeared from the back room, wheeling a wire model on a platform.

'My latest invention, madam,' Fairclough said with pride. 'I make the model to the dimensions of the customer. Then we can get some idea of the overall impression without troubling the customer for tedious fittings. Dare I ask what you think?'

Gertrude was a little confused, though she could see the sense of the wire model which, after all, was no different from the dress-making dummy of straw and calico she herself used to make her own garments. What confused her most was the gap where the face should be, the stiffness of one arm bent outwards while the other hung down. Fairclough stepped in and moved the position of the arms, which appeared to be arranged on some sort of swivelling device. The figure was wearing a suit in heavy black woollen cloth, with breeches, a frock coat that came to the knees, a waistcoat of best calico that reached midway down the thigh. The empty head was covered by a tricorn hat of black, braided with red and blue piping. Gertrude reached forward to touch the cloth, examining the stitches of one of the outside pockets of the frock coat.

'Have you ever seen such stitching, Mrs Fossett?' Fairclough asked with pride.

'Aye, Mr Fairclough,' she said, 'I have. If any of my girls ever turned such an irregular hand for Mrs Edgecombe, I'd send her packing straightway.'

He reddened. ''Tis a heavy cloth, Mrs Fossett, as you requested. One cannot expect the same fine work as in lawn.'

'And why not, Mr Fairclough?' Gertrude asked imperiously. In truth, she was nervous as a kitten for she had never spent such a fortune on garments in her life and, in her confusion, thought only to emulate the manner of Mrs Edgecombe herself when dealing with tradesmen.

'Of course, madam. It will be taken out and re-stitched this very day. Mark my words, I'll chastise the one responsible in fullest measure.'

Gertrude felt a pang of remorse; all too often she'd been on the other end of that stick. Something in her Aysgill blood prevented her being too much of a martinet when dealing even with the servants in Mrs Edgecombe's household and she suspected that some took advantage of her leniency. But she knew she must harden her heart; today she was dispensing coin her dear husband Luke had earned during his long and arduous voyages.

'Yes, see that you do that,' she said, 'if you wish to retain my husband's patronage.'

'Damned servants,' Fairclough was thinking though he would not have dared express himself in these terms; 'they get a bit ahead of themselves and are harder to deal with than their masters and mistresses!'

'Certainly, Mrs Fossett,' he assured her unctuously, 'you may place your reliance in me in that, as in all things. Would it be forward of me to enquire when we might hope to see your gallant husband himself, for the final fittings?'

162

'He could be here by morn,' Gertrude said, unable to keep the pleasure of anticipation from her voice. 'They lay off Ravenscar and the Customs will be aboard within the hour. With luck they'll cross the bar on the morning tide.'

'I greatly look forward to that, madam,' Fairclough said. 'And you may rely on all of us. Not a word—!' With the air of a joint conspirator, he showed her to the door after she had examined all the garments she had ordered in the greatest detail, indicating points that didn't please her, seams that must be done again, stitching that needed reinforcement, bands that had not been sewn precisely parallel.

Luke will be home on the tide tomorrow, Gertrude kept telling herself as she walked back along the street, regardless now of life bustling all about her as men handled the trolleys with their creels of fish, pulled out nets, coiled and recoiled ropes, the gallimaufry of the life of a busy fishing port which played its intimate scenes all around her.

Luke would be home on the tide!

She suddenly stopped, gazing down the length of the harbour to the bar where, the following morn, the vessel carrying her husband would appear. Until quite recently, she would have climbed Abbey Hill for a first glimpse of his three-masted vessel, the *Dandelion of Whitby*, but an onset of rheumatism had made such a climb a painful matter.

'You are fifty-three years of age, Gertrude,' she chided herself, blushing somewhat along her cheeks, 'and here you are waiting for the return of your man like some love-sick lass!' But she did miss Luke so when he was away on his long voyages, even though she had the workings of the house to keep her fully occupied. Nowadays, Mrs Edgecombe had permitted her to take an under-housekeeper, who attended to the supervision of the twenty-servant household. Mrs Edgecombe herself was over sixty, and the Captain nearing his seventieth year. Gertrude's three sons

163

were now grown men. Walter, her first-born, had recently married a girl called Nancy who, like Gertrude, spent her time waiting for her husband to return from voyages, while Reuben worked in the shipyard and shared a tiny cottage with his younger brother Daniel, who was 'prenticed to a ship's carpenter.

Such a family of grown boys, and here she was conning the horizon as if it were her husband's first landfall!

She turned and walked briskly back up the hill to her employer's house, and to her own cottage built into the stable-yard. She'd be happy to put her foot on a stool, drink a cup of the tea that was now all the fashion, and hear reports about the state of the household prior to the evening supper. Tonight was a small affair with food for twenty; the Captain had cut down considerably on his entertainment of late, and much preferred to eat in his study, conning his nautical books or reliving his voyages of the past. He sometimes joked that he would engage another clerk and use his scribing to write a book of his own. He'd been vastly amused by Defoe's novel, '*The Life and Strange Surprizing Adventures of Robinson Crusoe of York, Mariner, who lived eight and twenty years all alone in an un-inhabited Island on the Coast of America, near the Mouth of the Great River of the Oroonoque . . . written by himself.*'

'I'll write such a book of *my* adventures,' Captain Edgecombe threatened. 'And 'twill sell more copies than Defoe, I'll be bound, for I'll not be so mealy-mouthed about what may befall a man in these foreign places!'

Mrs Edgecombe would smile and nod and say, 'Take no heed of the Master, Mrs Fossett, for he has in mind, I believe, to give us nobbut a man's version of *Moll Flanders*! If he could have sailed with James Cook on his adventures, he'd have gone, quick as a shot from a bow.'

The Captain would splutter and protest. 'You go too far, ma'am,' he'd say, but no offence would be meant or taken.

164

For, with the advancing years, his former quarter-deck manner had abated like a spent storm, and the household knew only tranquil waters. Many retired sea-captains, Gertrude had observed, grew choleric with age and loss of command; Captain Edgecombe grew more benign as the years slipped by.

When Gertrude had drunk her tea, she replaced her slippers and went into the main house across the stable-yard. Cook, now nearing seventy and with three other cooks, two pastry-maids, three still-room maids under her command, could spend most of her day sitting at the table with a glass of rum by her side. She had grown gross over the years Gertrude had known her and now needed the two pastry-maids to lift her to her feet. She greeted Gertrude as she came through the kitchen.

'All's right as a trivet, Mrs Fossett,' she declared, though, without teeth in her mouth, her voice was sometimes hard to understand. 'I've given the lad his head tonight, and you're to have some French concoction the like of which *I've* never seen.'

'*Faisan farci*,' said Paul, the newer cook.

'That means pheasant with force-meat stuck up its afters!' cackled the old woman. 'Seems to me he were just putting back in what had but recently come out!'

Gertrude's eyes flicked from side to side as she progressed swiftly through the house. She'd changed into her evening wear; Mrs Edgecombe had always insisted that Gertrude be dressed finely, and this evening she wore a deep blue gown, with white Flanders lace at the collar and cuffs, and a lace-edged mobcap set in her hair with pins. She saw the last scurryings of the maids as they set everything in order. The long large table was set with porcelain the Captain had recently acquired from Josiah Wedgwood; the silver candelabra stood on the sideboards, waiting to be lit just before dinner began, and sweetmeats had already been put out on the sideboard and covered with a light muslin cloth. Nellie, Gertrude's assistant, had done her job well and Gertrude could find no cause for complaint, other than a couple of knives on the table that needed straightening, and one bowl of fruit in cut crystal that bore, horror of horrors, the mark of a finger.

'Nellie,' Gertrude said, 'you must insist the girls wear their gloves when they handle the crystal, for there's nothing so draws and distracts the eye as a finger mark.'

'Yes, Mrs Fossett,' Nellie said, her face worried.

Gertrude touched her on the shoulder. 'Don't trouble yourself so, Nellie,' she said. 'No one is going to eat you. You must just learn to use your eyes more carefully.'

'I will, Mrs Fossett, really I will,' Nellie said fervently.

Gertrude passed on her way with Nellie following in her wake as she examined every detail of this house she had come to know so well over the years of her service. She knew she could have sat in her own cottage, closed her eyes, and told Nellie where every single thing went in the entire premises. She could still enter a room and within seconds tell which articles were out of place, even though new furniture, new vases, new pictures, new sculptures, new looking glasses, were being bought and installed constantly.

Mrs Edgecombe was in her boudoir when Gertrude went to make her report, and the maid was pulling at the cords of her corset, to try to cram her excessive figure into it. Gone for the moment were the loose-fitting garments that flowed in an unbroken line from shoulder to hem; now a lady of fashion must demonstrate a narrow waist and a generous endowment of bosom. To that end, gowns, made of the new stiff brocade, were supported by whalebone pieces which further confined the flesh beneath.

'Nay, lass, I think I'll dine this even in my nightgown,' gasped Mrs Edgecombe at last. ''Tis nobbut a few friends and intimates.'

166

The maid gave up the uneven struggle and brought in Mrs Edgecombe's voluminous wrapper, made of a fine, multi-layered gossamer gauze that seemed to float on its own. Gertrude knew the simple-looking garment had in fact cost more than a hundred pounds, a vast fortune, but it was the garment in which her mistress was always the most comfortable. Then, as she watched the continuing toilette, Gertrude felt a sudden unease. Was it her imagination, she asked herself, or was Mrs Edgecombe eyeing her in a most curious manner, as if checking her own apparel for fault? She looked down, wondering if the passage through the house had stained her dress, or if a tape were untied. Did her mistress perhaps think she was being immodest, since she'd set her mobcap with two pins, the head of each of which was a small pearl? Her mistress herself had given Gertrude the mobcap pins many years ago and Gertrude had worn them over a score of times, but usually only one at a time.

'I've checked everything, Mrs Edgecombe,' she said. 'I trust you will find everything to your satisfaction.'

Again that strange look, that half-smile. 'I'm certain I shall Mrs Fossett,' Mrs Edgecombe said. 'I trust you may say the same when the time comes.' She turned to the stand mirror on her dressing table as if dismissing Gertrude summarily from her presence.

'What could that mean?' Gertrude asked herself as she left the room and returned downstairs. *I trust you may say the same when the time comes* . . . A feeling of foreboding swept through her. Her instant thought was that she had performed some disservice for which she was to be punished, but she knew of nothing, could think of nothing. Why, that very day, returning from the shops, she had thought how well Nellie was running everything, how smoothly the affairs of the house were being managed. For the first time for a long time, she'd balanced her household accounts at the first proving, and had not needed to spend an hour on her arithmetic – never Gertrude's strong point, especially since there were so many disbursements and purchases to be accounted for, so many servants' wages to be reckoned up each quarter day, though the actual payments were made by Enoch Farthingale, Captain Edgecombe's steward.

These days, a small room had been set aside for Gertrude's use on the ground floor, near the front door. When not actively employed on any specific task she would take her ease there with a piece of mending or embroidery. She had furnished the room with goods her employers had discarded in favour of the new styles, including a comfortable chair, a dark wood table, and a couple of hard-wood chairs for other servants to sit upon when she was addressing them on some minor matter. It was here that Gertrude now retired to consider Mrs Edgecombe's words, while awaiting Nellie's call for dinner.

Suddenly she heard the jangle of the bell on the wall that indicated her master wished to speak to her. She glanced at the row of bells to determine which was ringing. 'How strange he should be in the drawing room at this hour,' she thought as she climbed the stairs, her rheumatism as ever causing her twinges of pain.

The door to the drawing room was closed; she tapped upon it, opened it, and went in. A dark-clad figure was standing by the marble fireplace, warming his hands at the coal blaze, but of Captain Edgecombe there was no sign.

'I beg your pardon, sir,' Gertrude said, not able to discern his features in the flickering firelight since none of the candles had been lit. 'I thought the Captain was in here.'

'And so he is,' the man said forcefully as he turned towards her.

'*Luke!*' she exclaimed, immediately fearful that he was

bereft of his senses to stand here in the Master's drawing room, as if he owned the place. 'What are you doing in here?'

'Waiting for thee, Gertrude,' he said. 'Didn't you hear my ring?'

She was utterly confused, especially when he held out his arms and, as if propelled by some undeniable cosmic force, she walked across the room to be embraced by them. The smell and feeling of him were so familiar that for a brief moment she lost all fear at the impropriety of them embracing in the Master's drawing room; she felt his strong arms about her, crushing her somewhat, pressing her to the rough tweed of his jacket. His beard, as ever, was stiff after the voyage; the first contact with it, as he laid his face alongside hers, made her tingle with pleasure and then prompted the immediate thought of how she'd soap it and oil it and comb it to a fine smoothness before he sailed away again.

He smelled of salt, of sea-wrack, and of strange and exotic odours, doubtless of the cargoes his ship had carried, for this time he had been on the Eastern run and doubtless had brought spices and exciting goods from India and China.

Then she felt his lips on her cheek and she panicked. 'Nay, my dearest'! she gasped. 'We mustn't be caught here in such conduct. Whatever would the Master say if he discovered us abusing his household—'

'He'd say, gi'e thy man a buss on his lips after his voyage,' the voice of Captain Edgecombe boomed behind her.

She broke Luke's embrace and, covered in confusion, attempted to straighten her gown where Luke's arms had disturbed its folds. 'Captain Edgecombe, sir . . .' she stuttered.

The Captain was smiling hugely. 'What do you think o'

169

your fine man now, Mrs Fossett?' he asked.

Luke Fossett was also smiling, as if the two of them held some conspiracy. 'I didn't yet have the opportunity, Captain Edgecombe, of acquainting Mrs Fossett wi' the bad tidings.'

'Bad tidings?' she said instantly. 'Anyway, what are you doing here now? They told me the Customs were going aboard the *Dandelion* off Ravenscar, that you hoped to make the morn tide . . .'

'They put a new first mate aboard, along wi' the tide-surveyor and the tide-waiters, and brought me off in the Customs cutter.'

'They never! Tha's not lost thy berth, husband?'

Captain Edgecombe laughed. It was the first time she'd ever thought him cruel and so unfeeling as to laugh at another's great misfortune.

'Aye,' Luke Fossett said, 'I suppose you could say I've lost my berth aboard the *Dandelion*.'

'After all these years – they've turned you off?' Gertrude couldn't believe her ears.

''Tis true, Mrs Fossett, 'tis true,' Captain Edgecombe confirmed, though still smiling in, she thought, that monstrously unfeeling way.

'I've lost my berth aboard the *Dandelion*, I've lost my appointment as her first mate,' went on Luke, apparently enjoying the situation.

'But *why*, husband? In the name of all that's right, *why*?'

Captain Edgecombe could restrain himself no longer and began to chortle, his double chins bouncing with jollity. 'Because, Mrs Fossett, your good husband has been appointed Captain of the *Spring Rose* – that's why!'

Suddenly it dawned upon her what a cruel joke the two men had played, permitting her to believe that her beloved Luke had been discharged. Luke had always been the man for a practical joke, with a great fund of humour, but he'd never before deceived her so cruelly. The tears sprang unbidden to her eyes as she remembered the fears that had flooded her soul when she had thought him set aside.

''Tis all right, sweet lass,' Luke said, further confounding her sensibilities by putting his arm around her again, before the Captain's very eyes. 'Captain Edgecombe and I are to be partners in a venture. The *Spring Rose* is coming from the yards soon for commissioning, and I'm to have command of her, with a part-share. But that's not the best news. For a year or two, we're going to try the coal run. The *Spring Rose* is to be a collier.'

'Your good husband is off the long-distance run for a year or two,' Captain Edgecombe said jovially. 'You'll have him more at home to warm your feet on o'nights!'

'Captain Edgecombe!' she cried, scandalized that he should talk so to her especially in the presence of her husband.

'Tha' needn't go so red in't face, madam,' he said. 'Captain Fossett has graciously consented that you shall both sup wi' us this even. I warrant tha'll hear worse talk than yon over't table.'

Now Gertrude understood why Mrs Edgecombe had regarded her so critically and examined her garb; doubtless she too had been party to the plot and would have made some mention had she considered Gertrude's dress not fitting for supper. She couldn't resist, however, raising her hand to her hair. 'Oh dear,' she said, 'I shall need a little time.'

In all the years Gertrude had worked for the Edgecombes she'd never found herself seated at table with them; such a thing would have been considered most improper. Now she saw the servants eyeing her covertly, wondering what had happened as she entered the salon where everyone was waiting. She had not intended to be the last and had no motive of making an embarrassing entrance, but fixing her

171

hair had taken longer than she'd meant and the room was already filled when she arrived. Mrs Edgecombe beckoned to her and patted the cushions by her side.

'Ah, here comes the Captain's wife,' she said in a loud voice. Gertrude was mortified as she walked across to Mrs Edgecombe, the cynosure of all eyes. 'Come, sit by me, Mrs Fossett,' Mrs Edgecombe said, 'and tell me what you think of Mr Thomas Gainsborough. The Captain would have my portrait done by him, but I reckon as Hogarth could con a better likeness of my countrified features?'

'I think Mr Thomas Gainsborough would find much to interest him, Mrs Edgecombe, were you to honour him with a sitting.'

Mrs Edgecombe, seeing none other near enough by, closed one eye at Gertrude and opened it again, in a wonderfully conspiratorial wink. 'We mun give our menfolk their little games,' she said. 'They may parade and posture themselves, but they're nobbut great babbies at heart.'

When at last the supper was over and Luke and Gertrude were able to escape to their own little house, the questions flooded from her. Luke denied her all answers until, as he said, he'd 'got the feeling of her again'. He held her close in his strong arms, and kissed her cheeks, her nose, her eyelids, her lips with a strong love. Finally she was obliged to draw away from him to take breath, so hungry with love was he.

'Nay,' she said, 'we mustn't behave like youngsters . . .'

He looked deep into her eyes. 'My love for thee, Gertrude, will keep me young all my days,' he said with the utmost sincerity.

She gave him a hug. 'God bless thee for that, Luke,' she said. 'Looking round the room tonight at some of the lasses, I was thinking of how unkindly the years had dealt wi' me.'

This provoked a strong denial, and another round of kissing, which saw them finally in bed together. Only after Luke had satisfied his manly lusts was he able to speak about the events of the evening.

'Captain Edgecombe and I talked this over when last I was ashore,' he said. 'I left a sum of money on deposit with him to buy an eighth of the *Spring Rose*. He has the other seven-eighths – well, they're sixty-fourths but that's no matter. I'm a ship-owner, Gertrude, a ship-owner in my own right!'

She was so pleased she couldn't speak. To think that Luke had been a footman when first they'd met and it was only her initial rejection of him that had persuaded him to go to sea! Later, she and Captain Edgecombe had encouraged him to study, first for his sailor's papers, then his mate's tickets, then for his command. A captain, however, is appointed to a vessel, and there had seemed but little opportunity for him to find a vessel, since the newly founded Mariners' School was turning out so many qualified men and education was blossoming everywhere. Many young lads of stalwart middle-class families were going to sea for a few voyages, then coming ashore for book-work at the private academies run by retired sea captains.

The shortest path to a command, for those who had been prudent with money they'd earned from their voyages, was to buy shares in a new vessel. Gertrude had had no idea that Luke had been doing this, for he had always drawn a veil of masculine independence over their family accounts, providing such money as had been needed for the education of their sons, their clothing, their daily expenses.

'Now I understand about Mr Fairclough,' she said. 'I couldn't think why you'd want a suit of such thick cloth since you're always telling me how hot it is in these foreign parts. It is for your coastal runs, is it not?'

'Tha' gets to know everything in good time, Gertrude,' he said, sleepily. 'Now us'll have no more questions till the morn, for I'm powerful tired.'

She gave him a little tweak in a private place. 'Tha' means, power*less* tired,' she said playfully and, dare it be said, hopefully.

But he was already asleep.

The following day, the two partners and their wives met in the Edgecombe library. Each partner had talked in advance with his wife – now all that remained was to resolve their mutual dilemma.

'I'd not thought,' Captain Edgecombe said, somewhat grumpily, 'that by taking a partner in a venture I'd be losing my good lady her housekeeper.'

The arguments on each side had raged all morning. Mrs Edgecombe had come to regard Gertrude's services as indispensable. The Captain had pointed at Nellie, who was becoming efficient enough for him. 'But not for *me*,' Mrs Edgecombe had said forcefully, though she was not normally a woman to disagree with her husband nor overtly challenge his authority. 'Mrs Fossett is become more than a housekeeper to me. She's become a cousin in all matters, and I'll not see her cast out because you menfolk wish to earn a little carrying coals.'

'Then what do you suggest, woman?' he'd roared. 'Make her your cousin, by all means. Make her your lap-dog, for all I care.'

Gertrude herself had spoken out boldly. 'I'll not leave Mrs Edgecombe who has been so good to me all these years,' she had said, 'until I know she is settled with Nellie, and suited. I shall remain in her service as her housekeeper for so long as she wants it to be so.'

The problem had arisen because Captain Edgecombe had offered to sell them the cottage in Robin Hood's Bay – the sweet cottage in which Gertrude and Luke had spent the few days of their honeymoon all those years ago, and many chance days since then – with a deferred payment. He'd take a note of hand for the fifty pounds, and the note could be discharged from the collier's profits, a percentage with each run. The cottage was solidly built of best stone with a firm stone roof and would serve them well, both knew. But it would remove Gertrude to a distance from Mrs Edgecombe. Finally, over a half tumbler each of fiery rum from the barrels Edgecombe always kept in store, the two men had decided to call the women in so that they might have a discussion.

'Now, ladies,' Captain Edgecombe said in an attempt to mollify the two wives and disarm them, 'you're to feel quite free to tell we poor menfolk just what's in your minds, for we both declare we cannot see the rights of it. Luke Fossett is become *Captain* Fossett and a ship-owner: there's no denying that. It is neither meet nor proper that a ship-owner and captain should demean himself, either by giving his wife into the service of another or by sheltering beneath someone else's roof in a cottage at the back of a stable-yard.'

What he said was correct according to the social morality and hierarchy of the day, and none could deny it. Gertrude felt herself trapped, as did Mrs Edgecombe. Neither wanted to separate from the other, since a strong bond of sisterly affection had grown between them over the years; how many times had they conspired together to thwart what they considered the natural excesses of their men, the childishness, the extravagance of all kinds?

'I have the solution,' Mrs Edgecombe announced at last. 'You shall be my *companion*, Gertrude. And as to the cottage at the back of the stable-yard – well, we can build another wing there, beyond the drawing room. It'll be self-contained yet you can still have access to our house. So far as the rest of the world is concerned, you shall live in your own town-house, which will be built and furnished as befits the residence of an owner and captain!' Beaming round at them all, she pressed Gertrude's hand as she went on. 'And I shall dip into my patrimony and will settle such a sum upon you, the interest of which shall be equal to your present wages. In this manner I shall give you naught, shall pay you no wages, but you will be able to – how shall I say it? – help and assist me in all those small necessities for which I have come to depend on you over these many years.' She sank back on the settee, mopping her face in triumph.

Both men gazed from one to the other in perplexity. A house to be built contiguous with the present house? An investment yielding an annuity? Access between the two houses? Edgecombe, in particular, was aghast. He firmly believed a man's home should be his castle, and neither he nor Fossett, he knew, would welcome a castle with a breach in the walls, however friendly they might be disposed towards each other, no matter how well they might pull together in the harness of a partnership.

Mrs Edgecombe realized from their expressions that they were opposed to her plan, and looked to Gertrude for help. Gertrude had made up her own mind but did not dare to speak it. She loved her husband with patience and passion. She had served him to the best of her ability all the years of their married life. But theirs had been an unusual marriage. Though she had given her husband three sons, his voyages abroad had been long and she had spent far more of her life with Captain and Mrs Edgecombe than with her husband. She felt she owed them an enormous debt of gratitude and, being Gertrude and an Aysgill by birth, she intended, come what may, to honour that debt. Her voice was a whisper only as she spoke, her eyes beseeching her husband for understanding and forgiveness.

'Since I am the one most directly concerned in this

176

discussion,' she said, 'in which you, Captain and Mrs Edgecombe, have honoured me by permitting me to speak as an equal, and you, my husband, have dignified me by asking me to express my point of view, I would like to ask if the present arrangement could continue exactly as it is, in all particulars, until such time as Mrs Edgecombe and I can agree that a replacement has been found, trained and given sufficient experience so that at my going Mrs Edgecombe will feel no loss – though it may sound immodest for me to make such a statement, for I have never so highly valued those few services I am able to provide. I mean no dishonour nor demeanment to my husband, but though I feel my staying here may not be in accordance with the feelings of the day, I cannot accept a morality which does not permit individuals of humble decency to respect what they themselves feel are commitments to duty and, if I dare say it, friendship.'

Captain Edgecombe had lost himself in her convoluted phraseology but had gathered the import of what she had said. Mrs Edgecombe was beaming with pleasure.

But, Gertrude asked herself, what was the reaction of her dear dear husband? Had she lost his love and respect by her statement? Would he feel himself demeaned?

Luke Fossett sighed. 'I'm nobbut a simple sailor,' he said, 'who seeks to better himself wi' diligence, hard work and prudence wi' money. Sometimes it seems to me there's no rhyme or reason in what a man will and won't do. Both Captain Edgecombe and myself have seen men flogged before the mast for imperilling the lives of their shipmates by being asleep on watch; other times we've seen a man leap to certain death to try to salvage a mate washed overboard in a following sea. I no longer believe that one person can say what's in another's mind. I'll not be stubborn, missis, and force you against your will to gratify social custom, which says what a man may do and may not do in the ordering of his life. I'll have my name on't ship's papers behind the name of my benefactor, Captain Edgecombe, aye—' and here, a smile on Luke's features relieved all the anxiety Gertrude had been feeling, 'and I shall have my name on't deposit slip when the partner's share of the profits is put into't Mariners Trust Bank. I reckon as I can make do wi' that.'

Captain Edgecombe coughed. He hadn't taken part in so much speechifying for as long as he could remember. 'Aye, you're both strong of principle, I reckon. We'll leave it all to Mrs Edgecombe. It's *status quo*, madam – which, if you can't recall your Latin, means that everything shall continue strictly as before. And now, *Captain* Fossett, since you're a younger man than I am, I'll leave you to pull that cord and see if this benighted house can't offer us summat to sup.'

As in all matters of conscience, a final compromise was reached. The funds Captain Edgecombe had promised to advance the Fossetts for the purchase of the cottage in Robin Hood's Bay were now used to buy and furnish a cottage in Whitby itself. It, also, was built of stone and formed one of a row in which two retired sea captains had taken up residence. Each cottage in the row had a patch of ground before it and one captain had erected a whale's jaw-bone to form a gateway into his property. The entire row was known unofficially as Captain's Row. Gertrude was delighted with the place. It was close enough to the Edgecombes' house for her to call in on Mrs Edgecombe daily, and above all her husband now had a home befitting a captain and small ship owner.

Shortly after the Fossetts moved into the cottage, their son Walter returned from a long voyage east. His young wife Nancy had been invited to live with her parents-in-law, and she and Gertrude spent a busy week preparing for

Walter's return. On the day itself, all the Fossetts were at the quayside when the tri-masted *Southern Venturer* came across the bar under reduced sail and made its way along the channel. It had called into Madeira on its way home from the Indies, and carried a number of barrels lashed to the deck, to the great inconvenience of the sailors aboard. The Customs tide-surveyor was stationed next to the barrels; it was not unknown for smugglers to slip out to a boat at anchorage, waiting for the tide, to steal on deck and siphon off some of the wine or brandy by first light, often with the connivance of the ship's crew if not its officers. They all knew the tide-surveyor would have spent an anxious and wary night watching over his charges as if they were his own responsibility.

Walter Fossett was standing at the wheel in the forward wheelhouse; for the first time ever, he was helming the *Southern Venturer* to its berth. Captain Bishop was standing beside him, watching every move the deck crew were making as the vessel came slowly down the current with the wind fortunately on its bows. If Walter handled her well, he should be able to drift her gently sideways to lay her alongside with hardly a scrape; had the wind been behind them, he'd have needed a complex two-masted go about to achieve the same manoeuvre in the running tide, a job to task even the most accomplished captain.

'Steady as she goes, lad,' Captain Bishop said. 'We haven't come all this way to ram ourselves on the quayside. That's it, feel it in your hands.'

How Walter could feel anything with that enormous wheel to hold was beyond him; he'd seen his wife and parents waiting, his own father watching critically, and sweat ran into his palms as he muttered his prayers. 'Dear God, don't let the wind change in this last moment!'

The wind held steady; the *Southern Venturer* was losing way nicely, with its mizzen and its part-reefed foresail

179

acting as braking forces.

'Tighten starboards, let ports!' the Captain called to the sail-mate, who bellowed his instructions to the four sailors handling the ropes in their sheaves. The two to starboard tightened as the two to port slackened off; the sails changed their direction five degrees. Now the wind that had been acting as a brake began to edge the boat sideways.

At the same time Walter pulled the helm over slowly and progressively, so that now the bow appeared to want to go out into mid-stream, the stern to go towards the quayside. It was a tricky manoeuvre in which all the elements of wind, of tide, of helm and sail needed to be closely coordinated.

Captain Bishop grunted in approval. As the *Venturer* was headed, she'd lay herself alongside without cracking eggs, as they said. He gave orders to clear sails; they came rattling down the masts with their hoops clattering as the young 'prentices swarmed along the yards to secure them ship-shape. The lines snaked out from the boat to shore and were secured to the heavy cast-iron bollards which had been set into the quayside itself. Then, using the winches aboard, the *Venturer* was slowly hauled in to the quayside, where it finally came to rest against the fenders of thick plaited ropes – safe, snug, and home once again.

All the spectators were in one way or another connected with the vessel: wives or mothers of members of the crew; Customs men waiting to inspect the cargo; chandlers concerned with the order for the refit and provisioning; shipwrights who'd solicit any repairs that might be needed; investors with a share in the vessel itself or its cargo. They all knew that much work must be done before any man might come ashore, or go aboard, with the exception of the Captain and the tide-surveyor, who'd go to the Customs Hall to make declarations of the vessel's contents.

There was a swirl and bustle as the two-horse carriage of

the principal owner arrived on the quay; he looked at his vessel without even dismounting from his carriage, then called to his driver who turned the horses and brought the carriage away. The owner and the Captain would meet in the Customs Hall; then, by tradition, they'd go up to the Marine Merchants Club where the Captain would be fêted in drink for his safe return. Such investors as were members of the Club would be there to congratulate him primarily, but also to try to prise from him an estimate of the value of his cargo. Investing in cargoes was, at the best of times, a lottery. Goods could be purchased abroad, but could be lost at sea, could deteriorate or be spoiled, could be stolen by pirates. It was, however, a lottery which could pay much more dividend that many other forms of investment. Depending on the skill of the many men who'd gone to foreign parts to act as local agents, selecting unusual goods of high fashion or enhanced value, a cargo could fetch a hundred or more times the price for which it had been purchased. The manifests and bills of lading said but little: 'Forty Cases of Piece Goods' could either be Indian cotton or Chinese silk; 'A Bale of Feathers' could be either goose-down to stuff someone's mattress, or brilliant-hued pea-cock feathers for decorating the fashionable hats and head-dresses of the aristocracy.

'Well done, Walter,' Captain Bishop said when the *Southern Venturer* settled against the fenders of the quayside with nary a scrape. 'And good luck when tha' comes before the Board of Examiners. I s'all have my report to them first thing i' the morn. If tha's successful, tha'll have a berth waiting for thee.'

Walter swelled with pride, but didn't forget his manners. 'I owe it all to you, Captain Bishop,' he said fervently. 'If you hadn't skelped me to my books a time or two, I'd never have settled down to it!'

181

Walter, at twenty-one, had filled out and grown taller even than his father or his brothers. The sea life had agreed with him from the first moment. Captain Bishop, over the years, had kept his word, had made the lad apply himself to his studies as well as teaching him all manner of practical things. He'd taken a liking to Walter and, on many an expedition in foreign parts and ports, had taken the lad with him. He'd instructed him in languages and manners. Walter had always possessed a quick ear, and now had a competence in French and Spanish many a nobleman's son would have envied. He could converse in Portuguese and Dutch, curse in Arabic and Chinese, and even sing a few love songs in several of those tongues, to his own lute accompaniment. Captain Bishop had seen how perceptive had been the schoolmaster who'd said Walter would never learn from books. Many times, in the early years, he'd been obliged to take a rope's end to Walter to get him to con his studies, but anything he could learn by doing came naturally to him and he had a sensitive feel for all the delicate settings of a vessel under full sail. In the same vein he had learned his languages by speaking them with people they had met in foreign ports, and all this had given him the confidence of his graceful bearing. He was a handsome lad, with strong features and hair that the sun and salt-spray had bleached to a light corn colour, a broad sweep of shoulder, and a body from which all the puppy-fat had been trimmed by the exhausting work on board an ocean-going three-master trimmed for heavy cargo.

Gertrude's eyes opened wide as she watched Walter straighten from behind the wheel. 'Lord!' she said to Luke. 'He's grown twelve inches in height, I swear it!'

Luke hadn't seen his son for six years, since their times in port had not coincided. He noticed the strengthening of muscle, the increased assurance in his son's bearing, the manly way he accepted Captain Bishop's hand and shook it. Luke had noted the skill with which his son had brought the *Southern Venturer* safe alongside, with no anchor down for security as many a less confident captain would have insisted.

He caught his son's eye and each smiled at the other, perhaps shyly, perhaps in a tentative way. Luke knew he'd have to get to know his son again; six years of a lad's youth could see a vast difference in the ways he thought on life. All that, however, would have to wait. When his son came ashore, his wife Nancy would have him for an hour or two, to say all the things a wife says when her husband has been away for a year. And then, Walter would, probably, be conning his books as long as the candles lasted.

Tomorrow he was going before the Board of Marine Examiners. Tomorrow he was sitting the final examination for his mate's ticket.

CHAPTER FOUR

Stanley Ottershaw was twenty-three years of age; he'd celebrated his birthday the Sunday before Jonas Clegg called him into the office and bade him be seated. The large ledger in which he kept account of all transactions, other than purely monetary ones with which the clerks dealt, was open on the table before him. Stanley knew the book well; every creative thought he'd ever had about the machinery processes was in that ledger, carefully drawn to scale, with a full detail of the process for which the drawing was intended, accounts of the methods of manufacture, the effectiveness of the part, its triumphs or failures. Over a quarter of the pages of that ledger had, in recent years, been entered by Stanley himself, once Clegg had instructed him in the delicate matter of scale drawing, perspective, projection, shading to show form, the use of dotted lines to show function.

'I've been looking at your work,' Clegg said. 'I must say that in the thirteen years since you came to me, you've made a great success of everything you've put your hand to. As you are well aware, many of your ideas have been incorporated into the workings of the machinery. I reckon as John Kay would never have perfected his flying shuttle if you hadn't worked out the spring return mechanism for him. Aye, and hadn't gone to Huntsman's Foundry to learn the making of his crucible steel for the springs themselves. You'll never see a penny piece for it, of course, since Kay has taken out his patent, but you've many other ideas up your sleeve, I've no doubt.'

Indeed Stanley had. In the time they'd worked together, Jonas Clegg had taught the younger man everything he knew about the theory of metal in all its forms and the methods of working it. Stanley had learned to take an aesthetic delight in seeing something so hard, so strong, so implacable, worked to man's will, turned into useful objects and forms that could fit together to increase the power of man's elbow, to accelerate the processes on which modern machinery output depended. Where other men exclaimed over the beauty of nature, in a world where men were creating landscaped gardens that extended as far as the eye could see, Stanley adored machinery. While George Stubbs spent his time in shambles, studying the finest details of putrefying horses, the better to draw them on canvas in greater accuracy, Stanley Ottershaw studied metal form with the same practical and aesthetic eye, the better to represent its strength and function. Nothing in nature or art was so wonderful to Stanley as a man-made machine which worked. Now they had a spinning jenny which actually worked all the time, carrying sixteen spindles. It was Stanley's own adaptation of the machine Sleightholme had bought, and had not been able to keep running. By patient study, by shaping and reshaping the moving parts, by constructing them of better materials and using his own invented machine tools to fashion them smoother and of greater accuracy, Stanley had improved the invention of Hargreaves beyond recognition.

The only problem in Stanley's life at the moment concerned his benefactor, Jonas Clegg himself. Clegg was an engineer of the old school; though he had developed new devices and processes, he lacked the inventive, speculative, experimentalist mind that can soar into new directions unfettered by tradition. There were many avenues that Stanley wanted to explore but Clegg, always the traditionalist, hampered him and his thinking. He knew, for example, that if Clegg hadn't held him back, he'd have come out with the flying shuttle a year before Kay of Bury patented it. He'd had the idea for the boxes that formed the shuttle's run-way several years before but Clegg had refused to let him work on it to the detriment of their other manufactures.

Clegg was a wonderfully kind man, and had come to love Stanley as his own son. Now that Stanley's father was dead and his mother was working long hours at the hospital to try to recover the capital she'd lost in her Holland venture, Stanley and Clegg spent more and more time together. They would always go to the tavern to eat of an evening after work was ended for the day, and sometimes spent hours sitting after their meal listening to the general conversation. It was an age of talk; people everywhere were expressing new ideas; people were travelling about the country more since the toll-gate system had so greatly improved the roads.

At first, Stanley had been fascinated to learn of people's adventures on the new highways, but gradually, as his engineering work began to interest him more, he grew to resent the time he and Clegg wasted over the tavern tables. He longed to leave Clegg to his ale drinking, to return to the business and complete some interesting work he'd been doing when his employer dragged him away for supper.

The last thirteen years, Stanley realized, had not dealt kindly with Jonas Clegg. No doubt because of the perpetual maladies of his wife, he went home less and less frequently, drank more ale than was good for him, had increased greatly in weight, and had become most repetitive in his speech. It saddened Stanley to watch the gradual deterioration of the man who was, after all, his benefactor and his mentor, but it irked him too, to have to waste so much time listening to the same conversations, to feel that his inventive powers were being held back and frustrated by Clegg's traditionalism. How often these days, it seemed to Stanley, Jonas Clegg would say: 'It'll never work like that, lad, don't let's waste time and brass on trying.'

All Stanley ever wanted to do was to *try* – to try new ideas, new methods, to invent easier and faster ways of doing things. The well-spring of Stanley's eagerness was not only his love of metals and machines, nor even his desire to make more profits. Daily he saw the drudgery of human work, of men and women doing mindless tasks which, once learned by rote, demanded no more skill and gave no satisfaction. He greatly objected to the human animal being nothing but a pack-horse, a beast of burden, a mindless supplier of inefficient energy. He'd read stories of the building of the Egyptian Pyramids, and of Stonehenge, though of course he'd seen neither of these great monuments to man's wasted energy. For Stanley, the earlier gods had been the men who first conceived of the lever, a simple device to increase the power of man. Or the inventor of the pulley, whereby a man could multiply the strength of his muscles.

Once the dull repetitive processes could be done by machine, Stanley told himself, man would be free to think loftier thoughts, to seek to better his mind. How could any woman, committed to the drudgery of fourteen-hour days standing by a loom, be expected to know even the simplest facts about the nature of life itself? When, once, he'd tried to express these thoughts to Jonas Clegg, his master had been horrified.

'Is that what Titus Waverley taught you in school?' Clegg had said. 'There are too many of these dangerous ideas abroad with Wesley, with people agitating, with the Whigs in Parliament, without you seeking to apply them to daily work, to our factory systems. Lad, some of us was put on this Earth by Almighty God – not the God of the Papists, the Jacobites, the Wesleyans, the hundreds of other religions, all of which will perish in time. We were put on this Earth by Almighty God to work, work, work, without cease so long as we have strength in our body. Don't you realize that?'

It was the first time Stanley had realized that his master was a high Tory masquerading as a Christian only because that was the established order of things. It was the first time, too, that he had begun to understand what his Uncle Matthew said in his preaching.

'We mun all help each other to the best way of life,' he'd said, and had left it at that, determined to speak no more to Clegg of his secret feelings. Thus had a breach been formed between them, which over the years had only grown wider.

Stanley knew why Clegg had called him into the office; he sat still with his hands in his lap while Clegg conned the ledger of his ideas and achievements, all of which were clearly written and drawn for any man to understand.

'I've been thinking about the future,' Clegg said finally as he lifted his eyes and worked his chin to lubricate his speech with spittle. In the last few years he had lost most of his teeth, and his mouth constantly worked while he tried to speak. The resulting noises were very often unintelligible, but Stanley had learned to be patient, though it wasn't always easy. 'I think I should do something formal about your apprenticeship,' Clegg went on. 'Perhaps bind you to me for a few more years wi' a Deed of Contract. That way, you'll know your future lies secure in my hands.'

Stanley's heart sank. It was normal, of course, for a master to want to bind an apprentice to him with a Deed of Contract, so that the apprentice couldn't carry himself elsewhere.

'What would you say to sixteen shillings a week, eh? Wouldn't you say that was uncommon generous of me?' Clegg said, smiling ingratiatingly.

'Yes, Master, I'd say it was,' Stanley said, cursing himself under his breath for all the dreams he'd built over the past years. He'd believed Clegg when he'd said he thought of Stanley as a son; he'd served his time by trying to behave like a son to him, sitting with him in the taverns and listening to his ramblings, seeing him safely into his carriage when he'd had too much to sup, taking extra responsibilities in the factory when Clegg, because of the previous night's drinking, had been unable to leave his office. He'd dreamed that Clegg might settle part of the profits on him, even – and this was his favourite dream of all – leave the factory and the business to him when, as surely soon must happen, the over-drinking and over-eating killed him.

'And shall we say a seven-year indenture?' Clegg now added quickly.

Stanley was caught. What could he do? Sign himself to Jonas for the next seven years at a journeyman's rates while all his new ideas became the life's blood of the enterprise? Clegg wasn't contributing a single new idea; all the improvements in the processes came from Stanley and were carried out by the other skilled and semi-skilled workmen. Now they employed two lads just to do the drawings for the ideas which flowed from Stanley in a constant stream as he applied his mind to all the modern problems that demanded machines of ever greater sophistication. Many years ago Stanley had had an idea for a boring mill that would enable the inside dimension of a circular device to be cut with great accuracy, but Clegg had not permitted him to develop it. Stanley knew he could so greatly enhance the performance of the Newcomen Engine, could also reduce the cost of its manufacture by such a great amount, that he would earn a fortune from his invention if only he could patent it under his own name. There could be little point in giving it to Jonas Clegg in exchange for a further seven years of virtual slavery at a journeyman's wages.

'I'm greatly honoured by your suggestion, Mr Clegg,' Stanley said, 'but I'm obliged to speak to my mother about it. You know how we've always been a close-knit family, and I'd not care to offend her by taking such an important decision without her knowledge or approval.'

'*Approval*?' The sound that emerged from Clegg's tooth-less mouth was more of a shriek that a roar. 'What's there for a woman's approval, Stanley? Don't tell me a man can't take his own decisions wi'out referring to the ladies?'

'I shall take my own decision, Mr Clegg,' Stanley said firmly, 'as I always have in most things. But I feel duty-bound to my own mama to do her the honour and courtesy of speaking with her on the matter before making that decision.'

Jonas Clegg was badly put about, Stanley could see. 'You'll not keep me waiting,' he said firmly, 'while you run around somebody's petticoats, when I thought thee a grown man! I'll know by one week today – or else . . .'

The threat was left in the air; both knew it lacked the force of conviction, though Stanley knew that Clegg could be spitefully vicious, like many weak men, when he felt himself thwarted.

They didn't go to the tavern that evening, and Stanley hurried home through the gathering twilight. For once, his mother was back from her work at the hospital and was already eating supper with Claude and Jennifer.

'Well, saints alive!' Dodie exclaimed as Stanley came in. 'We never thought to see thee this side o' midnight. Tha' hasn't had a row wi' thy carousing friend?'

Stanley smiled affectionately at his mother. The years had treated her as well as they'd treated Jonas Clegg ill, and, at fifty-five, she was still a handsome woman. Working at the hospital had given her a stature and a personal dignity many women lacked at that age. He glanced at Claude, who hadn't paused in his eating, gnawing at the rabbit haunch regardless of his surroundings. Claude was a disappointment both to their mother and to him; still employed as a messenger boy for the same firm of solicitors, he'd done nothing to improve his life, nor, it seemed, ever would. Jennifer, on the other hand, was the prize bloom of all their lives.

Undoubtedly, Jennifer had become the most beautiful young woman and already, at twenty years of age, had a certain poise. Though it had meant the rest of them making sacrifices, she'd never been sent out to work, never sweated in a factory, a mill or a sewing shop. Most of the time she kept house for her mother and brothers, but Dodie had bought her a lute and she had learned to play and sing very sweetly. In the last year or so she'd taken a renewed interest in learning, and could speak a very pretty, if somewhat limited, French. She'd read a number of plays from recently published copies, and knew the work of Garrick in London as if she'd seen it herself. Since Dodie always bought the *Leeds Intelligencer* for her to read, she was kept fully acquainted with the doings of Parliament in distant London and, what was more important to her, the Yorkshire social scene. She could discourse quite freely on the terrible events that were happening in the colony of America, or on the policies of King George III and his current Prime Minister, Lord North. She was particularly interested in what was happening in America; that distant, exotic, colonial country had held her attention ever since she'd read an article in the *Intelligencer* about the opportunities this rich territory offered.

For Jennifer had learned one lesson from the example of her Uncle Peter: that humble backgrounds and origins would always tell against anyone trying to rise through the social scale. Many had done it, of course; the wife of Sir Dolby Chisholm had been a seamstress, for instance, and he had married her against all opposition, against the threat of being disinherited. Jennifer had read a book which all were saying was a thinly disguised account of the tribulations of Sir Dolby: *Love will Always Win*. It was one of the flood of new novels that Jennifer devoured voraciously, since many dealt with the subject of marriage between girls of humble birth and gentlemen of the upper class. Apparently, the way to lose the stigma of one's origins was to take one's husband off to the colonies, where his grace and manner – and his money, of course – would quickly establish him as a gentleman of quality on a large estate. Jennifer was determined to find such a man. She did not know how this would come about, but in her mind the conviction grew with each day that such a meeting was ordained. When her opportunity came, she was determined to be prepared for it and, above all, to keep herself pure. 'But, sir – I am a *good* girl!' was a phrase she had taken to heart from the many romances in which, often to the detriment of the housework, she had immersed herself.

Dodie watched Stanley as he sat at the table to eat the portion of stewed rabbit Jennifer had placed before him.

'What's this?' he asked, eyeing the cotton square that Jennifer was busily tucking into the open neck of his work shirt so that it hung down in front of him.

'It's a napkin,' she said. 'Surely you know that? It keeps the grease from your shirt and serves to wipe your hands when you've eaten. All the gentry use them.'

Now Stanley noticed that his brother Claude was wearing one and, to judge by its stained and crumpled appearance, had been making great use of it. He adored Jennifer and had no wish to thwart her often pretentious aspirations. 'Aye, Jennifer,' he said, 'I reckon as that's a good idea.'

'Lord North always uses one,' she said with conviction.

'Then if it's good enough for the Prime Minister, it's good enough for me,' Stanley said, smiling at her. His mother had spread her napkin across the lap of her coarse cotton gown, smiled approval at him, and returned to picking delicately at her food. No doubt about it, Jennifer had learned to cook tasty food, if of a fairly inexpensive and routine kind. It was better than greasy tavern plates of meat with congealed gobs of fat floating on top.

Dodie let him finish his meal before she spoke to him. She'd dismissed Claude from the table to help Jennifer clear away the earthenware bowls they'd used and now gave Stanley all her attention. 'There's summat amiss, lad, isn't there?' she said. 'Tha'd better tell me about it.'

'Aye, I reckon I better had,' he said, and went on to explain what Clegg had offered. His engineering work had taught him a disciplined method of thinking. He presented the facts about his situation in a perfectly logical order, building his case as methodically as he would the part of a machine. The conclusion, however, was not something that could be tried by experiment, proved either to work or not work, depending on the efficiency of his design and construction. 'If I refuse to sign, the chances are that Clegg will dismiss me from his service, despite any loss to himself. Over the years I've found him to be a very difficult man when thwarted, with a streak of spiteful cruelty. If I sign the Deed, then I am bound to him for seven years at a journeyman's wages, and can say goodbye to any hope of improving myself.'

'You are confident in your abilities?' Dodie asked quietly.

'It's no secret, Mam, that Clegg has put nowt of value in the ledger this past six months. Every drawing, every idea, every page of instructions is mine. And at least sixty per cent of my suggestions, when translated into machines or methods of working, have proved successful.'

'Aye, tha's served him well,' said Dodie. 'But what about the future? Do you think you're knowledgeable enough to go out and stand on your own?'

'Nay, Mam,' Stanley said, 'th'art dreaming. First and foremost, standing on my own needs money, a lot of money—'

'I wasn't aspiring for you to have your *own* factory,' she said hurriedly. That would be beyond all expectations. 'I was meaning to stand on your own in the matter of seeking employment with someone who'd give you better treatment for your ideas – someone, perhaps, who'd recognize your abilities by giving you a part-share of the profits.'

He shook his head. 'Nay, Mam, that'd never work for me. I've seen it with Jonas Clegg. An inventor needs must stand on his own, take his own risks, go his own way. It's always difficult to explain to anybody why you do a thing in a certain way. It's inside, an instinct. You just know, beyond all reason, that it will work. Take the turning lathe as we're building now, wi' more orders than we can cope with. When I saw the new gear-cutting machine, I said to myself, if we can cut gears on the *outside* of a wheel, we can cut them *inside*. If we make the wheel into a ring, with the gear inside, we can mount it on a spindle and turn it so that the outside wheel turns.'

'I know nowt about wheels and gears, I'm afraid,' she smiled.

'Neither did I until I thought about it, then I realized we could make a wheel with gears on the inside so heavy that its own momentum would keep it turning against the carpenter's tool.' Stanley paused; his mother had a quick understanding of most things but could not grasp mechanical theory or practice. 'The point is, Mam, nobody knows nowt about it until they start, and then they go two ways. One lot can do anything they see anybody else doing; they can learn skills like carpentry or machining just as easy as they can learn to shovel coal or build roads – there's nowt special about it. But there's other folks who go way out ahead, and they think in *thoughts* only, not in practices and customs. They forget all about how other folks do things and work out for themselves, by thought alone, how a thing must best be done. They are the *inventors*, the improvers, the dreamers.'

'And you're one of them, Stanley – is that what you're telling me?'

'I reckon it is, Mam. Once I've done a thing, I'm not

interested any more. I want to improve on it, to find a better way of doing it. Just doing it I leave to the others.'

'And you've enough buzzing round in your head to find things to improve?'

'Mam,' he said despairingly, 'the thoughts are buzzing round in my head like bees. I know there's so many things I could improve on. So many new things waiting to come out of me, so many inventions. But I can't do it wi' Jonas Clegg standing by my shoulder, breathing ale fumes all o'er me and saying "That'll never work, lad." And I don't think I could do it wi' any other Master. There's nowt else for it, Mam. I've got to find my own way, the way of being my own master, else I shall burst.'

Dodie didn't sleep that night, and neither did Stanley. She could hear him tossing about on his pallet in the corner of her bedroom, the straw creaking beneath him every time he turned. Jennifer had the other bedroom to herself – Stanley and Claude shared Dodie's room now that their father had died. Dodie lay in bed as long as she might, but her brain was so fevered with thoughts about Stanley's future that she could find no ease in rest, and long before dawn she climbed from her bed and dressed herself before going down to gather water from the pump to wash. There was a slab of oatmeal cake in the cupboard in the corner of the room; she took a chunk of it and broke her fast, still thinking about what she could do.

Finally, she decided. She knew she had but scant chance of success, but her determination compelled her to try against all the odds. Donning her dark blue woollen overcoat, she set off through the streets now streaked with the light of a cold dawn. She knew it would be better to go later in the day, when tempers would be mellowed by the sun's warmth and a belly full of breakfast, but each hour would see the determination seep from her.

She had never been to her brother's bank before. It was a grand two-storey edifice in Boar Lane, with a wide portico in which stood a man dressed as a beadle, scanning those who would enter. The principal room of the bank was high and imposing, lined with marble, with many bronze sconces for candles around the walls, and gilt-framed mirrors. In the middle of the room was a rotunda behind which an elegant young man in a fashionable dark frockcoat sat on a stool; the rotunda was surrounded by a chest-high bench which carried ink-wells of pewter and quills for writing. There was one table in each corner of the room, with a screen along one side and a low bench along the other; each table formed an area of tranquillity and carried an ornamented candle-holder, though the windows high in the walls gave ample light to see the ledgers in which each clerk was busily writing. There were ample chairs about the room, though several of the men seemingly preferred to stand. Along one wall a number of newspapers had been clipped to special stands, and some of the customers were perusing them, no doubt for the latest market intelligence and news of vessels and cargoes.

A door of solid brass, or so it appeared to Dodie, stood at the centre of the far wall; from time to time a servant would appear, approach one of the sitting or strolling men, and lead him through into the inner regions. The whole atmosphere was that of an exclusive club for gentlemen, though Dodie noticed she was not the only woman present. The other females, she thought timidly, might better be termed 'ladies'; without exception, even at this early hour of the morning, they were elegantly dressed and be-jewelled. Though she couldn't know it, the only time one could guarantee to see Peter Aysgill, the banker, was before ten o'clock. After that hour it was well known that he could be anywhere in the city.

She approached one of the desks in the corner when the man who'd been speaking with the clerk left. The clerk looked up at her, his opinion of her garb as clearly written on his face as anything in his ledger on the page.

'What may I do for you, madam?' he asked haughtily, not bothering even to rise.

'I wish to see Mr Peter Aysgill,' she said firmly.

'So do many other people, ma'am,' he said with an airy wave of his arm that embraced the entire room. 'Not many of these waiting gentlemen will be privileged to see Mr Aysgill himself, but must needs transact their business with others.'

'I *must* see him,' Dodie insisted.

'I'm afraid that is quite out of the question. Should you so desire, you can give your name and address to one of the runners, who will doubtless see that it reaches someone inside. If Mr Aysgill wishes to see you, I've no doubt you will be brought to him in the proper time.'

Dodie stood firm. 'Send someone in, or go yourself, to inform Mr Aysgill that someone out here wishes to see him urgently concerning his nephew. It also has to do with the *Leeds Intelligencer*, and Lord Barthwick.'

Despite his hauteur, the clerk was impressed by the latter name. He wasn't to know, since he was not privy to the details of his master's personal life, that Lord Barthwick, who had frustrated Peter Aysgill's attempts to become an Alderman in 1760, was the man his master most hated. He held up his hand and one of the runners came immediately across. The clerk penned a few lines on a piece of paper, which he dusted then folded before handing it over.

'This lady would like to see Mr Aysgill,' he told the runner. 'Take this to Mr Percy's assistant and do whatever he says.' He turned to Dodie and this time his face cracked with a diffident smile. After all, he was telling himself, one couldn't know with whom one was dealing these days, and so many people, making money on ventures, took no trouble with their apparel. 'The runner will come for you if Mr Aysgill is able to see you,' he said.

Dodie smiled back. 'Thank you very much for your

courtesy, young man,' she said. The smarmy upstart was no older, it seemed to her, than her own boy Stanley . . .

To the astonishment of everyone who had witnessed this exchange, and had amusedly speculated that the drably dressed woman would quickly be evicted from the premises, the runner came back almost immediately and led her through the brass door into the inner sanctum. The corridor beyond was lined with other doors in the new dark mahogany and the floor was shiny with beeswax. Dodie followed the runner along it to the far end, to an enormous door set with a doorknob so huge it would have taken two hands to span it. The runner knocked, then pushed the door open. He stood in the doorway and beckoned for Dodie to pass him quickly, hurrying her into the presence without delay.

Peter was sitting at the largest desk she'd ever seen. 'I guessed it was you, Dodie,' he said.

His voice contained no warmth, his eyes no joyous recognition. Peter had cut himself adrift from his family, or perhaps it would be more true to say he'd cut his family adrift from him, leaving them to float as best they might wherever the wind might take them. He had not seen Dodie since that disastrous night in 1760 when he'd lost the nomination for Alderman in the Philosophical Society.

'I was sorry to hear about Mark Ottershaw, Dodie,' he said. 'I can give you five minutes, and no more. Sit down, will you, and state your business.'

'Is that the way it was when our brother Simon came to borrow a few pounds to buy himself a little business?' she asked. 'You know, if you'd advanced him that money, he wouldn't have killed himself.'

Peter sighed as he leaned back in his chair. 'Dodie, I wish no reminders of any other member of our family. I have agreed to see you because you said your business had to do with two of my interests: Lord Barthwick and the *Leeds Intelligencer*. I care naught for my nephew, nor any other of our clan – surely I've made that clear over the years. Now, do not waste my time nor your own. Tell me what business you and I could possibly have, discussing Lord Barthwick and the *Intelligencer*.'

Dodie seated herself across the desk from him. The years, and doubtless his great wealth too, had given him an assurance. She knew that, though he conducted much of his business from the bank he and Sir Ian Clether had founded, his other concerns – his great trading company, the manufactories he had bought, the shares in Hull Docks, his canal-building enterprises – had all made him one of the richest men in Leeds.

'We are in no hurry, Peter,' she said complacently. 'Give me news of my nephews Gavin and Robert, and of your dear wife Tessa. Gavin must be sixteen years old now, and Robert fourteen. Gavin has gone to Semple's, I hear, and Robert to Eton—'

Peter exclaimed in exasperated irritation. 'Come, Dodie, do not waste my morning with prattle about children.'

'Shall I rather tell you of one of my patients, Theophilus Cryton?' she asked, keeping her voice light, her manner gentle.

'Cryton's a blackguard,' he snapped. 'I hope you have nothing to do with men of his sort.'

'A blackguard? Is that the best you can say? You don't think him a scandal-monger?'

'It is by no wish of mine that we have a free press, sister,' he said, 'in which a man like Cryton can write any sort of blackguardly scandal and get away with it.'

'But he can only write as he does if he has information, dear brother,' Dodie smiled.

Peter had dismissed one of his messengers for double-dealing, taking coin both from himself and from one of his rivals, Lostein, for the same information. In revenge, the messenger had talked at length with Cryton at the *Leeds Intelligencer* about Peter's business methods, detailing the way he acquired confidential information from a great variety of sources before making a business decision. Luckily, that particular messenger had been one of the less trusted ones and the information he had to impart had not ruined Peter's reputation, though it had occasioned him some embarrassment in the coffee-shops. Cryton had written a scabrous lampoon, depicting Peter as a greedy opportunist; accompanying the lampoon was a cartoon which showed an unmistakable Peter Aysgill with his eye bent to the keyhole of a boudoir, in which a tart was hiding money within her intimate garments while pleasuring a customer. The caption to the drawing, which was viciously witty in its line, read 'He Stoops to Conquer', after the title of a play by Goldsmith then all the rage in London and in Leeds. Peter had thought to take the newspaper and Cryton to court but his barrister had strongly advised against it. 'For a man of your importance to take them to court, Aysgill,' the barrister had said, 'would multiply their circulation ten-fold overnight. Many of these provocations are committed for that very reason.' It had irked Peter to accept the jibe since he greatly lacked humour, especially in a joke against himself. 'If, for example, he were to gain information about Lord Barthwick's intervention in your vain attempts to have yourself elected Alderman, if he were able to inform members of your own family who share your flesh and blood . . .'

Peter now made a steeple of hands, and gazed over its pinnacle at his sister. He'd always known she was a determined woman; now, he realized, he was to experience that determination at first hand.

'You've explained one of the names on your list,' he said. 'The *Leeds Intelligencer* – by which you mean Theophilus Cryton. Are you going to couple such a villainous name with that of my dear nephew Stanley?'

Dodie smiled back at him. 'You play games brother,' she

said, 'but I am not unskilled in that pastime. I link the name of my son with those people only, I pray, to his advantage. You haven't seen your nephew these many years, Peter. He is grown strong and intelligent. He has studied Latin, Greek and Mathematic, and has now served thirteen years of apprenticeship with an engineer, from whom he has learned many skills with machines.'

'I heard he'd gone to Clegg,' Peter said, surprising her with his knowledge. 'I heard further that Clegg would likely have gone under without young Stanley's fertile brain keeping a supply of inventions in the ledger.'

'I am astounded that you take such an interest in your nephew.'

'Do not delude yourself, Dodie. I take an interest only in commercial enterprises. Jonas Clegg wished to transact some business with me, and I naturally sought to discover how soundly based was his commercial knowledge.'

'And you found him lacking, I'll be bound,' suggested Dodie.

'It is not the custom of the bank to disclose such information, even to kith and kin, dear Dodie. Won't you now after all these tedious preliminaries, let me know the reason for your visit?'

That Peter had not the slightest spark of humanity in him, Dodie had long been aware. She'd arranged her appeal to him to avoid any demand on his humanity. However, she'd been repeating the words of Thomas Gray to herself as she'd walked along the street, and from them she derived strength.

'*Too poor for a bribe, and too proud to importune, he had not the method of making a fortune,*' she quoted now. 'Is that how you think of me, brother?'

'It may surprise you to know that on occasions I read poetry, too,' Peter said. It was the truth, but in his case done for quite different reasons than hers. It helped in social intercourse, it assisted him to bridge the gap in conversations in which he had no interest, longing always to pass to more commercial matters. It was a good way of disengaging oneself from importuning wives and daughters. It gave him an air of culture which few could recognize as only a façade, a coating on the rough surface beneath. 'I must confess, however, that I find your Thomas Gray a little romantic to my taste, and infinitely prefer Mr Goldsmith. *Friendship is a dis-interested commerce between equals; love an abject intercourse between tyrants and slaves.* Shall brotherly love make me your tyrant, Dodie, or your slave? Can we not return, in friendship, to a commerce between equals? I can see that you have demands to make upon me concerning your son Stanley. I also see that, if these demands are not met, it is your intention to disclose as much scandal, gossip and malignity as you can scrape together to a man prepared to impugn others more successful than himself, Theophilus Cryton. I care naught for Cryton, nor for my nephew. But if you can give me a sound proposition, I'm willing to listen to it and forget your criminal intent towards me, for I do believe that blackmail stands high on the Statute Book as a felony. Remember, however, that any proposal must, *ipso facto*, benefit *both* parties. What benefits can you offer me?'

Inwardly Dodie applauded his tactics. He's carried the battle to his own field, she thought; what do I know of benefits, of advantages in the machine world? Aloud she said: 'The financial benefits, dear brother – and I believe you mean no others – will obviously be in proportion to the terms of the arrangement, will they not?'

'You're fencing with me, Dodie. Tell me plain – what do you want for the lad, and what are you prepared to offer in exchange?'

'I want to see him set up in a business of his own, developing his own inventions, making his own machines, enjoying the fruits of his own patents.'

'And in exchange?'

'A suitable share of the profits.'

Peter laughed. 'Oh my dear sister! What would you consider suitable? Fifty-one per cent? With a lien on all the patent income, a debenture on the premises, a first charge on all the assets, no doubt.'

As he had intended, Dodie was lost in this terminology. 'I'd want what's fair for the lad,' she said. 'Nothing more, nothing less.'

Peter was already tired of the game. For the truth was that he had heard excellent reports of the work Stanley Ottershaw was doing for Jonas Clegg. His informants had told him, when Clegg came to borrow money from the bank, that the only asset Clegg possessed was the fertile inventive brain of his apprentice. Peter's own factories had need of new machines, new processes, new engines. If the lad did nothing more than modernize the Aysgill enterprises, then he would be worth a small controlled investment.

'All right, Dodie,' he said. 'Tell Stanley to set out a scheme of what he needs. I'll want to see all the papers, all the figures. I shall want to see his suggestions for the future, the avenues in which he will work, the problems he will seek to solve. If I like what I see, I'll finance him. We shall go into partnership as Aysgill and Ottershaw.'

Dodie rose in her chair and clasped her reticule to her. 'I can see you haven't understood me,' she said firmly. 'There has been no talk of partnership nor ever will be. The lad will draw up a scheme, as you request, but you'll finance the needs of it, Peter, with a fair return for your money and nothing else. I'm quite certain that Theophilus Cryton would agree with that approach.'

'Damn Cryton to all hell!' Peter burst out, realizing she had bested him and he could neither browbeat nor trick her. 'Very well then. Send the lad to see me, with his papers.'

CHAPTER FIVE

The bulk of the three men filled the room, and Matthew remembered the number of times, when first he and Mildred had been married, when folks would flock in to hear him read from the Scriptures, to listen to him talk about the Future of Mankind or other such heart-lifting subjects. Now he was fifty-five years old, yet still it seemed people wanted to listen to him. He looked at Mildred, who smiled encouragingly at him. He looked at his son Frank, sitting with his wife Sylvia, with six-year-old Keith on his knee, and Frank nodded his approval.

'Matthew, you do no good tramping the moors from place to place with your Wesleyanism, when the likes of us need you here more than ever,' Alf Stokely was saying. 'That's what we've come to tell you. Aye, and we've come to ask you to come back among us, to take your old job back down't mine, and see if you can't organize a bit of sense into things for us. Matthew, there's women and bairns dying down there because the conditions is so bad, and there's none to speak about them for fear of losing the pennies we earn. You're needed *here*, Matthew, not tramping about the four corners of the country.'

Sam Shaw and Bill Thorn, who formed the rest of the mine delegation, both agreed.

'You wouldn't believe the conditions down there, Matthew,' Sam said. 'You know the devil's never changed yon engine? Half the time we're splashing about in water, else we're gasping for breath on the second level.'

'It ain't much better on the first level, either,' Bill Thorn added, 'but there's nowt Broadley will do. As he grows older he seems to grow meaner; he can't thoil't brass for cwt in the way of improvements, even though we are bringing out as mucn coal as ever. Now that the seams are growing wider, he's got more men at't face, more women and kids drawing, and his pile grows ever higher.'

For some time, Matthew had been growing discontented with the constant travelling, with the impersonal business of making speeches to strangers, none of whom he was likely to see again to discover if his words had had any effect on the quality of their lives. Wesleyanism had now grown so widespread, with so many people deserting the established Church, that there was a great need for travelling preachers. Certainly it was much easier to travel these days, now that the roads were being improved, but it was still a tiring and scarcely rewarding way of life, walking to the remotest parts of Yorkshire to address a crowd, probably suffering violence on the way there, during the address and on the way back, without even the satisfaction of knowing you'd *achieved* something. There were so many alternative religions now that Matthew had begun to wonder if people were interested by what he specifically had to say, or if they were just seeking a diversion from the conventional parish churches and clergy who cared more for hunting with the gentry than caring for their flock.

'At least, if you come back, Father,' Frank said in his soft voice, 'you'll know the people you're dealing with.'

'Aye, and you'll not have so much travelling to do,' Mildred put in. She missed her husband dreadfully when he was away, especially now that her second son Richard was no longer at home. Frank's wedding to Sylvia had been a blessing, giving Mildred young Keith to look after while Sylvia went to work in the mill. At fifty-three she was the constant victim of crippling rheumatism that prevented her working, or even walking very far, and though he was a handful the youngster helped her while away her days waiting for the return of her husband.

'There's a job to be done, here and now,' Alf Stokely persisted. 'Surely you'll agree that your own folks has as much a claim on you as anybody else. We're all starting to move now, you must have seen that. It's becoming a strong nation-wide movement. Aye, some are calling us radicals, but I was at a meeting the other night held in secret at the back of the Bull and Bear, and I heard a fellow as were just off the coach from London, telling how they'd formed a Bill of Rights Society, and were getting men in Parliament to stand up for it. Most of it was beyond my comprehension, but it did seem to mean as we'd all be represented with a voice in Parliament. It sounded to me as if, at last, somebody was waking up to the needs of the common man, such as thee and me, such as all of us here. It's not right that them above can impose their will on them below, to the detriment of health and strength, aye, and often lives. This fellow was saying that yon man Wilkes, as made such a story a while back, was refused election to Mayor of London, even though he had a majority of votes. What we need, Matthew, is people of your ability all over the country to gather the force of their own folks behind them and try to get things done.'

'And where better,' Bill Thorn added enthusiastically, 'than down the mine, back where tha' started from.'

Matthew immediately saw one problem. 'Broadley would never take me on again,' he said. 'He knows me as a preacher – he'd never have me back in't mine.'

Alf Stokely was grinning hugely; he knew they'd started Matthew thinking about joining them. 'Aye, well, that's summat we've thought on,' he said. 'Broadley's getting on, you know, and he journeys to Harrogate every week's end to take the waters for his stomach. The mine goes on working, o' course, while he's away. Broadley's taken on a young man as a mine-manager; he's no higher than twopenn'orth o' copper and though he knows a bit about mining I don't reckon as he knows much else. Saturday morning he takes on a few folks, according to the list Broadley leaves wi' him – he gets them clamouring at the gate, as always, and lets the first two or three in. Tha'll be first at't gate on Saturday, we can promise that. George Alverthorpe, that's the mine-manager, doesn't know thee from Adam. Wi' thy name on't book, and a shilling advance in your pocket, Broadley won't dismiss you, come Monday, will he?'

And so it was decided. Matthew would go back down the mine; he would stop travelling for the Methodist Wesleyans and would live at home again. Mildred wept silent tears of joy when she realized her man would no more go a'roaming, as one of the new songs said.

When the meeting had ended and only the family were sitting round the table, Frank asked his father, 'Would you like us to find a place of our own, Father, now that tha'll be at home all the time?'

Matthew shook his head. 'Nay, lad,' he said, 'I can see from the way your mam holds her grandchild on her knee that she'd not like to be deprived of his company. If tha's a mind to, tha' can stay. Mam and me, we'll sleep down here, and you and Sylvia can have the room upstairs wi' the bairn. It'd been different if God had spared t'others.'

Frank and Sylvia had had four children since they'd been married. Keith was the sole survivor. Each of the other babies had died within a year of birth, and the marks of sorrow were clear on Sylvia's face. Already she looked much much older than her twenty-six years. She worked a jenny in Sleightholme's Mill and the winding of the wheel placed a heavy burden on her back as it drove its eight spindles. The machine was constantly breaking down, and her cousin by marriage, Arthur, was not always able to steer her to alternative earning, careful that Mr Tomlinson, the overseer, should not think he was favouring a relative.

'At least there'll be another wage coming into't house,' Matthew said, 'and nowt going out for my travels. How I mun have been a burden to you all!'

'Nay,' Frank said instantly, 'it's not my way to speak back to my own father, but tha' mun't ever say owt like that again. Tha' were never a burden to any of us. Tha' wert an inspiration to us all.'

'Even Richard?' Matthew said unhappily. He missed his younger son, of whom they heard only snatches of news from time to time. Travellers had reportedly seen him in some tavern in the dales in the company of doubtful men; people who'd been riding the mail-coach had seen him pass by on horseback. Once, at the Hunslet Feast, Frank thought he'd caught a glimpse of his brother through the crowd. He'd pushed his way through as quickly as he could but when he came to the fist-fighting booth before which he thought he'd seen Richard, he could discover no trace. He'd even gone into the booth, without success.

'Aye, even Richard,' Frank said, 'before he took the whim to go adventuring. Don't worry, Father, when he knows you're back at home all the time, he'll come around. Us'll have him by our side once again, mark my words.'

The object of all their thoughts was cantering happily along the Wakefield Road at that very moment, riding a powerful pure-bred Arab stallion that had been loaned to him specially for the occasion, looking occasionally into the window of the family coach beside which he was riding, seeing the stunningly beautiful face of the Honourable Miss Cecily Throwton, and thinking how much more pleasant it would be to be bouncing on her rather than on the horse. She was wearing a lilac-coloured silk outfit that couldn't have been bought, he supposed, for a penny less than two hundred pounds: the long skirt worn without hoops for the convenience of travelling; the fine woollen shawl she'd thrown around her shoulders to keep out the draught; the bonnet worn wide of her face, trimmed with a small posy of flowers on the left and a feather which hugged the line of the top. Now that they were on the road she wore no jewellery of any kind; he remembered the flash of her rings when she had hired him, the glint of the diamond encircled by rubies on the heavy gold chain that hung between her breasts.

Richard had derived an enormous enjoyment from watching her the previous evening and had learned much, too. It wasn't only the slut who could coquette a man into helping her; the lady of quality could get up to the same tricks, too.

Richard had been sitting in the main room of the tavern. Since he'd broken with Joe Grice and his depleted gang, he'd set his cap at any adventure likely to yield him profit, with no concern for scruples, but no stomach for violence. Joe Grice and he had parted over that issue, for Grice had always wanted to top his victims to avoid them later recognizing him. Richard had restrained him once, when Grice had been about to slit a packman's throat; they had come to blows and shortly afterwards Richard had left. Dick Berry, John Hirst and Stephen Lumme had all been caught by the peace-officers, he had since heard, and were transported to America. Richard was happier on his own, living more on his wits than by violence. He'd grown into an engaging fellow, now twenty-nine years of age. So far he'd avoided matrimony, though there were beds across the wold and weald where he could sleep in love and comfort.

He was aware of the Honourable Cecily Throwton examining his features as he rode along; aye, well, many a lass had told him he was no beauty, that his nose was bent too much to the side and that his eyes were too wide apart. 'If you don't like what you see,' he'd always told them, 'you can

209

always close your eyes and enjoy what you feel!'

As he'd been sitting in the tavern, speculating on what might become his next venture, he'd heard a coach rumbling into the yard. The tavern was the collecting point for the London coach, and many other new coach lines converged here, discharging passengers on their way to or from London.

The door had opened to admit a large florid gentleman, dressed in London style, bellowing for the steward. He'd seated himself without so much as a glance in the direction of anyone else in the room, and had proceeded to command a meal, drink, a bed, and even warm water for a bath.

The tavern steward had bustled about, recognizing the newcomer as Sir Charles Lakeby on his way back from a short season in London. 'I trust all went well for you, Sir Charles?' he'd asked with due deference.

'London's become a damned impossibly expensive place,' Sir Charles had growled. 'I'll go there no more for a twelve-month.'

'Lady Lakeby is not with you, Sir Charles?'

'No, her ladyship has gone to Bath for the waters. We shall enjoy a month of peace and bachelor solitude afore we suffer the chatter of the ladies again, since she's ta'en her daughters wi' her, thank the Lord.'

It was at this moment that the door had opened again to admit the most beautiful woman Richard had ever seen. Her fine complexion was enhanced by the cold, her skin delicate and fragile as ivory, her large eyes luminous with the tears caused by the biting winds outside. Even Sir Charles, when he looked up and saw her, had felt constrained to rise, to move himself along the bench so that the lady might share the warmth of the log fire that roared in the chimney breast.

''Tis no night to venture abroad, ma'am,' Sir Charles said, 'if I might make so bold. Lakeby's the name – Sir Charles Lakeby, at your service.'

She had obviously been moved and amused by the gawkishness of his gallantry, seeing him instantly for what he was: a high-born country bumpkin more accustomed to horse and hound than to the niceties of Society. She inclined her head delicately. 'Cecily Throwton, Sir Charles; the Honourable Miss Cecily Throwton.'

'Charmed, madam, charmed,' he said. 'Might I invite you to share a board of humble fare wi' me? I'm on my way back to my house, Lakeby Manor, but have no wish to travel by night. My coach will come for me i' the morn.'

Her eyes had clouded over, and she raised a speck of finest lawn to wipe away a tear. 'Lucky, indeed, is the man with a home to go to, his own fireside, his favourite chair, his dog to sit beside him, his steward to fill his glass, his wife and family to sing prettily to him . . .'

'My wife and family are at Bath for the waters, ma'am. There'll be no madrigals till they return. Though, truth to tell,' he added hastily, not wishing to seem a churl in matters of music, 'sometimes they do pluck their instruments and sing their songs most commodiously.'

Richard had been watching these exchanges in silent amusement; he'd rarely seen a man react so swiftly to a lady's charm, and could only speculate as to what she would do with her prize trout, once she had coaxed it to land. For coax it she most certainly did. Pretending to sleep at his bench, Richard heard the entire story of how her father had gambled away his patrimony in London's gaming clubs. She embellished her story with details of how her father had staked ten thousand pounds on a card at White's; the shock, apparently, had killed her poor dear mama who, fortunately, had left her small fortune to her daughter, safe from the father's depredations. All else had been lost, she tearfully reported. The mansion in Wiltshire and the London house in Albemarle Street had both gone to pay creditors and now her father, in disgrace, had sailed for Bermuda where he

211

hoped to secure a position in the Army or the Colonial Administration.

'Leaving you, my poor morsel, destitute?' Sir Charles, who by now was pressing her hand to comfort her, was visibly moved by the recital.

'Hardly destitute, Sir Charles,' she said. 'I have sufficient funds to buy myself a small cottage somewhere in the country. I despise Society and London so greatly for what it has done to my poor deluded papa that I long only to live out my days in the serenity of the countryside. I care not where it is, so long as the foul vapours and tawdry humours of city life are far away from me.'

'You never married?' Sir Charles asked deferentially.

She shook her head slowly. Truly, it was a performance worthy of Mrs Cibber, playing opposite Garrick, Richard thought. 'Alas!' she said. 'The only man I ever loved was taken from me by a highwayman's bullet when, with foolhardy courage, he tried to stop a gang robbing the Wiltshire Mail. He was ever thus – to think naught of himself, to give all for others!'

Sir Charles gulped with embarrassment, not knowing how to address such a paragon of all the virtues as this beautiful independent young woman. 'My dear lady,' he said, 'I wish I could help you in your distressing situation. My house is, needless to say, at your disposal. You'll need a base from which to conduct your search for suitable properties, and the inns hereabout are frequented by the lowest types. I myself am seldom at home since I dispose myself about the property hunting, shooting, even a little fishing. My servants will tend you as if you were their mistress – which you shall be in all but name, until my dear wife returns from Bath.'

'I thank you kindly for your offer,' the lady responded, 'but without wishing in any way to impugn or offend you, I'm bound to say that virtue and modesty do not permit me to accept.'

Virtue and modesty had taken but one hour, a full belly and a head of wine to assuage, when it was agreed that the Honourable Cecily Throwton would accompany Sir Charles on his morning journey to Lakeby Manor. If the coach had already been to hand, it was quite apparent to Richard that the enflamed and impassioned Sir Charles would have insisted on leaving that very night, despite the wind and cold. Then, when Richard went across the room to relieve himself in the yard, he found himself the subject of scrutiny by the lady. On his return she beckoned him imperiously. He approached her and bowed politely.

'Richard Aysgill, ma'am, at your service,' he said.

Sir Charles cast a disparaging eye over him. 'What is your occupation, man?' he asked grumpily. 'You dress like a wayfaring scamp, I'll be bound.'

Indeed, Richard's garb fitted no correct order of things, being neither a workman's uniform nor a gentleman's habit. The breeches of fine buckskin had come from a hunting Earl obliged to leave a doxy's bedchamber via the window; the waistcoat, heavily encrusted with beads, had been found in a bag of jewels that Joe Grice and Richard had taken from the York stage coach; the shirt, of finest lawn, had been taken from one of Grice's victims, though dead of a heart attack and not of a shooting for that would have stained the fabric. His hat had been blown from the head of a gentleman fleeing from the Grice gang; his watch and fob had come from the same source after the gentleman had been captured and hanged. The boots he wore were of fine Northampton leather, soft as doe-skin, and they too had been provided by a doxy though she was coy at revealing the circumstances.

Richard had but one answer to this question which was often asked him in taverns he frequented. 'I am an officer in His Majesty's Service,' he said with as much hauteur as he could command, 'but I travel on leave and incognito. You, sir, may call me Lieutenant.'

It was apparent that Sir Charles wanted naught to do with the 'Lieutenant', or with any other man, so long as Cecily Throwton was nearby. She, sensing the antagonism between them, interrupted to prevent an outbreak.

'Lieutenant, did I hear you say that you are an officer?'

'Yes, ma'am, that you did.'

'Then I wonder . . . Would it be too much to ask . . . Dare I impose on your good nature?'

'Madam,' Richard said gravely, 'I am yours to command.'

Still she seemed to hesitate, then patted the bench beside her. 'Pray, do sit down,' she commanded.

Richard sat on the bench at a respectable distance from her, his back ramrod straight in what he hoped looked like a military bearing.

'Tomorrow I am to travel with this gentleman, Sir Charles Lakeby,' she said. 'I cannot travel alone with Sir Charles, for reasons of propriety which you will naturally understand, being yourself an officer and *a priori* a gentleman too.'

'I do, ma'am,' said Richard gravely.

'Then, I wonder, would it be possible . . . ?'

'You wish me to accompany you?'

'There you have it, in a nutshell, as they say. I will, of course, fully recompense your time and your trouble.'

'A gentleman never reckons time or trouble, ma'am, whilst he is in the service of a lady,' Richard said. 'I'll be more than happy to accompany you, to act as your chaperon, to guard and defend you should it become necessary. I shall be greatly honoured to be your champion in all matters.'

Thus, despite Sir Charles's patent disapproval, was it arranged. When the family coach arrived the following day, the groom had also brought Sir Charles's Arab, knowing how eager Sir Charles would be to cock his leg over a saddle, and not certain if Lady Lakeby might not also have arrived. Sir Charles therefore had a choice: to ride the horse and miss the opportunity of travelling with this devastating lady, or to offer the horse to the 'Lieutenant'.

So now Richard Aysgill found himself astride that most wonderful of beasts, riding along beside the coach. No man is ever content – prior to this journey he would have believed it his greatest ambition to ride such a creature; all he could think at this moment was of a form of riding greatly removed from that he was now enjoying. That the Honourable Cecily Throwton had some kind of venture afoot, he was quite convinced. He'd go along with it until the time came when he could advantage himself, playing his role conscientiously and faithfully until the time came to abandon his imposed 'principles'.

And if a tumble with Cecily could be included, so much the better.

Two weeks later, Richard was still acting the chaperon to Cecily at Lakeby Mânor. Each day he escorted her around the countryside, looking for somewhere to live. It was apparent that her legacy must be sizeable since the only properties which interested here were vast, each secluded in its own grounds. Sir Charles would usually accompany them on these rounds, though they could see he was aching to follow his hounds across the moors and through the glades where stags still lurked.

Richard was never anything but courteous and deferential, for it was part of his plan that Cecily did not realize how much he had guessed of her intentions, though the details of any plan she might have continued to perplex and elude him.

The two weeks had been otherwise dull for him, though he'd discovered one of the Lakeby Manor chambermaids prepared to oblige him, albeit in a bovine way. His quarters were in the Manor's stable block; he ate his meals with the head servants, the housekeeper, steward, gamekeeper and head gardener in the staff dining room next to the kitchen, listening to their gossip about the Honourable Cecily

Throwton. The housekeeper, completely won over by her, pronounced her 'charming, a tragic lady, a mite who's suffered, a paragon, an angel'. Richard realized that Cecily must, discreetly, be spreading coin around and regretted that so far none of it had come his way.

From the beam that came to Sir Charles's face, and the softening of his manner towards the 'Lieutenant', Richard supposed that some good fortune had befallen him. Then one evening, sitting beneath a chestnut tree in the Manor grounds, speculating about the affair in hand and wondering if he should persist with it or pursue advantage elsewhere, Richard saw the candle light move along the corridor from Sir Charles's quarters in the west wing to those occupied by Cecily in the east, and divined the source of his contentment. That night Richard couldn't sleep, and the chambermaid learned more of what she'd come to call his 'strange foreign ways'.

The following day, Cecily and Richard rode out alone, to visit yet another house. None of the ones they had so far seen had pleased her – and often he'd remarked that the excuse she'd given for not making a purchase had seemed somewhat flimsy. On this occasion she rode one of Sir Charles's finest black mares. She was wearing a full pink riding habit lined with apple-green silk, over a silk waistcoat, with a full pink petticoat in heavy cotton below it. Her cloak was of camlet woven with alternate silk threads; thrown back from her shoulders, it glistened in the cold morning sunlight.

She sat the horse well and had obviously been trained to it, and Richard had watched her a few days before at the butts and seen how well she handled a bow. She'd taken much trouble to learn country pursuits, that much was apparent. He was wearing the same rig as before, since he carried only a change of undergarments with him; but the chambermaid had sponged and pressed his clothing and they made an attractive pair as they set out across the dewy grass of the

Manor fields, between lines of chestnuts that one of Sir Charles's ancestors had planted as rides and coverts for birds. Most unusually, Sir Charles had not even come to the door to see them off; on the few occasions he'd not accompanied them, he'd always stood on the Manor steps and a groom had accompanied them, doubtless acting under his master's instructions. Richard could only suppose that carrying the candleholder along those lengthy corridors had tired Sir Charles beyond belief.

'At what secret pleasure do you smile so contentedly?' Cecily now asked, seeing the expression on his face.

'A thought of no consequence, ma'am,' Richard said. 'Perhaps the beauty of the morn. Perhaps the clarity of the day. Perhaps the scent of the dew like wine beneath the trees.'

'And nothing to say about your benefactress?'

'Only, ma'am, if you'll forgive the liberty, that your beauty surpasses all descriptions.'

They cantered and galloped, trotted and walked for an hour across the rolling landscape. Cecily could jump her horse as easily as any huntsman and nothing barred their progress. They started to climb a long steep hill, and Richard guessed they were heading for the architectural folly that stood atop Tewkley Hill, a Temple of Diana built a hundred years before by a local squire who had died without issue and whose servants had buried him there. It commanded a wide aspect over fields, moors, forests and rivers; they dismounted there and Richard tethered the horses beneath a nearby tree whose single line of foliage enhanced the beauty of the somewhat stark outline of the Temple.

'What sort of man are you at heart, Richard the Lieutenant?' Cecily asked him, seating herself on the stone bench at the centre of the Temple. 'Are you a bold man? Are you honest, virtuous and God-fearing? Or are you an adventurer?'

217

The absence of preliminaries did not worry him; he had felt a tension mounting between them as they rode out that morning and had already guessed that their relationship was reaching a climax of some sort. He had no knowledge in which direction the lofted arrow would fly; ever since they had departed, alone, she had been like a bow being stretched slowly by events.

'I am, I hope, as you would wish me to be, ma'am, since I am in your service.'

'You turn a pretty phrase,' she said. 'I would dearly like to entrust you with a secret, but am mightily afeared . . .'

'I am, ma'am, as much at your service for the guarding of secrets as in all other matters that touch upon your honour.'

She laughed, somewhat roughly. 'A fig for my honour!' she said. 'Can you truly believe a lady of *honour* would shelter beneath a stranger's roof in the absence of his wife and family, were she concerned with *honour*? Can you truly believe a lady of honour would ask a man she met in a tavern to be her chaperon and defender? Can you truly believe that, Richard Aysgill, former associate of Joe Grice and Tod Lackley – aye, and a few others the peace officers have taken?'

'You conned me from the start?' he said, laughing out loud, 'and I deluded myself I had the measure of thee.'

'Very well, Richard Aysgill. What *is* my measure? Am I a Molly Cutpurse? A Moll Flanders? What am I?'

'Th'art an adventuress, for a start. We're two from the same purse, I'll be bound.'

'Aye, I know that. But what's my adventure? What's afoot, as they say in those taverns you frequent?'

'Don't forget I first me *thee* in such a tavern,' he exclaimed angrily.

Cecily patted the bench beside her. 'Don't let us quarrel, Richard. After all, we have a common victim, a rooster ripe for plucking – and, I can promise you, he will yield more flesh beneath those dowdy feathers than you've ever dreamed of. Sir Charles is a well-known miser, who hoards his coin. When we met, Sir Charles had just been to London to see doctors who warned him to avoid exertion of all kinds, though riding is said to be good for him. He hasn't come with us today, nor issued instructions to his groom to accompany us, because when he left me in the early hours of this morning he was incapable of either. Now, Richard, here's the rub. I know where he keeps his store of gold and coin, as well as the jewels bequeathed to him by his father which he is too miserly to permit his wife to wear even to the smart salons of Bath.' Cecily smiled, watching Richard's face. 'What you witnessed in the tavern was no chance encounter. I had planned every last detail of it. There lies the difference between us, my dear. I do nothing on impulse, as you and Joe Grice did. I lay my plans only when I've thoroughly conned the lives of my victims. I read the newspapers to find out which men's wives go where and when, which men are in London, which men are travelling. I mount a campaign against them, and carry off the booty. One a year, two a year – but never hastily, at the end of a pistol. I never lie with a man and cut his purse; I'd rather lie with him a time or two and then cut out his *inheritance*!'

Richard was amazed. He'd never thought of adventuring on such a scale. Of course, given Cecily's beauty, her winning ways, her dramatic abilities, how could it not work? No doubt her horse-riding ability and her skill with the bow were just a part of her self-imposed training and discipline. No doubt her wardrobe, her elegant garb, was all part of it too.

'Where do you live when you're not adventuring?' he asked, but saw at once from her expression she was not yet ready to give him *all* the truth.

'In London, of course,' she said innocently. 'Where else could I gain such information as I require to see a successful conclusion to my efforts?'

'And is Cecily Throwton your true name?'

'Is Richard Aysgill your true name?' she countered.

'It is.'

'Then you are a fool, Richard. I venture only under the protection of a *nom de guerre*, lest one of my victims lay information against me. Though you would be surprised how many men fail to do so! I imagine they are reluctant to confess to their wives that they have shared the family bed with the first beauty who came along. Wives in Bath, or Harrogate, or any other watering spa – they are my protection!' Cecily fell silent, looking intently at him as if to penetrate his thoughts. 'You realize that no one would ever believe this conversation,' she said. 'I have taken care to provide myself with impeccable documentation and could have you transported for a slander should you gossip to anyone about my activities.'

She had revealed herself to him as a hard woman, determined to work her way in all matters. He could only admire her strength and her competence, which far surpassed anything he'd ever imagined possible in a woman. What a partner-in-crime she would make, he told himself. How well the two of them could work together! And if a tumble now and then helped seal a bond between them . . . !

'I'm no lick-spittle gossip,' he said. 'You must know that by now. Tell me what you have in that inscrutable mind of yours, and we'll endeavour to see if we can't the better advantage each other by partnership than by enmity. In such matters we can only succeed by mutual trust. You have mine, Cecily, or whatever your name is – may I not have yours, and your hand on it?' He approached her and held out his hand.

'Kiss me, dear partner,' she said. 'Contracts last longer signed by lips than by hands.'

He flung his arms around her and placed his mouth on hers. She was enchanting, bewitching, sweet-breathed, smooth-cheeked. Her back was straight beneath his hands as he drew her to her feet and hugged her close. She was light as a feather when he picked her up in the temple, carried her across the grass to the tree, and laid her down beneath its whispering foliage.

A full hour passed in scenes of urgent passion, tender administration and sweet culmination before, finally exhausted, they broke apart from the mêlée of intertwined limbs.

'Are we partners now?' he asked.

'Partners? Indeed we are partners,' she said dreamily, 'and I pray our crime may succeed as forcefully as our passions.'

'Amen to that,' Richard said.

'We have but little time for our venture,' Cecily said, as they rode side by side back to the Manor. 'I had hoped to find Sir Charles's hidden wealth long before this, but the old goat proved as stubborn in yielding information as he was persistent in his rutting. Now I have the location of his strong box beneath the floorboards and a carpet, and we can take all tomorrow night. You must go to the coaching house and there hire a fly, which you must conceal in Dolby Wood. We'll lift the box an hour before dawn, head for Dolby Wood afoot, then make our escape.'

'But they will be looking for the fly,' Richard protested. 'It will give us away.'

'I have a scheme for that,' she said. 'I'll inform you of it at the correct time.'

He reined in his horse and stopped. Seeing him behind her, she circled round and came back alongside him.

'What's amiss?' she asked innocently.

'The correct time is now, if you trust me,' he said. 'If you don't trust me the right time will never come and I'll gallop out of your schemes o'er yonder hill.' He'd realized he would have to employ strength if he was not to be bested by this strong-willed woman. If they were to have a partnership, one

221

must take the command. He intended it should be himself, for the rest of this enterprise. 'The fly will give us away,' he repeated. 'News of its location, the direction of its travel, will be known by every peace-officer and constable on the road. We will hire an ostler, pay him good coin to proceed to York as fast as he may, with a promise of more coin if he arrives promptly. We'll give him a piece of paper that we'll say is an urgent message to the Archbishop. We'll tell him that religious dissidents may try to prevent his passage, but he's to stop for no man. That way, the fly will draw the peace-officers from us. We, meanwhile, shall travel quietly as man and wife, with a small matter of disguise, on a varied route that will eventually take us to the Port of London. Provided the wealth we con from Sir Charles is as you say, we can then embark for foreign parts, and spend a few weeks away from the hue and cry. Is all that understood?'

'Bravo!' she exclaimed in admiration. 'I didn't realize I'd partnered a thinker, my dear. It shall be as you say, in every particular.'

That night, Sir Charles drew upon his final reserves of energy, and as Richard watched the candle proceed along the corridor he suffered bitter twinges of jealousy. He resolved that future enterprises they might make together would not include the use of Cecily's loving arms as bait, nor her divine body as the hook.

The following morning, Cecily did not appear for riding, and sent a message to the 'Lieutenant' to explain that she had the vapours, would be staying in bed all day, and would not require his services as chaperon. Would he please be so kind as to go to the coaching house, to enquire if a parcel she was expecting from London had yet arrived? The purse which accompanied the message jingled with coin and the servant gave Richard a knowing wink as he handed it over.

'I'll wager there's plenty more where that came from, eh, Lieutenant?' he suggested with a lascivious leer.

Richard raised his riding crop and slashed it across the servant's face. 'Take that for an impudent churl,' he said, 'to speak thus of a noble lady!'

He mounted the hack he usually rode when he ventured alone, and set out for the coaching house in the village. Hiring the fly was a simple transaction, though he rejected the first one offered as being too weak and insubstantial, with the iron band on one wheel already beginning to slip.

'Who will the fly be for, Master?' the coachman asked. 'Sir Charles Lakeby's guests,' Richard said impatiently.

'There's powerful strange,' the coachman said. 'Sir Charles has two flies for his guests to use, and the family coach to boot.'

'This may be needed in excess of the others,' Richard said placatingly.

'Ah, I thought as Sir Charles had given up having a house full o' guests.'

''Tis naught to you what Sir Charles does or does not do,' Richard said, knowing that if he didn't close the man's mouth he'd be there all day. 'There's a guinea for your trouble. Sir Charles will settle the balance of the account in person.' Richard handed over the coin, seeing in the man's eyes his intention of using it to line his own pocket.

'Very well, Master, if that is how it is to be.' The coachman briskly invited Richard to inspect a second fly. It was satisfactory, and the transaction was complete.

The transport Richard had chosen was little more than a padded bench set between two high wheels, with a leather hood on brackets that could be opened and closed by pushing it to the back of the bench. With a good horse ahead, it would make the journey to York as fast as any other vehicle, and almost as quickly as a man on horseback. He drove the fly to Dolby Wood and hid it securely in the undergrowth. He tethered the horse to the trunk of a stout tree with enough grass growing beneath to keep it happy for the few hours. Then he returned to the village.

His next point of call was at the vicarage, where he asked to speak to the parson privately. The parson had obviously breakfasted late and heavily; the front of his black suit was stained with grease and dotted with pastry crumbs, which he tried unsuccessfully to remove with a cotton handkerchief.

'May I entrust you with a secret, Parson?' Richard asked abruptly.

'I'll have naught to do wi' confessions,' the Parson said, evidently suspecting his visitor might be seeking to trap him into revealing Papist tendencies or High Church ritual.

''Tis naught to do with confessions anyway,' Richard reassured him. 'I'm not at liberty to disclose my identity to you, nor to tell you the correct nature of my appointment. His Grace specifically forbade me to disclose anything of that.'

'His Grace?' The Parson swallowed. 'Of course, I understand . . . In what way can I be of service to you and His Grace?'

'I need a man I can trust,' Richard said. 'He must be a God-fearing Christian, a contented member of your flock, with no digression from the Church along the Papist or the Wesleyan line. He must be able to drive a horse hard. He must be courageous, and loyal to His Grace.'

'I have such a man in mind,' the parson offered. 'I would trust him with my life.'

'Ah, but would you trust him with His Grace's life, against foul plots and villainy?' Richard asked, enjoying himself hugely in his play-acting.

'I would, I most certainly would,' the Parson said.

'Then have him wait for me in the church porch shortly before tomorrow's dawn,' Richard whispered, looking about him that none might overhear.

'May I give him any information as to the nature of his task?' the Parson enquired. He, too, was whispering and looking about him though there was no one within earshot.

'You swear before God you'll reveal this to no other?' Richard demanded fiercely. 'On the Bible—?'

'I am a man of God,' the Parson said, mustering some of his lost dignity, 'and have already sworn on everything I believe holy to preserve the faith in whatever manner the good Lord may decide. No word of what you tell me shall pass my lips.'

'Then tell your man he will be away from home for a short while, and that he is to go to York with a sealed letter. But swear him to silence first. Now, have you got that?' The Parson assented. 'Very well then,' said Richard, 'I will be here before daybreak tomorrow. Remember: reveal this to no one!'

Richard's next task was to send a lad from the ale-house to book two seats on the London coach departing at eight o'clock on the morrow, in the names of Mr and Mrs Farthingale. Though the journey was reserved as far as the London coach terminus, he planned that they should leave the coach at the first stage, from where they would travel west, away from the London Road. Well pleased with the progress of his day's endeavours, he ate a satisfying meal of game pie, mutton chops and a neck of lamb, washed down with two or three tankards of fine porter, then mounted his hack and permitted it to carry him, stuffed with food, drink and great expectations, nodding back to Lakeby Manor.

'I hope your day has been as successful, Lieutenant, as that of the mistress,' said the groom slyly, as Richard toppled off the horse with over-indulgence and fatigue.

Richard was forming a noncommittal response when the groom's words struck him. 'The mistress? A successful day? What do you mean, you churl?'

'Shortly after you disappeared over the horizon, her ladyship descended in a flurry, asked for the Arab stallion to be saddled, and left, heading north.'

'Her ladyship has gone?' Richard asked incredulously, all sign of fatigue vanishing instantly.

'Aye, Lieutenant, she went . . . But she's returned,' the groom added. 'And I've never seen yon Arab in such a lather as when she came back. Lord, she must have galloped him for miles! I were a bit worried, tell the truth, wi' you being absent and Sir Charles being laid up wi' what ails him, and her ladyship leaving on her own. I wanted to ride wi' her, but she'd have none of it and was so vehement in the manner of her refusing that I feared to give offence by insisting. Jamie, the ostler's lad, was telling me only the other day of a fella sleeping rough in the Forty Acre Spinney this last few days and nights.'

'Forty Acre is east, and you said her ladyship went north,' Richard said with a puzzled frown.

'Aye, that's so. Had she started east I'd have risked offence by following close by her wi' a piece in my belt.'

Mystified, Richard went to his quarters to freshen himself after the long ride. Someone had put a wooden tub of water by his chair and he stripped off and washed himself in it, before starting to dress again. He'd stepped into his drawers and was pulling on his vest when suddenly the door swung open and he felt mutton-chop arms embrace him and a hungry wet mouth close on his neck. It was Bessie, the chambermaid.

'I can spend tonight wi' ye!' she cried excitedly. 'Flo's having dreadful pain wi' her womanlies and is to sleep away from us all. I'll be able to slip from my bed when t'others are asleep. Flo allus makes me sleep by the wall and I can never climb over her to get out for fear o' waking her. Just think, we can go at it all night long, if you've a mind!'

Richard had to think quickly. The last thing he and Cecily wanted that night was chambermaids creeping round the corridors when the whole house should be enveloped in the peace and tranquillity of rural slumber.

'All night long, if you've a mind!' Bessie repeated ecstatically.

'I've a mind, my lass,' Richard said hurriedly. 'Nowt would please me more. There's just one thing against us, tonight.' He was trying desperately to think of some excuse that wouldn't arouse her suspicions. 'Today, when I were going into the village to enquire for her ladyship's parcel, I felt the horse hobbling. I stopped and dismounted, thinking it must have a stone in its hoof. It was a bit of stick wi' a sharp end that were pressing into the horse's pad. When I pulled the bit of stick out, the horse must have felt summat, for he kicked back. Right here he got me,' Richard said, exposing his parts. Bessie wasn't to know they were reddened from the vigorous soaping and wash he'd given them in the cold water.

'My, they do look all swollen,' she said, reaching out her hand to stroke and comfort him.

'No,' he said with fear in his voice, 'tha' mustn't touch 'em or I shall be in such agony.'

When Bessie had finally been persuaded to go back to her labours, which were light in the absence of Lady Lakeby and her daughters, Richard settled back on the bed to pass a few hours in grateful slumber, in anticipation of the arduous adventure that lay ahead of him.

'This time tomorrow,' he told himself as he slipped into sleep, 'I shall be a rich man.'

CHAPTER SIX

It was a cold night but there was no moon, only the light of stars. Richard realized that Cecily had even taken the phase of the moon into account in her planning. Truly, with her ingenuity and his courage . . .

She was waiting behind the door that led into the back of the still-room. She slipped her hand in his and he heard the whisper of her clothing as they walked slowly along the corridors of the basement which, at the back of the Manor, was below the ground level of the front. He had seldom been in the Manor House itself; Sir Charles had made it abundantly clear that he didn't want the man he ungraciously called 'the mercenary' within the house. Well, Richard thought, smiling grimly, after this night Sir Charles would never see 'the mercenary' again.

There were three staircases to the upper floors. One was the ceremonial staircase in the centre of the south-facing front; the other two, used by family and servants, were situated in the east and west wings. The room in which Cecily had been living, the principal guestroom suite, stood above the library, the 'tiring room and the Master's sitting room. They walked along the corridor of the first floor, past closed bedroom doors, along the length of floor-covering that deadened the sound of their footsteps, then Cecily led the way into her own room. They stood by the bed, looking down at the pink blob that was the naked body of Sir Charles Lakeby, seventh Baronet Lakeby of Lakeby. He was snoring loudly.

'I gave him laudanum in his port,' Cecily whispered to Richard, 'but he still had ambition enough to cock his leg o'er me. It'll cost him a coin or two when the chambermaid finds him in my bed i' the morn!'

They left the snoring Sir Charles where he was, and walked back along the corridor. The candles had long since guttered out in their sconces and a smell of burnt wax hung in the air. Richard felt a cough starting in his chest and Cecily must have heard him snuffle for she stopped and placed her fingers across his lips, commanding him to silence. A small light of stars gleamed through the front windows which overlooked the Manor courtyard, sufficient for them to see to make progress.

The master bedroom was at the end of the corridor, and occupied the entire corner of the angle with the west wing. The quarters consisted of a morning room, a room containing a tin bath and tiled floors, even a contraption in the corner above a hole down which Sir Charles could relieve himself into a pit dug in the ground below, and a dressing room filled with clothing of all descriptions. However mean Sir Charles might be, he had certainly equipped himself to dress for all occasions; Richard quickly counted thirty pairs of boots of all types standing on wooden boot-trees against one wall, and as many jackets and pairs of breeches of all materials from high-quality buckskin to serviceable worsted broadcloth. An abundance of wigs stood on wig-stands at the back of a long bench above which was a mirror glass; some were short and rounded for riding in the field whilst others, which showed few signs of wear, were long with many curls, doubtless for country balls and rallies. Sir Charles had official duties within the parish and Richard pictured him sitting on the Bench at the Leet Court and Sessions wearing the most elaborate of the confections, with hundreds of tight-bobbed curls itching on his bald head.

Cecily dragged Richard's arm and led him to the side of

the bed. She moved the enormous chamberpot, then bade him roll back the carpet as far as the bedposts. In the centre of the floorspace thus revealed, a ring had been cunningly set beneath a square of wood, almost invisible to the human eye in that light. Cecily removed the piece of wood with a pin from her hair and showed him the ring. Richard inserted two fingers and pulled, and a piece of floorboard lifted beneath his hand. Inside the cavity little could be seen, but neither cared to strike a light that might have attracted unwanted attention. Richard groped around inside the space, a bare fifteen inches deep. Within it he encountered an iron box, which took all his efforts to lift, and a couple of wooden boxes almost as heavy. He hoisted them out one by one and stood them on the carpet.

'Are we to carry these by hand to Dolby Wood, dear partner?' he whispered. 'We would have done better to arrange a pack-mule to carry them – and us.'

She chuckled. 'Come, Richard, you've given me proof already of how strong you are!'

He stripped the sheet from the bed and made a sling with the boxes hanging on each side. When he put the sling around his neck, he could stand upright and support the weight on his shoulders, though he knew the journey to Dolby Wood would be long and arduous carrying such a burden.

'You must leave instanter,' Cecily said. 'I must fetch a small bundle of clothing I have left prepared in my room, and will overtake you on your way to the wood. As I approach you, I will make the sound of a curlew. You will reply in like fashion. Understand?' He nodded, already moving towards the door.

The trek to Dolby Wood was, as Richard had anticipated, long and wearisome, and several times he slipped on the muddy ground and dew-soaked grass. He had barely reached the wood when he heard the curlew call behind him.

With relief, he dropped his burden and hid behind a tree until he could locate and identify his pursuer. He cursed under his breath when he saw the approaching figure of a young boy carrying his bundle on a stick across his shoulder like Dick Whittington, swinging jauntily along as if he had no care in the world.

As the boy neared, he paused, and formed his lips to emit the song of a curlew.

Richard, baffled, returned the signal but remained where he was, hidden in the shadow of the trees. He knew it would not be dawn for an hour; he could hide successfully until it became light, by which time the lad would be well on his way. But how strange that of all sounds to cheer him on his way in this cold pre-dawn he should have chosen the note of the curlew.

'Is that you, Richard?' the lad called as he drew near the tree behind which Richard was hiding. The figure was that of a lad; the voice was that of Cecily!

Richard came, dumbfounded, from behind the tree.

Cecily was laughing at the success of her stratagem and his discomfiture. 'Did you not say "some small manner of disguise"?' she asked. 'Well, will this suit the occasion? They'll be looking for a lady – no one will think to look twice at a lad, will they?'

He slapped his leg in appreciation. 'Cecily,' he said, 'th'art a wonder in all tha' does! I'd ne'er have thought to dress thee as a smooth-faced 'prentice.'

They proceeded together into the wood to where he had parked the fly. She examined it critically. 'You chose well,' she said, 'and now we must quickly away from here. I saddled the Arab and the hack and turned them loose; when the men find them missing from the stable they'll think we are riding them. The first alarm will be for those two horses, which by now are probably halfway towards the Temple of Diana. It will give us yet a few more hours of grace.'

They drove the fly sedately into the village. Entering the

231

staging tavern, Richard announced himself as 'Mr Farthingale' and demanded a room and a bed for the few hours before the departure of the London coach. The servants scarcely glanced at the traveller's 'boy', who helped carry the boxes up the stairs. Richard asked if trunks had arrived for Mrs Farthingale, and was told they had been lodged there from the London coach three days ago.

'Take them to my room,' Richard commanded; then, pinching his 'boy's' shoulder, he said, 'You get up there, you young scamp, and guard them with your life!'

Richard now went out again, driving the fly to the back of the church he had visited the day before. An intense-eyed young man was waiting for him in the deep shadow of the porch. There was no sign of the Parson.

'You've been given your instructions, lad?' Richard asked.

'No, sir, only that perhaps I am to go sharply to York on God's business.'

'Lad, this is it. Mark my words carefully, and don't disclose what you are about to hear even though the Dissenters pour boiling oil on your kneecaps. You're to go to York as quickly as you can. You must stop for nobody, no matter what disguise or ruse they may use to deceive you – some of them, the enemies of the true God, are even dressing these days as soldiers, peace-officers, constables and the like. You are not to change horses, only hide in the woods until your mare has had a chance to blow herself cool again. D'ye understand?'

'Aye, sir,' nodded the young man solemnly. 'I understand. And when I arrive in York?'

'You are to go to the Chapter House, knock on the door, and to the servant who comes say naught but the following words: *I hear tomorrow, by God's Grace, will be a fine day.* Can you commit that to memory, not varying it by one syllable?'

'That I can,' said the young man, and he repeated the message word for word.

'Here's coin for you and your journey,' said Richard. He knew the amount he was giving the young man would more than compensate him for any inconvenience or suffering the voyage might occasion – the damage to his reputation, with the help of the Parson, would be slight. 'Right, lad, away wi' ye – and the Blessings of Our Lord Jesus Christ be wi' ye!' It was the only form of blessing Richard at that moment could recall.

When he returned to the coaching inn Richard went straight upstairs to the room he had hired. There he found Cecily sitting on the chair beside the bed. She had unpicked the hessian sewn around the trunks that had awaited her, one large, and three small.

'Where's the booty?' he asked hungrily, but she raised a finger to her lips.

'Walls have ears, my dear,' she said, 'especially in coaching inns. I'd as soon invite the landlord to share as to open even one box here.'

'I'm aflame wi' impatience,' Richard said, gathering her into his arms. 'Not only for the booty, but for another go at thee!'

'You must wait,' she said, eluding his grasp. 'What would the chambermaid think if she came in here and found you locked in the embraces of a boy? No, wait, my sweet coz. We'll change coaches at the next stage as you proposed; I shall go to our room, bathe and anoint myself with the sweetest perfumes, then lie and await your pleasure.' She pecked his lips. ''Tis a promise, my dear, a promise.' She reached under the bed and produced one small box from which she took a ring. 'These are a few personal baubles I couldn't bear to leave behind,' she said. She put a ring on his finger. 'It's a small token of no value, save that it binds my heart to thine.'

Whoever had made the paste fake had done a marvellous work, Richard thought, as he looked at the enormous diamond set in the centre of matched rubies in a heavy gold setting. He wouldn't have been able to tell it from the real thing.

'All your beautiful clothing?' he asked. 'You left it behind?'

'Aye,' Cecily said firmly. 'I dress myself for each role I play as an actress would stepping on the stage. Fortunately, I have access to a warehouse in Eastcheap where one never asks the origin of the goods. You wouldn't believe the number of fine ladies whose husbands deprive them of money, and who sell items of wardrobe to pay a lover's pleasures!'

He tried again to seize her, to tumble her across the bed, but she thwarted him.

'When we arrive at the next stage,' she said, 'I promise you you will be astounded by the use I shall make of you . . .'

When the London coach arrived, Richard and Cecily climbed into the carriage together. They were running a risk, of course, by not having the 'lad' sit with all the other young folk on the roof.

'He's in delicate health,' Richard explained to their fellow travellers. 'I'm taking him to St Bartholomew's Hospital in London since Dr James's Powders don't seem to do him any good.'

'Aye, he looks a bit pale and sickly to me,' observed a gentleman sitting in the corner of the coach, peering short-sightedly at the 'lad' through his quizzing glass. 'I hope he has naught of an infectious nature?'

'Nay, your lordship, 'tis only to do wi' the circulation of his blood,' Richard said.

'Goose-grease on the soles of the feet works wonders,' offered a grandam sitting in the other corner. 'I've had twelve bairns in my time and treated them all with goose-grease. Not one of them had a day's sickness until he died . . .'

Cecily was able to sit with her head cast down for most of

the way, and even dozed comfortably against Richard's stalwart shoulder. When the coach arrived at the first staging post, she sat still on the seat while all the others disembarked. Then, while the coachmen were caring for the luggage of those who were not proceeding, or who were joining the coach, she drew Richard to one side.

''T'would be better,' she whispered, 'if you stroll through the village until the coach departs. Just before it leaves, I will be able to say you've missed it, that we'll have to wait for the next one, and get them to take off our baggage.'

He winked at her. 'I'll just take a stroll, lad,' he said loudly, 'to stretch my legs. I'll see you anon.'

Richard was in a euphoria of expectancy as he walked around the village, pretending to examine the church's architecture, the trees on the village green, the cottages that surrounded it. He shooed away a gaggle of geese that swirled, cackling, around his legs, patted the rump of a cow being led to its byre for milking, stood still while a flock of sheep bustled past him. In truth, he had no taste for this rural scene, though he pretended delight. He was resolved that once he had taken possession of his share of the booty and had the delicious Cecily on his arm, he'd set himself in style in the city and no more venture abroad – save, perhaps, to the watering spas for the entertainment. Provided the sum they had gained was large enough, he might even talk Cecily out of further schemes, and invest his money in some legal enterprise. He conjured up pictures of himself as an *owner*, a *master*, to whom the workers would touch their forelocks in respect. His imagination didn't stretch so far as to tell him what the workers would be doing when they weren't touching forelocks, but that detail didn't trouble him; Cecily would think of something, he had no doubt.

He took care to be out of sight of the coaching inn when he heard the horn that heralded the coach's departure. He heard it again, more urgently, then it was heard no more. Instead he heard the neighing of the team of horses as they set out on the next stage of the journey, and knew it was safe to return.

To return! To his blessed Cecily who lay, washed, unguented and perfumed in the bed, awaiting his pleasure! And later the division of the spoils!

'Can you show the way to the room my lad has ta'en?' he asked the pot-boy, who was cleaning tables after the coach's departure.

'We've nobbut one room,' the boy said. 'It mun be that. At the top o' yon stairs, then sharp right.'

Richard bounded up the stairs, two at a time, turned right, flung open the door and entered. Sitting on a chair beside the bed was a man he had never seen before. There was no sign of Cecily. The man was wearing a long black top-coat with silver facings, black breeches and black boots to his knees. In his hand he held a cocked pistol.

'Richard Aysgill,' cried the stranger, 'th'art taken!'

Richard whirled round. Another man stood in the open doorway behind him, and he too carried a cocked pistol.

'Tha'd better come quietly,' the second man said, 'else tha'll come wi' a ball in thee!'

They tied his hands behind his back with a leather thong. As the first man was making the knot, he spied the ring on Richard's finger, slipped it off and examined it. His companion took over the knotting while he held the ring to the light of the window where it glittered prodigiously. He whistled.

'Tha' has a good taste in jewellery,' he said.

Now everything fell into place in Richard's mind, and disconnected events took on a pattern. He'd been had for a fool, of that he was quite certain. The man who'd been lurking in Forty Acre Wood must have been Cecily's true, unseen, accomplice. Yesterday morning, while she was supposed to be in bed with the vapours, she had doubtless ridden the Arab to meet him when Richard had been in the village making the arrangements, as she had told him.

As to him walking round the village – her real accomplice had no doubt taken his seat on the coach – she had most probably changed her clothing and reverted to appearing as a woman.

Cecily, Cecily, he thought, his heart grey with sorrow, why did you use me so? Why not venture in trust with me?

The peace officer had ceased his examination of the ring and was now looking at Richard. 'Well, lad,' he said with a smile on his face, 'aren't tha' going to tell us a story? Alf and me, us enjoys the stories as much as the reward!'

Richard said nothing.

'Nay, Richard Aysgill, don't do us out o' our bit o' pleasure,' the second man said. 'Aren't tha' going to say as it's all a mistake, that tha's innocent? Aren't tha' going to plead wi' us that tha' has a missis and bairns to feed, that tha'll make recompense, that tha'll pay the two of us owt to let thee go?'

'Th'art disappointing,' the first man said. 'We heard as tha' were violent. Why we've got the place surrounded wi' peace officers, all armed wi' cudgels – we thought we were going to have a bit o' sport taking thee!'

'I've nowt to say,' Richard said, standing erect and speaking out firmly, though his heart was racing within him. Perhaps if he had not been fortified by his self-rage, by his chagrin at permitting himself to be so easily duped and deluded by a woman he considered to be no more than a high-class doxy, he might have been overcome by fear and unable to vouch for his actions. The penalty for theft was quite clear. He'd be lucky to escape with his head. The least he could hope for was transportation. Mercifully, they'd stopped chopping off people's hands for stealing. 'I'll say nowt,' he said, 'until I'm brought before the right person. You're charged wi' making an arrest, and there's no denying you have the better of me. But I'll not whine to you, nor offer you nowt in the way of violence *or* bribes.'

The peace officer stopped his badinage and his face took

on a more serious mien. 'Tha's a sensible lad,' he said, 'on all counts except thy thievery and flaunting part of thy spoils on thy finger. Us'll be taking thee to Wakefield, where tha'll come before the Magistrate. Tha'd do best to prepare a likely story for thyself, if tha' likes to keep a head on thy shoulders. The last man we took was hanged – but that could have been because he had the misfortune to rob a relative of the Magistrate himself.'

Richard's head was buzzing with contradictions. Could he believe Cecily had laid an information against him? That she had deliberately planted one of Sir Charles's rings on him to provide evidence? If he now told this to the peace officers, they might still be able to stop the coach and apprehend her with the rest of the jewels and coin – and, presumably, her accomplice. Or would it go worse for him if the eloquent Cecily were in the dock by his side? Certainly no magistrate would believe that Cecily, and not he, was the instigator of the plot. What could he say in his own defence if she accused him of being the ruthless leader of the enterprise, the man who'd forced her, against her wishes, to pursue a life of crime? Magistrates were notoriously susceptible to a pretty face telling a convincing tale – might he not make matters worse for himself? His own story was being formed in his mind. It would not save him, that he knew, since the peace officer had found him in possession of stolen property, but it might reduce his sentence from one of hanging to one of transportation.

He spoke not one word in his own defence all the way to Wakefield, nor when he was incarcerated in the gaol awaiting the magistrates' pleasure.

After a week in the cells in the stinking company of cut-purses, highwaymen, house-robbers and footpads, Richard was brought before the court. With no opportunity to wash or to clean his apparel, he knew he looked a scurvy knave at best. The Magistrate's glance fell upon him; he saw the man's face wrinkle with distaste at the spectacle he knew he must present in his soiled clothing, with the dirt of the floor of the cell covering his hands, face and hair.

The peace officer who had arrested him stood in the witness dock and swore his oath on the Bible. The charge was read out – that Richard Aysgill, of unknown address and style, was hereby accused of the theft of a quantity of jewellery and coin from the home and person of Sir Charles Lakeby, of Lakeby Manor. That the accused had been apprehended at the coaching inn at Scoresby, due to information received. That the accused had been discovered in possession of a ring, verified as the property of Sir Charles Lakeby. That the accused had offered no violence. That the accused had volunteered no information.

'Have ye any information to volunteer now?' the Magistrate asked him.

'Yes, sir, I have,' Richard said quietly, trying to speak in his best voice the better to impress the Magistrate. 'I was engaged in the employ of a lady whom I encountered in the company of Sir Charles Lakeby—'

The Magistrate held up his hand to stem the flow of words. 'You are aware,' he said ponderously, 'of the penalty for slander? I hope your statement will not increase the trouble in which you now find yourself.'

Richard fell silent. Was he to be permitted to make *any* statement?

'With my warning in mind,' the Magistrate said, 'pray continue.'

Richard took a deep breath and began again.

'I was engaged by a lady I came to know as the Honourable Cecily Throwton—'

Again the Magistrate interrupted.

'In what capacity was this *engagement*?'

'I was to be her chaperon and bodyguard,' Richard said.

'You mean to tell this court that a lady of quality engaged a lout like you to be her chaperon?' the Magistrate said. 'I find it hard to countenance that any lady of quality would consent to stand within a hundred paces of you.'

''Tis true, sir,' Richard said desperately, realizing that the Court had already been turned against him by the Magistrate's obvious repugnance. 'I carried out my duties faithfully. I escorted the lady on the coach to Scoresby. She paid for my services with the ring I wore on my finger. I never believed it to be a *real* diamond, nor even *real* gold.'

'It is reported,' the Magistrate said, 'that you represented yourself as an Officer of the King. Did you practise this deception in the hope of gain?'

'I did it to preserve the lady's good name!' Richard protested.

A titter ran round the officers of the Court, and someone in the public benches guffawed out loud. The interruption was ignored by the Magistrate, who was reading a rolled paper he held on the desk before him.

'Did you leave Lakeby Manor in the company of this . . . *lady*?' the Magistrate asked quietly.

'Yes, sir.'

'And was *that* to preserve her good name? Sometime before dawn on the morning in question, you left the house by stealth – after robbing the man who had fed and befriended you – to accompany and chaperon this lady?'

'I was following her instructions,' Richard said. 'The lady had engaged my services, not the master of the house.'

'Are you claiming, Richard Aysgill, that this lady, whom you represent to the Court as the Honourable Cecily Throwton, robbed Sir Charles Lakeby *without your know-ledge*, and that you merely followed her instructions as to the time and manner of departure, without wondering why she should choose to leave at such a clandestine hour?'

'I am so claiming,' Richard said, trying to muster the remains of his dignity, despite his appearance, despite his desperate circumstance.

'I find that quite preposterous,' the Magistrate said. 'It is my conviction that you, falsely representing yourself as an

Officer of the King, together with a person unknown representing herself as a lady of quality, conspired to rob Sir Charles Lakeby, your benefactor. I understand that you have stubbornly refused to disclose any information, either about your accomplice and her whereabouts or about the whereabouts of the property stolen from Sir Charles. You are an exceedingly plausible rogue, Richard Aysgill, but this Court is not deceived. It is within my power to sentence you to death for the heinous crime you have committed. Should you choose to repent, and to use your best endeavours to restore the possessions you so basely stole from Sir Charles Lakeby, I could be inclined to leniency. Do you so repent? Will you speak, now, and disclose the whereabouts of your ill-gotten gains?'

'I do, in truth, repent, sir,' Richard said, as convincingly as he could, 'but can say naught of the jewels and coin, since I know not where they are, nor where Cecily Throwton might now be.'

The Magistrate looked at Richard with eyes that could have pierced a barrel's staves. 'You persist in representing yourself as the innocent victim in this matter?' he asked, his voice ominously quiet.

'I do, sir.'

The Magistrate glanced down at the scroll, then looked up again at Richard's earnest face. 'Despite my better judgement, I am inclined to believe there is some truth in what you say, though not all of it,' he said. 'I therefore will not invoke the supreme penalty of death, as is within my power. I sentence you, Richard Aysgill, to be transported for life. We'll see if honest toil in His Majesty's Colony of America will make something of a man of you.' He turned his head to the clerk. 'I will now hear the next case.'

Richard had slumped in the dock. The gaoler seized his arm to drag him away, but Richard straightened himself.

'Thank you, sir, for your mercy,' he said, then turned and, with his head erect, walked from the dock to a life of slavery.

241

CHAPTER SEVEN

Though Dick Oxby and Tam Trenton were only fourteen and fifteen years old respectively, Richard Aysgill found more strength in them than in any of the other condemned villains along the chain which had been shackled to each man and woman's ankle.

All twenty-five of them were lying on the straw-covered floor of a barn, one day's ride from the Port of Liverpool where they would be embarked for America when a boatload had been assembled. They travelled each day in the back of a long waggon; ten of them could ride in the waggon while the remainder took turns to hobble alongside, impeded by the chains which they had to hold in their arms or drape across their shoulders to prevent them dragging. Each man had an individual length of a yard of chain which connected to the main one; the shackles had been cold-forged round their ankles by the blacksmith and, they had been informed, would be removed in America when they were disposed into working gangs. Dick Oxby had been chained in front of Richard, Tam Trenton behind him. The two lads had been taken in Sheffield for stealing a gentleman's watch; only the intervention of the gentleman's wife and their own youthfulness had saved them from the gallows.

They lay side by side in the straw, waiting exhaustedly for sleep. Suddenly they heard a rattle of chains at the far end of the barn, and felt the pull of the main chain along their ankles.

'I don't know where they get the energy,' Dick whispered.

'She were walking half the day, and he were walking t'other half!'

'Once a whore, allus a whore,' Tam whispered back. Then he tugged at Richard's elbow. 'Can tha' keep a secret?'

'Aye,' Richard said, 'if keeping it will advantage me.'

'I'll promise you that,' Tam said. 'They never searched us, so they don't know I've hidden a bar down the leg o' my breeches. It's what Dick and me used for forcing doors at night – Dick has one, too. I've been thinking. If the three of us works together, happen we can break the links of our chains.'

'Let's see it,' Richard said, immediately excited. The metal bar was about twelve inches long and half an inch wide, with a blade at one end and a point at the other. 'Why didn't you speak about this before?' he demanded, testing its strength between his thick hands as Dick produced his bar too. The bar didn't bend; it must have been made, he thought, from one of the new steels he'd heard about.

'I wanted to get well away from Sheffield,' Tam said. 'My face is too well known in them parts, and wi' a shackle already round my ankle I'd ne'er stand a chance.'

Richard had already inserted the bar in a link of Tam's chain. 'Lean over,' he whispered to Dick, 'and stick the point of your bar through the next link to mine, That's it. Now, the two of you grab this one – that's right – and twist against me.'

They did as he bid them, and the link of the chain began to twist under the immense pressure they were able to bring to bear with the aid of the bar.

Richard glanced covertly along the line. Only one of the three guards was on duty, and he was looking the other way. Most of the other prisoners were already sleeping with exhaustion; only at the end of the line could he see the rhythmic movement of buttocks, and knew they'd have no interference from that quarter.

'Now twist it back,' he whispered. 'We'll have to work it

243

backwards and forwards – we'll never do it wi' one twist.'

It took only a few minutes of twisting to and fro before the iron of the chain grew fatigued, and finally snapped. Richard was free! With increased enthusiasm they renewed their efforts, prising the links apart. Twenty minutes later, Richard and Dick were free from the main chain, too, though each still had about a foot of chain dangling from the shackle clamped firmly to his ankle – a heavy bracelet three inches wide and a quarter of an inch thick.

Their boots had been removed when the shackles were fitted, and their feet were now raw and bleeding with cuts.

'We'll need to tie the rest of the chain around our legs,' Tam said, 'until we can get somewhere safe.'

Richard didn't reply; he was busy scouting a way out of the barn.

The end of the chain had been passed round a post set in the ground, and the guard was lying on the other side of the post, on a pallet set above the ground where he could look over the entire scene. At that moment, he appeared to be watching the activities of the man and woman at the end of the line, leaning over the edge of his pallet and leering down upon them. Each of the three guards had pleasured himself with the woman several times along the way and she, no doubt counting on future favours from them, had made no objections. Certainly she had fared well in the distribution of the daily food, usually getting a knuckle and a handful of meat from the evening stew while the rest of them made do with the vegetables, oats and stock. No one had begrudged the woman her extra portions; all realized that by pleasuring the guards she was making things easier for the rest of them, since the guards seldom harried them by using the heavy whip.

If only the guard would choose this night to pleasure himself, Richard thought. A lamp carrying candles had been set on top of the post. Some of the candles were low and already guttering.

'We'll have to wait,' Richard said, 'to see if the guard replaces the candles.'

The waiting was agony for each of them; they bound the chains round their legs with strips of cloth torn gently from their clothes, afraid the rending noise would alert the guard. Fortunately, he'd settled back on his pallet – he was either asleep or gazing up into the wooden rafters of the barn, festooned with hay dust which clung to the giant cobwebs. The candles burned lower and lower, until just the one was left. Its last feeble glimmer seemed to persist for hours.

A cow in the stall at the end of the barn mooed softly, but the guard didn't move. Richard jangled the cut end of the chain and still the guard didn't move.

'He's asleep,' Tam whispered. 'Let's go now rather than wait. The minute it's dark, he'll be more alert.'

There was sense in what the lad said. Tam flopped over and started to squirm on his belly. The rustling noise he made sounded like thunder to the other two. Richard tapped his back to indicate he should get up on all fours, like a dog. Crouched in this position, the three of them made their way out of the straw on to the firm stones along the centre of the barn. It meant crawling through animal piss and dung, but at least their progress was silenced.

The door at the far end of the barn, by the cow stalls, was part open; they slipped easily through it and into the field behind the farm which had been chosen as a way-station for convicts being taken to Liverpool. They made for the nearest hedge and ran along in its shelter, running and running until they were breathless, then flopped together in the corner of a wood some two miles from the farm.

'Now,' Richard said, 'all we need is an honest blacksmith.'

'Don't you mean a *dis*honest one?' Dick laughed.

'Nay, an honest one as doesn't agree wi' transportation of human beings in chains. A dishonest one could sell us for five pounds each to the peace officers – aye, and win a special dispensation for his own crimes,' said Richard grimly.

As they rested, the dawn began to appear over the wood in which they lay. The night had been cold and there had been but little chance of sleeping, but not one of the three of them minded that. They were free!

The first rays of light stole among the trees until the edge of the world before them was illuminated by a brilliant aureole. It was, somehow, a symbol of their new freedom, their new life.

'Aye, do you know what today is?' Dick said, after counting on his fingers.

The others shook their heads; the passage of the days they'd spent in captivity had meant little to them.

''Tis New Year's Day!' Dick said joyfully.

He was right. It was New Year's Day 1775.

Part Three

CHAPTER ONE

The funeral procession wound its way slowly up the hill, Stanley and Claude Ottershaw walking in front of the coffin, with Arthur Aysgill, son of Simon, and Frank Aysgill, son of Matthew, walking behind it. Following Arthur came Amelia and Sally, while Matthew and Mildred walked behind their son Frank, holding the hand of his son Keith. To the surprise of everyone, Peter Aysgill was there too, with his sons Gavin and Robert, though they followed the rest of the family at a distance.

No one knew why Dodie had died; each had his own theory, his own belief.

Matthew believed it was the will of God, and therefore unquestionable. Mildred believed that, once she had established her first-born son in his own factory, admittedly with financial help from Peter, Dodie had had nothing else to live for. Dodie had dedicated herself to one proposition: that her sons would have a chance to better themselves. Claude, they all knew, would never do so; but Stanley, with his own factory, would certainly succeed. Jennifer, her head filled with romantic visions of the afterlife, believed that her mother, quite simply, had gone to join her husband Mark in Heavenly Bliss. Being an engineer, Stanley used the same principles in measuring human action and reaction as he would in gauging metal; he knew his mother had worn herself out, had died, as metal will die, of fatigue.

Titus Waverley was standing by the grave-plot behind the

church; tears ran down his face as he saw the simple wooden coffin approach up the small hill that led to the cemetery. Though Dodie had never acknowledged it, Titus had been the only man who loved her purely for herself. Mark Ottershaw had wanted a wife when she had wanted a husband; their marriage had never been more than convenient. Titus, while beginning the relationship because of his lust for her body, had come to learn to love Dodie for her human values: her indomitable courage, her unfailing loyalty to her family, her constant questing for knowledge, her perpetual good humour. None of them knew that he had contrived to meet Dodie at least once each two weeks since her husband died, to plead with her to marry him. Constantly, and he knew not why, she had refused.

'I loved your mother,' Titus told Stanley when the interment was completed, the coffin had been covered, and the mourners were walking away through the cold February day. 'She was a fine woman.'

'I know you loved her,' Stanley said, proffering his hand to his old tutor, 'and I believe she loved you in like manner. I pray you and I will always be friends, not master and pupil.'

'I hope we shall be,' Titus said, as he turned his head to avoid revealing his tears and walked away down the hillside.

'Hello, cousin Stanley,' Gavin said, dutifully offering his condolences.

'Hello, cousin Gavin,' Stanley said, 'and cousin Robert.' He shook hands with them both.

Peter was standing behind them. 'Your mother was a wonderful woman,' he said to Stanley. 'In many ways, the best of the Aysgill family! You owe everything you are to her, you know. Don't tarnish her dreams of what you might one day become.'

'I shall not, Uncle Peter, you may rely upon that,' Stanley said.

Peter spoke to no one else, and none spoke to him as he

gathered his two sons to his side and walked away rapidly down the hill. He'd come to honour Dodie from his respect for her – that respect didn't extend to any other member of the family.

Slowly the others made their way down the hill and back to the Ottershaws' house. Jennifer had made a bit of a spread for her mother's funeral with pasties, ham, pies, soup, and cooked vegetables. Claude had sufficiently stirred his lazy self to go to the ale-house for jugs of beer, though there was a shortage of beakers and mugs from which to drink it.

Stanley, carrying out his filial duties as master of ceremonies, made a short speech about his mother.

'I'm not one for talking much,' he said, 'but I'd like to say thank you to everybody who's come, even though some didn't come to eat afterwards, but never mind that. No offence meant, nor taken. My mother, our mother, your sister, your auntie – whichever is right – was a noble woman who spent all her life in the service of her family and her husband. There can't be nowt better than that in life, I reckon, so I don't need to say owt else, do I?'

He sat down, picked up a pie and started to eat, indicating to the others that they should do so too. After a while he noticed that Matthew, his son Frank and Frank's wife Sylvia were sitting in the corner of the room having what appeared to be a quiet but heated argument. Stanley stood up and walked across to them.

'Nay, our Frank,' he said, 'aren't tha' going to have summat to eat and sup?'

'I will, when she gives over and lets me,' Frank said.

'Nay, cousin Stanley,' Sylvia said, 'what do you think? Matthew's been blacklisted from work on account of his union agitation, and now Frank wants to take up where Matthew left off! Afore we know where we are, Mildred and me will have both of them out of work, neither capable of earning a penny piece. And what shall we live on then, eh?

Matthew says the Good Lord will provide – but I reckon that these days He's too busy to bother wi' the likes of us!'

'Tha' moan't blaspheme,' Matthew said weakly.

It had taken Jabez Broadley, the mineowner, only a week or two to discover what Matthew Aysgill was doing. Thanks to his many informers, he learned about the secret meetings at which Matthew urged the men to band together, to force Broadley into repairing the mine machinery. Everyone knew that Broadley ran the mine at the lowest cost consistent with pulling out the maximum of coal, but none dared face up to him. Any man who'd done so in the past had been beaten into insensibility by the mineowner's bully, Tarn Fowles, a vigorous brute of a man despite his increasing years. They had the constant reminder of Job Bentley before them; Job had been one of Tarn's victims and now was barely fit to maintain the pumping engine. Some said that Broadley only kept Job on as a constant reminder to the others of what could happen to them if they dared to voice their protests.

Now that Broadley had taken on George Alverthorpe as mine manager, he himself attended less and less often. Alverthorpe was mortally afraid of Broadley and would do nothing to offend his master. He was a mouthpiece, no more.

Within a month of returning to work in the mine, Matthew had persuaded the rest of the workers to agree to concerted action. The final straw was when a woman in the last stages of pregnancy had collapsed in one of the distant tunnels; she had lain for an hour in the stream of water – water that the pump was too weak, too poorly maintained, to remove. On being brought to the surface it was discovered that she was dead.

George Alverthorpe had argued with them for days, while, to give him a fair chance to approach the master, the miners continued to work. When they'd seen no action for five consecutive days, they refused en masse to go down the shaft, even blocked the shaft to prevent any who might be weak-

willed from descending. This had brought Jabez Broadley
fuming to the mine, at the head of twenty or more men he'd
hastily recruited, including a Peace Officer, a Constable and,
for good measure, a Bailiff. The Peace Officer had looked at
the determined faces of the hundred and fifty miners, had
looked back at his band of twenty men, and had hastily
withdrawn, taking the Constable and the Bailiff with him.
Civil disturbance, he quickly explained, was a matter for a
detachment of soldiers, not his puny band of men.

On that occasion, Jabez Broadley had backed down; he
had ordered the pump to be completely repaired, with one of
the new barrels that, being milled to a finer accuracy, had
greatly increased efficiency. The work had cost him three
hundred pounds, money he bitterly resented having to spend,
so he docked a coin from each man's earnings to pay it. The
men turned on Matthew in their ingratitude, and that fact,
too, was reported to Broadley.

At last Broadley had seen a way he could discredit
Matthew, since the workers would not understand, and
certainly would not agree, if Matthew's innovations cost them
money. He therefore engaged a doctor and a nurse, who
attended the mine daily and sat in a room he put at their
disposal, awaiting patients. Anyone who went to them with
anything other than a specific mine-caused injury would be
sent to the Free Hospital, a walk of over seven miles.
Broadley deducted twopence from each man's pay for the
doctor, a penny for the nurse.

'You see how generous I am being, Matthew Aysgill,' he
said, 'to provide at your request all these new things you
require! If you need anything else, don't hesitate to ask
me . . .'

'Us can't afford nowt else,' one of the miners growled. 'Us is
already spending fivepence a week on luxuries us could do
well wi'out.'

Feeling had quickly mounted against Matthew. He had

253

become powerless, and would remain so as long as Jabez Broadley bested him.

One of the traditional methods of paying for the coal involved each man reckoning up how many skips he cut from the face, how many skips he dragged to the assembly post. The women and children tallied how many they dragged. Each skip was paid at a fixed agreed wage, or was supposed to be. That wage was never paid in full, since a tally was kept at the mine-head of the amount of shale and rock picked from the actual coal before it was despatched, and the skip-rate was reduced accordingly. It was a simple matter for Broadley to bully a few of the men into deliberate inefficiency when separating coal from shale and rock, so that this would force down the price per skip. The other men knew nothing of this; they knew only that they were working as hard as ever, taking out as many skips as usual – if not more, now that the pump was working properly – yet their weekly wage was diminishing rapidly. On top of that, they now had what they called in derision 'Matthew's Mite' as a further deduction.

Matthew set his bow at the wrong target. He demanded that the men be paid one hundred per cent as the skip rate. If a man hewed fifty skips from the coalface, he should receive the pay for fifty full skips, with no percentage deduction for shale. Of course the men were wildly enthusiastic at first. It would immediately increase their money by ten or twelve per cent. Matthew called a vote and they agreed to stay at the mine top the following morning to press their claim. That day, Broadley's toadies were active, filling their skips with pure shale and rocks, throwing only a few cobs of coal on the top to escape detection.

The following morning, George Alverthorpe took the meeting, though they knew that Broadley had arrived early and was sitting in the office. Alverthorpe listened to Matthew's argument with great politeness and no sign of dissension.

'We cannot always discern in the dim light underground which is shale or rock, and which is coal,' Matthew pleaded, his voice now much practised since his travels as a Wesleyan preacher.

Many of the men were embarrassed by the tone he took, by the too-easy fluency of what he was saying, as if he were lecturing to a small child instead of a man qualified as a mine manager and engineer.

'We try our best to separate shale from coal, rock from coal, but, in all conscience, we cannot guarantee to be successful all the time,' Matthew went on, feeling the full flow of rhetoric. 'Since an equivalent amount of labour is required, irrespective of the contents of each skip, we ask only that we receive God's just reward for our labours, for our toil, for the sweat of our honest brows.'

'Just let him talk,' Broadley had told George Alverthorpe, 'and he'll hang hisself, mark my words.'

When Alverthorpe could see the men were shuffling their feet restlessly, he held up his hand to stem the flow. 'Yes, Mr Aysgill,' he said, 'I quite agree with what you've said. But may I ask one or two questions, if only for my own information. When did you announce that you intended to place this matter before the mine management? Yesterday morning?'

'Yes, we came to agreement when we first went down to the lower level,' Matthew said.

'So, for the whole of a working day the men have known that you intended to ask for the same amount of pay, no matter what was brought from the mine?'

'Yes, I suppose so,' Matthew agreed, mystified by Alverthorpe's line of questioning.

'And you believe, you all believe, that to be entirely correct and fair?'

'Yes, we do, we all do. The Lord has united us all in his wisdom,' pronounced Matthew.

255

'Well, Mr Aysgill,' smiled Alverthorpe thinly, 'I don't know too much about what the Lord does, since I have to run a mine. All I would ask of you is to come over here and examine yesterday's production. This is what comes from the mine when you all suppose that you'll be paid your coin, even though you drive the Master to ruin.'

They walked across to the mound of coal that had been collected the previous day, and surged around it; George Alverthorpe sent the pickers into the mound and they began to separate the rock, stone, clay and shale from the genuine saleable coal, throwing each towards a separate pile.

The pile of true coal grew at a much slower rate than the pile of waste.

When half the mound had been separated George called off the pickers, went to stand by the pile of waste and indicated it with his hand. 'Is it fair and just,' he asked, 'is it the wisdom of the Lord, that the Master be ruined by losing more than half of his production each day – just because you do not separate the coal properly before you drag it all the way to the surface? Nay, Mr Aysgill, decent men will have none of *that* wisdom, I'll be bound!'

Alverthorpe looked round the faces of all the miners. None would meet his eye. All were experienced enough to know that such a pile of waste should never be brought to the surface, and never would have been if the men below were working conscientiously. All knew instinctively that this new demand they were making was outrageous and they felt in some way demeaned by it. Furthermore, the actual sight of the wastage started a dispute between those engaged solely in bringing the coal out of the mine, and those working at the coalface, who bore the sole responsibility for what went into the skips.

'If you lot took more care,' one of the women draggers shouted, 'us wouldn't have our pay docked so much!'

Her cry was immediately taken up on all sides, with the

women mostly blaming the men and the men unable to defend themselves. Soon they'd gathered together in a mob, glad to move away from the pile of so much wastage.

Alverthorpe found himself standing beside Matthew as they listened to the heated arguments all around them. 'I'm afraid you've lost the command and the respect of your disciples, Mr Aysgill,' he said, entirely without malice, without gloating. 'I reckon your usefulness in this mine is over, for you, for the workers, and for the management. I reckon you'd best sign off, and look for fame and fortune elsewhere.'

'Are you ending my employment?' Matthew asked bitterly.

'I think you've ended it yourself,' George Alverthorpe said mildly.

Stanley had already heard the story of his uncle's dismissal, but now he heard it again in the passionate words of Sylvia, Matthew's daughter-in-law. Matthew Aysgill would never be employed again by any mine or mill master. He'd been labelled a dissident, an agitator, and no one wanted such a man in his place of business.

'Now my Frank wants to go the same road!' Sylvia cried angrily. 'He wants to follow in his father's footsteps, to try to *organize* the men, to make them band together. What do you think, Stanley?'

'It's no good asking cousin Stanley what he thinks,' Frank said bitterly. 'He's on t'other side o't fence.'

Stanley's little factory now had five employees, so Stanley was a master, albeit in a small way as yet. 'I reckon as men should be able to talk over their grievances with the master,' he said. 'But I don't relish all the violence that's being unleashed these days in the industrial cause.'

'*Of course* you wouldn't,' Frank said. 'Violence means loss of profit for you, less of a chance to screw the most you can out of them as works for you, while giving 'em the least you can.'

Stanley would not be provoked. On the few occasions the members of their families met together these days, the conversations were always dominated by Frank, who'd taken on all Matthew's evangelistic fervour with none of his mildness, none of his human charity. Stanley reckoned his cousin Frank was a pompous tub-thumper who relished the sound of his own voice, a browbeater who'd brook no opposition to his own bombastic views. He'd tried discussing matters with Frank in the past, but had failed to get his cousin to accept that an objective view is sometimes required.

'I do the best I can,' Stanley said. 'I pay my men good wages. They're all indentured to me, so they can be sure of employment.'

'So you can bind 'em in slavery,' Frank sneered.

'I wouldn't know about slavery,' Stanley said. 'It was by their request that I indentured them.'

'Damned fools don't know they're being bound,' Frank said, 'but that's because they haven't all been given the advantage of your education.' It was a sore point with Frank that his Ottershaw cousins had attended school, while he'd had to pick up all his knowledge at nights, by the weak light of a candle. He'd been working down the mine when Stanley had been conning his books. Now, seven years older than Stanley, he knew he'd never outpace him. Stanley would always be richer, better educated, more successful than Frank could ever hope to be.

'It seems to me, cousin Frank, that we've had this discussion before,' Stanley said. 'Now, if you'll excuse me, I have to go see to the rest of the family. I don't think our mam would want any disputes at her funeral, somehow.'

'Th'art right, cousin,' Frank said, suddenly contrite. 'We mun respect your mam.'

'That doesn't answer my question of what we're going to do if and when, as surely must happen, you lose your job,' Sylvia persisted.

Frank's answer was simple and forceful. He smashed the

back of his hand across her face. 'Shut thy gob, woman!' he said. 'Speak when tha's spoken to!'

And that's the man who says he wants freedom for all, Stanley thought, as he crossed the room to pick up a plate of meats to hand around to Dodie's mourners.

Now that Dodie was dead, much thought was given to the future of her daughter Jennifer, since it would not be fitting for a single unattached girl to live on her own, even though she was keeping house for her two brothers. Mildred and Matthew invited Jennifer to come to live with them, but Frank objected, asking why they should take into their already overcrowded accommodation a young lass who'd been brought up beyond her station, with fancy ideas of dress and manners.

Jennifer, however, had no intention of going to live anywhere else. The house that Dodie had found for them was in a respectable, middle-class neighbourhood. A tradesman lived on one side of them, a journeyman on the other, and several carriages were kept in the street. And, best of all, Jennifer was frequently invited to the home of Mrs Tester on the corner of the street. Mrs Tester's husband was a retired merchant, quite well connected in the city. He kept a coach and pair in his stables and welcomed the sight of the pretty girl who, at twenty-two, would surely have been married had she met the right person.

'I'm a-waiting, Mr Tester,' Jennifer would say brightly. 'Someone as handsome as you, and as perfect a gentleman, must surely come along!'

Once shortly after Dodie's death, Mrs Tester had invited Jennifer to live with them. Jennifer had been tempted, since Mr and Mrs Tester had become like father and mother to her, but she felt a duty to look after the house for her two brothers. Claude had never developed his career and was still content to be in the solicitor's employment, performing the identical job he'd held since he went there. The seeds of education

Titus Waverley had planted within him had withered and died without bearing any fruit. He had no ambitions of any kind, other than to do his job, then spend his evenings in the corner of a tavern or ale-house with a single drink lasting him until it was time to come home to his bed. He never gave offence to anyone, hated no one, nor loved anyone enough to call him friend. And Stanley was rarely seen in the house except when he came home to sleep. Starting his own enterprise demanded all his waking time, since he was determined to make a success of it and already had patented a couple of small items which, he hoped, would bring in regular income. So Jennifer would have spent much of her time alone, had it not been for the friendship of Mr and Mrs Tester.

From time to time the Testers asked Jennifer to their small dinner parties, and sometimes for afternoon tea parties – a practice that was becoming very fashionable among middle-class people and gentry alike. It was at a tea-party that Jennifer had first encountered Sir Arthur Brearley, though the manner of their first meeting was not propitious, since Jennifer accidentally poured a cup of scalding tea over his waistcoat and breeches.

Sir Arthur, recently widowed, had heard of Mrs Tester's 'salon', and had determined to attend a tea-party in the hope of finding a lady fitting to replace his dear departed. He had come with a clear picture of the lady he hoped to find. She should be about thirty years of age, five years younger than himself. She should be of independent wealth, though not necessarily as wealthy as himself. She should be a widow and thus accustomed to a man's ways – he had no patience to take on an inexperienced spinster, he told himself. He hoped the lady would still be of a breeding age, for his wife, always delicate, had not been able to give him issue, and he would dearly like an heir. Sir Arthur's money derived from land, of which he owned fifty thousand acres in the region of Huddersfield yielding him a goodly income. In addition, as Mrs Tester eventually told Jennifer, he possessed a personal fortune of some twenty-five thousand pounds.

After Sir Arthur had left to change his tea-soaked clothing, Mrs Tester and Jennifer sat side by side discussing him. When Jennifer heard the catalogue of Sir Arthur's requirements, her heart sank. From the first moment of seeing him, realizing his intentions, she had determined to set her cap at him. If only she hadn't stumbled over the edge of the woollen rug, she told herself bitterly. If only she hadn't been carrying a full cup of scalding tea. If only . . . The list seemed endless as she lay on her bed that night.

The following week, Sir Arthur came again to tea but gave Jennifer a wintry cautious smile and kept a distance between them. She looked covertly across the room at him, engaged in animated conversation with two ladies who hung on his every word. Both, Jennifer knew, were widows, both were in the age span in which Sir Arthur was interested, and both had independent incomes. She could cheerfully have thrown boiling tea over both of them. When she turned her head away, blushing at the extravagance of her thoughts, she found Mrs Tester looking at her. Mrs Tester leaned forward, patted the cushion on the chair beside hers. Jennifer went to sit with her, took a proffered cake and nibbled at it.

'They wash out a barrel with strong spirits,' Mrs Tester said innocently, 'before they put the delicate wine in it – had you heard that, Jennifer?'

'No, I hadn't,' Jennifer replied, wondering what on earth she meant.

''Tis true. They wash it out wi' spirits.'

'And what do they do with the spirits, pray?' Jennifer asked politely.

'They save them and use them for washing out the next barrel!' Mrs Tester chuckled wickedly, watching the girl's eyes stray across the room. 'Them two as you have your eyes on have scoured out many a barrel this last year or two. Many a barrel that's now sweetly contented with delicate wine . . .'

Understanding dawned on Jennifer's face. 'You could turn

a girl's head with your talk, Mrs Tester,' she said, blushing.

'Not if the girl had her head screwed on right, and were not impatient. Have you read *Julius Caesar*, lass?'

'No, Mrs Tester.'

'Then you ought. You must borrow the copy in Mr Tester's library. "*There's a tide in the affairs of men which, taken at the flood, leads on to fortune.*" Yon's not yet at the flood – he's running this way and that like a neap-tide i' the wane o' the moon!'

'It would be too tempting to believe you, Mrs Tester.' Jennifer raised her cup to her lips and sipped delicately. Over its rim, she saw Sir Arthur looking directly across the room at her, despite the animation of the two ladies sitting with him. She held his gaze for a moment, and he smiled at her, as if to forgive her the scalding tea. She lowered her eyes chastely, the picture of him clearly imprinted within her head. My, he was *handsome*, especially when he smiled. No wonder the two ladies had set their caps at him, doubtless fighting each other with all the feminine subtlety at their command.

'Mark him well, Jennifer,' Mrs Tester was whispering in her ear, like the voice of temptation. 'Mark him well. One day, if you've a mind to it, yon Squire will be on his knee before you, a-pleading to be your husband!'

CHAPTER TWO

Mr Tomlinson of Sleightholme's Mill was accepted into the Leeds Guild of Weavers in August 1775, after a lifetime spent producing cloth. He had been sponsored by Sleightholme himself, who'd been in the Guild for thirty years or more. Now that Sleightholme had reached seventy-five years of age, he wanted to see a Guild man at the helm of Sleightholme's, knowing that he himself couldn't continue much longer. It had been the greatest sadness of his life that the only son he had sired, along with the twelve daughters who'd come each year with dreadful regularity, had died six months after he was born. There were sons aplenty among the partners, but he'd had a lust to pass the mill along one line of succession. He didn't like any of the progeny of the other partners; they'd all been brought up to the monied life and none showed the slightest interest in working the mill, the source of much of their present-day prosperity. All seemed more interested in manipulating the new money markets which had opened to all with venture capital; a number of prosperous banks had opened in Leeds which successfully managed speculations in Government loans, in the finances of the Bank of England which had been responsible for sorting out the financial mess that had followed the South Sea Bubble all those years ago. A number of insurance companies had also opened branches in Leeds itself, and insurance was becoming big business, with banks and speculators combining to form what they were calling 'syndicates'.

Sleightholme himself, thanks to good advice from his own

banker, Peter Aysgill of Aysgills – the largest bank in the city of Leeds by this time – had spread his funds across a variety of interests. In truth, he seldom knew where his money was at any one time. He trusted Aysgill completely. Of course Aysgill was a parvenu, but since he sought acceptance in social circles, he was careful to remain the very acme of respectability. Sleightholme knew he could retire at any time and still have more than enough to launch each of the four daughters who remained alive; his oldest girl was already engaged and dowered in the sum of five thousand pounds to a man who'd come into twenty thousand acres when his father died.

Sleightholme took Tomlinson into his office after the Guild meeting, sat him down, and gave him a glass of hollands. The strong spirit stung Tomlinson's throat – he'd never been a drinking man but lately had started to take a glass each morn and night to soothe the ague in his bones.

'Beg pardon, Master,' he said, as the coughing overtook him.

'You're getting old, Tomlinson,' Sleightholme said, 'as I am myself.'

'Aye, Master, I reckon I am.'

'When was the last time you climbed to't fulling press?'

'I haven't been there for a week or two,' Tomlinson confessed. He knew the question was asked without malice or reprimand. 'Arthur is my eyes and ears up there,' he said, 'and I make my judgements on what is achieved. He's got them working a sight faster than ever I could, to judge by what comes down.'

Sleightholme thought for a long time while he and Tomlinson sat in companionable silence. Finally, he shuffled the papers on his desk as a preliminary to what he was going to say. 'You know that young Ottershaw has perfected a spinning jenny since he left Jonas Clegg and set up on his own?'

'I had heard,' nodded Tomlinson.

'I went yesterday to see it operating in Barton's. It works a fair treat. I'm thinking to place an order wi' him for six – pull out the old ones and put in Ottershaw's new ones. I like the way Stanley Ottershaw does things.'

'If you think so, Master.'

'There's only one thing,' mused Sleightholme. 'I understand there's a bit of trouble over patents. You know Kay's had a lot of trouble wi' his flying shuttle?'

'Everybody had them, Master, and nobody pays royalties.'

'It could be the same thing wi' Hargreaves and his jenny. Ottershaw was telling me he's patented a few of the improvements he's installed in his jenny, but he'll never be able to patent the machine itself. That'll go to Hargreaves, I'll be bound – there's a Commission sitting on it right now.'

'Us'll have to be careful we don't get caught between the two if we buy them.'

'I reckon it's worth the risk. But there's something else that worries me, Tomlinson. One man can handle the jenny wi' only a lad or two to help him. Happen a woman could handle it even. Wi' sixteen, thirty-two, mebbe forty-eight spindles, as Ottershaw has promised, we'll be able to cut down on the labour force. The hundred or so folks we have spinning for us will no longer be needed. Us'll have to get rid of them.'

'We mun move wi' the times, Master,' agreed Tomlinson sadly, 'but there's work a plenty in other occupations.'

'Now that we're embroiled in a war in America, there'll be a great need for cloth, if only to clothe the soldiers. I'd hate to see all that lost to us by not moving wi' the times. I think we'll have to do it, Tomlinson; we'll have to put in Ottershaw's jenny, and get rid of our workers.'

'Then we shall do it, Master.'

Sleightholme was now looking directly at him. 'There's a new spirit abroad, Tomlinson. There's a great unrest at the arrival of all these new machines. Folks are talking back to their masters, even threatening them. The Wesleyans are everywhere as big a threat to stability as were the Jacobites in their time. I'm worried, Tomlinson, and have to ask you a straight question for a straight answer. Your Arthur Aysgill has liberal thoughts. I know, though I've never talked wi' thee about it, that he can be very lenient wi' some of the workers. I've heard tell he even lets some of them sit down to work!'

'Aye, I cannot deny that he does have free-thinking tendencies,' admitted Tomlinson. 'I had occasion to talk to him a couple of years back when we indentured him. I thought that he'd improved his ways.'

'It's not my way,' Sleightholme said, 'to talk behind a man's back, as I hope you know, Tomlinson.'

Tomlinson did know. All his working life he'd known Sleightholme for a hard taskmaster – there was none harder – but a fair man in all his dealings. He had a will of iron, and God help the man who crossed him, but his principles were fair, even though rigid.

'Aye, Master,' he said, 'I know.'

'Then you'd better know about your protégé. If anything, he becomes more lenient as time goes by. He lends or gives money to all and sundry. He lets other workers help those who are sick, to the detriment of their own production. And here's another matter. It ill behoves me to speak of a man's private life, but since Arthur Aysgill married and went to live in his new house, he rarely goes home of an evening when his work is done. He goes to the ale-house, sits there and drinks himself into a stupor before he staggers home to bed.'

Tomlinson's heart sank. He'd seen Arthur a time or two in the mornings arriving late and the worse for his previous night's drink. Sometimes, he thought, Arthur looked as if he hadn't been home at all and stank as if he'd come straight from the ale-house or a whore's bed. But he hadn't realized that Sleightholme knew about this.

'His father was the same,' Tomlinson said gravely. 'I had to stop his employ when he became incapable through drinking.'

'It's the curse of the modern generation,' Sleightholme

said, his lips compressing tightly as if to prevent any of the
damned liquid passing them; he couldn't abide a man who
drank to excess. He shuffled his papers uneasily; he knew
Arthur had been Tomlinson's favourite, and he respected
Tomlinson's opinion in all matters save this one. 'I don't
believe Aysgill will be strong enough to carry out the changes
we must make if we are to stay ahead of the new times,
Tomlinson,' he said. 'There's going to be unrest when we get
rid of over a hundred spinners. Dammit, one of them is
Aysgill's own mother, if I remember correctly.'

Tomlinson nodded, not trusting himself to speak since he
knew what was to come.

'I must ask you straightways,' Sleightholme finally said.
'Can you *guarantee* that Aysgill is man enough for it?'

Tomlinson could not and would not lie. He'd watched
Arthur's deterioration which seemed to have been accelerated
by his marriage. He'd seen his failures about the Mill, usually
in time to correct them. He remembered the lengths of cloth
that had gone to the croppers as goods to be finished, and the
croppers had sent them back – so poorly woven, with many
unjointed ends and coarse crude knots, that the croppers
knew they'd be blamed for ruining the piece when they tried
to shear it. On each occasion Arthur, contrite, had promised
to be more careful in his supervision. Tomlinson knew that
many of the weavers were being lazy because they knew they
would escape unchecked. Now that the flying shuttles were
speeding up cloth production, the need for supervision was
greater than ever. Each time Tomlinson reprimanded Arthur
for his personal condition, and sent him to the stream behind
the Mill to cleanse himself, Arthur had promised to reform,
and for a few days had improved. Tomlinson knew, however,
that what had afflicted Simon, Arthur's father, and had
driven him eventually to kill himself, also afflicted the son.
Arthur was an Aysgill and carried the strain that Tomlinson
knew must be cut out ruthlessly or it would destroy him. And
there was nothing Tomlinson could do if he were to remain

faithful to the Master who had always dealt fairly with him.

'Nay, Master,' he said slowly. 'I fear I cannot *guarantee* Arthur Aysgill. I do not think he has strength within him for the difficult times ahead.' The great sadness welling inside him showed clearly on his face.

'I'm sorry, Tomlinson,' Sleightholme said. 'I know the lad meant much to you and that you had great hopes he might one day climb the ladder to success. I fear you must pay him whatever is owing to him. *If thine eye offend thee, pluck it out.*'

'*And cast it from thee . . .?*'

'Yes, Tomlinson, *cast it from thee.*'

'You've a bit put by, Arthur?' Sally asked anxiously. 'It's quarter day next week and we mun pay half a year's rent since we missed last time, though why you had to give our rent money to yon slattern to feed her bastards, I'll never know.'

Arthur looked around the home that Sally and Amelia had so lovingly furnished, with frequent help from Nancy Boothman. But he didn't see the carefully sewn curtains with their embroidered tassels, the cloth covers for the chairs, the polished wood of the furniture that had claimed a coin or two. He didn't see the two new babies, William and Elizabeth, lying in their improvised cots. William was a year old, Elizabeth barely two months, and both were whimpering, as if sensing the evil tidings Arthur had brought.

There'd been nothing owing to Arthur in the way of wages, for he'd drawn against the ledger; in fact he owed Sleightholme two pounds ten shillings in pay he'd taken in advances. Tomlinson had taken one look at Arthur's face, stricken by the news of his dismissal, and had cancelled the bookkeeper's ledger entry. He'd paid Arthur a notional two pounds – if the Master queried it, Tomlinson knew he'd need to pay the money out of his own pocket and would be reprimanded for his generosity, but the sight of Arthur's woebegone countenance was such that he couldn't turn him away with nothing in his hand.

Arthur had gone straight to the ale house and had drunk a mixture of brandy, brought in from the shop for him, and ale. Now a shilling had gone from the precious store of money, in drink, and a mite to eat. He thrust the remainder of the money into Sally's hand.

She counted it, tightlipped. 'And what am I supposed to do wi' this?' she asked.

'Guard it well,' he said, lucid in his mind but wobbly on his legs. 'It's all we have.'

'Tha's saved *nowt*?' she asked, unbelieving.

The two babies, hearing the tone of her voice, sent up a concerted wail. Amelia, who'd been sitting quietly in a corner, fearful of exposing herself to her son's vituperation and drunken abuse, gathered them quickly in her arms and held them to her breast, rocking them gently from side to side, crooning softly to them.

'Nowt,' Arthur said, forcing a smile of bravado to his face. 'Tha's had it all in good food, in clo'es for thyself and yon old drab, in furniture and covers and cloths for this damned prison you've made between you.'

More and more it had become a prison to him, with the three women cackling around him with their sewing needles and bodkins, telling him he couldn't sit in this chair with its new clean covers, that he couldn't rest his arm on this table since they'd just polished it wi' mutton fat and beeswax, that he couldn't step on that floor since they'd just swabbed it wi' water. It was in desperation that he'd first sought the easy comfort of the ale house, where he could loll on a bench supping his ale in comfort, where folks had summat to talk about other than scraps of cloth, curtains and clo'es.

Sally had quickly realized that Arthur was not a nest-builder. In fairness to her, she'd begun by trying to make everything nice for him to come home to, then, seeing that Amelia shared the same interests, she'd let the house gradually take over until, if she were being honest, she'd have to confess that it occupied all her waking thoughts. She knew it had become an obsession which Amelia, who'd never had a decent home of her own with Simon, had come to share. Sally hadn't meant to drive Arthur away from her and had been happy when, after several years of trying, she'd conceived their first child. Surely, she'd reasoned, with a babby in the house, Arthur would settle down, would begin to face his responsibilities at home. He hadn't changed then, nor had he changed when Elizabeth had arrived a couple of months ago. Arthur had never picked up either of his babbies, had never comforted them or loved them the way a natural father will. Rather had he tended to stop away from home, more and more often, and she'd begun to smell other women on him as well as the ale, brandy and vomit – aye, and ordure too, for he'd become less and less careful about his personal cleanliness of late and often disgusted her.

But Sally resisted the temptation to fly at him, to upbraid him for his failings. 'Husband,' she said, 'if you find any discontent in this prison as you say we've made for you, then I require you only to tell me where I err. It has ever been my wish to please you, to be as good a wife to you as I may. I want no other, my dear, than to love and serve you in any way I might. So now, we mun set on our thinking caps and work out how we're to find new employment for you, and quickly, since we have to meet a double rent on quarter day, and neither your mam nor I have any coin set by.'

How she regretted the last purchase she'd made of material for curtains for the windows! It had been expensive and had taken all her store of coin. Now it was all cut and seamed, and she couldn't even think to take it back to the draper.

'Aye,' Arthur sneered, waving his arm about him, 'we're sitting down among a fortune wi' nowt to put in our bellies. We can't eat covers for chairs, ma'am, nor table-legs, nor your fine clo'es.' He knew that was unjust when he said it. Sally and Amelia bought material cheaply wherever they might, a cast-off scrap from the milliners, a bit of Flanders lace if they were lucky. Sally used all her skills to fashion

270

garments from them, and once or twice, when sober, Arthur had marvelled at the miracles she wrought with her needles and thread. She always looked after his garments impeccably, and he never lacked for a button, nor had a tear nor a frayed edge to disgrace himself.

She bit her lip, determined to say nothing to provoke him further. Her mind raced actively. She could perhaps go back to the milliners – she hadn't been able to work since William's birth, which had practically crippled her with the cramps. She'd been barely over them when Elizabeth had arrived, and even now she was still weak. Perhaps she could work a day, sitting at the sewing bench? She knew that, in her present condition, it would be hard and since the milliners paid only piece-work, wages only for what the workers achieved, she'd have to stick hard at it to earn a competence. Amelia was still working at the spinning, but they'd all heard rumours that spinners were being thrown out of work by the new inventions. If only she could keep Arthur clean and decent, so that he could present himself for employment. She put her arm around him despite his ale-house stink.

'Us'll work summat out, Arthur,' she said. 'I'm sorry if I've been amiss, if I've made this a prison for you. That were never my intent. I nobbut wanted to make you a comfortable home as you'd be proud to come to at nights when your work was done. Now, why don't you go out into't yard and give thyself a sluice while I make thee a bit o' summat to eat?

'Aye, too mucky for you, am I?' he said, pulling himself away from her, determined to take offence at anything. 'I weren't too mucky when you pulled me on to't sofa afore we were wed!'

She knew he was past reason. Amelia had told her many times how things had been with Simon, Arthur's father. It seemed the Aysgill men all had a massive pride they could not subjugate. When that pride was injured, or when they fancied it to be injured, they struck out in anger at whomsoever happened to be nearest. Amelia had told her how she feared to see Simon come home drunk, how he would beat and abuse her, interfere with her sexually in bestial ways. Well, Arthur hadn't come to that, thank God, but this was the first big knock his pride had taken, and the Lord alone knew how he would react to it.

'Happen Blind Jack o'Knaresborough is looking for more men?' Sally now suggested timidly. 'You were happy working wi' him.'

'And now you're trying to get me out of the way, is that it, woman?' Arthur roared. He was being monstrously unfair but there was a devil driving him, a devil he knew not how to deny. Truly, he loved Sally. So far as she could, she'd tried to be a good wife to him. He knew he ought to have stood up to her more in the early days, taken command a bit more in his own house, stopped the woman coming to such a passionate love of the inanimate things with which they'd imprisoned him. At first he'd been indulgent. If that's the lass's way, let her have it, he'd said to himself. He'd been indulgent, he now knew after Tomlinson had tongue-lashed him, in all his transactions with people; he'd been afraid to incur people's enmity, to be firm in his refusal of their too many, too outrageous requests. He knew the women at the mill had taken advantage of him and, though they were always happy to take a coin from him, would never give him a harder day's work in gratitude. 'Folks will always advantage themselves from you,' Tomlinson had said before he turned Arthur away from the mill. 'They'll be like the leeches that suckle off another's blood. Unless tha' develops a hard heart and a deaf ear, my lad, tha'll be sucked dry.'

Arthur knew that, quite simply, he'd never had the courage to say no.

'I'll go wash mysen, lass,' he muttered after a moment, and stumbled out of the room into the back yard. The fresh air hit him a blow in the chest and he staggered. A wave of nausea rose in his gullet and, before he could stop it, the bile and vomit burst from him as he fell to his knees in the cold wet slime of the yard. His chest heaved and heaved until there was nothing left in him to come away. His eyes had clouded over and his back sagged with disgust of himself. Then he felt a cool damp cloth wiping his forehead, a strong arm round his shoulders, pressing him close.

'Tha'll be all right, love,' he heard Sally's voice softly saying. 'Tha'll be all right . . .'

'Go away and leave us alone,' he said, still gasping. 'I'm not fit to be seen.'

'Tha's my husband,' she said, 'through thick and thin. I'll not let thee down again, I promise thee that.'

All doors were closed to Arthur Aysgill, for his reputation had gone before him. Workers had talked to workers over the years about the 'softie' who managed them, and word had gone upwards. Sleightholme himself had been told about Arthur by Barton, who had heard it from his manager, who had heard it from his workers. Nobody wanted a 'softie' as a manager, supervisor, foreman. And nobody wanted, as a worker, a man who'd shown such liberal tendencies. Might he not, in turn, affect their own workers with his liberal views?

So Arthur tramped further and further afield, as he had once before, seeking employment, but this time he encountered no Jack o'Knaresborough to help him. Sally went back to work for the milliner but, working as hard as she might in her tired condition, she could earn no more than they spent on meagre food, and could put nothing by for the rent. Fortunately the agent gave them a month's grace, since he sympathized with Sally's situation.

Then, at the end of that month, Amelia was dismissed from Sleightholme's, along with eighty other spinners. Now they knew their plight was desperate, since there was no hope that Amelia would find other employment at her age; fifty years old, she was a thin broken stick of a woman. When the agent regretfully ejected them from their house, taking the furniture and curtains and covers on which Sally had lavished so much love and care in payment of overdue rent, they all moved back into the hovel they'd been living in when Sally and Arthur first met. It was so tumbledown that no one had cared to live in it during the intervening years, save the occasional gypsy who'd squatted there for a night or two before moving on.

Sally had hoped to be able to profit by her aunt's home, but Nancy Boothman had had the good fortune to marry a widower the same age as herself a couple of years before, and had sold her house and moved to London with her new spouse. On the night they moved into the hovel, with all five of them in the same room under the leaking roof, Sally walked round to her aunt's house, remembering the gracious room she'd occupied there, all to herself. The front door was open and she could see the gleam of the fire within and the glow of candles. She was drawn forward as if spellbound, until she was standing on the outer step sniffing the rich odour of roasting meat, feeling the warmth flowing out from within the comfortable home, seeing the brightness and the cleanliness of the interior.

She imagined that she could hear the laughing voice of her aunt, Nancy Boothman, who always had joy on her face and a chuckle in her heart. She remembered the halcyon days she'd lived there, in warmth and affection, with no care in the world. She tasted again the first fresh kisses Arthur had given her, recapturing the innocent pleasures of his courtship, the deep satisfaction of their first fumbling love-making.

All that love, warmth, happiness and devotion – where had it all gone? Why had it all run away, like water from a cracked pot?

The door suddenly opened wider and the man who stood there was wearing the black suit, short bobbed wig, polished boots, and sour suspicious face of a typical clerk.

'What does tha' want?' he asked brusquely.

'Nothing,' Sally stammered, caught unawares.

'Then what's tha' doing here? Hoping to steal summat, I'll be bound.'

'I used to live here . . .' Sally said, fighting the tears.

'Well, tha' doan't live here now!' he said, and slammed the door tight shut in her face.

Amelia lasted only six months back in the hovel. The constant damp and dirt worked on her spirit and her body; when she fell ill of the ague that winter, she had no courage left with which to fight it. She simply faded into death.

Arthur had found no employment and, since he had removed across the parish boundaries, he had lost his entitlement to assistance for his mother's funeral from the Poor Law funds. So it was that Amelia was buried early one morning in the cemetery on Middleton Fields, with no person save Sally to say a few words as the dead body, wrapped in sacking, was lowered without ceremony into a pauper's grave.

Arthur had so alienated the rest of the Aysgill family with his drunken borrowings during the previous six months that Sally, with the remnants of her pride tight about her, had refused to notify any of them of Amelia's death lest they offer her charity to bury the one who had become her friend. Arthur himself was too drunk to attend his mother's funeral. So Sally pushed the cart up to the burial fields herself, and paid the two burying men with coin she'd obtained by selling one of the fine dresses she'd sewn for Amelia in their days of prosperity. Arthur was still snoring when she returned home.

CHAPTER THREE

Jennifer Ottershaw went swiftly along the street. What could Mrs Tester require of her that demanded such an urgent summons, she asked herself, at such a late hour? When the pot-boy had knocked on her door she had been inclined to ignore the sound, for neither Stanley nor Claude was yet at home and darkness had already fallen.

'I'm to conduct you to Mrs Tester,' the pot-boy had said, grinning in his urchin way, 'and I'm to take care of you along the way, else I shan't receive my coin.' He'd replaced his familiar cloth apron and jug with a stout blackthorn stick which spoiled its own effect by being far too long for him to wield.

Jennifer had kept him waiting only an instant while she dashed cold water on her face and placed her woollen cloak around her shoulders. It was an exciting summons, and she was agog with curiosity.

Mrs Tester was waiting just inside the open door, which she pulled wide when she saw Jennifer appear at the gate leading through the tiny garden to the house. She pushed the coin quickly into the pot-boy's hand with an injunction to spend it on improving himself, and almost dragged Jennifer in to the house.

'There's not a moment to lose,' she said, 'if we're to be ready in time.'

'Ready for what, pray, Mrs Tester?' Jennifer asked. She'd never seen her friend and benefactress in such a – well, lather wouldn't be too strong a word.

'For the masquerade!' Mrs Tester cried. 'Sir Arthur Brearley is to give a masquerade, and we are invited! He specifically said, when he came for tea today, that I am to come with a young chaperon – even suggested that you might be a suitable person to perform that task. My dear, that is every bit as good as a command!'

A masquerade! Jennifer, of course, had read about the masquerades that were sweeping the country as the fashionable form of entertainment. They had been known for some time as part of the family entertainment at grand country houses; Jennifer had read in the newspaper she still devoured so avidly of ones that had been held in public, often by subscription. Hundreds of masquerades had been given in 1768 in honour of the visit of the King of Denmark; only the previous year, she remembered reading, Lord Stanley had given a *fête champêtre* at the Oaks, near Epsom, and had appeared dressed as the artist Rubens! Some people were calling them *fiera mascherata*, in the Italian style, and all the guests would vie with each other to see who could produce the most original costume, some going as nymphs, some as common country girls – one lady, Jennifer had read, had appeared dressed as a country shepherdess and leading a sheep! Many took a favoured character from a painting and had garments specially created to be an exact replica. Lord Byron's wife had appeared at one masquerade as an Arcadian princess, while the Marchioness Grey had appeared, as the *Intelligencer* described it, in the Haymarket in a handsome '*pretty habit . . . what we call Spanish . . . composed of a pink satin curtained petticoat trimmed, a black satin waistcoat trimmed also with silver with close sleeves slashed with p.nk, and a small hat and feather. Lady Mary Capell was the fine Van Dyke with her hair hanging about her ears . . .*'

'You see what it says,' Jennifer had read aloud to Mrs Tester, '. . . *but somehow, it did not suit her!*'

Both of them had laughed. They'd conned every word they could find about masquerades since the evening Mrs Tester had sent the pot-boy for her, but were still in a dither as to what they should wear at Sir Arthur's house.

''Tis a most *grand* establishment, you'll see,' Mrs Tester said, 'with an enormous ballroom built as a separate wing in a garden. Not quite as enormous as some I've seen,' Mrs Tester added, seeing the sparkle in the young girl's eye, 'but it'll do for a provincial gentleman.'

'Oh, Stanley!' Jennifer had said to her brother. 'Sir Arthur Brearley is to give a masquerade, and I'm to go with Mr and Mrs Tester!'

Stanley had huffed and puffed. 'I should've been consulted,' he said. 'Don't forget that I am your guardian now that our parents are both dead. I should've been consulted . . .'

'Oh, don't be so *serious*,' Jennifer had pleaded.

'You'll need garments to wear.'

'Mrs Tester will provide all that.'

'Nay, Jennifer, if you're to attend such a grand occasion, you should go in your own colours.' Stanley had offered to pay for the garments; he was making a small profit from his business these days, even though he was obliged to pay his uncle Peter a heavy interest on the capital he had borrowed and had no cause to spend the money on himself.

'You'd better hold your purse-strings tight until we learn what the garments are likely to cost,' Jennifer had said.

Now she and Mrs Tester were trying to make a final decision, since they'd wasted too many evenings in speculation, had pored over too many accounts of what the fashionable folk were doing.

'Why don't we wear dominos?' Jennifer proposed. 'Dominos are quite in keeping with the fashion. We can either wear the French one with the hoop, or the Venetian one without a hoop.'

'What's the Venetian one like?' Mrs Tester enquired, 'for I've no mind to swirl around in a hoop all evening, unable to sit comfortable.'

278

''Tis exact the same as a parson's gown,' Jennifer said, 'and will cost but little to make, yet we shall be in style and fashion. We can wear a multi-hued mask, and that will relieve the severity of our garments, and have our hair plain-dressed with a simple cap. There's virtue in simplicity, Mrs Tester,' Jennifer said with an assured authority.

Mrs Tester looked at her protégée. 'You've learned a lot these few months, my girl,' she said, 'as if in readiness for the grand challenge. It is my fervent wish that cruel fate shall not intervene to dash your hopes and give you cruel disappointments.'

Surely, she told herself, Jennifer had come on apace since first she'd met her. What a sweet girl, filled by virtue's tenderness! She was certainly a beauty; no man with eyes in his head would gainsay that. But she also had a cultivated mind and a forthright stance on matters of principle. Would that weigh against her in the cruder reality of life? Were men, as was commonly supposed, averse to knowledge in a woman? *Her* husband had never had that problem to consider. She had always lacked the finer points of intelligence, though she could discourse on the matters of the day with vigorous energy. This slip of a girl had a mind, an intelligence that perhaps could militate against her. A man could feel himself challenged by her, and that would never make for repose and contentment.

'Would you take it amiss were I to warn you,' she said diffidently, 'that there are many who seek only acquiescence in others?'

'And would have only slaves and servants about them?' Jennifer asked, though the twinkle in her eye removed any suggestion of impudence from what she said. 'I fear such people can never be happy if they would surround themselves only with assenters. Hasn't Mr Handel taught us that from a thoughtful discord can come a greater harmony?'

Mrs Tester laughed. 'I know nor care nought for such

bandying of words,' she said, 'though I enjoy to hear Mr Handel's Messiah well sung, and his Water Music well played. Philosophies of harmony and discord are far too much for my simple mind to grasp . . . We shall go to the masquerade in dominos, as you propose. In that we shall be in harmony. As to the discord, I shall raid my jewellery on your behalf, and you shall wear my fine diamonds to relieve the simplicity of your costume.'

Jennifer, Mrs Tester and her servants spent all the day of the masquerade in preparation for the evening ahead. Mr Tester had ordered a waistcoat specially for the occasion; it was a fine garment of green watered silk trimmed with silver lace. Above it he wore a double-breasted surtout coat, without his cape. His breeches were of fine Manchester cotton velvet, and his boots of delicate Northampton kid had been waxed to a high gloss.

The carriage had been cleaned and polished; the horses were brushed and oiled to perfection, with the leather and metal accoutrements all shining. They set off at three in the afternoon for the two-hour drive to Brearley Manor which lay along the road to Otley, across the hill known locally as the Chevin. It was a cold afternoon but neither of the ladies felt the least chilly; they were aglow with the excitement of the day, and nothing could lower their temperature in the slightest degree.

Mr Tester observed Jennifer most carefully, remarking the beneficial effect she always had on his wife, who seemed to grow younger in the girl's company with every hour that passed. He regretted he and his wife had never been able to create a family of their own – he suspected the fault was his own, since he'd had a bad infection in youth and had since heard from apothecaries that a man's virility could thus be impaired. Jennifer, he saw, was the daughter Mrs Tester had never been graced to bear; the delight she took in the companionship of the young girl was as real as a natural mother's. He had a whim to indulge the pair of them in any way he could. Though the masquerade meant nothing to him, he was delighted to escort them. Doubtless he and a few cronies would settle somewhere for a game of whist, leaving the masked pair of them to wander at will through the glittering throng.

The throng was larger and even more glittering than he had supposed. Since none of the higher echelons of Society had been invited, the guests, mostly from the wealthier middle-classes and squires, doubtless felt less constrained to formal behaviour. Laughter greeted them at the door and the lively buzz of conversation, and Sir Arthur himself awaited their arrival in the hall.

Jennifer had never seen such a house, so filled with people, so decorated with marble pillars and painted friezes, with family portraits on the walls, urns bursting with flowers, even a marble pond in which she caught the glimpse of golden fishes.

Sir Arthur greeted Mr and Mrs Tester civilly, took Jennifer's right hand in both of his, and welcomed her. She curtsied as prettily as she might, having practised the complicated motion for hours before the glass in Mrs Tester's dressing room. How could he possibly have recognized them, since they had donned their masks before leaving the coach, Jennifer asked herself.

She was not to know that Sir Arthur had demanded details of their costumes from Mr Tester when he'd met him the previous day; Mr Tester had shown him the diamond brooch that Jennifer would be wearing in her elaborate coiffure. In the event, he had no need of the symbol. Sir Arthur had thought long and often of this pretty young wench in the previous months, dispelling his objections one by one. She did not, in any manner, conform to the design he'd laid out for his future bride. She was not a widow but, as Mr Tester assured him, an innocent maid. She was not independently wealthy, though Mr Tester had reassured him she was no wanton spendthrift. Finally, he'd told himself, she was too young for him. She'd have a young girl's mindless prattle to dull his senses. She'd be too fly-by-night for him.

Mr Tester had helped him overcome that ultimate objection. 'You'll find, Sir Arthur, that Jennifer Ottershaw has an older head on her tender young body; she's versed in modern literature, if not in the classics. She can talk intelligently of the philosophies of England and the Continent of Europe – she's well versed in the failings of Lord North and his Imperial Majesty in our American Colony, can even discuss the merits and demerits of the Peace of Paris with critical understanding . . .'

'I' faith, Tester, you make her sound too much a paragon for me!' Sir Arthur had protested. 'Will she sit silent by my hearth, and comfort me down my days? I'll have no debater at my board, no waspish woman wi' a mouth full of theory!'

'Let me only say,' Mr Tester had assured him, 'that I have never been bored by her discourse, nor troubled by vehemence. Though I have delineated her as a spirited filly, with a mind to shy at times, I have never been embarrassed by any vehement expression of liberal points of view. Her parents were humble God-fearing people, who brought her to an exploration of her own mind and the intricate beauties of artistic creation.'

'Next you'll be telling me, man, she's a work of art herself!'

Tester had smiled. Aye, he'd thought to himself, you might throw up a screen o' words, but if you hadn't found her a work of art you wouldn't be sounding me out as to her virtues. He knew Sir Arthur had been smitten by the lass; he saw clearly that Sir Arthur had struggled for many a month against the infection of love, but had not succeeded, or Jennifer Ottershaw would not have been so pointedly suggested for this evening's masquerade.

Sir Arthur quite simply had fallen in love. He'd tried to forget Jennifer Ottershaw, had even avoided taking tea at the Testers' for four weeks, until hunger for the sight of her beauty and the hope of talking to her had driven him back. He'd told himself countless times that she would be in every way an unsuitable match for him. His parents had both died of the plague and he had come into guardianship of the Brearley land and fortunes at an unseemly young age; then his young wife too had died, only two years past. Now he was thirty-five; the estates and fortune had multiplied under his careful ministration, but he was a lonely man, with more time to think of his private life, his personal comfort.

Many of his friends had advised him that he'd be dropped by Society if he married someone so unsuitable. 'Take her for your doxy, by all means,' they said. 'Pleasure yourself with her, but marry someone who already has the entrance to Society.'

It had been good unselfish advice and Sir Arthur had tried in vain to heed it. Why should he not take the lass for his pleasure? He could settle an income on her quite easily, even set her up in a discreet little house somewhere. He could marry any one of the ladies he met frequently at the homes of friends – ladies who already had a name in Society. In truth, after a few stimulating conversations, they all began to bore him. The cup of their knowledge, he realized, was all too quickly drained to the bitter lees of scandal and gossip for which he had no stomach. Jennifer Ottershaw possessed a freshness of mind, a discourse unburdened by social familiarity.

'Good evening, Miss Ottershaw,' he said, retaining control of her hand in his. 'I am most happy to welcome you to my home.'

'And I, Sir Arthur, am most pleased to be here,' Jennifer smiled. 'I thank you for your kind invitation.'

He seemed reluctant to let go her hand, but the press of new arrivals forced him to do so and she and Mrs Tester went forward into the room that had been provided for the ladies' cloaks. It had been especially fitted with long mirror glasses in which the ladies could see to repair travel damage to coiffures and head-dresses. With the certainty of youth, Jennifer spent little time preening herself – her long hair, worn without wig, was so artfully pinned into position that little could damage it. Mrs Tester pinned more diamonds into it from the bag her husband had given her before he left them to look for the men's smoking room. When she had finished, Mrs Tester looked quizzically at her protégée.

'You'll do,' she said. 'Your hair has no need of further adornment, nor you either. If you were my age I would tell you to powder your cheeks, but the ruddy glow of health well becomes youth if not age. Were my cheeks of such a colour I'd be taken for a milk-maid, I'll be bound!'

They went together on what Mrs Tester called 'a promenade', visiting all the rooms and galleries in turn, seeing the glittering displays that awaited them, but more fascinated by the motley they encountered. Jennifer had dreamed of this evening for many nights but not even her most fevered imagination had conjured such a wealth of styles, fabrics and colours as now she saw about her. Many people had decided to humble their apparent station of life, and Jennifer saw a score or more of seeming country lasses and lads. Others had taken pictures as their inspiration and there were several Van Dykes of which, she'd been told, Henry, Lord Irwin, had a full gallery in his mansion at Temple Newsam. Vermeers abounded, she was told by Mr Tester whom they met on their promenade, as did Holbeins and Titians. The style of the ladies, culled from the works of these painters, excited her ambition one day to see the paintings themselves.

'That's the Duchess of Urbino, Eleanora Gonzaga,' Mr Tester said, indicating one lady wearing a dark brown dress covered in ochre patterns, with a pleated fine lawn chemisette covering her neck and shoulders, and a rounded bonnet.

'The *real* Duchess of Urbino?' Jennifer asked.

'No, my dear, merely Titian's representation of her. I remember the painting well from my journeys to Florence in Italy to purchase silks.'

'One day,' Jennifer said hungrily, 'one day how I would love to travel to Florence in Italy to see such a painting for myself!'

The dress of the 'Duchess of Urbino' was such a magnificent concoction that it excited her interest beyond words. She could imagine ladies wearing such exquisite gowns walking through the Courts of Europe in elegant ceremony and luxurious disdain – such a gown, she knew, must have cost more to reproduce than she could imagine any husband earning within a year. But then, she chided herself, she must not reduce everything to petty thoughts of coin and earnings.

Soon all such thoughts were forgotten as she and Mrs Tester began to have their hands taken for the dancing; large men and small, short men and tall, all demanded and were granted a quick whirl round the dancing room. Though Jennifer had never learned the steps of formal dances, she quickly applied herself to moving gracefully in time with her partners, all of whom had obviously benefited by training in the matter and were able to lead her. The press of bodies about her was such that no one had time or occasion to look at feet; hands were held in immodest grasps, arms went naturally around waists in a rumbustious style more suited to a country rout than a formal ball.

Once, exhausted by the vigorous movement, she and Mrs Tester took themselves to the refreshment rooms.

'You must not accept an offer of refreshment from any man,' Mrs Tester warned her, 'lest he take that as an acquiesence to improprieties in other matters.'

Jennifer imbibed a delicious cordial made with fresh fruits, then joined her friends at the enormous buffet table and picked at what remained of the hams, the legs of pork, the barons of beef and haunches of venison, the pies, cakes, biscuits, the dishes of syllabub and sweet confections at whose exotic ingredients, they could only guess.

All the while Jennifer watched Sir Arthur, the only man not wearing a mask, as he danced with this lady and that, as he strolled though the rooms greeting everyone with an air of proprietorial assurance, as he laughed amidst a group of men at some quip or sally. She felt a growing discontent as the evening wore on without any approach from Sir Arthur, either to herself, which she hardly dared expect, or to their mutual friend, Mrs Tester – which surely might be expected, since he spent so much time drinking Mrs Tester's tea on so many occasions? She began to feel a boredom grow within herself, and twice refused to dance, even though the man who approached her seemed young, nimble and ardent in his wish to claim her. Mrs Tester, enjoying herself hugely, accepted all invitations and was much in demand since she could romp vigorously with the best of them, her own gaiety enhancing the pleasure of her companion as they swirled across the polished wood floor in time to the ten or twelve musicians who appeared to have been playing non-stop for many hours on fiddles, pipes, sackbuts, lutes, viols and mandolins. Standing beside one of the pillars that adorned the length of the magnificent ballroom, providing an arcade and promenade from the dancing area, and trying to simulate an interest in the proceedings which were in truth already wearisome to her, Jennifer suddenly heard a soft voice at her ear. Turning around, she had already begun to phrase a polite refusal when she recognized Sir Arthur himself.

'Are you not dancing, Miss Ottershaw?' he said quietly. 'I must not say your name out loud, since all are to hide in secrecy until ten o'clock, when we shall have the ceremony of unmasking.'

She smiled at him, all thoughts of boredom vanishing like overnight vapours. 'I have danced so much,' she said, 'that I fear to lose my feet!'

'We mustn't risk such dainty pretty appendages,' he laughed softly. 'Could I perhaps tempt you to partake of a glass of cool wine with me?'

She remembered the warning of Mrs Tester, but surely those words couldn't apply to their host? 'That would be my delight, Sir Arthur,' she said, 'though I must look out for Mrs Tester.'

Sir Arthur indicated Mr Tester, who was standing not six feet away, watching his wife swirl about the ballroom with obvious pleasure. 'I think Mr Tester has come to claim his wife,' he said. 'I asked him if you might be excused your chaperonage for a moment or two.'

Her eyes flashed at him. 'You were so certain, sir, that I would accept your invitation to take wine?'

'I came with a full quiver of arguments,' he said ruefully. 'I had hoped that at least one might hit its mark.'

'And what is that, if I may make so bold?' she asked.

'To permit us a few words of conversation, Miss Ottershaw,' he said.

'And if I had preferred to remain alone, in silent solitude?'

'I would have called others to my assistance to help carry you away,' he smiled.

'Others . . . ?'

'Mr Milton would have been one. *Beauty is Nature's coin, must not be hoarded, But must be current, and the good thereof consists in mutual and partaken bliss!*'

Jennifer laughed daintily. 'Sir, though you flatter me so, I must confess to a small thirst for a glass of cooling wine, and a soft seat so that I might rest my weary legs.'

As they moved off, side by side, Sir Arthur placed his arm about her waist. In any other situation it would have been an unseemly and over-familiar act, but most couples were thus engaged as they strolled through the promenades and it seemed a natural thing to do. Jennifer was conscious of his arm, but had prepared herself in her dreams of this event against expecting too much, of reading too much into

287

anything that might happen. It did, however, seem to her that they were hurrying through the motley with somewhat indelicate haste . . .

Her feelings of growing anxiety were not assuaged when, at the centre point of one of the corridors, Sir Arthur used a key from a fob to unlock one of the doors. He flung the door wide and beckoned for her to enter the room within. She looked about her, then at him, before stepping across the threshold. The room was deep, and almost filled with books; she had not known that so many books existed in the entire world as were lined like soldiers on the shelves which stood along the walls. There were three tables in the room, each with chairs. At the far end, she saw a sofa facing two deep arm-chairs, with a low table between them.

'This is my reading room,' Sir Arthur said, watching her reaction.

Jennifer walked around the room, glancing at the spines of the books in the shelves, unsure of the custom. Would he consider her impolite if she examined the gold-blocked titles more closely, or studied the large map spread on the centre table, or turned the pages of the large volume propped open on the far desk? The room smelled of tobacco and beeswax; a fire had been lit in the marble fireplace, though now the logs had burned to a hot glowing ember with no flickering flames.

She noticed two glasses on a silver tray on the low table at the near end of the room. Between the two glasses was a decanter in fine cut glass, which threw rainbow colours in the flicker of candlelight. The top of the decanter was ringed by silver, with a delicate spout. She stood still and exclaimed aloud with pleasure. The picture composed by the table, the decanter and glasses in the foreground, the dark wine-coloured rug extending to the window, the glow of the park beyond in the last light of a setting sun, was so incomparably beautiful that she wanted only to stand still and absorb it, drink it in like some heady potion. So much beauty, so much refinement . . .

She turned as he came to her side and read the look of

amusement on his features. 'You waited for this moment, Sir Arthur,' she said softly.

'Aye, lass, I must confess it. 'Tis my favourite time of the day, when I most like to sit here, taking my ease with a glass of wine, looking out across the trees that have been there for all my ancestors to admire.'

'I am grateful to you, sir,' she said, 'for showing it to me. For sharing such a treasure with me.' She turned from him and both were unmoving and silent as they looked out across the sward, seeing the swaying tops of the trees, the gentle slope of the ground away from them, the flocks of birds bustling in and out of tree-tops, or flying in wheeling formations that outlined them blackly against the last of the sun's light.

At last, a sigh of contentment escaped from her. 'I think you do Mr Milton a disservice – if you do not think me bold in expressing an opinion?'

'Nay, Miss Ottershaw, speak as you will,' Sir Arthur smiled.

'Perhaps his words were meant to express the beauty, not of a maid, but of all God's unmolested creation,' she said. *'Beauty is Nature's coin, must not be hoarded . . . and the good thereof consists in mutual and partaken bliss.'*

'You have a good memory,' he said in wonderment.

'Nay, Sir Arthur, I had a good mama – departed this life, alas – who made me familiar with the works of Milton from an early age.'

'I' faith, I must look to my memory,' he said. 'A false quotation could fast lead me into the literary quagmire!'

'I think not,' Jennifer said seriously, respecting him for his modesty. How could any man with access to such a library doubt his literary perception? 'And now, if you will excuse me, I fear I must return to Mrs Tester. I cannot do so, however, without thanking you for the great honour you have given me in permitting me to enjoy such "*mutual and partaken bliss*". I shall never forget the view from the window of your reading room, so long as I may live.'

'And the lonely man who sits here, and cannot read for

thinking of *you* . . . Will you remember him?' The words were said quietly, with no undue emphasis, no play-acting pathos. 'At least take a glass of wine with him, to give him a remembrance to match your own, for I confess the only failing in this vista is its lack of animation. Come, Jennifer, take a glass of wine with me, i' good faith.'

'In good faith I accept, Sir Arthur,' she said and seated herself in one of the comfortable chairs.

He poured a glass of wine, placed it on a silver platter on a small table beside her, did himself a similar service, then went to sit across from her on the sofa, resting his arm along the sofa's carved wooden back, gazing at her.

'This is the only modern piece of furniture in this room,' he said, trying to make conversation to verify his words, 'i' good faith'. 'I cannot make up my mind as to whether it is fitting in the style of decoration to have it here. These sofas have become all the style in the Court of King George, so I'm told. But I need the taste of a discerning woman to inform me in this, as in so many other vital matters.'

'This is a delicate wine, Sir Arthur,' Jennifer said, avoiding his eye. 'I have had little experience of wines – could you kindly tell me about it? In this, as in so many other matters, I have need of the information of an honest and unselfish man . . .'

He laughed out loud. 'Touché, mademoiselle! I can see we shall have an alliance of common and uncommon needs to talk about,' he said. 'The wine is newly brought from Portugal. I confess I find it a little green for my taste but it can refresh if chilled in running water for a brief while. It quenches the thirst more satisfactorily than some of those heavy Spanish sherries or French clarets from Bordeaux.'

'And will it make me lose my senses as quickly?' Jennifer asked.

'I doubt anything would make you lose your senses, Miss Ottershaw,' he said with a smile. 'I find you a most composed young lady. Now, fair is fair. I have given you the benefit of my honest knowledge in the matter of wine. You must give me the benefit of your taste in the matter of my sofa. Do you find it too modern an apparatus to be lodged here?'

She examined it carefully, stood, walked back into the room and examined it again. Then she sat down again, carefully smoothing the folds of her domino, longing to take off the mask which was pinching the sides of her cheeks, but not daring to suggest it, since he had not.

'It is a commodious piece of furniture,' she said gravely, 'in that it is conveniently suited to its purpose. I think you would have a better regard for it were you to – oh dear, you will think me a spendthrift – were you to strip off that covering and replace it with a material of warmer texture, perhaps a woollen cloth, dyed to the same colour as your floor covering. Since the sofa is covered in silver material with a light green stripe and a shiny surface, it stands too readily in the eye, inviting criticism. Were it covered in a material which didn't shine, which blended into the colour of carpet and curtain, you would not be assailed by the sight of the piece, and would thus be able to judge it on the merits of its comfort.' She looked anxiously at him, lest she had offended him with her forthright remarks.

He got up, walked to where she had walked and looked back at the sofa. He walked all around it and examined it. Then, as if to obtain another angle of view, he came and stood behind the chair in which she sat, resting his fingertips lightly on its back.

'You know,' he said, 'I do believe you've hit the target with the first arrow! The sofa is too apparent. It commands one's attention. It should, like a faithful servant, stand silent and unseen, waiting to serve. How can I thank you? You have done me a great favour, Miss Ottershaw . . .'

She had turned to look at him as he paused, and found his eyes locked on hers.

'All this talk of wine and furniture,' he said, 'when all I want to say to you, with every fibre of my being, is that I love you and want you to marry me.'

291

CHAPTER FOUR

When Arthur Aysgill awoke, he could not imagine how he came to be lying in this bed of clean bleached calico sheets with the brass rail at the foot of the bed gleaming in the light of the day. He glanced around him, despite the pain in his skull when he turned his head. The room was bright and airy, simply furnished with a chair at one bedside and a table at the other, a cupboard against the far wall between the windows, and clean bare boards testifying to the fact that the room had recently been cleaned.

His head throbbed unmercifully and his mouth tasted dreadful. There was a jug of water on the bedside table; he grasped it and gulped it down – then knew he had to leave the bed or burst. He quarter-filled the pot beneath the bed in one continuous stream before he felt the relief in his belly.

Where on God's earth could he be?

He was not unused to waking from a drunken sleep and finding himself in strange surroundings, since the last stages of his nocturnal meandering could take him anywhere, but usually he was lying in the straw of some coaching-yard, or in the dirt and squalor of a doxy's bed. The cleanliness of this room revealed it belonged to no doxy nor whore-house but, beyond that, Arthur had no idea where he might be, nor even what day or time of day it was. Latterly the days had tended to merge into each other as his craving for drink had led him on for as long as he had a coin in his pocket.

Sally had gone to work again for Mrs Little, the milliner,

and was earning money. She'd found a woman living nearby who was happy to look after the two babies for a coin. Arthur himself had ceased to look for a job, since all had learned about his drunkenness and none would employ him. Sally left a coin on the table for him each day; it was sufficient to take him to an ale-house where he could sit and get drunk. Sometimes he'd have the good fortune to find someone who wanted a bale portered, or a trunk carried, and that would earn him an extra coin with which he could carry on drinking through the night, until fatigue and insensibility overcame him and he'd either find his way home or, what was more likely, fall into a sleep at the back of some ale-yard.

Though Arthur couldn't know it, since he had neither the desire nor the opportunity to gaze at himself in a glass, he already had the face and manner of a man twenty years older. None would believe he was only thirty years of age; he had the fat fleshy jowls of a man of fifty, and a loose ponderous belly. His skin was engrained with dirt since he seldom bothered to wash and he didn't know that, on the rare occasions he went home, Sally would strip his drunken figure and scrub him all over in an attempt to get the lice from him.

He looked down at his frame now, and realized he was wearing a cotton nightgown he'd never seen before. His feet, protruding from the end of it, were also clean. Where could he be? In some almshouse? Some hospital? Hardly likely, for such institutions crammed their inmates together without privacy.

The problem was solved for him when the door opened suddenly, and Tomlinson stood there.

'I heard you moving about, Arthur,' he said.

Arthur hung his head in shame; now he realized what must have happened. 'You found me somewhere?' he asked. 'This is your home you brung me to?'

Tomlinson nodded. 'Aye, and a right grand state you were in, too. Lying in't gutter! I should have left you, and would

293

have too, if I hadn't remembered your dad Simon, your mam, and that wonderful lass as has given thee two bairns and never a word of reproach. I brought you home; we had to wash you down in't yard and we've burned all your clothes. You were as dirty as a dog's dropping, Arthur, and my good lady needed a de'il o' persuasion afore she'd let me bring you into't house. We had to clean your hair wi' sulphur, so lousy you were, and rub your skin wi' the same to get rid of infection. As it is, Mrs Tomlinson will not come into't room for fear of the plague or the ague. Get thee back into bed, lad,' he commanded. 'I'm going to gi'e thee a right talking to.'

First, however, Tomlinson called to a lass who helped around the house and a moment later she brought a bowl of gruel, with oats and potatoes mixed with bits of meat and fat. 'Eat that down,' Tomlinson said, 'while I talk to you. You'll need summat in your belly.'

During the next fifteen minutes, Tomlinson used every term of vilification he could lay his tongue to, none of which would have served in polite company. He spoke of Sally, whom he regarded as an angel even to tolerate 'a lump of ordure' as vile as Arthur had become. He invoked the memory of Amelia, lying cold in a pauper's grave, unmourned by her ingrate son. He was even more scathing when he talked of Arthur's son and daughter, innocent babies on whom the curse of 'a drunken loutish pig of a father' had been laid.

'Tha'll take no more to drink, Arthur Aysgill!' he thundered. 'Tha'll not shame thy wife nor thy bairns, tha'll not shame thy dear departed mama, and tha'll not shame me, who once had the misguided foolishness to put his trust in you! Tha'll clean thyself, put on the suit of clothes I'll lend you, and go back home to beg the forgiveness of that sweet angel who was daft enough to marry you! Tha'll stay at home this e'en; if tha' goes to an ale-house or brandy-shop, I'll come looking for thee wi' a stick in my hand and I'll beat thee insensible! Tomorrow, tha'll come to't mill and I'll set thee on again. The road will be hard; tha'll have no privileges and tha'll do the hardest and the dirtiest work I can find for thee until tha's proven thysen to be sober, God-fearing and industrious. Tha'll get the minimum wages until such time as tha' improves thysen. Is that clear, man?'

'Yes, Mr Tomlinson,' Arthur said humbly.

Arthur couldn't know the difficulty Tomlinson had had to overcome, persuading Sleightholme to take Arthur on again; he had been obliged to stand as personal guarantor of Arthur's good conduct before Sleightholme agreed to the return of the man he called 'that wayward radical'. Nor could he know that his wife Sally had sought out Tomlinson, and had pleaded with him to come to Arthur's assistance, to help him overcome the dreadful consequences of his excessive drinking and profligate way of life. Tomlinson had been most reluctant to intervene, but, as an ardent Christian, he had finally been persuaded by her passionate eloquence on her husband's behalf.

True to his word, Tomlinson gave Arthur all the heaviest and dirtiest tasks to perform about the mill. Arthur began by being grateful to his benefactor and obeying him in everything. He even succeeded in giving up drinking, and spent his evenings quietly at home with his wife and family.

But Sally could see how restless he was and how he ached to visit his cronies in the ale-houses. Previously she had been prepared to work any hours for Mrs Little, the milliner, to earn any extra coin. Often ladies would want an item of millinery to be readied quickly for some social event. They never seemed able to order their new things sufficiently in advance to permit the seamstresses to proceed at leisure with the orders. The work was always hustle and bustle, and Mrs Little had been happy to find one worker, in Sally, who wouldn't seek to return home when darkness descended. Nowadays, though, Sally made a point of never staying late at the milliner's, no matter how urgently the hat or headdress on which she was working was required. She earned less money, of course, and Mrs Little's disfavour, but she felt that was preferable to the risk that her husband, finding her not at home, would seize the opportunity to go out to some alehouse or tavern. Sally did not ask much of life; all she wanted was to keep her husband, the father of her children, by her side in peace and contentment.

For many months after his reform, Arthur would gaze at the slight, chestnut-haired, strikingly attractive woman who sat across from him at the fireside, tending his family, carefully and conscientiously sewing a garment for him, and he would bless his good fortune. 'Th'art a good wife to me, Sal,' he'd say, and the simple words would repay all the struggles, all the difficulties, all the hours she spent working to keep her small family together.

Tomlinson was having great problems at the mill. A group of workers had been listening to the Wesleyan preachers, and to the other speakers who came from London seeking to enrol workers into a 'Lodge'. 'United We Stand', was their message. In other parts of the country, they said, workers had successfully combined to secure better working conditions and higher wages for themselves. The instrument they had used against the factory owners was the riot. Tomlinson himself had heard stories of riots in the cotton industry, where machines like the spinning jenny had thrown many people out of work. Such stories, of course, raised immediate echoes in the minds of the workers at Sleightholme's Mill, for Sleightholme had been very progressive in installing the new machines and never hesitated to lay off workers who were no longer required.

In London, the Lord Mayor Thomas Harley had called upon master tradesmen to 'keep their journeymen and apprentices off the streets', and reminded Freemen of the City of their pledge to prevent journeymen 'going abroad' in times of disorder. In 1768, so these agitators informed them, the weavers of Spitalfields, fearing a loss of work from the introduction of new looms, had risen as a body and had entered several shops and cut to pieces and destroyed the silk works then being manufactured on nine different looms.

Arthur was leaving Sleightholme's Mill one night when he saw a crowd gathered outside the main gate, and a man standing on a box addressing them in a loud and obviously well-trained voice. He made to pass them, but a number of other men, all carrying staves, were ringed round; he would have been obliged to force his way through them, and one look at their faces persuaded him of the consequences should he try to do so.

'We've done it in London,' the speaker was saying, his voice carrying all round the crowd of workers. 'We've done it in Manchester and in Sheffield and we'll do it here in Leeds. As a result of the Spitalfields Acts – which permit us to appeal directly to the Magistrates to fix wage-rates and enforce them, so that no thieving Master can do us down on pay – we've formed a permanent body which we call the Union. Through the Union we have a voice with the Justices and our piece-rates are enforced by them. We've brought the tyrants finally to heel!' As he said this, the man pointed dramatically at Tomlinson, standing just outside the factory gate.

Tomlinson gazed bravely back at him, showing a serene countenance, without the least sign of fear.

'It's not just wages we're concerned with,' the man continued. 'Some of you may have heard that we've organized bread riots, when those thieving rogues in the Corn Exchanges have artificially forced up the price of a crust on which our daily lives depend. They say the Assize of Bread guarantees a fair price, but let me ask you this: how long is it since you last saw a ha'penny loaf? Answer me that, my friends!' There was an angry murmuring in the crowd; no one needed reminding of the cost of bread.

Arthur had to admire the way – crude though it might be – in which the speaker had allied the price of food to the amount of wages a man received, and had wrapped it all in an approval of the Union with all its threat of violence. As he began to make his way home, after the speaker had said his last words and pamphlets had been distributed, Arthur decided that the agitators would have no great effect on the slothful workers at Sleightholme's Mill. They were all content enough to be in jobs at a time of great unemployment, a time when folks were flocking in ever greater numbers into the towns now that the roads had been improved, seeking employment. Sleightholme paid adequate money, nothing more, and nobody would ever be able to build a store of coin in his employment. Tomlinson was a fair man, and didn't carry a whip around the mill with him, as did so many other overseers. Sleightholme's only distinguished itself in the number of machines it employed, in the way in which the Master actively sought out any improvement that made work easier and more productive, with less hands needed. Tomlinson had once explained the Master's attitude to Arthur: Sleightholme didn't see why human beings should be made to do the heavy, dull, repetitive work of animals, he'd said, when the application of machinery could lighten their load and give them a more interesting task. 'Our Master is humane in his thinking,' Tomlinson had insisted, 'and wants only to improve the conditions of the workers along with his production.' It was just unfortunate that many machines Sleightholme had installed had not worked safely or correctly, and that some workers had been horribly maimed, even killed, in accidents when limbs and hair had been trapped in rotating wheels and cogs.

Sally was anxiously awaiting Arthur when he arrived home tardily – she looked into his face to determine he'd not been drinking. He'd kept a pamphlet in his hand and gave it to her to study. She sat near the candle and scanned it hurriedly.

'Nay, Arthur,' she said, new worry showing on her face, 'you're not getting yourself involved wi' the likes of these, are you?'

Arthur laughed. 'I'm no firebrand,' he said. 'It's got nowt to do wi' me. I've got enough to do just to keep my job, and keep myself going. Would you believe it, the old devil has got me scrubbing out the lye-vats this week!'

'You mustn't call him that – the old devil – Arthur. Mr Tomlinson has been good to us.'

'I'll grant you that,' he said, 'but he's also taken back in full measure. I've repaid him the suit of clothes he loaned me, and I've given him a day and a half's work all the time I've been back.'

'Stick it out a bit longer,' Sally said. 'You watch – soon you'll have your old job back.'

They were not destined to find much peace that even. Scarcely had they eaten their supper than there came a knock at the door. Arthur opened it to admit four hard-looking men whom he recognized from the meeting. They'd been taken on by Tomlinson during Arthur's drunken spell and he had not had the opportunity to get to know them since his return to the mill.

'You used to be working by Tomlinson's side i' the old days, we've been told,' one of them said, with no preliminaries. 'You must have a good knowledge of what goes on in't office. We're thinking of making a Combination for ourselves and starting some sort of action against Sleightholme. Seeing the rotten jobs Tomlinson has been giving you of late, we reckon as you'd want to join wi' us, to get your own back on him.'

Arthur had indeed become angry at some of the jobs Tomlinson had given him recently, as if he were trying to cleanse the transgressor with fire. 'He's a sanctimonious old bugger,' he said now, without much thought, and saw the men's eyes gleam.

'Then you're with us?' the man asked eagerly.

Sally stood up, cradling baby Elizabeth in her arms. 'No, he's *not* with you,' she cried. 'Mr Tomlinson has been an angel of mercy to us, and we'll do him no harm, nor join in any combination against him.'

The man who'd spoken looked at Arthur. 'We didn't know as the hen ruled thy roost,' he sneered.

Arthur smiled weakly at him. 'Aye, my missis likes to have her say,' he said, 'though I'm not obliged to listen.'

The men got up. 'Us'll come back,' the leader said, 'after tha's taught thy wife not to interfere when *men* are talking! If she were mine, she'd taste the strap end and that's for sure!'

The men came back four times to persuade Arthur to join them, but each time he refused.

'If the men are joining together,' he pleaded to Sally, 'it'll mean more wages for everybody.'

But she remained adamant. 'Aye, and mark my words, it'll be the beginning of worse things,' she said. 'Mr Tomlinson's always been fair to us and I'll not see him done down.'

Arthur knew something was brewing in the mill, for he often saw the same four men talking earnestly with others in corners, a whispered word here, a whisper there. The men were always silent when he chanced nearby, eyeing him warily. But suddenly one day he found they all had smiles for him, all greeted him as if he were a sheep returned to the fold.

'There's summat amiss,' he told Sally when he went home that night. 'One of yon men slapped my back today and said "tha's a good lad, Arthur" – though I've no notion what he was talking about.'

'Tha' mun watch thyself,' Sally said. 'Happen you ought to go and see Mr Tomlinson at his house, and tell him what's been happening.'

'But I know nowt,' Arthur protested. 'I know nowt at all . . .'

He'd had supper and was still pondering the events of the day when there came a knock at the door.

'If that's them again, send them away wi'out letting them in,' Sally said firmly.

Arthur went to the door and opened it a crack. ''Tis nobbut a pot-lad,' he said, opening the door wide to admit the boy carrying a candle in a lanthorn.

'Are you Arthur Aysgill?' asked the boy.

'Aye, that's me, lad.'

'Then you're to come quickly. Mr Tomlinson wants to talk to you in private in his office in the mill.'

'He must have heard summat,' Sally said quickly. 'Now's your chance to tell him all you know, to repay his many kindnesses to you.'

'Nay', Arthur said, 'I don't welcome the role of informer . . .'

'Tha'd better,' Sally said fiercely, 'else I'll go do it! And tha' mun come straight home, after.'

Arthur clapped his hat on his head and followed the pot-boy's lanthorn down the street. Halfway towards the mill the boy veered to the left.

'I go this way,' the boy said. 'Do you know where to go?'

'Aye, I do,' Arthur muttered and went hurriedly down the darkened lane.

When he arrived at Sleightholme's Mill, the front gate was part open and there was no sign of the gate man who usually looked after the premises during the hours of darkness. Arthur went through the opening and crossed the waggon yard to the door into the side of the weaving shed, a shorter route and one more familiar to him these days than the front entrance, which he assumed anyway would be closed at this time of night. The weaving shed was eerie at night, though he knew every part of it. Shadows seemed to flit about, but he chided himself for a foolish coward; it was nothing more than the clouds moving across the moon, he told himself, throwing shade and light through the long high windows.

Tomlinson's office lay ahead as Arthur crossed the shed. Suddenly, one of the shadows took on a more tangible form. It was moving towards him. He stopped, aghast, chiding himself again for being afraid of shadows – but this was no shadow cast by the moon. It looked like a crouched human, or a vast dog.

'Go away!' he shouted in desperate fear, and the shadow vanished. He heard a chuckle – but was it a chuckle, or water running into some vat? He heard a scuffling sound, like shoe leather on the planking of the floor. But was it a foot in a shoe, or rope rubbing against a pillar? 'Go away!' he yelled again, wondering why his shouts didn't bring Tomlinson from his office.

Then, away in the corner by the new machine, with its pile of coils all waiting to be set in the morning, the machine that would spin forty-eight spindles simultaneously, he saw the first flicker of a flame. He heard the breath as someone blew on it, and now there could be no mistaking the outline of the man he could see crouched there against the fast-growing flames.

'Hey, you!' Arthur cried, starting to run forward.

He hadn't taken more than two steps when he heard the swish of a cudgel and felt the blow on the back of his neck that sent him sprawling on his face, unconscious. Around him, the flames began to rise as the men moved about the shed with their oiled rags, placing masses of them at the foot of the wooden pillars that supported the roof of the weaving shed. Finally, before they left, one of them bent over Arthur and placed his extinguished brand in Arthur's limp hand.

Tomlinson had not been able to settle that night. For days he'd sensed an atmosphere of malice in the mill, a defiant militance showing itself on the faces of some of the men that seemed to promise evil to come. He had intended to retire early to bed, since his age was beginning to tell heavily with him, but decided at the last minute to take a walk around. Thus it was that he happened to be walking across the yard to the mill when the first flames showed through the window.

He dashed inside, calling for the nightwatchman. There had been so many fires in mills of late that he had ordered wooden vats filled with water to be placed around the walls. He shouted repeatedly for the nightwatchman, while he ran around dipping a pail into the vats and sluicing water over the flames, which had not yet gained a good hold on the thick timber beams. His heart pounded as he ran here and there with the pail but he didn't stop to regain his breath. When the last flicker had been extinguished he sank exhausted on the side of one of the vats, breathing deeply, though the acrid smoke from the oily rags bit into his lungs. He was still sitting there, wondering where the nightwatchman could be, when he heard the moan of someone in pain. He crossed the shed hurriedly, and helped the man he found on the floor to his feet. Only when moonlight struck the man's features did he recognize Arthur Aysgill.

'Arthur!' he exclaimed. 'What in God's name are you doing here at this time o' night?' Then he saw the brand in Arthur's hand. 'It were *thee* who set the fire? I'd heard as the agitators were meeting at your house of an evening, but I never thought as tha' would . . .'

Tomlinson's anger was so uncontrolled that he struck out at Arthur was his ham-like fist.

Arthur saw the blow coming and put up his hand to ward it off. He hadn't meant to hit Tomlinson, but as Tomlinson lurched forward Arthur's blow took him on his chest, just above the heart, and he stopped as if pole-axed. His mouth was working but he couldn't speak. His eyes looked imploringly at Arthur, with sorrowful pleading. Arthur dropped the brand and threw his arms wide to embrace Tomlinson, to assist him in whatever way he could, but Tomlinson slowly crumpled to the ground. At that moment, Arthur heard the shout from the doorway.

'Stay where you are, you blackguard, else I'll blast you to hell and back!'

Arthur turned and saw a man whom he recognized as Probyn, the husband of Tomlinson's servant, carrying a flint-lock musket. He heard more voices outside and the doors opened wide to admit a crowd of men and women, folks who lived in the Mill Cottages who'd been attracted by the noise of the shouting.

'It's Aysgill,' they were saying, 'he's tried to set fire to the mill!'

303

They surged forward at him and Arthur found himself backing against the wall. Soon they were gathered about him but none came in to attack him, fearful, no doubt, of the weapon Probyn was holding. They lifted Tomlinson and carried his inert body back towards his house.

'Aysgill, trying to put us all out of work!' Arthur heard them saying. 'Trying to burn down the mill . . .'

'I never!' he shouted. 'It weren't me!'

'Aysgill, killed the overseer who befriended him . . .'

'I *never*!' Arthur shouted.

Someone had found the brand and brought it to the front of the crowd. Though the evidence was circumstantial, they were working themselves into a frenzy, ready to rush him, kill him, hang him from one of the beams.

'I had nowt to do with it!' Arthur screamed. 'It were all a scheme to make it look as if I did it!'

The crowd were not listening. These were people Arthur had known for most of his life, but when he looked into the screaming faces before him he couldn't recognize them for the blood lust that had been aroused. They were like animals, seeking a moment of weakness to dash in and mangle their victim.

'I never had nowt to do with it,' he moaned in despair.

'Aysgill, killed the overseer, wanted to do us all out of a job . . .'

The crowd was growing as more and more people living in the neighbourhood were attracted by the noise. Suddenly, one voice sounded louder than the rest, in a terrible piercing scream. The movement was rapid, and Arthur couldn't see the details through his tear-filled eyes, but the left side of the crowd came in rapidly, and a weaver he knew reached out his hand and locked it in Arthur's hair. Arthur punched out but felt his arm being held and twisted. He felt a boot against his shins and the horrible pain that ran into his kneecap. Now he was screaming and felt his last moments had come once this wolf pack engulfed him.

The sound of the piece being fired shocked them all into silence. Sally had followed her husband after she'd left the babies with the neighbour, and had arrived in time to see him menaced by the crowd. It was she who'd emitted the first scream, who'd seized the piece from the hands of Probyn. She pushed her way forward through the crowd and stood before Arthur. Then she turned, spread her arms wide and shouted at them.

'If you kill him, you kill me, too! Come on, you cowards – kill a woman, will you? A woman as has bairns still suckling at her breasts?'

The crowd, stunned, were still.

She reached up to her neck and tore open the bodice of her dress, exposing her breasts to the mob. 'You'd kill a woman as still gives suck?' she shouted.

Now they drew back, and the murmur began again.

'Us'll kill no woman,' Probyn said. 'Us has no quarrel wi' thee, missis.'

Someone must have run to fetch the Constable and all now heard the clatter of the galloped horse outside. The Constable forced his way through the crowd, taking in the scene with a few piercing glances.

'We'll have no mobs nor riots,' he said, loudly but firmly. He pointed to Probyn. 'You,' he said, 'stay here and tell me what this is all about. The rest of you disperse outside – else I'll call out the troops!'

The crowd began to shuffle backwards; the last time troops had been called out, to handle the bread riots in Briggate, thirty men had ended up with broken heads and the two men believed to be ringleaders had been killed.

'He tried to set fire to the mill and killed the overseer,' Probyn told the Constable.

'You were witness to this?' Sally asked rapidly.

'I saw him kill Mr Tomlinson with a blow to his chest,' Probyn asserted.

'I'll ask the questions, young woman,' the Constable said.

'And you'd be advised to cover your modesty as best you can afore you catch an ague. Or, from this crowd, summat worse.'

'I'm not afeared of a group of cowardly louts such as yon,' Sally said, her eyes flashing contempt at the mob.

'Hold your tongue, missis,' the Constable retorted, 'else I shall run thee in and charge thee wi' breaching the King's Peace.' He turned to Probyn. 'You saw him strike a blow to the deceased?'

'To Mr Tomlinson? Aye, I saw him.'

'Afore the blow, Mr Tomlinson was alive?' went on the Constable.

'Aye, he struck out at yon.'

'After the blow, he was dead?'

'Aye, he just, like, fell to the ground . . .'

'And you are prepared to swear on the Bible to what you've just said?'

'I am that.'

'So be it. Now, get us both out of the mill by the back way, sharp as you can—'

'Where are you taking my husband?' Sally wailed.

'I'm taking him to the cell beneath the Magistrates' Court,' the Constable said. 'He'll appear before them in the morning.'

'What are you charging him with?'

'*I'm* charging him with nowt,' the Constable told her firmly. 'It'll be up to the Magistrates to call for whatever evidence they require and then they'll charge him.' He turned to Probyn. 'You'd better be at the court i' the morning, nine o'clock sharp, else we'll send somebody to fetch you, understand?'

'Yes, I understand,' Probyn nodded, 'though there's much to be done afore then.'

'Then show me the way out, and tha' can get on wi' it,' the Constable said, as he took Arthur Aysgill's shoulder and led him out of the mill.

Probyn was not the only one who busied himself during the

night. When the Court assembled the following morning, in the presence of Mr Justice Barnard and Mr Justice Collingbrooke, Sally had already sought out the Clerk of the Arraigns and engaged him in urgent conversation.

Sleightholme had been summoned from his home; he appeared dressed entirely in black, even with a black bandeau on his arm, in mourning for his faithful servant Tomlinson. He was a most impressive sight as he took his place in the Court, glaring at Arthur Aysgill when he was brought from the cells below.

The Clerk of the Arraigns had placed himself behind and between the two Justices and spoke urgently to them for a considerable time before resuming his normal seat below their Bench. Both Justices were wearing their long full-bottomed wigs and scarlet robes; neither looked as if he had slept well, or welcomed being called at such an hour to commence business but, Sally thought as she looked up at them, those could be their normal expressions and mien, since neither gave the slightest sign of being burdened with good humour.

When order had been obtained after the public, mostly workers at Sleightholme's Mill, had been given entrance to the gallery, the Clerk rose to his feet; the Court Usher banged a mallet on a piece of wood to demand silence, and the proceedings began.

Arthur Aysgill was charged with murder, and with maliciously setting fire to the property of one Thomas Sleightholme; to wit, the premises of a mill.

How did he plead, the Clerk asked Arthur.

Arthur pleaded not guilty.

Was he represented by counsel, the Clerk asked.

Arthur said that he could not afford counsel and, in any case, proposed only to speak the truth in which case he had no need for counsel.

That elicited the first smile from the Bench. It was not the first occasion on which both Justices had heard similar words of bravado.

Probyn was called as a witness. He described how he had entered the mill on hearing unusual noises from within, how he had seen the accused holding a firebrand in his hand, how he had seen Mr Tomlinson of dear memory aim a blow at Aysgill, how Aysgill had aimed a blow back, which had struck Tomlinson in the chest, and how . . .

At this point he was interrupted by Mr Justice Barnard. 'You say you saw the deceased attempt to strike the accused?' he asked in a cold clear voice.

'That is so, your lordship.'

'Prior to this, had the accused attempted in any way to strike the deceased?'

'No, your lordship,' Probyn said decisively. 'The accused was just, like, standing there.'

Mr Justice Barnard bent his head towards his colleague on the Bench and they whispered together. Then, sitting upright again, he addressed Arthur. 'Mr Aysgill,' he said, his voice betraying a certain warmth of anger. 'You have been wrongly charged with murder. Clearly, if Mr Tomlinson – God rest his soul – struck you first, you cannot be said to have murdered him. Either you struck a blow to defend yourself, or you decided to engage him in a bout of fisticuffs to pursue your as yet unproven design of burning down the mill. Now, think carefully before you answer this question. Why did you strike Mr Tomlinson?'

'But I *didn't* strike him,' Arthur said desperately. 'I only stuck out my arm to ward off his blow, to prevent him from striking me. He sort of – in a manner of speaking – ran on to my arm. I had no desire to strike him. He was my benefactor and my champion; I wouldn't even think of striking him a blow.'

The Justices conferred again, then Barnard addressed Probyn. 'You've heard what the accused has said. Would you say that the blow you saw was struck in the manner of an attack, or was the movement which you observed consistent with one man trying to fend off the assault of another?'

Probyn thought about it for a long moment. He looked at

Sleightholme who was glaring across the court at him, the malice in his eyes quite apparent. Probyn knew he was taking a risk upon himself of losing his job, of losing his cottage and his livelihood. But he couldn't lie. 'Yes, your lordship,' he said quietly, 'it could have been as Aysgill said, that he was trying to stop Mr Tomlinson hitting him.'

Sleightholme groaned with rage, and both Justices looked severely at him.

'In that case,' Justice Barnard said, 'the Bench is agreed that the accused has no charge to answer on the first count of murder. However, I would take this opportunity of warning the accused that, if it will be established that another crime was committed, and that Mr Tomlinson died as a result of the instigation of that crime, then other charges will, most certainly, be formulated.' He leaned across the Bench and addressed the Clerk. 'This witness can be released for the moment,' he said. 'I understand you wish to call another witness?'

'Yes, your honour,' the Clerk said. 'Call Mrs Sally Aysgill.'

A murmur of surprise ran through the public gallery. Arthur turned towards the door at the side of the Bench which had opened to reveal his wife. She was dressed plainly in an old brown calico dress with a cowled hood which hung behind and framed her chestnut hair. Her face glowed with health and recent scrubbing and she looked so fresh, so sweet, that his heart went out to her. What had the lass done this time, he asked himself.

Sally stood in the witness box and took the oath on the Bible in a clear though quiet voice. She looked at the Justices as if eagerly anticipating any questions they might care to put, determined to answer them as honestly as she could.

'You are Mrs Sally Aysgill and you are the wife of the accused?' Mr Justice Barnard asked gently.

'I am, your honour,' she said, avoiding the mistake Probyn had made of calling him 'your lordship'.

309

'And you have something to tell the Court?'

'I have, your honour.'

Suddenly, Arthur knew what she was going to do and the words burst unbidden from his lips. 'Sally, don't!' he cried. 'Tha' mustn't!'

'The accused will refrain from speaking until I ask him a direct question,' Mr Justice Barnard said sternly. 'Now, Mrs Aysgill, what have you to tell us?'

'I can produce evidence from the family of Mr Tomlinson,' she said firmly, 'that for some time Mr Tomlinson had been complaining of pains in his chest. They say the doctor says—'

The Justice was holding up his hand. 'I do not want to stop you, Mrs Aysgill,' he said in a kindly manner, 'but normally we cannot take account of what other people say. You are not to know this, but such evidence is called "hearsay" and cannot be accepted in a Court of Law. However, on this occasion since I have been informed of the steps you have taken, I will admit what you say, though I shall use my own judgement as to whether I shall count it as conclusive. Do you understand what I mean?'

'You'll listen to me, but you may not believe me unless I can prove it,' Sally said.

Both Justices now smiled. 'Madam, we could all take lessons in clarity of speech from you. Pray continue.'

'The family of Mr Tomlinson told me that he had recently consulted a doctor, who said Mr Tomlinson was having trouble with his heart.'

Justice Barnard nodded. 'Well, that is something that can easily be proven,' he said. 'Do you wish to say anything else?'

'In the matter of setting the fires, your honour. My husband was approached on five separate occasions by men who asked him to join with them in a combination. Each time, he refused them. A pot-boy came to our house last evening and told us Mr Tomlinson was wanting to see my husband at the mill. My husband went to see what Mr Tomlinson wanted, and that's all.'

'And you are certain your husband never entered into collusion with these men?'

'Never!' Sally said vehemently. 'Of that I am quite certain.'

'And the names of these men?'

Arthur again wanted to shout, 'Don't do it, don't do it!', but he held his tongue.

'I don't know all their names,' Sally said in a clear voice, pointing an accusing finger. 'But three of them are sitting up there in the gallery right now.'

The Court erupted in a storm of whispering. There was no need of names. The three men knew at whom she was pointing, and made the mistake of standing up to try to leave the Court.

'Beadle, detain those men!' Mr Justice Barnard said loudly, his voice carrying above the sound of the mallet being pounded on the block of wood to restore silence and order. He turned to Sally. 'You know, my dear,' he said admiringly, 'you've just done a very sensible, brave, and possibly foolish thing. And I am inclined to believe your evidence. The Constable will go into this matter more thoroughly, especially with the men you have identified. If, as a result of those enquiries, we are able to get to the truth of this matter, I shall be most pleased to release your husband to you. At the same time, I shall recommend from the Bench that no action of any kind is taken by your husband's employer to the detriment of your husband's welfare. I think that Mr Sleightholme, who is not unaccustomed to the manners of the Court, will heed our words most scrupulously. You are to be congratulated, Mrs Aysgill, for your spirited defence of your husband. I wish you well, and you may now step down.'

'And my husband . . . ?' Sally asked hopefully.

'I think we shall keep him with us for a day or two, until the Constable's enquiries have been completed. I remand the accused in custody, to appear before us again in twenty-four hours.'

CHAPTER FIVE

The year of 1776 brought two happy events for Gertrude Fossett. The first occurred when her son Walter passed his examinations and was offered a berth as mate on one of the vessels owned by her employer Captain Edgecombe, engaged on the West Indies run. She had earlier hoped that Walter would take to the sea with his father, Captain Fossett, engaged in the collier trade with his own command of which he also had part shares, but father and son agreed that Walter would gain greater experience of the sea and the world by spending a few years on the long-distance foreign runs. Though it meant parting from her son for many months at a time, Gertrude finally had to agree, since both men had set their heart on it and Captain Edgecombe, her employer and benefactor, had agreed with them.

The second happy event, which fortunately happened before Walter set sail and when her husband Luke was at home while his ship was being unloaded in Whitby Harbour, was the marriage of her youngest son Daniel at twenty-three to a local Whitby girl, Mabel Turnham, the daughter of a journeyman carpenter who made masts for the larger ocean-going vessels. Daniel had learned much of his carpentry skill from Mabel's father, and now found steady employment in the local shipyards where he could turn his hand and his tools to a variety of ship's requirements. He was extremely skilled in making sheaves and sheave-boxes and even contemplated setting up his own business to make them for supply to all the yards since he'd earned such a reputation. Luke Fossett had insisted his son take a grounding in *all* manner of ship's carpentry before he'd agree to invest any of the family money in a speculative venture, though he was certain the sheave-box would succeed.

The wedding was a grand affair in Whitby parish church; Mabel was her father's only child and he wanted to see her – in his own words – 'launched in style upon the sea of matrimony'. A reception and luncheon was held afterwards at the Ship Inn, at which all who knew the two families were invited to eat and drink their fill. Captain and Mrs Edgecombe graced the occasion by putting in an appearance for half an hour, for the whole of which time Captain Edgecombe and Fossett discussed their joint maritime venture. Only when Mabel, a sprightly young bride, dragged them apart did Luke Fossett take his glass to join her father, who by this time was very much the worse for drink. Tears were running down Turnham's cheeks as he morosely told anyone who would spare time to listen of his pain at losing his 'only lass'.

Luke slapped him on the back, filled his glass with rum, and took him out to the back of the hotel to get some fresh air. When Turnham had vomited away the mixture of rum, beer and brandy he had consumed, he began to feel more cheerful. Thereafter the celebrations continued in thoroughly satis-factory fashion, and Turnham hardly noticed the departure of the newly-weds.

Daniel and his bride had decided to travel to York for their honeymoon, to observe the bustling life of the northern capital city for a few days. Mabel was consumed with excitement as the coach drew near to the wonderful city on the plain, with its Minster soaring into the sky as a landmark for many miles around.

They put up at a hotel in Micklegate and spent the first night of their marriage in passionate lovemaking. Next morning Mabel was too excited to stay indoors, and dragged her husband out through Ploughswain and Badgergate, to Fetter Lane where the felters worked, through Coopergate to see the coopers busily employed in making their barrels. Next they must go and see the site of the former royal castle of which only Clifford's Tower remained and the earthmound known as Baile Hill. The newly married couple wandered, often hand in hand, past the new construction of Burlington's Assembly Rooms and Mansion House, with Mabel declaring at each step that she had never seen any buildings so magnificent, any sights so enthralling.

Daniel was prepared to be patient with his new bride – though, truth to tell, his desire was to take her back to the hotel. The previous night's lovemaking had served only to increase his passions and make his wife the more desirable. Finally, as the light began to fade, he was able to lead her back towards Micklegate by a devious route and to express surprise when they came within sight of their lodging.

'My feet are so sorely tired,' he complained, 'that I needs must rest a while in our room.'

He led her up the stairs. Mabel was unused to such luxury as the hotel offered and when others passed them on the stairs, for it was the customary hour for dining, she blushed at the certainty they would be recognized for newly-weds.

When they arrived in the room, Daniel took off his boots and flopped on to the large feather-down mattress of what seemed to Mabel to be a most enormous and wicked bed. A virgin when she had married, she knew it would be some time before she could accept a man in her room with equanimity. Especially since her first encounter with a man's passions had given her certain problems.

'Come lie by my side, sweeting,' Daniel said, seeking to cajole her on to the bed. 'We'll take our ease for an hour before we go down to sup.'

Mabel could divine his intentions from the look on his face. 'Husband,' she said hesitantly, 'I must crave your indulgence in a small matter . . .'

'Anything your heart desires,' he said tenderly.

She came to sit beside him on the bed, but when he reached

314

for her she drew away from him. 'Dear husband,' she said, 'I am troubled to know how to speak what is in my mind . . . Please do not hold me, for when I have said what I must, your love will quickly turn to hatred.'

'Nay, lass,' he said, pulling himself up on the bed so that he was sitting, 'nothing on God's earth nor in the heavens above could make me hate thee!'

His apparent affection merely served to increase Mabel's distress. How could she bring herself to speak of a matter so intimate? 'Last night . . .' she began nervously.

'Last night was the ultimate point of my happiness,' Daniel said ardently. 'It was but an indication of the rich quality of love which awaits us for the rest of our lives.'

'Let me *speak*, husband,' she protested.

He was surprised to hear a rasp to her voice, a note of some exasperation, and to see tears forming at the corners of her eyes. He leaped from the bed and, despite her protests, gathered her tenderly into his arms. 'What ails thee, my love?' he said. 'Only speak to your dear loving husband . . .'

'That is the trouble,' she said. 'Last night's loving was so painful to me, in . . . in the bodily sense, that all intimate pleasure was removed. Now I ache so in my tender places that I can hardly bear it. I have walked and walked this day, hoping to alleviate the distress my pains have caused me, but without success. I am so . . . Oh God give me strength to speak of these things! I am so pained that I can hardly bear the touch of my undergarments on . . . on that part of my body. Husband, I have no wish to refuse you, to fail in my wifely duty – but in truth I cannot . . . I could not . . .' Unable to continue further, she burst into a fit of wailing and weeping that tore at his heart.

'My love,' he said, seeking to comfort her but failing in words. 'There, there, my love. It was never my intention to cause thee pain, tha' knowest that.'

Daniel cursed himself for a blundering fool. Mabel had been so small in her parts, and he so large with lust, that she had screamed when he had thrust himself into her, and he had seen the blood on her lower lip which she had bitten to stifle her sounds of distress. He'd known several women before, all doxys, and when they commented on the size of his parts he'd assumed they were flattering him to increase their payment of coin. His brothers Walter and Reuben had warned him that matters didn't go easy the first time if a man married an inexperienced girl. Clementine, Reuben's wife of three months only, had apparently suffered greatly the first time, but according to Reuben had shown signs of pleasure the second and third times and now was always enthusiastic to retire to bed with her husband. Last night, after the wedding, Daniel had made love to Mabel some four or five times, consumed with passion and longing for her tender body, and stimulated by the joy of the wedding and the following feast. Had he been too demanding, he now asked himself?

'Have no more fears,' he said. 'I am quite prepared to wait until nature heals yours pains. I love you greatly, Mabel, and being together in the bed is only a small part of that.'

'But if I can't please you, you'll cast me out,' she wailed.

'You *do* please me, in all matters,' he said. 'We must be patient in that one aspect of our marriage. You have no cause for fear, sweetest one.'

'You'll cast me out! I know you will!' she insisted between sobs. Cradling her in his arms, Daniel picked her up and laid her tenderly on the bed.

'I cannot . . .' she sobbed. 'I cannot . . .'

'We will not even try until such time as you are mended again,' he said, seeking to comfort her. 'I shall go to the apothecary now and try to find some soothing balm. Then I shall leave you alone while you endeavour to cure your aches with it. Take your ease, my love. I shall soon return.'

'You'll not leave me here?' she wept. 'You'll not abandon me?' Daniel bent over and gently kissed her brow. 'Rest, and try to sleep,' he said, 'I shall be back before you awaken.'

* * *

Daniel descended quickly to the street, wondering which way to proceed to find an apothecary. A military gentleman was passing by and Daniel recognized the same uniform he'd been seeing all day on their perambulations. The man was doubtless garrisoned in York, and would know all its inhabitants.

'Excuse me, sir,' Daniel said, 'but could you direct me to an apothecary? I am but recently arrived in York with no knowledge of its establishments.'

The soldier stopped. 'An apothecary . . . Have you an ache or a pain? I am not unskilled myself in some matters concerning the human body.'

'Nay, 'tis not for me,' Daniel said quickly. 'The good Lord has given me the best of health. 'Tis for my newly married bride.' He hesitated, but then reasoned that a soldier would be a man of the world. He indicated the part of his body which corresponded to the source of his wife's discomfort.

'Ah, I see,' the soldier said knowledgeably. 'Newly wed, eh? Right, I'll march thee off to an apothecary fast as fast can be.'

They had gone but a few yards down the street when Daniel saw the filled jars in a shop window that denoted an apothecary's premises.

'Ah, here it is,' he said. 'I'm greatly obliged to you, sir.'

The soldier took his arm. 'Yon fellow would be better in a shambles than as an apothecary,' he said. 'One of my men went to him wi' a toothache and the cure fetched every hair out of his head! I know of a more skilled one, specializing in the ailments of women. We'd fare better wi' him than wi' this quack.'

'It was my good fortune to meet you,' Daniel said warmly, 'else I should have been dosing my wife with poison, likely.'

'Likely so,' the soldier agreed. 'Now, we'll just step out this way . . .'

The soldier set a smart pace and all moved aside as he strode along the pavement beneath the overhanging balconies. His was a commanding figure in shining black boots, white buckskin breeches, short red jacket cross-banded by two white leather straps, massive epaulettes trimmed with fur at the shoulder, cuffs of a bluey-grey with buttons and white facings. On his head he wore a high matted woollen hat into which a chain had been fastened. Daniel wanted to ask which regiment he belonged to, and what was his name and rank, but was so intimidated by the man's haughty bearing that he hesitated to seem inquisitive.

The soldier now turned sharply left off Micklegate into a small alley. 'It's through here at the far end,' he said. 'This is a shorter route than going round the streets.'

Daniel followed obediently. They were halfway down the alley when suddenly the soldier stopped and turned around.

'You wouldn't be interested in joining the First West York Militia, would you?' he asked ingratiatingly.

'I fear not,' Daniel said, smiling. 'I'm but newly married, as I told you, and a carpenter by inclination, with no desire to become a soldier.'

'I thought not.' The soldier abruptly raised his voice. 'Right, lads – sharp about it! Here's another for you!'

Within a trice, Daniel was surrounded by other soldiers who'd been lurking in the shadows of the alleyway.

'Nay, what's this?' he shouted. 'What do you want with me?'

'We want you for the Army,' grinned Daniel's erstwhile friend. 'Now, you can come quietly, else we shall have to take you by force and you won't enjoy that, I'll be bound!'

'You're the press gang!' Daniel shouted.

'That we are,' the soldier said. 'I'm happy tha's so intelligent as to work that one out, for we have sore need of intelligence in the Regiment – eh, lads?'

Daniel made up his mind quickly; he lowered his head and butted the nearest man in the face, winded the second one with the crook of his elbow, kicked the third one with the side of his boot, and attempted to run out of the alley, shouting as loudly as he could. The soldiers were laughing. One put his gun between Daniel's legs. Another slammed the weighted butt of his weapon on the back of Daniel's neck.

'Steady, lads,' the first soldier warned them. 'We get nothing for dead uns!'

Daniel heard the jeering voices, felt the rifle-butt descend a second time on his neck, then knew no more as he toppled forward into a hellish nightmare of oblivion.

Daniel sat shivering in the hold of a vessel that was, reportedly, taking him to America from the port of Liverpool. Other new recruits, similarly clad in the red and white of the Militia, were sitting along the long bench that extended amidships below decks. Each had a different story to tell of the press gang. Some had been taken in brothels, others from the street in broad daylight, others shortly after dark. Daniel learned that his captor had been Lieutenant Sampson, a notorious pressganger who had a hundred new soldiers to his credit from the city of York alone; Sampson was growing rich on the bounty the Army paid him for each new recruit. Since the night Daniel had enlisted Sampson's aid to find an apothecary his life had been one long nightmare. To all his entreaties that at least a message should be given to his new wife, to tell her he had not voluntarily deserted or abandoned her, Sampson's men had turned a deaf ear.

'You'll go fight in the war,' they laughed, 'and become a hero wi' battle honours! Your wife will hear soon enough what a stout fellow you are!'

Foolishly, Daniel had even tried to explain to one officer the special circumstances that had prevailed, the intimate reason he had set out to find an apothecary. The officer had laughed, told the men under his command, and Daniel had become a laughing stock. Unable to help himself, for his hands were cruelly bound behind him as he rattled with other pressed men in the back of the cart taking them to Liverpool, he had watched impotently while the soldiers exposed his private parts and made a joke of his size.

'Yon's a fearsome weapon to carry into battle!' they had scoffed. 'Show that to the Americans and they'll run screaming to lock up their wives and daughters!'

At Liverpool the pressed men had been assembled in a shed surrounded by armed soldiers. The bonds had been released and they had been given uniforms to wear, while their other items of clothing had all been taken away. An officer had read an Article of Enjoinder over their heads and each man had been given a coin. On pain of an immediate-beating, all had been made to recite the Oath of Loyalty to His Gracious Majesty, and had then been informed that they were now soldiers.

'If any man tries to escape,' the officer had warned them, 'he will be treated like a deserter and summarily shot. If any man offers resistance to the orders of superior soldiers or officers, he will be tried by Courts Martial and sentenced in strict accordance with military procedures.'

The non-commissioned officers had regaled the new conscripts with stories of men who had disobeyed simple instructions and had been tied across the muzzles of cannon before the cannon had been fired, to be blown away by the guns. 'That's the least they do if they even suspect mutiny,' they were told.

Most of the new soldiers were resigned to their fate and resolved from that day forward to make life as easy for themselves as they could in the Army. Daniel himself would have followed the same course, for he had never been a man to seek the impossible, save for two worries that nagged him. Firstly, Mabel might believe that, because of her lack of sexual prowess, he had run away from her to seek a more compliant wife. Secondly, when they arrived in battle, would he turn out to be a coward? He had never been particularly brave as a boy and his two brothers had often laughed at him. He knew his parents had wanted him to take to a sea-faring life, and he would dearly have liked to do so himself, except that he felt always afeared when he heard stories of storms at sea, men lashed to the yard-arm to prevent monster waves from washing them overboard, or putting into strange places for water and being attacked by natives. He knew he had no stomach for danger of any kind and all his life had nursed a feeling that perhaps the good Lord had made him a coward. If he proved a coward in battle, would he be tied across the muzzle of a gun and blasted away? Many times he resolved to try to escape, and would have done so before the ship sailed from Liverpool had not another of the pressed men attempted to flee and been captured. In the centre of the barrack square of the Militia's camp two horses had been tied, one to each leg of the recaptured fugitive, and, while all the other pressed men were forced to watch, the horses had been spurred on to tear the unfortunate victim bodily apart.

In his heart Daniel knew it was already too late to make amends to Mabel. By now she would have solved her problems at the hotel and have returned to Whitby. By now his dear mother and all his intimates would have begun to believe he had run away – he had no doubt that Mabel, who had become close to Gertrude during the months before the wedding, would have disclosed something of the nature of what she believed to be his reason for leaving her. Would his own mother believe he had been so base, so vile? He doubted that any enquiries they made in York would lead to the truth, that he had been pressed into the Army. He would have to accept what life brought him during the next year or two. Perhaps, if he waited a few years and served His Majesty loyally, the Army would relax its vigil and he might be able to escape to return to Whitby. But would he survive? When the American guns began to shoot at him, would he turn tail and run, only to be killed for a coward and deserter?

The fruitlessness of such speculations didn't prevent them haunting Daniel night and day during the passage across the Atlantic Ocean to join the American Revolution.

* * *

The boat on which Daniel and the other pressed men were travelling, in the company of a thousand regular soldiers of the British Army, was a hotbed of rumour and misinformation. One thing, however, did emerge clearly. The Americans, always prior to this time separated into different colonial factions, had finally joined together and had formed a Continental Army, under the command of a man quoted as a brilliant soldier and tactician, George Washington. It appeared that an action had been fought near Boston, at a place called Breed's Hill in Charlestown with the British under the command of General Gage.

The Continental Army had posted 1,600 Americans at the top of the hill – mostly untrained farmers and backwoodsmen, they did have the advantage of what was being described, no doubt fancifully, as the most fearsome weapon in the world, the 'Kentucky rifle'. This weapon used a smaller bullet held into position by a greased band. The inner walls of the rifle had been grooved so that, after the rifle was fired, the bullet spun to its target. Such was the stability and accuracy this spinning gave to the bullet that it was claimed a rifleman could hit a man's head at two hundred yards' distance.

The men on the hilltop, so the shipboard rumour ran, had been short of ammunition. General Israel Putnam of Connecticut, one of Washington's four leading generals, had recognized this and issued an order that brought a chill to every Britisher who heard it. '*Men, you are all marksmen,*' he was reported as saying, '*don't one of you fire until you see the whites of their eyes!*' With its terrifying implication that the Americans could actually put a bullet through a man's eye, the phrase had shivered the very marrow of the British soldiers. They had, however, advanced bravely on Breed's Hill, and over a thousand had been killed, including nearly a hundred officers.

This consignment of new soldiers, including Daniel Fossett, was intended to make up the Army's deficiency.

There had been hope that the war would end; Mr Dickinson

of Pennsylvania had drawn up an 'Olive Branch Petition' which Congress sent to London, but it was rejected by King George and Lord North, who said they could not accept the existence of such a body as the American 'Congress'.

When the vessel was three days out of Liverpool, the pressed men were released from below decks and permitted, as were the other soldiers on board, to take a turn round the decks from time to time. Daniel quickly discovered that a large percentage of the men on board were mercenaries from the German States – a murderous-looking lot, prepared to fight for any who paid them. They wore strange uniforms and seemed to have no respect for the bright-coated Militia. Daniel learned to avoid them; he took his fresh air in the scuppers, away from their swaggering walks, and contemplated the wake behind the vessel that daily lengthened to carry him further from his country, his home and his wife.

He was sitting thus one day when a youth of about sixteen, wearing the colours of the Militia, diffidently came and sat beside him.

'I hear your name is Fossett,' he said.

Daniel looked at him curiously. 'Aye, but what is that to you?'

The youth shivered, but whether with cold or fear it was impossible to tell. 'I have relatives called Fossett,' he said, obviously seeking a bond of companionship.

'Aye, it's a common enough name where I come from,' Daniel said. He too had need of a confidant, though his treatment so far had taught him to be suspicious of all who ventured close to him.

'Where's that?' persisted the youth.

'Whitby,' Daniel told him.

'My relatives live in Whitby. I've never seen them, but I have heard speak of them.'

'What's your name, then, lad?' Daniel asked.

'Aysgill. Robert Aysgill.'

'Well, I'll be damned!' Daniel said. 'Th'art my cousin, then

– if thy father's name is Peter Aysgill?'

'So it is. You must be one of Auntie Gertrude's sons, then?'

'That I am!' Daniel was so pleased to find a kinsman aboard, that he hugged the lad to him.

Robert was equally delighted. 'Nay, cousin,' he said, ''tis one of God's miracles to find you here!'

'Can the Devil's work be called God's miracle?' Daniel laughed bitterly. 'I was taken on my honeymoon, and my bride of a day was left abandoned in York to fend for herself.'

'I was taken in York,' Robert said.

'Lieutenant Sampson?'

'The same.'

The relief both lads felt at having found each other amidst this motley of foreign troops, pressed men, brutal Militia and indifferent officers was so great that neither could speak for a while. But then Robert ventured a remark.

'It were my own fault,' he said. 'I've wasted my life, you know. I've always had too much money from my father, who sent me to Eton where I learned many sophisticated ways, and little else. I was travelling through York with, as usual, my pocket full of money. I decided to essay a few hands of cards and a few rolls of the dice. A girl in the gambling hall enticed me out with promise of her favours – I'd had too much to drink or I'd have seen her for the slut she was. The press gang took me from her room while she, laughing coarsely, boasted I was the fourth she'd lured that way for coin. Aye, and the baggage stripped my purse, though the press gang took the money from her before each enjoyed her services, with me bound and gagged and obliged to watch in a corner of the filthy room. Aye, you see beside you a lad who has ill-spent his years and a considerable portion of his patrimony.'

The two cousins became inseparable companions during the long voyage to America, each lending fortitude in adversity to the other. It appeared to Daniel that his cousin lacked naught in bravery – several times, despite his lack of years, Robert faced down German mercenaries who blocked his path. One thing he had learned at Eton was a most haughty and imperious manner and even the regular soldiers quailed before him when he turned his piercing eyes on them. It was a great comfort to Daniel; he would be less liable to turn and run in the face of the enemy if he could have Robert bravely by his side to inspire him. He felt himself growing in stature beside his cousin, feeling larger in his reflected light.

'We will fare well,' Robert would say. 'When we arrive at our destination, we will quickly establish ourselves in the Regiment so that none shall subordinate us. We shall make ourselves known to the highest general and, using his good offices, we will send a message to England to my father, who will provide the funds to buy us an honourable discharge.'

Daniel eyed this hopeful young man with admiration. Though six years younger than himself, Robert had the self-confidence of a man twice his age, a tongue as sharp as a rapier and a devastatingly destructive wit. In so many ways he made Daniel feel like a coarse provincial, of neither birth nor breeding. Daniel did not object; he was so happy to have the companionship of his cousin on this dreadful voyage that he forgave him his occasional bouts of ill-humour, when his tongue could truly sting like a bee.

An event occurred when the vessel was fifteen days out of port which completely secured Daniel's loyalty to his younger cousin. Daniel, with his interest in ship's carpentry, had visited the carpenter's locker and had cajoled the man into giving him a piece of oak and the use of a knife with which to carve it. Since they had nothing to do aboard ship to while away the hours of the passage, he spent his time carving the piece of oak into a heart-shaped bas relief which carried the so-well-remembered face of Mabel surrounded by intertwined oak leaves.

Robert watched the careful work proceed with some scorn. 'You'd serve yourself better,' he said, 'to forget the past for the time being, and think of our immediate future. Since you appear to have the peasant skill, why don't you carve the insignia of the Regiment on a plaque? We could present it to one of the officers as a token of our loyalty and thus earn immediate favour and privileges.'

Daniel would have liked to accede to his cousin's request but could not put the face of his beloved Mabel out of his thoughts. Carving her likeness seemed to lessen his nostalgia for her – each hair was separately chiselled, each feature of her fair remembered face, her gentle profile, her tender mouth and smile.

He was sitting carving in the scuppers one day when a group of German mercenaries walked by. They stopped to admire his work, then decided they would have sport with him.

'Vot you are making?' one of them asked in his guttural voice, and snatched the carving from Daniel's knee. 'Ah, it iss a girl . . .'

'His sveetheart!' the second said, laughing.

The first man threw the carving to the second. The second threw it to the first, who threw it to the third.

'Give me that,' Daniel said furiously, springing forward as it spun in the air from one to the other.

The Germans started teasing him, enticing him forward, then throwing the carving over his head at the last moment so that Daniel could not retrieve it. A crowd quickly gathered to watch and Daniel found himself the butt of all the laughter and jokes. Each time he jumped the crowd jeered and laughed again. One of the German mercenaries was standing in the scuppers and each time the carving came in his direction he pretended to miss it. Daniel saw, with sinking heart, that each time it was thrown to that man it became more difficult for him to catch it, and now the other two, as well as evading Daniel, were trying to best the third. Should they succeed, as inevitably they must, the carving would go over the side into the ocean, lost for ever.

'Please stop,' he said. ''Tis the image of my dear wife from whom I was rudely separated by the press gang.'

If he had hoped this plea would draw mercy from them he was mistaken. He raced about trying to catch the precious carving, stumbling over coiled ropes on the decks, banging into windlasses and sheave-boxes, while the mercenaries deliberately attempted to trip him whenever they could, taunting him as he sprawled on the deck, waving the carving near his face, then tossing it rapidly away when he tried to grab it. He feared that soon he would have no more strength to continue and then they would ruthlessly throw it overboard, bored with the game. He had to continue for as long as he could. He approached the man cautiously, advancing on the carving that was held out so temptingly before him. He saw the man's eyes taunting him. Which way would he throw it, left or right? Would he be able to read it in those eyes? The man was now passing the carving from hand to hand, swaying on his feet from side to side. Left or right, Daniel asked himself. He thought he saw a flick of the man's eyes to the right and threw himself in that direction. The man, however, had only feinted: the carving went spinning to the left. Daniel whirled round to where the first mercenary stood, his feet planted firmly apart on the deck, his hands wide waiting to catch the spinning carving. Daniel knew it would be hopeless to try to dart across the deck – the carving would have been caught and thrown long before he could snatch it.

Then, suddenly, Daniel saw the steel of a marline-spike appearing between the mercenary's opened legs. The spike was pointing upwards, thrusting up with an immense force. The man screamed as it drove through his breeches and he fell forward in agony, clutching at his middle.

The carving whirled above the man's bowed head and would have spun overboard had not Robert, standing a little to the side, caught it in his hand and quickly hidden it behind his back.

The two other mercenaries dashed forward to their compatriot, whose breeches were running with blood. One of them took the marline-spike in his hand and pulled it out, and blood gushed from the opened wound.

No one had seen who wielded the spike; or rather, none of the pressed men standing around watching the sport would admit to having seen who had wielded the weapon.

The mercenary died within the half-hour and was unceremoniously tipped overboard to a watery grave while the officer of the watch read a couple of verses from the Bible.

When Robert returned the carving to Daniel he said, in his best Eton voice, 'I believe this damned thing is yours . . .'

Daniel clasped his cousin's hand. 'Cousin,' he said fervently, 'I am forever in your debt and in your service.'

'Then you must put that carving aside and start on some token of the Regiment with which we can flatter one of the officers,' Robert told him.

'I will beg a piece of wood immediately,' Daniel promised, 'and start to carve it at once. Meanwhile, if you give me your tunic I will endeavour to clean that blood from the sleeve facings.'

328

Part Four

CHAPTER ONE

'There's a gentleman here to see you, Mr Ottershaw,' Wormsley said with a worried frown upon his face. Wormsley always wore a worried frown. Stanley had hired him to be office manager, clerk and book-keeper in his factory enterprise and had never once seen Wormsley looking happy. Now he stood at the side of the machine on which Stanley was working, wringing his hands as if he brought news of Doomsday.

'What sort of a gentleman?' Stanley asked, not paying too much heed, preoccupied with the movement of the cutter on the metal face before him.

'I think, Mr Ottershaw, 'tis Mr Aysgill,' Wormsley said.

'Ah, Uncle Peter . . . Tell him I'll come at once.'

Stanley straightened his back, nodded to the apprentice who'd been working the treadle and fiddle motion that kept the machine head turning, and wiped his hands on a piece of rag he kept hanging from his belt for that purpose. He followed Wormsley to his own office but Peter Aysgill was not there, he was in the outer office, standing at Wormsley's desk with the ledger open before him, scanning the records of past transactions. When he saw them he closed the book without embarrassment, stepped through into Stanley's own office and sat down.

Stanley sat behind his desk, clearing the papers to one side with hands still soiled and smelling of the liquid lubricant he used for the cutter head.

'Now then, Uncle,' he said cheerfully. 'To what do we owe the honour of this visit? You've not been here for a twelvemonth.'

Most surprisingly, Peter Aysgill had turned out to be an admirable silent partner once Dodie had persuaded him to invest his funds in Stanley's business. The interest on the loan had been paid with scrupulous accuracy on each quarter day, as stipulated in the agreement. Granted, there had not been many profits to divide, though Stanley reckoned his uncle must be getting about four per cent on his money, which couldn't be a bad investment. At least he'd lost nothing and still had his equity in the buildings, the machinery Stanley had bought or made, in the good stocks of metals he carried, in the royalty income from the improvements Stanley had been able to patent.

All this time Peter had kept Stanley at arm's length socially. Once, when Robert had mysteriously disappeared, Stanley had called at his uncle's house to offer his condolences but, to his shame and surprise, had not been granted admittance. He knew from other sources what had happened to his cousin Robert, for his uncle had engaged the services of a peace officer on a private account, to investigate the disappearance. It had not taken the peace officer long to find out that Robert had been seized in a brothel and press-ganged into the Army for service in America. Though not part of his duty, the peace officer had provided his employer with a list of names of the other men Lieutenant Sampson had taken; glancing down it idly, for he had no interest in the matter once he knew his son had been taken, Peter Aysgill had come upon the name of Daniel Fossett, and had sent a letter by special messenger to his sister Gertrude in Whitby. She had thanked him by return, and since then they had had no further correspondence on the matter. Stanley Ottershaw knew that to mention his regret at the press-ganging of Robert would only be to invite a rebuke, as would any conversation of a personal nature.

'I've come about my investment,' Peter said coldly, 'for I reckon it's lain fallow long enough.'

'Fallow, Uncle? Nay, 'tis earning four per cent on top of the interest. Yon can hardly be termed *fallow*.'

'If I had placed my money in the India trade, I should have trebled it by now. At the rate you're going, I reckon I shall be lucky to double it in my lifetime.'

'Nay, Uncle, I reckon we are doing most well. The patents are all paying handsomely, the buildings and the stocks are worth summat, and I'm not yet finished wi' inventing, you know. I've got that many orders for my borer. Half the water frame of Arkwright is made of my invented parts.'

'Yet he has the copyright,' Peter pointed out.

'Aye, but *we* get the work to make the new parts and that yields us considerable profit.'

'Of how much, may I ask?'

'How much, Uncle? I don't know that, do I? I leave it to Wormsley to work that out. Why keep a dog and bark yourself, that's what I say.'

'What figure does Wormsley work on?'

'How would I know that, Uncle? He books down what it costs in materials, in labour and time, and he puts a bit on.'

'And who pays the factory expenses?'

'Well, I do, of course. It's my factory. I pay the factory expenses out of what I earn – leastways, Wormsley arranges the payment, and that's that.'

'Who buys the materials you use, Stanley?' Peter went on.

'Well, you know how it is. When we need summat, we send out and buy it. If we get an order and know we're going to need summat to make whatever it is that's ordered, well, we buy what we're going to need.'

'So, you can buy today materials you're not going to use for a year or two.'

Peter's relentless questioning was beginning to annoy Stanley. 'Well, if it's a big order and takes a lot of time . . . I wouldn't like to run out of supplies and have to let somebody down, see. They'd soon go elsewhere if I started that lark.'

'And where do you buy your materials?'

'Damme, Uncle, I don't run around chasing every peck o'

brass! We buy the stuff we need from wherever we can get it. Some of it comes from Kirkstall Forge if it's a special forged iron, some comes from the steel smelter, some comes from't brass founders . . .'

'And if you have to buy a lot of materials, what do you do about the bills that come due the next quarter day?'

'Well, you know about that, Uncle. Wormsley comes and sees Binns, and they arrange between them that we borrow a bit more from your bank. You made the arrangements yourself. I don't know nowt about that; so long as the bills are paid, and my name stands good wi' the folks who supply me—'

'Stanley,' Peter interrupted impatiently, 'do you know anything at all about business? Do you know anything about the office? Do you know anything other than inventing pieces of machinery that will do things for you?'

'But that's not my interest, Uncle,' Stanley said reasonably. 'I'm an engineer, and – wi'out boasting – a damned good one. I know about metals and machines, and that's all that interests me. I took Wormsley on because you said I needed somebody, and I leave that side o' things to him.'

'I said to take Wormsley, or someone like him, to keep your *books*, Stanley, not to run your *business*. Wormsley, it seems to me, has no business training. Why, the man's a counting-house clerk and nothing else! He's good at his job – and believe me if he hadn't kept such an immaculate ledger, I'd have been round here long afore this. The time has come, Stanley, when you've got to learn to run a *business*. Other inventors, other engineers, are making fortunes for themselves. Aye, and earning honours while so doing. They're saying that yon fellow Arkwright – whose name means more to you than to me, since you say his machine uses many of your inventions – will one day be given a knighthood for his endeavours. Certainly he is a very wealthy man already with his water-powered mills at Cromford and elsewhere.'

'You've been studying him,' Stanley muttered resentfully.

'Of course I have,' Peter Aysgill said, 'in the way *you* should have been studying him if you hope to succeed. Look at the state of you, Stanley. You're covered in oil and grease from head to toe.'

'An engineer has to get his hands mucky, Uncle Peter.'

'I'll grant you that, Stanley, but surely much of what you are doing out there could equally well be done by an apprentice under your supervision. And surely, once you had trained him and others like him, certain tasks could even be completed *without* your direct supervision, simply following your design and standards. I've heard how you are working day and night, killing yourself because you insist on doing everything yourself. I've heard of how you've been found in the mornings, asleep over your drawing board. You must learn to train other folks to use their hands on your behalf, Stanley, so that you can use your mind on my behalf and your own. Stop being a machine-minder, and become a business man! I mean that most sincerely. You have six months to turn your interests around, and if I do not see signs of improvement, I shall pull out my money.'

'Pull out your money, Uncle? Nay, you'd never . . .'

'Don't put me to the test, Stanley. I am a business man, not a charity. You're locking up money which I could use elsewhere to greater profit. Unless you show sign of matching those profits, I shall end our relationship. Now, you and I will sit down together, and we'll go over your accounts. Then we shall see what we can do to make your business more profitable.'

'I've got machines working out there!' protested Stanley.

'Then let the damned things work, for me, and for you. First, let's begin with your purchases of raw materials . . .'

Stanley's business education began at that moment. Peter Aysgill stayed six hours with him that night, and Stanley was in a state of total bewilderment by the time they finished.

Though darkness had fallen, Peter made no move to invite Stanley to sup with him, or take a drink at an ale-house. His coach, with horse and coachman standing ready, had awaited him all that time. He made no apology, climbed into the coach, and told Jenkins to take him home.

Stanley watched him go, then turned to re-enter the factory from which all the workmen had gone for the night. Wormsley was standing just inside the door, rubbing his hands together nervously.

'I trust there is naught amiss, Mr Ottershaw,' he said. 'I hope no errors have been discovered in my work?'

Stanley placed his hand on Wormsley's shoulder. 'Nay, Wormsley,' he said, 'the only thing amiss is your Master. I'm to go back to school, Mr Aysgill says, and learn the alpha and beta of being a businessman. Damn him – I'll do it! I'll show him! But, my dear Wormsley, I'll need thee and thy head for figures to help me . . .'

The next months were difficult ones for both Stanley and Peter, in which each refused at first to concede a foot of ground to the other. Peter was adamant that no man could run a business from the side of a machine that others could be trained to work equally well. Stanley was equally adamant that his integrity, his reputation and hence his business would decline if he were not personally responsible for everything that left its doors.

'You must do as I do,' Peter insisted. 'You must find the best man for each task, ruthlessly eliminating those who do not match up to the highest standards. Having found the men, train them, and leave them to get on with whatever task you have entrusted to them. Of course, you must learn to supervise, to check what they do constantly, for no man who works for another is ultimately to be trusted. All will be tempted to pinch and scrape, to steal and to cheat.'

'Nay, Uncle,' Stanley declared more than once, 'I cannot countenance such a pessimistic view of mankind.'

'Then you'll die poor and a fool!' Peter retorted. 'The

debtors' prisons are filled, not with villains, but with optimists who would tell you they love all of mankind!'

Gradually the lessons Peter was teaching Stanley came to make some sort of sense. Why should he, for example, borrow money to pay for a consignment of steel to be delivered all at once when, with a little foresight and advance planning, he could arrange for the material to be delivered when he most needed it, and paid for stage by stage? Thus he would not owe so much money to the bank, and would not need to pay so much interest. Once he had invented his water wheel with concentric drive to take off power at a right angle to the main shaft, why should he bother to make each concentric drive himself when he could train a man to copy the one he had designed and had watched being made by one of his older engineers, a man he'd trained himself over the years to work a machine with fine accuracy? In fact, Stanley grudgingly admitted, the man was able to work more accurately than he himself. Why should he not ask his customers, when placing an order, to make him an advance of at least the cost of the materials? Why should he bear their financial burden until the machine was completed?

At first, Stanley had thrown up his hands in horror at such suggestions. He told Peter that he would lose all his customers if he asked them to pay money when they signed an order, but, to his great surprise, none of them jibbed at his request and all thought it reasonable. Almost overnight his borrowings from the bank were greatly reduced; he was able to pay back a part of his loan, thus reducing the interest and increasing his profits.

Why should he laboriously produce his own drawings, Stanley started to ask himself, often working all night to do so, when he could give a draughtsman the figures and a rough hand drawing and instruct him in the technique of turning this into the meticulous drawings from which the engineers worked?

More and more, Stanley found himself approaching Peter's point of view about money and materials, though he could never agree with his uncle about the nature of men and the impossibility of trusting them. It wasn't long before Stanley discovered how little he was needed on the floor of the factory, and how the output increased radically if he directed the men in the right way and then left them to get on with the work. He also found that he shed the great burden of fatigue that had diminished his efforts during the years he had stuggled to make the factory successful.

When his sister Jennifer asked permission, which he had granted, to live with the Testers, Stanley had bought a house near the factory for himself and Claude who, he realized, would always be dependent on him since he lacked ambition to prosper on his own. More and more he began to use the house. He'd installed a housekeeper who kept the place clean and tidy, cooked for him and Claude, and then retired to her own little cottage in the house's garden. It became a great pleasure to him to leave the factory each evening when darkness came and to sit with the candle lit at home, re-reading the classical books he had studied at Titus Waverley's school.

He also discovered that he enjoyed the mathematical side of making the business profitable. It was interesting to him to plan his money income and debt repayments, to so arrange his manufacture that he had as little money tied up in stock as possible. He began to curse himself for not having learned business before; quite soon the loan from his uncle had been considerably reduced, for the factory had much work on hand, and he knew that by the third quarter of the year he would be entirely out of his uncle's debt. When the debt ended, the interest he was now paying would go to swell his profits, which he could put back into the business in the way of more and larger machines. He had invented a boring machine and saw now that if he could extend the scope of it,

338

the factory could start to manufacture a steam engine of considerably greater power than the one in use at present. The smoother bore would make for a more efficient retention of steam. Perhaps he could even fulfil Jonas Clegg's dream of harnessing a steam engine to the processes of spinning and weaving. Already he used water power effectively in his factory, taking the Aire river as his source, but think what he could do with steam, which would make him independent of the river . . .

Now Stanley devoted each morning to the business side, each afternoon to inventing. Thus the practical side of his nature was satisfied; he could get his hands as mucky as he liked during the afternoon. Since he spent the whole morning thinking only of figures and business methods, he came to the bench fresh each afternoon, and many problems of a technical nature, which for so long had bedevilled and defied him, suddenly fell easily into a solution. For a long time he'd worked at a scheme to transfer power from a spinning object such as a water wheel into other forms of motion. Soon, from his water wheel by means of gears that he made himself – or rather, under the new regime, his engineers made for him – he could turn the spinning-motion into any combination of other motions. He had invented his own screw-cutting lathe, with a head that moved along parallel to an axis while the cutting head spun around. He could cut threads inside and out, could turn all manner of elegant but practical shapes.

Some of his time was spent keeping up with other people's inventions and he began to spend time in the Leeds Patent Office, to see what others were doing. He had been thinking of patenting his lathe, but already someone else had taken out a patent for the basic motion, and he knew he would not succeed. He also needed to keep abreast of all that was happening in the field of metals, since new irons and steels were constantly being produced, new amalgams to make brass and bronze more malleable, or more strong in the section. The wire trade had been known a long time and had succeeded because of the need for wire to card wool. Now, new metals made wire a most useful commodity, and new drawing techniques made wire of many different cross-sections. It was no longer necessary to roll steel in the forges to give it a sectional shape in the thinner pieces, though lines were already being forged along which waggons could be drawn by horses. One horse could pull a weight that formerly required three, now that waggon wheels could roll along forged iron rails and didn't have the enormous friction of stony roadbeds. It was one of Stanley's dreams that perhaps, one day, he might be able to build a machine that could roll along such lines, drawing waggons behind it. The machine would need to be made to work by steam power, of course, but Stanley's gearing inventions could be used while the machine was moving, to transfer the power from the steam piston to the motion of the wheels.

It was a dream that won him the reputation of being a fantasist from his uncle, who told him quite firmly that the horse could never be superseded. Peter had invested money in blood-stock, bringing Arab horses into the country from which a new strain could be bred. He made a lot of money from his importations, since all the gentry wanted an Arab these days.

'One day,' Stanley would retort, 'your horses will be old-fashioned – kept only as specimens, as wild animals are kept in zoological parks, for folks to pay to gawp at!'

It was a frequent arguing point between them, though such arguments were now carried out in a much better atmosphere. Stanley had acquired a greater understanding of his uncle, though it contained no affection as yet. He could see that Peter Aysgill remained faithful to his own beliefs; however financially ruthless he might be, he never cheated a man. Stanley himself began to understand that if a man entered into a transaction with him, the rules of that dealing became as harsh and inflexible as the rulers and etiquette of a duel. Nothing was

340

more frustrating than when a supplier, bound to him by written contract, let him down, and caused him in turn to let down his customers. He began to see that business affairs were a chain of confidence that, if broken, would damage the structure of the whole of the new community of invention and progress. Change was all about them and would inevitably lead to chaos and financial ruin if men could not be relied upon to meet their obligations.

Stanley saw this as a state of affairs that went from the lowest to the highest, a new hierarchy of dependence that would, he believed, in time become as important as the social and aristocratic hierarchies which had ruled the land for so long. It was a fact that many of the new men, of no great birth or breeding, had so far advanced themselves socially as to be greater leaders of the community than the traditional squires and land-owning lords. The Merchant Guilds, the Craftsmen's Guilds, the Aldermen of the City Council – such men were now more powerful than any duke or earl in the financial affairs not only of Leeds but of the whole country. And Stanley learned from Peter about the subscribers to the Bank of England, few of whom were former rulers of the land, rather they were successful merchants and politicians who'd used their power in office for personal profit.

All Stanley's engineers were bound to him; he had given them a wage on which they could live with decency in a suitable style. They were assured of a job, and he was assured of their services. Thus, for him, the chain started. He had found good suppliers and discussed prices with them, so that he was assured of a plentiful supply of the necessary raw materials, such as bronze, brass, iron and steel. He had no problem designing his final productions; there was a big demand for his kind of practical machinery which could be applied to cotton, silk, woollen manufacture with equal facility, save that wool was always the most intractable material and required particular handling.

341

Now that he was learning business sense, Stanley realized how right his uncle had been to take a strong line; in the past he had paid insufficient attention to the background to his activities and, in consequence, had not earned a just reward for his own or his men's endeavours. Once he had mastered those recondite matters of the office and the business, he knew he would forge ahead and become a tolerably wealthy man. The burden of gratitude he felt to his uncle opened the paths of understanding between them; though they could never become friends, since Peter Aysgill scrupulously continued to avoid any form of social intercourse with his brothers' and sisters' families, they could at least respect and admire each other's qualities.

On several occasions recently, despite the meticulous cleanliness of his apparel, Peter had even ventured into the machine room with Stanley and had watched some of the processes for himself with an apparent fascination. The world of practical matters, the delicate movement of machine parts one upon the other was obviously a revelation to him, though he had a great knowledge and respect for the saleability of the finished products. Peter grew to respect Stanley for his ability to see engineering problems in the abstract, and then to deduce a mechanical solution based on the various properties of the raw materials. It had never occurred to Peter that a metal could vary in its constitution; he thought of all metals as being hard and heavy substances, without realizing that some could be bent and some could not, that some could be polished hard and smooth and some could not, that some had great strength and others great flexibility. So Peter too had received an education; he now realized that though Stanley, in the early days of his tutelage, had been a hopeless business man, he had always possessed qualities of great imagination and sound practical commonsense. Now that Peter's business acumen had been grafted on to that sense, he recognized that Stanley would become a powerful person. And Peter revered power and those who could exercise it for financial gain more than any other human quality.

Such thoughts of human power derived from mechanical efficiency would often occupy Peter's mind as he was driven home from Stanley's engineering works after their sessions on business management. Peter had never considered that many of the mechanical allusions were also related to human experience, though, without realizing what he was doing, he had sometimes used the same principles in his business dealings. He now recognized, for example, that he had often used small sums of money to acquire larger sums, very much in the way a lever works, where a long and short handle work in concert. On these journeys to his house it amused Peter to cross-refer these allusions; money loaned out to a man to start a company meant the man paid interest back to the bank, which then loaned him more money for more interest, in an ever increasing spiral. Some of his bank's most lucrative accounts had started with as little as a hundred pounds, paying interest and secured by a debenture – many of those accounts were now in the thousands, with the difference being taken up by the skill, time and work of the borrower. He likened this to a pulley Stanley had shown him, in which the same piece of rope, passing over and round a number of wheels, greatly increased the power of the apparatus, enabling a man, for example, to lift many times more weight.

One evening, Peter came to a resolve. His son Gavin seemed to lack practicality in his education. The tutor Peter had engaged was a personable young man, but taught Gavin only such subjects as would form him into a gentleman. The tutor himself was of high birth though his family circumstances, due to the peccadilloes of his father, were so greatly reduced that he was obliged to earn his living as best he could. Such a man would normally have gone into the Army or the Church, but John James Neville had been born with defective eyesight and a lack of physical courage that effectively kept him from the Colours, and a cynical disbelief in the Almighty inherited from his carousing father that no amount of pretence could disguise. Neither a man for the camp nor the cloister, then, he was eventually reduced – when the bailiffs had seized his family's estate near Tadcaster and his father had escaped to France with a high-born lady of ill-repute who had been banished from King George's bedchamber because of her mendacity – to earning a livelihood by instructing young men in the art of gentlemanly behaviour.

As befitting a man who mourned former glories now lost to him, Neville painted a gilded picture of the life of the high-born and wealthy for his pupil, and Gavin was fast becoming a thoroughgoing convert.

Peter resolved that he would give Gavin the shock of his life: he would make him serve a term of apprenticeship to his cousin Stanley. 'That should teach the lad practicality,' he told himself.

Gavin was eighteen years of age and thus far had shown no aptitude for anything save the gentlemanly pursuits of gaming, dancing, gossiping and drinking. John James Neville, who had early asked for the full appellation, had told Peter once that no teacher could turn Gavin into a linguist, still less a great thinker.

'He's weak in the classics, Mr Aysgill,' Neville told Peter, 'and nothing I can do will persuade you otherwise. I fear that unless Master Gavin acquires some expertise in your world of banking and business, he will remain an adornment to society but little else.'

Peter had respected John James Neville for the honesty of his assessment; he had formed the same opinion himself and had despaired of finding improvement. Of one thing he was quite certain: he would never let Gavin loose on his business affairs, for that would quickly lead to the ruin of them all. He settled a sizeable income on the lad by way of rentals of property Peter had acquired in a default; the property could not be sold and therefore the capital would remain untouched. So far, Gavin had kept within his income, though his account at the bank hovered always near the danger line of insolvency since Peter had forbidden him to draw against future expectations. He would put the youth into Stanley's works and let him soil his hands for a month or two. That would teach him something of a mechanical nature, just as Peter himself had learned.

When he arrived home on this particular evening, Peter went to his study to await the housekeeper, who always came to him with an account of the day's domestic affairs. Mrs Pocock had been with him for a number of years, ever since his wife Tessa had misbehaved herself over the matter of her first pregnancy. After he had made his wife pregnant with Robert, his second child, Peter had ceased having relations with her, and she now remained a virtual prisoner in her own part of the house. Peter had not even seen her for over two months , having returned home late every night, by which time she was presumably already in bed. Mrs Pocock's daily account of the household activities, including those of his wife, sufficed to satisfy his interest. His butler, Chambers, presented himself first.

'I will take supper in an hour, Chambers,' Peter instructed him. 'When I have seen Mrs Pocock, I would be obliged if you will send Master Gavin to see me. When he has gone, I shall see Mr Neville.'

'Very good, sir,' Chambers said. 'Shall you be taking the claret tonight with the game?'

Peter hated wine and drank it only as a form of social observance when others were around. 'No,' he said, 'I shall take a pot of ale.'

He could see the disapproval on Chambers's face but was beyond caring. Peter had abandoned all forms of social pretence for himself, when he was alone. The loss of his candidacy for Alderman had persuaded him that he would always be socially vulnerable and, while he was prepared to play the game by social rules when others were about, he felt himself secure enough now to do as he thought fit with his intimate life. Drinking ale with his meals, when he ate alone, was one of his favourite indulgences, especially since the ale was brought from Smith's brewery at Tadcaster and reputed to be one of the finest in the land.

When Mrs Pocock arrived Peter saw immediately that she was troubled, though she began her account in the usual way, reporting that there was nothing unusual that he should know about the domestic situation. There seldom was; she ruled the house with great efficiency and all the staff went in fear of her, with instant dismissal the usual punishment for any transgression. Peter had abdicated those rights to her – he wanted nothing to do with such matters and refused to let his wife interfere in the household. Meticulous in maintaining the household accounts, Mrs Pocock's end-of-quarter ledger was a model of precision. Peter was convinced that she had never stolen so much as a penny from him, nor taken financial advantage of her situation in any way – unlike many housekeepers, who swelled the bills their masters paid by arrangement with the tradesmen.

Then she started telling him about the acquisition of new linen for the beds, since she had found the old linen no longer capable of repair – 'even by Nellie Fostle, Master, and a better hand with a needle we've never had below stairs'.

Peter always insisted on being informed of any domestic outlay immediately, though he made no attempt to interfere in such expenditure. He knew that her remark about the old bed linen would be an understatement; in the past, he'd often had to encourage her to throw old things away and purchase new ones. Such was her assured position in the household that she would even chide him respectfully and charge him with extravagance when he insisted, for example, that she should re-clothe all the servants in new uniforms.

As Mrs Pocock went on, Peter noticed her distress seemed to be mounting, as if she regretted approaching an unpleasant destination. When, finally, the report was ended, she seemed quite perturbed but still reluctant to leave. Peter watched her with some amusement, knowing how seriously she tended to view the most harmless of domestic misfortunes. Was she going to report a breakage, perhaps, or a small theft, the discharge of one of the servants, a case of below-stairs misconduct?

'Now what it is, Mrs Pocock?' he asked. 'You are hopping from leg to leg like a boy wi' the itch!'

To his utter amazement and chagrin, his jesting remark caused her to break down completely, and she began to wail and cry. He did not know what to say. She tried to turn and flee but the scrap of cotton she was pressing to her eyes effectively prevented her seeing.

'Now, Mrs Pocock, do control yourself,' he said, rising from behind his desk and showing her to a chair. 'Sit down, Mrs Pocock, and do control yourself . . .' She made an attempt to resist but was overwhelmed by her tears again, and could not rise. 'Now, Mrs Pocock,' he said, his voice taking a more commanding note, 'you must *control* yourself. I'll not have you behaving like a squalling brat, or a between-stairs maid. You must regain your dignity, madam.'

Her years of self-discipline stood her in good stead; she did as he had commanded, controlled her tears, stood up and regained her dignity, though nothing could hide the marks the tears had made on her cheeks or the redness of her eyes.

'It is with great regret, Master,' she said, 'that I must report a circumstance to you. I have been derelict in my duties – though in my own defence, sir, I can only indicate the cunning of those who set out deliberately to deceive me and the skill with which the deception has been practised.'

'I am none the wiser,' Peter said, resuming his seat. 'If you have some misfortune to report, I beg you to do so without treating me as a child from whom all nature of unpleasantness must be concealed.'

Mrs Pocock swallowed hard. 'I have the proof of what I am about to say, Master, but since you insist I will give you the conclusion before the proof. I fear that Mr John James Neville has been deceiving you with Mrs Aysgill, and she has been rewarding him for his vile services with her jewellery, a goodly portion of which is missing.'

'Proof,' he snapped, as if asking for the last line of a balance sheet.

'Because of a rumour in the Servants' Hall which I wished to end, I concealed myself in Mrs Aysgill's apartment. I observed Mr Neville commit acts of an indelicate nature with Mrs Aysgill which I cannot bring myself to describe. I observed her give him the ruby and diamond ring from her jewel box.'

'Do they know you observed them?' Peter demanded.

'No, Master.'

'Have you spoken of this to any other?'

'No, Master.'

'Nor shall you. Do you swear that?'

'I swear I shall never speak of this matter again to any living soul.'

He paused. 'Mrs Pocock, this day you have done me a great service. For my part, I shall repay you by settling such a sum on you tomorrow that you will never know financial want for the rest of your life, such sum to be yours when health and advancing years make it impossible for you to continue in my service. All I demand, as a further token of your service, is that you honour your vow never to speak of this matter again, to anyone.'

'I do so vow, Master,' Mrs Pocock said.

Following this unpleasant scene, Peter abandoned his plans to see Gavin and John James Neville on the matter of the change of education. He sent instead for Wallaby, his first footman.

'Wallaby, I have a special duty for you, which I pray you will carry out with your usual loyal efficiency.'

'Rely on me, Master,' Wallaby said. He was a large man to be in service, with little of the grace the gentry seek in those who serve them. But Wallaby had his special uses for Peter Aysgill, and they had a strict bond of understanding.

'I want you to keep an eye on Mr Neville,' Peter said. 'I want you to watch his every move from this moment forward. I think your surveillance will last a few hours at most, but I wish to know precisely where he is and what he does. If you are obliged to leave the house, you will take another footman with you, without disclosing the reason for so doing, and you will despatch the footman back here to inform me should Mr Neville settle himself anywhere. Is that absolutely clear?'

'Abundantly so, Master,' Wallaby said. 'From this moment forward, I'm to keep my eyes on Mr Neville and not lose sight of him till you tell me otherwise, and I'm to keep you informed of his whereabouts should he leave this house.'

Peter nodded, thinking deeply. 'Now, send a message to Sugden to attend me here as soon as possible.'

Sugden was the peace officer whom Peter had used to discover what had happened to his son Robert, an investigator of enormous skill and resource. He was duly sent for and came post-haste to Peter's house, knowing the summons could lead only to a lucrative commission.

'I have every faith in your discretion,' Peter began, when Sugden was seated in his study, 'and in your skill. I have reason to believe that my son's tutor, John James Neville, has purloined a quantity of jewellery from the possession of my wife. The circumstances will become evident to a man of your perspicacity, so I may as well be the one to inform you that Neville has been conducting an adulterous relationship with Mrs Aysgill, for which I shall devise other stratagems of punishment. Your task is to locate the jewellery – which, I believe, will have been removed from these premises. I cannot think Neville would be so foolhardy as to keep such precious and identifiable objects in his room or about his person. My housekeeper has prepared a list of the missing jewellery to the best of her knowledge. You are to take whatever steps are necessary to locate the jewellery and, if you can do so without alerting Neville, to restore it to me. Is this task within your compass?'

'This Neville, Mr Aysgill . . . Would he be related to the well-known Neville family?' asked Sugden darkly.

'Yes, he is, though the relationship is somewhat attenuated,' Peter told him. 'He is the son of Sir Rupert Neville.'

'Ah yes, in that case I know him well,' Sugden snorted. 'I was charged with apprehending his father who, alas, had fled the land the previous evening and escaped from justice in that way. Is Master John James to be apprehended and charged, sir? It would be a pleasure to see him brought to justice.'

'Mr John James Neville will indeed be brought to justice,' Peter said grimly, 'but I charge you not to concern yourself with that matter. Your sole concern will be the recovery of Mrs Aysgill's jewellery by any possible means, without the knowledge of the cuckolding blackguard. Can you do it?'

Sugden was a man of few scruples in the matter of solving a crime, as Peter well knew; he was not above planting false evidence of theft on a few criminals against whom he had wished to secure a firm conviction.

'I have every confidence, Mr Aysgill, that you and your valuables will soon be reunited,' he said. 'I would enjoin you, however, to restrain your righteous anger for the moment, so that Neville will have no cause for suspicion, else he might fly the coop to join his father in France. Once I have seized the stolen property, I can then peacefully leave the dispensation of retribution and justice to you.'

'You will not be out of pocket by this,' Peter promised.

Sugden smiled his thanks, but in fact he would have worked for no financial gain, since he was passionately concerned to square the accounts with all evildoers. A man of the Church, Sugden saw himself as a flaming sword set on earth to exact righteousness, an evangelist of the inflexibility of the law.

'Neville has left the house,' Peter said, 'and I have word that at present he is in the Assembly Rooms. I don't doubt you'll find him there. If you are able to do so, you may take Wallaby and Tinsman into your service – I shall relieve them of all duties as footmen for the duration of this investigation, should you require them.'

'If you do not object, Mr Aysgill, in a matter as delicate as this, I prefer to work unassisted.'

'And unobserved, no doubt,' Peter remarked, with one eyebrow raised.

Sugden nodded, took the bag of coins Peter gave him by way of expenses, and set out in pursuit of his quarry.

John James Neville was allowed a free period each afternoon, during which time he was able to leave the house should he so wish. He had quickly established his own routine in the household. When his morning's teaching work had ended, he would go to the kitchen to collect a small plateful of cold food, then retire to his own room, presumably to eat his food at leisure and to repose himself. He would, however, use the time while the servants were eating their lunch to make his way unobserved to Mrs Aysgill's apartments. There he would stay for an hour.

Posing as a new footman, Sugden automatically acquired access to all parts of the house. On the second day, he noticed Neville disappearing upstairs, and quietly followed. Secreting himself in the same closet that Mrs Pocock had hidden in, Sugden found himself witnessing the couple's adultery. From his vantage point, Sugden had a clear view of Neville's face, registering unconcealed repugnance as he went about his task with some distaste. Lacking for exercise, Tessa Aysgill was so obese that her body was grotesque; she obviously over-indulged herself with all manner of sweetmeats, Sugden thought, and consumed an excessive quantity of wine and spirits. To bring her to a satisfactory conclusion demanded enormous energy and persistence, and Sugden could clearly discern how little Neville enjoyed the labour, though he was most skilful at simulating pleasure and satisfaction. Mrs Aysgill talked all the time, questioning Neville, forcing him to speak, an obvious distraction from the mammoth task in hand.

'My dear John James,' she said, 'you cannot realize how wonderful it is for me to have the companionship of a gentleman, after the coarse embraces of that lout to whom my father sold me in slavery! Tell me, tell me, do you find me beautiful?'

'Madam, you're the apple of my eye,' Neville said, pausing in his labours.

'There! What a wonderful gentleman you are, to be sure! Do you find me as witty and as amusing as I find you?'

'Madam, I am only surprised you haven't set pen to paper to leave your incomparable bon-mots to posterity.'

'Oh, John James, oh . . .'

Sugden, in his place of concealment, could not restrain a smile. The jouncing that was taking place on the bed was, without doubt, the most ludicrously lascivious act he had ever seen two mortals perform. He himself had never taken a woman, being disinclined to compromise his dignity for something as uncomfortable and grotesque as the sexual act. Neville looked like a small boat tossed on a wallowing ocean of substantial foam, rising and sinking between those billowing breasts, his buttocks bobbing and dropping like a tidal buoy, his toes scrabbling in the dunes of the bedsheets like the claws of a sand-crab.

The following afternoon Sugden forbore to watch the jousting, but stationed himself outside the house. When Neville left the servants' entrance he turned immediately right walking as briskly as his doubtless tired legs would permit. Sugden followed him unobserved, the coach he had ordered walking along behind him ready for instant use should Neville himself take a flyer. The two of them walked thus, with twenty paces separating them, to Briggate, where Neville turned into an alleyway. Halfway up the alley was a building well known to Sugden; he had taken several villains from it in his time.

Peg Milner, under the guise of a men's haberdashery, ran a

bordello in this house, in which the services of the so-called 'seamstresses' were available for hire. Her customers tended to be of middling class, men who might indeed be purchasing their wares from such an establishment. The ground-floor shop – capable, in fact, of supplying all manner of linens, waistcoats, even hose and hats – was managed quite profitably by Matt Milner, Peg's cousin and partner-in-crime. Peg Milner was also a receiver of stolen property, which she disposed of in the London market. Sugden had known of her activities for several years, but it had never been in his interest to bring her to justice, since her house formed a meeting ground for all manner of superior criminals whom he was able to observe without revealing himself. That Neville should be using her facilities, if not her services, surprised Sugden. He would have thought Neville too high in self-esteem to use such a bawdy thieves' kitchen.

He followed Neville into the premises and saw him disappear through the door marked 'Gentlemen's Fitting Room', his destination obviously the less public rooms above. Sugden knew at once he had a problem; it was unlikely that Peg Milner would keep the jewellery on her premises for any length of time, since she would be looking for a quick turn-round of any monies she might advance to Neville. Once the jewellery had vanished into the depths of the London market, there would be little hope of recovering it. Sugden made some small enquiry as to waistcoats and left the shop quickly, vowing he would be back when he had completed another task he had temporarily forgotten.

He waited along the alleyway until he saw Neville depart, then went back into the haberdashery. This time Matt Milner came forward and eyed the customer suspiciously. Milner had a nose for peace officers and similar men of the law, and this one didn't smell right to him.

Sugden regretted there had been no time to arm himself with a pistol, though he had no fear of Milner and knew he could acquit himself very well if it came to a rough-and-tumble.

'The weather is good for the time of the year . . .' Milner said politely.

'So long as the rain holds off, the streets will remain dry,' Sugden replied. This coded exchange was well known to him and should give the 'open sesame' to the upstairs apartments. He saw Milner hesitate. 'But we must beware of storms,' Sugden added. The use of the second code phrase succeeded where the first had failed in dispelling doubt. It implied that the user was here on a matter of business, not pleasure, a buyer or seller of valuable property rather than someone seeking temporary diversion with one of the doxys.

Milner beckoned for him to proceed through the fitting room door. Beyond the two changing cubicles was a staircase that led to the first floor, a door at its top. Sugden knew that Milner would give a secret tug on the bell-cord that hung behind him to indicate that the visitor had passed the first test.

Peg Milner herself was waiting beyond the door to admit him. She looked surprised when she saw him. 'I do not know you,' she said, obviously puzzled, 'yet you come fore-armed with words.'

'I have the strongest recommendations,' Sugden said smoothly. 'Before the peace officers took Wild Willie of Otley, he recommended you to me for any . . . delicate transactions requiring absolute discretion.'

'Wild Willie of Otley, God rest his soul! We don't see his like any more, now that he's danced on the gallows . . .'

'I was close to him towards the end, ma'am,' Sugden said, without revealing that he himself had been the one to apprehend the highwayman in the Wharfedale Valley, nor that, in an attempt to save his blackguardly soul, Willie had disclosed much useful information about local criminal elements, including the mode of entry into Peg Milner's salon.

Satisfied now, Peg took him to her own sitting room, a gilded confection of red plush, pink satin, white-painted tables and chairs, that gave an impression of sugared almonds then much in vogue by importation from Kandia in Crete.

'You keep a stylish apartment, ma'am,' Sugden said, 'in which it would be a pleasure to do business of many sorts . . .'

'I do my best to please in all matters and manners,' Peg said, gesturing to him to take a seat. A woman of some forty years with a trim and well-exercised figure, she would have been prettily attractive were it not for the hardness of her eyes and the sharp set of her mouth. Her hair hung loose down her shoulders and gleamed a red that was more a tribute to artifice than nature's art; it had been well-brushed and gleamed attractively doubtless with the fragrant oils that a certain style of woman was wont to affect. What her shoulders and bosom lacked in prominence, they gained in presentation since the skin was taut and delicately rose-tinted, dusted with a fine powder. Peg saw him taking the inventory of her assets, and marked him down as a possible customer, should his pocket prove as heavy as the lust in his eyes.

'I am here on a most delicate matter,' Sugden said, 'and must needs impose the most stringent conditions of secrecy, ma'am.'

'I shall take all my secrets to the grave,' Peg said solemnly.

'But not for many a long year,' Sugden said gallantly.

She tinkled a stage laugh. 'There's gallantry for you!' she said. ''Tis always more decent to do business, or pleasure, with a gallant gentleman. Pray tell me, are you a buyer or a seller?'

'At this moment, I am a buyer,' he said.

'And what is your pleasure?'

Sugden knew what would be Peg's pleasure and what caused her almost indecent haste. She had a lust to assay his coin before venturing more of her time on profitless dalliance. He reached into the pocket of his tail-coat and produced the coins Peter Aysgill had given him, now wrapped in a handkerchief. He used the handkerchief delicately to dab at his nostril, then put both back in his pocket.

'My mission is a delicate one, ma'am,' he repeated. 'It

concerns the honour of a lady, whose name I have no need to disclose, I think. This lady has committed, shall we say, a small indiscretion – a matter of a momentary aberration which, despite its pettiness, could involve her in most serious consequences.'

'And you are not at liberty to tell me this lady's name?' Peg asked curiously.

'I did not say, ma'am, that I was not at liberty to disclose it – merely that I had no *need* to disclose it.'

'For you think it known to me?'

'How perspicacious of you, ma'am!'

'It is someone with whom I am familiar, then?'

'I do assure you, ma'am – in the most intimate terms,' Sugden said, hiding a smile.

Her brow wrinkled; truly, it could not be said she was familiar with any woman in such intimate terms.

'The lady of whom I speak, ma'am, has two possibilities before her. If she agrees to give her confidence to one man – in strictest secrecy, I might add – she will be permitted to enjoy the comforts to which she has become accustomed. If she fails in that small matter, she will suffer shame and disgrace, penury and deprivation of the most sordid kind.'

'A terrible fate for a lady of quality,' Peg said, 'but I'm afraid you mystify me. I'm like the audience at a new play; I cannot see where the action will lead, nor tell which is the hero and which the villain.'

'You, my dear lady – 'tis you who are cast for all roles in this tight little drama! And the one man, the sole arbiter of your chosen performance, shall be myself!'

'Now you have baffled me completely,' she said, starting to rise from the chaise-longue.

He stood quickly. 'Enough of this stuff and nonsense,' he said. 'I know you for what you are, Peg Milner, a slattern and a moral slut. I know you have received jewellery from a certain John James Neville, a man cast in your own villainous mould. You will return those jewels to me, and that shall be the end of this matter. Or you will cry shame, weep, pretend to be a virtuous woman, and be dragged to the gaol in ruin and disgrace.'

'You're a peace officer?' she whispered, aghast.

'In this matter, I am Sugden, of whom you've doubtless heard. Sugden, who took Wild Willie of Otley and led him to the hangman's ball . . .'

'You're Sugden!' she said through a throat suddenly constricted by fear. His name was well known, his reputation fearsome. ''Twas you fixed Gertie Farmer . . .'

'A pox-raddled cut-purse!' he snorted.

'. . . by planting a Church Bible and an altar cloth beneath her bed!' finished Peg, her face a mask of horror.

'Neville's stolen jewels – shall you restore them to me, or shall I drag you away? And don't think your villainous cousin will help. I have surrounded the place by fellow peace officers and have only to shout from a window. Give me the jewels, Peg, and I swear I will walk out of here with no one the wiser. Refuse me, and I'll see you dangle at the end of a rope.'

'You'll strike a bargain?' she said, hope coming to her eyes. 'But what of Neville when he comes for the proceeds of the sale?'

'You have my word he shall not come for proceeds of any sale,' Sugden said. 'The jewels are to be restored to their rightful owner, and none save you and I will be any the wiser. If you do as I say in this matter, then you have naught to fear for the future. From time to time I shall call on you and seek information of your clients, and—'

'You'll use me for a tattle-tale, an informer!'

''Tis your choice, Peg Milner. Would you rather live to be an informer, or die as a receiver and whore-monger? The choice is yours.'

She didn't need to think long about the alternatives, but crossed to the corner of the room and swung aside a picture to reveal a strong box built into the wall. She opened the strong box and produced a wooden casket from within it. She laid the casket on the table between them, after re-fastening the strong box.

'This is all the property of Mr Neville, so far as I am concerned,' she said. 'He asked me to keep it in safe custody, nothing more. I can swear before any witness that not one farthing has passed between us by way of payment – I have committed no crime in this matter.'

'So shall it be, dear Peg,' Sugden said, smiling. He opened the casket and saw the quantity of jewellery within; he took a list from his inner pocket and checked it – each item was there, each wrapped separately in fine leather. 'You have proven your great sense to me this day, Peg, and acquired an ally.'

'I'd as soon coddle an adder!' Peg said drily. 'But you leave me no choice.'

John James Neville was busy at his tutelage when Sugden returned with the casket of jewellery and placed it on Peter Aysgill's desk.

Peter asked no questions but took twenty pounds from a drawer and gave it to Sugden. 'There'll be no word of this,' he said.

Sugden took the money and secreted it in his pocket. 'No sir, there'll be no word. I was merely committed to seeing that Neville did not escape with money for these baubles to join his father in France.'

'He shall not,' Peter promised grimly. 'Of that I can assure you . . .'

That night, John James Neville was taken in his drugged sleep, and never seen again after the milky mud of the lime-pit at the leather works had closed over his head.

The following day, four doctor friends of Peter Aysgill signed a paper declaring Tessa Aysgill to be of unsound mind. She was taken from the house in a closed carriage, and committed for the rest of her life into the Insane Asylum.

CHAPTER TWO

'You surely are not penning yet another letter?' Daniel asked Robert, who was sitting at the table in their quarters in the village of Trenton, a candle behind a glass providing illumination for his writing.

'I will not give up,' Robert said firmly. 'One of them must get through.'

Since they had landed in America and had joined the Regiment of Hessians, Robert had taken every opportunity to write to his father, urging him to secure his son's release from 'this hellish life'. The picture Robert had painted in each letter was far from the truth – indeed, they had seen little actual fighting so far since they'd been occupied to the rear of Howe's army. Most of their time had been spent marching and managing the supplies on which the more experienced and more efficient mercenary Hessians depended.

Now they were luxuriating in winter quarters in Trenton with fifty or so men occupying the houses and the rest of the 1,400 men in tented camps. Howe had taken the bulk of his men back to New York and Washington was reported to be wintering his American army across the banks of the Delaware River. Christmas saw a peaceful landscape, with the majority of the men content to enjoy such simple festivities as they could arrange for themselves. The Hessians were all prodigious eaters and drinkers; Daniel knew it would be a night of carousing and feasting, with all of the camp followers being in much demand. For his part, he just longed to get away from it all since he had no stomach for any of it and the memory of his beloved Mabel still lingered with him despite the months that had passed since he had seen her.

When the Sergeant of the Guard came round, Daniel was pleased to be given duty a mile before the village. Robert was not so pleased since he had hoped to pass the time lazily. He knew there would be gambling and perhaps he could add to his store of coin from the pay of the Hessians, who lacked finesse with the dice and cards as with all things. They shouldered their packs with the other six men and set off on a steady march through the icy landscape with its snow-covered fields.

A mile from the village, the Sergeant led them across a field to a small wood which occupied the crest of a hillock. They established themselves inside the wood, scooping out the drifted leaf-mould to form fox-holes that would serve to conceal them and keep them warmer. Each carried a blanket in which he wrapped himself.

'Four on watch,' the Sergeant said, 'and four to sleep behind them. You'll change over each four hours. You, Daniel Ottershaw, will be in command.'

'Where will you be, Sergeant?' Daniel asked.

The Sergeant chuckled. 'Why, you dummkopf – I shall be back in the village, enjoying myself until the time comes to bring out your relief in the morning. Now, you know the rules of watch-keeping. No open fires, no cooking. Four men watching all the time, four men sleeping.'

'And what do we do, pray, if we see the enemy?' Robert asked languidly.

'You won't see them – they'll be enjoying Christmas just as we will be. I hear that half of Washington's Army has gone home to wife and family and won't return till the spring.'

The Sergeant marched away across the landscape, as all save Daniel watched enviously. Daniel had no interest in the camp or the festivities. To spend Christmas away from his beloved Mabel was a terrible mockery for him.

He quickly pointed out which four men should stand watch and which four could relax. He estimated that they could see for at least a mile from where they were; in the unlikely event the American Army advanced, they would have plenty of warning, and could withdraw into the wood before setting off back to camp to sound a general alert. If what they saw was a small patrol in advance of the troops, they could possibly ambush the patrol hoping to take one prisoner back to camp with them to supply information.

Though Daniel was occupied in deciding his strategies in the event of seeing an enemy, his mind constantly strayed. Was it possible that not one of Robert's letters had got through to England? If one had got through, surely Peter Aysgill would have told Daniel's wife and mother of his predicament? If his uncle provided funds to buy Robert out, surely he would do the same for Daniel? Robert had written thus in his letters, but so far there had been no reply. Letters to soldiers were very rare, but some did come through. Anyway, Peter Aysgill was, surely, sufficiently well connected to make contact with a General, perhaps even Howe himself, and thus the message would be passed down the line. They'd heard nothing, not a single word, and when Robert had asked their Captain if any message had been received, he'd been rebuked for addressing an officer on such a trivial matter and lashed by the sergeant.

Life in the Army had been horrible for both of them, though they'd been spared the true horror of front-line engagement. Daniel still held his fear of his own bravery, and now he'd come to suspect Robert's. The fine manner of the boat had all but faded from Robert; contact with the mercenaries and the life of a soldier had coarsened him somewhat, leaving few if any of his fine airs and little of his self-confidence.

If they were in a bloody battle, would they both cut and run? This nightmare occupied Daniel's thoughts constantly, especially when the waggons carrying the wounded came back and they saw the number of head wounds the Kentucky rifles inflicted, the terrible slashes caused by the butcher's hatchets and skinning knives of the farmers and frontiersmen – who could, and often did, disembowel a man with one thrust and swing.

Howe's Army fought tactically, of course, in the military tradition. The men formed ranks and files, long solid lines. When they advanced, they did so in line, with bayonets fixed ready for the charge that had broken the hearts and the resolve of so many enemy forces throughout the history of the British Army. This war, Daniel had overheard a Hessian saying, was different from any other in which he'd fought. The Americans tended to split into small harassing groups, with men squatting in tree-tops and hiding in bushes, using their newly invented rifles with devastating accuracy to demoralize the British soldiers and the Hessians alike. Only the large set-piece battles, with artillery on both sides covering the foot-soldiers, were conducted by formal manoeuvres and then Howe's men frequently failed to take advantage of their numerical superiority to consolidate the positions they had won. After a few days of inaction, the British would be ordered to start the advance again, only to discover that the opposing generals had stolen away during the night with their troops and had set up impregnable positions on the next available heights. Howe, it appeared, was afraid of the lesson of what was now being called the Battle of Bunker Hill, when the advancing British Army under General Gage had been decimated. In these latter months of 1776 the British command had come to respect their American opponents, and from that respect had sprung elements of fear.

The night dragged slowly on. At midnight Robert, who was on duty beside Daniel, held out his hand.

'Happy Christmas, cousin,' he said ruefully. 'I never believed we'd still be in this God-forsaken land by this time.'

'Happy Christmas,' Daniel said, 'and nor did I.'

Robert produced a flask of spirits from his knapsack and offered it to Daniel. 'I won this from a trooper,' he said. 'We may as well take advantage of it.'

The spirits were burning to the throat, but Daniel gratefully took a deep draught that brought tears to his eyes. 'Word will come soon, Robert,' he said. 'Do not be despondent. In the

New Year we shall both be homeward bound, mark my words.' The younger fellow was so obviously low in mind that Daniel sought words with which to reassure him. 'In any case, this war cannot continue long. Rumour has it that approaches have been made to the Congress of the Americans for a peaceful solution to the fighting. There are reputed to be as many in Philadelphia opposed to the war as are in support of it. When the war ends, as surely soon it must, then we shall be able to seek our opportunity to return to England.'

'We could always desert,' Robert said half-heartedly. They'd seen deserters who'd been retaken, men who'd fled the enemy in cowardice, and had watched them being lashed to the mouths of cannon. It was a sight neither Daniel nor Robert would ever forget; they'd been forced to watch the executions with unblinking eyes, standing strictly to attention in a square.

Four hours later, the two friends were still on duty, since neither could sleep on that cold and miserable night, and Daniel had permitted two other soldiers to remain wrapped in blankets in their fox-holes. It was just after four o'clock when Daniel heard the first sound coming from the direction of the River Delaware.

'Did you hear owt, Robert?' he whispered.

Robert shook his head, too lost in self-pity and remorse to pay any attention to what might be happening across the field or along the road.

Daniel strained his eyes in the starlit night light; the air was so cold and the sky so crystal clear that he imagined he could see every shadow which moved. And there, suddenly, were many moving shadows. On the side of the road, in the copses, along the ridges of the fields, in all the folds of the ground.

The four sentries were spaced along a twenty-foot stretch, with Robert and Daniel in the centre.

'Keep your eyes alert, Robert,' Daniel whispered.

Were his eyes playing tricks with him? Were those shadowy figures human, inexorably advancing on their position? Was that the glint of a star on a weapon, that the shaking of one of the skin hats some of the frontiersmen wore? Daniel crawled rapidly to his left to where Krantz was on guard.

'Do you see anything, Krantz?' he whispered, then cursed as he saw Krantz was lying flat on his back, fast asleep. He started to crawl back after shaking Krantz's shoulder, then suddenly heard a whisper in the wood behind them, a rustling of branches. Now that these sounds were all about them, his fear had fled. He was concerned only with activating his small band of men to get them to the ready. He crawled rapidly to where the men were sleeping and woke each one with a whispered word. All trained soldiers, they came instantly awake and gripped their muskets as they rolled over.

'Ja, I see them,' Biemeyer grunted.

Nominally a waggoner, Biemeyer had long ago retired from active service, though he knew no other occupation but soldiering. He had been brought along by one of the band of Hessians as a general cook and helper; believing there'd be no action this night, they'd permitted him to serve on the night-guard. Biemeyer's eyes were glinting with anticipation; it would be good to get back into real fighting for a change. He pushed his musket forward, arranged his pack with his charges and ball by his side, and his powder.

'Let zem come!' he said 'Biemeyer iss ready for them.'

'Nay,' Daniel said, 'we're not to fight. We're to return post-haste to camp to warn the other men.'

'Run? Like cowards?' Biemeyer snorted. 'They are only tventy or zo . . .'

Biemeyer's eyes were playing him false, Daniel knew, for his sharper, younger sight could distinguish at least fifty men beginning an advance across the fields. Doubtless the rustlings he had heard in the wood in which they'd placed themselves were made by birds and other animals alerted by the coming humans, or perhaps by his own movements.

'Pack up, lads,' Daniel said, 'and prepare to withdraw through the wood.'

Reluctantly Biemeyer closed his pack again, and came up

into a crouching position concealed by a small stunted growth of bush. The men all bunched together, and Daniel signalled to Robert and Krantz to stay behind, to keep an eye on the men clearly seen to be advancing, but still a mile from them. Now he fancied he could hear also the rumble of gun waggons, and the heavy tread of many troops along the road.

'Right, lads, let's go,' Daniel said. 'Biemeyer and Smart, take the front flanks; I will take the centre. The rest of you spread out in this arrow-head – with you, Robert, behind me.'

Now that they were on the move, Daniel was astounded to realize he felt no fear. He was not running back to camp with his tail between his legs, he was executing a planned withdrawal with the purpose of carrying information. He liked the sense of power his small command gave him; he told himself he must remain constantly alert, for these men's lives depended on him. It was, in many ways, an exhilarating feeling, a totally new sensation.

'Keep further apart,' he field-whispered and was gratified when both Biemeyer and Smart – a burly man of at least thirty years, press-ganged in Manchester – obeyed him instantly. Thus they penetrated deeper into the wood, with the light rapidly lessening, and their vision shortening.

Perhaps a more experienced soldier would have realized that no army moves without scouts ahead; that the advancing army would, in all probability, be split into at least two columns, and that scouts would occupy the ground in advance of and between the two columns. Such had happened with the forces of George Washington after they had crossed the ice-choked and perilous Delaware at seven the previous night. It had taken eight hours to get the army of 2,400 men across. At three in the morning they had been formed into two columns, one under General Greene and one under General Sullivan, and the march on Trenton had begun. Irregular bands of scouts were detailed to travel before them, and one such band was now in position on the other side of the wood through which Daniel and his pitiful patrol was marching to carry the news of Washington's advance to Trenton.

The first shot took Biemeyer through the right eye. Daniel heard the crack and the thud of the ball, saw Biemeyer stop, then begin to fall. He ran across to him. Biemeyer was now kneeling; when Daniel cradled the old Hessian's shoulders and tilted his head back, he saw the hole where Biemeyer's right eye had been and felt the stickiness of Biemeyer's blood on his arm. It was his first experience of a casualty by his side. He unslung his loaded musket and went to ground immediately.

The second shot from the Kentucky rifle would have taken Daniel's eye too, if he hadn't had the good fortune to flop down just as the marksman was taking aim. He had been taught over and over again that it took longer to reload the Kentucky rifles than a conventional musket. As soon as he recognized the crack above his head and saw the stab of flame from a bush twenty-five yards in front of him, he rose instinctively to his knees and moved forward, the bayonet on his musket projecting before him. The man, dressed in a fringed buckskin jacket with a racoon hat dangling over his forehead, was still struggling to reload when Daniel's bayonet took him through the breast bone and his heart. Daniel, in his impetuous rush, carried on forward and would have overshot his own rifle had he not stumbled; he pushed his knee against his victim and pulled the rifle back towards him; the sucking sound as the bayonet came out sickened him more than the blood which followed it, or the surprised and agonized look on the man's face. Daniel whirled round, saw Krantz stick his rifle through another enemy, then suddenly realized he had not taken note of, but certainly had heard, the fusillade of rifles firing against them through which he must have dashed. Three of his men were down, presumably dead. Krantz took a shot in the neck, but charged forward like a bull and stuck his assailant on the end of his bayonet before he, too, slumped in death, the two figures entangled one with the other on the ground.

Then Daniel saw Robert. Robert was running, back through the wood, back towards the advancing troops. An

American had raised himself above the trunk of a tree and was taking a careful aim to put a shot between Robert's shoulderblades. Daniel threw himself forward; the American must have felt his approach for he half turned. Too late Daniel saw the second American behind the first and to the side, and his rifle was more free to swivel. Daniel jabbed his bayonet forward towards the first man, feinted with the butt and brought it round in a circle the way one of the Hessians had shown him. The butt smashed into the American's face and dropped him to the ground. Reversing his musket again, Daniel was just in time to see the wicked skinning knife the first American was about to use, despite the gash Daniel's bayonet had made on his upper arm; this time the butt of the musket came up under the skinning knife and sent it flying into the air.

'Robert!' Daniel shouted. 'Come back! For God's sake, come back!'

Though the second man had a broken jaw, he was still conscious; through the mists that fogged his eyes he saw the red and white of the hated Britisher in front of and above him. He pulled his skinning knife from his belt, gathered his strength, and struck upwards as the final act of consciousness. Daniel felt the knife slice into his belly. The first American was coming forward again. At point-blank range, Daniel fired his musket into the man's chest. The man staggered back, and Daniel staggered back, the musket falling from his hands as he clutched the handle of the long-bladed knife sticking from his belly.

Robert had stopped; he'd turned and was hiding behind a tree. He saw that the small American scout patrol, of probably no more than four men, had been destroyed. He saw that of his companions, six were dead and one was attempting to stagger towards him. It was his cousin.

'Robert, Robert! Help me, Robert . . .' Daniel was crying.

Robert looked around, afraid that other scouts might still be lurking, that a bullet might await him if he stepped from the shelter of the tree.

Still Daniel staggered on, refusing to fall. 'He was going to shoot you. Robert! In the back! Didn't I promise you . . . my life . . . was at . . . your . . . service?' He fell on one knee and the knife handle almost touched the ground. 'On the boat, Robert . . . I promised . . .'

Robert looked around. Dammit, were there more scouts waiting to put one through the whites of his eye?

'Robert, help me . . .' Daniel was pleading, rocking back and forth on his haunches with the blade of that terrible knife sticking from his belly, blood seeping past it and through his fingers, staining the white buckskin breeches of an Army he'd never wanted to join.

The American with the broken jaw suddenly gurgled and choked as blood blocked his windpipe. He half rose in a twitching spasm, then fell back to the ground, dead. Robert hadn't waited to see; at the first sound he had turned again on his heels and was bolting out through the wood.

'Robert, help me . . .' Daniel was still saying, but now there was a roaring in his ears, his vision had blurred, and all he could see was the sweet image of his dear wife Mabel printed on his unforgetting mind's-eye.

The letter came from the Second Earl Cornwallis, Major General, with the notation 'On Active Service in His Majesty's Colony of America'. It was addressed to Sir George Savile, Member of Parliament for Yorkshire, and begged to inform him that following stringent enquiries in the field, it had been ascertained that the soldier Daniel Fossett had been killed in action, that the soldier Robert Aysgill had deserted in the face of the enemy and, if apprehended, would be the subject of summary military justice in accordance with the King's Regulations.

Peter Aysgill read the letter with a stony face, then tore it up and flung the pieces on to the fire at which he was warming his suddenly old, cold and weary bones.

CHAPTER THREE

Arthur grumbled as Sally held him under the deluge of water that cascaded down from the jug she tilted above his head.

'Rub yourself with the soap, lazy devil!' she said happily, watching him splutter in the unaccustomed ablution. 'The coach will be upon us before you are dressed.'

Though times had been bad for Arthur, Sally had come back to an admiration of his indomitable spirit in the last years. When she had stood up in the court on his behalf, she had done so to save him from the hangman's rope which surely would have been his fate if they had found him guilty of murdering Tomlinson and setting fire to the mill. The men she had denounced had been seized and interrogated, and finally confessed that Arthur Aysgill had played no role in their plot to burn the mill. At their subsequent trial, all had been sentenced to be hanged, since the judge ruled that their actions in attempting to set fire to the mill had led directly to the death of the overseer.

Arthur had been happy when Sleightholme reinstated him in his job, even promising that if Arthur could only learn to cast liberalism away from him he might one day succeed to Tomlinson's job as overseer. He was filled with optimism the day he had set out to work after his release from gaol with all charges against him dropped. He had walked into the mill a few minutes late but as content as he could remember being.

The second Arthur arrived, all the other folk in the mill stopped working.

Sleightholme himself was there that morning. He walked

through the mill shouting to everyone to get back to work but finally Nellie Cross, one of the weavers, bobbed an ironic curtsy at the master.

'Begging your pardon, Mr Sleightholme,' she said, 'and meaning no offence to your person, us have all decided we'll not work wi' yon turncoat and traitor, Aysgill.'

It was the first ever concerted strike, and Sleightholme could do nothing about it. He blustered for an hour after sending Arthur into his office to await events, but the workers remained adamant. They'd devised the scheme whereby each spoke in turn, so that Sleightholme would see that they were in unison. No one came forward as a leader so that none could be summarily penalized. After an hour Sleightholme, realizing he had been beaten, went back into his office to speak to Arthur.

Arthur had already departed; the clerk gave Sleightholme the message Arthur had left. 'You've been good to me,' he'd said, 'and I won't see you suffer on that account. I shall seek work elsewhere and remain ever your humble and grateful servant.'

Word had spread round the whole district and Arthur had once again been unable to find employment. This time, however, he had kept himself decent and tidy, and had not taken a single drink other than a glass of cheap ale to wash down his meals. Sally had gone back to the milliners, and Arthur occupied himself by doing any small jobs of a temporary nature that he could find.

Sally had stitched a pair of breeches for him, and a new coat made from an old one inside out and resewn. She'd procured a pair of beige hose for him and cleaned his boots with mutton fat, spitting on them and rubbing them into a fine lustre. She'd sewn a new front on to an old shirt and had implored him not to take off his coat when there were folks about. She'd washed and brushed his waistcoat, and pressed it with a hot iron. She'd reblocked his hat on the bottom of an upturned pot until the felt brim was flat and the crown stood high and proud, with its ribbon and gleaming brass buckle. When she'd dressed him, she stood back to regard him.

'There, you are every inch a gentleman, my master!' she said.

Despite her protests he gathered her into his arms. 'And you are every inch a lady and a loving wife,' he said.

Sally was wearing a kerchief of embroidered cotton around her shoulders, a petticoat of cream-coloured flannel with a daygown in cream linsey-woolsey above it. On her head a plaited straw bonnet was decorated with cloth flowers she had sewn herself and a facsimile of cherries loaned to her for the day by Mrs Little. They had barely finished their examination of each other than suddenly they heard the clatter of wheels on the cobble-stones of the street outside their tiny house, and the shouts of boys. They heard the crack of the coachman's whip and Arthur remembered the number of times he, in his boyhood, had jumped on the back of a moving coach to drop off the second before the coachman's whip came whistling across the roof.

Today he was to travel *in* the coach!

Gertrude Fossett alighted from her coach on the steps of the house and was ushered inside by the footman who'd awaited her. She gave a small gracious bow, as she had so often seen her employer Mrs Edgecombe do, and hurried inside.

'My master sends his compliments,' the footman said, 'and will await you for departure in an hour.'

Gertrude saw her bags taken up the stairs and followed them. The room was large and airy, but she couldn't shake off the tight feeling in her chest which she attributed to the noxious air of Leeds, after the clean balmy sea breezes of Whitby to which she was accustomed. The coach ride across the Yorkshire moors been most uncomfortable and she had not been able to sleep properly, even though Captain Edgecombe had secured the corner seat in the stagecoach for her.

At one point, the coach had begun to gallop wildly, careering down the road. '*Highwaymen*!' the coachman had shouted and all had clung on. The threat had not been fulfilled for the three men who eventually overtook them on horseback were obviously two gentlemen and a groom.

Gertrude had brought a simple dress for the occasion. Over the years she had put on a little weight; now, at sixty-three, her figure was beginning to look portly if she did not pull it in rigorously with stays. A maid had awaited her in the room, and it took all her energies to draw the corset tight enough to please Gertrude. The gown was of silver and green stripes on a white background; she'd paid an extravagant two pounds for it specially for the wedding of her son, Reuben, four years previously. She'd worn it only once again, when her dear departed son Daniel had married. As ever, when she thought of Daniel dying on a soldier's field in America, her eyes moistened, but she had learned to control her sorrow. She regretted very much that Mabel had got married again, to the man in York who'd come to her aid when Daniel had been pressed. Gertrude thought the girl should have waited, but she'd married within two months of being told of Daniel's death.

Peter Aysgill had sent them a brief note: '*I regret to inform you that I just heard, by special despatch from America, that your son Daniel has been killed in action.*' He had said nothing of the fate of his own son Robert, and Gertrude knew better than to enquire.

'You do not think this gown too florid?' Gertrude now asked the maid as she looked at herself in the full mirror.

'Florid, madam? No. I think the colour suits your healthy complexion and reflects a quiet modest taste,' said the girl.

'Thank you, Hetty,' Gertrude said. Quiet modest taste, indeed! Whatever were the girls learning these days . . .

A knock came on the door. Hetty went across the room and opened the door a fraction, then she turned. 'Begging your pardon, ma'am,' she said, 'but the master awaits you if it is convenient.'

'Thank you, Hetty.' Gertrude took a last peek at herself in the mirror, though for reassurance, not from vanity, and walked slowly and deliberately from the dressing room to where her brother Peter awaited her in the hall below.

'Gertrude!' he said. 'How good to see you looking so well! Whitby most obviously agrees with you. I am sorry I could not be here to greet you, but a pressing affair of business . . .'

'I quite understand, dear brother,' she said. 'May I say how well you yourself are looking – despite this poisonous air of Leeds.'

'You're late again, Claude,' Stanley said in exasperation. 'If we don't make haste, the coach will have arrived before you're ready.'

'I'll go as I am,' Claude said in his usual lackadaisical manner.

'You'll do no such thing,' Stanley said firmly. 'You'll change into the new clothing I bought especially for you. You will cleanse yourself and put on the clean linens that are lying on your bed. And you will make haste!'

Stanley had long ago despaired of his indolent brother who seemed to lack energy to do *anything*. Even Lawyer Wormsley had finally lost his patience and had discharged Claude from his service when Claude had taken three hours to run a five-minute message, with the result that the case he was representing had to be held back for a later occasion due to lack of the documents Claude was delivering to the court. The Judge had reproved Wormsley most pointedly for his supposed 'lack of preparation' and Wormsley, quite rightly, had vented his anger on the runner who'd failed him. Now Claude spent his time at home. He had acquired something of an occasional interest in watercolour painting and drawing though, as ever, he was too lazy to study draughtsmanship and his works all lacked any form of symmetry in consequence. Stanley didn't mind indulging his younger brother, whom he

373

regarded as being barely above the mental level of an idiot, and gave him a quarterly pension. Claude invariably spent the amount within the first month, and then was content to remain penniless until more money came in. Stanley was grateful for one thing: at least there was no malice in his brother and no evil – sometimes, in exasperation, he felt his brother was just too damned lazy to be dishonest!

Stanley could afford to indulge his brother. The year of 1780 saw him prosperous, with all his debts paid to Peter Aysgill, all his debentures redeemed and a programme of expansion well under way. Though he had fallen behind Wilkinson in his invention of the cylinder-boring machine – having been mentally diverted by working on his multiple screw-cutter – he'd followed James Watt's work closely and had even supplied one of the special parts for the separate steam condenser that gave the Watt steam engine such startling efficiency. Now Stanley was building steam engines under licence, and had as many orders as he could handle, hence the expansion of his factory. Since he was obviously capable of handling business affairs, he'd been able to look around for further capital with which to finance his expansions, and had obtained loan rates far more advantageous than his uncle offered, with no debentures on his stock.

Peter had laughed jovially at him. 'I taught you all you know,' he'd said jokingly, 'and now the whelp turns against the fox . . .' Peter was not interested in making long-term low interest loans, no matter how well secured they might be; short-term ventures carried a much greater rate of interest, and Peter was concerned only to have his money working for him as gainfully as possible.

Stanley had joined a few of the clubs his uncle occasionally patronized in the way of business, but they never ever sat down socially together. Stanley knew that something in the past still rankled with his uncle. Though he suspected it was the manner in which Dodie, his mother, had persuaded his uncle to advance the first money to get his factory started, he had no details and therefore could not make an accurate judgement. Stanley had branched out in other ways, too, and now cut a pretty figure at one or two of the fashionable but middling sorts entertainments. So far he'd mentioned his desires to no one, but he'd met a certain young lady, Letitia Gainsborough by name, who had quite stolen his heart.

Claude was still upstairs when the coach arrived, and Stanley called up to him. He'd recently engaged the services of a houseman who, even then, was helping Claude to dress. The houseman came to the top of the stairs and said that 'Mr Claude' would soon be ready. Stanley went to the front door, opened it, and signalled to the coachman that they wouldn't be but a moment.

The coachman sat his box happily. He was muffled against the weather and quite accustomed to waiting for his passengers.

Frank Aysgill had decided not to go. To Sylvia his wife, to his son Keith, now twelve years of age, to his father Matthew and his mother Mildred, both of whom lived in his house, Frank stated that it was against his principles to go.

'I ain't spent all these years fighting privilege,' he declared fiercely, 'to waste my time on the foolishness of the rich.'

'Nay, husband, we're expected,' Sylvia said plaintively. 'Us can't back out now, not wi' the coach doubtless already on its way.'

Sylvia had laboured for weeks to make herself a dress that was decent. Mildred had dug into her store of clothes and found a heavy grey woollen gown that suited her age and her grey hair. Matthew had been dressed in the dark garb he had worn when he'd tramped the countryside preaching Wesleyanism; the two women had laboured over it with a wet cloth and a hot plate and now it gave Matthew a clerical air which greatly suited him. He wore his grey locks long, and as they fell over his shoulder they gave him a distinguished educated look.

The sufferings of the years had carved hollows in his cheeks, seemed to have sharpened his profile and tightened the skin of his nostrils, so that his expression was gaunt and ascetic, as befitted an unworldly scholar.

More and more Matthew had withdrawn into a private holy world of his own. Mildred had found a few pupils for him to teach; he went to their houses declaiming Latin and Greek, English Language and Literature to them, and thus managed to earn a few shillings each week which went into the common store of household monies. Sylvia worked in the mill with her son Keith, assisting on one of the mammoth spinning jennies that could handle forty-eight bobbins at a time. The work was exacting, since all the bobbins had to be kept in order and the machine spun at such a speed that both were constantly on the run.

Mildred had found herself a good job too, though it paid but little. When the printing shop had opened along Hunslet Lane, she had sought a position and was now one of those who read the proofs of the final work for accuracy of setting. Many times the wrong letter would be taken inadvertently from the font of type or the box would not be correctly squared. They worked in a large room at the top of the building which gave as much natural light as possible. Her wages of five shillings a week also went into the family fund.

Frank was not paid for his work as an agitator and an organizer of combinations, a leader of strikes, an industrial lecturer. He spent each evening tramping round Hunslet addressing meetings of workers anywhere he could assemble them. The peace officers were constantly on the look-out for him, but he managed to dodge them and, though they knew where he lived, they could not enter his home since he committed no crime unless he urged his supporters to violence. He had successfully organized a bread riot, and another riot against Sleightholme's Mill when the new jennies were installed, and had recently witnessed the death by heart seizure of his most hated enemy, Jabez Broadley, the man who had owned the mine in which he had first learned his revolutionary lessons.

Frank had been speaking to the men outside the mine gate, telling them that they were fools to work in such conditions of danger and ill-health. After the first use of gunpowder had caused many deaths in the colliery, Broadley had continued to use it – without, Frank argued, any regard for human life. In the middle of his harangue Broadley had appeared from the mine office. His toady and bully Tarn Fowles had been killed the previous month when a gang of the miners had thrown him head first down the shaft to the lower level. Broadley could have used his services as, brandishing his stick, his face scarlet with anger, he tried to drive his way through the crowd to assault his taunter, Frank. The stick had been raised and Frank had stood still, determined to take the blow and by so doing to strengthen his cause by martyring himself, when the scarlet of Broadley's face had turned to blue; his congested heart had finally thumped its last and he had fallen down, dead. The workers had carried his body back into the mine and had laid it on the ground outside the office. If Wilfred Oates, Broadley's informer, hadn't told the mine manager, George Alverthorpe, the body would have been left there for the scavenging dogs to find, so little was the regard they had for this tyrant.

'I had so looked forward to going,' Sylvia said, tears beginning to appear in her eyes. 'It would have made such a change . . .'

'Art saying this life ain't good enough for you?' Frank demanded truculently. 'We mun be faithful to our beliefs, not traitors!'

Matthew cleared his throat. 'I don't see how you can suggest treachery, son,' he told Frank in his firm though reedy voice. 'We shall not be betraying the cause of the worker. You must learn to be more precise in your use of the language if you seek to sway the minds of men. I for one shall go, and I have no doubt your mother will come with me. As to your wife . . .'

'She'll go nowhere wi'out me,' Frank immediately said. 'I'll not have a wife o' mine gallivanting around the countryside wi'out me.'

'Then you'd better make up your mind to come,' Matthew said. He knew his son so well. He knew that Frank always had to bluster, to put up a show of opposition. Whenever he listened to his son debate a social issue with other men, Matthew often noticed that his son would put up a proposition in his loud aggressive way, only to want the other men to oppose him, to appear to force him to do something he didn't want to do.

'I s'all go as I am,' Frank said. 'I s'all not dress myself like a mountebank.'

'I am quite certain,' Matthew said mildly, 'that no one will have any time to notice how *you* are dressed.'

'There!' Sylvia said anxiously. 'Didn't I tell you as the coach would be here before we were ready?'

'It can wait,' Frank said stubbornly, 'until us is ready.'

'Spoken like a true aristocrat,' Matthew said, chuckling.

It was Jennifer Ottershaw's wedding day, the day she was to marry Sir Arthur Brearley. The coach carrying her to the church was pulled by two pairs of white horses. Each horse bore a fine silver decoration on its noble Arab brow. Jennifer was dressed all in white in the gown which had been Mrs Tester's wedding gift to her. Mrs Tester was in the coach beside Jennifer, and Mr Tester sat on the bench seat facing them.

'Two finer looking ladies,' he was saying, 'it has never been my privilege to see!' He himself was wearing a light grey outfit with a plum-coloured waistcoat, and a light grey hat perched atop his tie-wig with short curls above his ears. A silver stripe edged with plum-coloured silk was piped down the seams of his breeches, which were tied with a silk bow at the knee.

Mr Tester never knew when he'd been happier, unless it be

when he had married his own bride. He had conceived such a fond affection for this pure unspoiled maid that could not have been surpassed, he'd told his wife that morning, if Jennifer had been their own daughter. Mrs Tester had agreed with her husband; her joy at the forthcoming wedding was only tempered by the knowledge that Jennifer, who had become such a good companion to her these past couple of years, would no longer be lodged beneath their roof.

Sir Arthur Brearley, out of his affection for the Testers and his gratitude for the role they had urbanely played in his courtship of Jennifer Ottershaw, had kindly suggested that, instead of them all repairing to some dusty lawyers' chambers, the marriage contract be signed in their own drawing room – 'since that is the birth-place of our affections,' he said, the twinkle in his eye reminding them all that the genesis of his interest had been the cup of tea Jennifer spilled over his clothing.

It had long been agreed that Jennifer's brother Stanley would yield pride of place to Mr Tester, who would act *in loco parentis* to the young bride-to-be. Stanley and Mr Tester had combined to provide funds for Jennifer's dowry, though Sir Arthur had required no such, and had insisted the funds be placed to Jennifer's account, to provide for her financial independence in a small way. Thus she would have the use of an income of the interest from a capital of two thousand pounds, and would not feel completely beholden to her husband. Since Jennifer had little other property the marriage contract was a simple affair and, to Jennifer's sorrow, concerned mainly with what would happen to Sir Arthur's goods, property and chattels if and when he should pre-decease her.

''Tis a morbid subject to be tackling on our wedding day,' she confided to Mrs Tester, and was relieved that Stanley and his lawyer, Mr Tester and his lawyer, and her future husband with his lawyer, were the ones to debate it. There had been small ground for disagreement – Sir Arthur was anxious that all his worldly wealth would pass to Jennifer, save for the customary bequests to loyal retainers who had been long in his service.

The contract had taken only an hour to complete; they'd eaten a light snack once the lawyers had left, and were now proceeding to the ceremony which would be held in the parish church in the village owned almost in its entirety by Sir Arthur.

The day was fair. Jennifer hugged her happiness to herself, as tangible as the smooth silk of which her gown was made. How she wished Dodie could have survived to see this day, to see how all her ambitions and high hopes for her daughter had been fulfilled. 'You shall ride in your own carriage,' Dodie had promised her all those years ago when Jennifer had conned her books, the newspapers, the foreign language tracts, to prepare herself for this wonderful moment.

She looked out of the side window of the coach and tears of joy rolled down her cheeks. Could there be a happier person in this entire world, she asked herself, to be married this day to a fine man she could respect and, she devoutly hoped, love? She thought of the myriad arrangements that had been made for their happiness, the suite of rooms Sir Arthur had placed at her disposal in their house, the way he had asked her to attend to its redecoration and refurbishment. She was going to have a wonderful time when they returned from their foreign travels, making a home for her husband and a life for herself.

She turned to Mrs Tester, a new joy on her face. 'I shall be Lady Brearley,' she said simply.

'Aye, missie, 'twill be twopence to speak!' Mrs Tester said as she placed her hand upon the girl's with the light pressure of love.

Jennifer smiled at her benefactress and at Mr Tester. 'I owe it all to you,' she told them, then turned away to look out of the windows again.

They had left behind the bustle of Hunslet streets, and now

were out in the country crossing the heath. The road was but lightly used, since most of the waggons now followed the London Road which had recently been so well surfaced by Blind Jack o' Knaresborough and turnpiked. Thinking of the turnpike road brought Jennifer to think about her living relations. How wonderful that Sir Arthur, that dear sweet kind wonderful man, had permitted her to invite all of them to the church ceremony and to the repast at his house afterwards! She looked forward to seeing Arthur again – he had worked occasionally with Blind Jack's men in the turnpike construction. She had the best memories of him when she had been a small girl; he'd always been a lad of mischief and boldness. She'd always been somewhat afraid of her severe Uncle Matthew and Aunt Mildred who, she felt, had disapproved of what doubtless they considered her frivolity. She wondered if she'd have to suffer a sermon from Uncle Matthew on the duties of a good God-fearing wife. She had never taken to cousin Frank on the few occasions she'd met him. It always seemed to her that he spoke too much of freedom for a man who imprisoned the ideas of his own wife and family in his mean narrow way. Still, he was her cousin, and she was happy to know that Sir Arthur had sent a carriage for them all and that they would be waiting when she arrived at the church to witness her wedding.

Jennifer had only the vaguest memories of her Aunt Gertrude and wondered if sorrow over Daniel's death would have affected her strongly. It would be good to sit and converse with her about the Fossett arm of the family, about which she knew so little. Uncle Peter had been kind enough to accept the invitation, though he would not be able to attend the wedding feast afterwards, due to business pressures. Ah well, she told herself, it was a feather in her cap even that he had consented to come and bring her cousin Gavin and Aunt Gertrude. So many relations, so much to look forward to, so many pleasures to share . . .

She was startled from her reverie by the sudden quickening

of the horses' pace.

'We've time a-plenty,' Mr Tester said, 'without shaking ourselves on the way!'

'Aye,' Mrs Tester said, 'we don't want to arrive at the church disturbed. Tell him to go more slowly, husband.'

Mr Tester reached up and unbolted the small wooden panel that would give him access to the coachman. Jenkins was bending down and obviously had been about to shout to them.

'I fear we've picked up highwaymen, sir,' he said gravely. 'And I am unarmed.'

Mr Tester reached into the leather box strapped inside the coach and found the piece that was always kept there. He busied himself loading it with a charge of powder and a wadding, though the rapid movement of the coach impeded him greatly. The coach was now swaying from side to side, for this road had not been finished as well as the turnpike road since it led only to the village on the other side of the heath.

Now they could hear the drumming hooves of the highwaymen's horses, growing closer and closer.

Mrs Tester began to wail. 'Today of all days!' she sobbed. 'On such a day . . .!'

Jennifer found that she was quite cool, quite calm, though filled with a fierce anger that these louts should seek to destroy her pleasure. Mercifully she was not wearing many of the jewels Sir Arthur had bestowed on her, since she wanted to approach the church altar and her wedding in simple style. Mrs Tester had followed her example and was wearing only a brooch at her bosom, a thing of comparatively small value.

'I'll get the blackguards!' Mr Tester cried, pushing the wadding tight home, taking a ball from the leather pouch in the gun-case. The bouncing of the coach over the crudely finished surface dashed the first ball from his hands and before he could extract a second, they heard the voice of the highwayman.

'Stand and deliver!' came the chillingly familiar call.

Jenkins was unable to disobey without getting a bullet through his back from the highwayman's pistol. The coach trundled to a stop and they could see the gang of highwaymen numbered only three, unless others were waiting at a distance. The first man, half his face hidden behind a black mask, crossed to the door of the coach and opened it with some flourish. He saw the piece Mr Tester had been trying to load, seized it, turned it upside down and banged out the charge of powder and the wad.

'You'll not be needing that, good sir,' he said. Then, to their surprise, the man directed his attention to Jennifer, reached in and deftly caught her hand, raising it to his lips.

Jennifer prayed he would not discern that she was wearing her diamond engagement ring, which bulked inside the glove. His pistol loomed large in his hand, pointing directly at her breast.

'Villain!' Mr Tester cried, but the highwayman silenced him with a wave of that fearsome weapon, looking over Jennifer's hand directly into her eyes.

'Sir,' she said, 'sir, it is beneath my dignity to beg of you. I am a virtuous girl, e'en now on my way to be married with the man I love. Today has been a day of joy for me in the anticipation of my future happiness . . .' Though her voice seemed to quaver of its own volition, she was resolute in her determination to address him. 'Sir, if you have a spark of decency left in you, if you have even a memory of better times when you yourself anticipated happiness . . . I am on my way to be united with my future husband, to be reunited with my family – my aunts and uncles, my dearly beloved brothers . . .'

'And your cousins, Jennifer Ottershaw!' he bellowed, breaking into laughter, and tearing the mask from his face. 'Hast no memory of me, thy cousin Richard – lately turned highwayman but this day your humble servant? Dearest coz, I would have been by thy side i' the church, had I not had word your dearest husband-to-be has engaged peace officers to guard your person and his jewels, your honour and your modesty during your nuptials. I kiss thy hand, Jennifer Ottershaw, and wish you well in your life to come. To you – and to you, ma'am – I offer my humble apologies lest my style of approach in any way has offended your pride.' He backed from the doorway, closing it behind him. 'Fare thee well, dearest coz!' he cried. 'We'll ride guard on thee, my lads and myself, till we see you safe and sound within sight of yonder steeple. Coachman, drive most careful, I charge thee – thou hast a valued cargo aboard!'

The coach lumbered away with the three highwaymen, Richard Aysgill, Dick Oxby and Tam Trenton, riding slowly behind it.

Jennifer, unable to speak, had rested her hand in her lap and opened it slowly. In her palm, where Richard had stealthily concealed it while pretending to kiss her glove, twinkled a beautiful ring, a large diamond set about with rubies.

The Aysgills, the Fossetts and the Ottershaws, gathered outside the church, pressed forward as Jennifer's coach arrived but she, looking out of the back window, raised her hand to the horseman just in sight.

The horseman raised his arm in return, then wheeled and galloped away across the heath as Sir Arthur Brearley came forward to claim his bride.